Due Unto

Denmark Vesey's Story

K. F. Jones

two harbors press

minneapolis, mn

Two Harbors Press
322 First Avenue N, 5th floor
Minneapolis, MN 55401
612.455.2293
www.TwoHarborsPress.com

FIRST EDITION
1. Vesey, Denmark, ca. 1767-1822 --Fiction. 2. Vesey, Denmark,
approximately 1767-1822 --Fiction. 3. Slavery --Caribbean Area --Fiction.
4. Slavery --South Carolina --Fiction. 4. African Americans --History
--Fiction. 5. Abolitionists --Fiction. 6. Caribbean Area --History --Fiction. 7.
Charleston (S.C.) --History --Slave Insurrection, 1822 --Fiction. I. Title.

PS3519.O435 D8 2013
813.6 --dc23   2013905116

ISBN-13: 978-1-62652-732-4
LCCN: 2013905116

Distributed by Itasca Books

Printed in the United States of America

For Emma

'A knight errant—to cut a long story short—is beaten up one day and made Emperor the next.'

Don Quixote,
By Miguel Cervantes (1547-1615)
Translated by J. M. Cohen

Table of Contents

PROLOGUE   1

Part I.

ONE: *What's the Count?*   7

TWO: *The Mystic Worker*   13

THREE: *Pigs*   22

FOUR: *Dangling*   24

FIVE: *Que Sais-je?*   26

SIX: *Anticipation of the Unknown*   36

SEVEN: *Tabula Rasa*   42

Part II.

EIGHT: *Fresh Graves*   59

NINE: *Knock and Run*   64

TEN: *Metaphor in Motion*   76

ELEVEN: *There's Always Trouble*   89

TWELVE: *We?*   95

THIRTEEN: *Prince of Abissinia*   106

FOURTEEN: *A Pugilistic Battle: My name is Koi*   110

FIFTEEN: *Our Little Speck*   122

SIXTEEN: *The First Salute*   121

SEVENTEEN: *Life, Liberty…*   123

EIGHTEEN: *Statia*   127

NINETEEN: *No Man's Land*   132

TWENTY: *Macabre Seascape*   139

TWENTY-ONE: *For God's Sake*   141

TWENTY-TWO: *The Red Kerchief*   149

TWENTY-THREE: *A Surreal Mark of Time*   153

TWENTY-FOUR: *Living State of Dead*   157

TWENTY-FIVE: *As for the State-less Rabble*   161

TWENTY-SIX: *Treasure*   169

TWENTY-SEVEN: *My Juliet*   175

TWENTY-EIGHT: *To Survive*   181

TWENTY-NINE: *One Eye Open*   186

THIRTY: *Dashed!*   190

THIRTY-ONE: *The Other Half*   204

THIRTY-TWO: *If I were a Slave*   212

THIRTY-THREE: *Grand Mal*   218

THIRTY-FOUR: *Newly Christened*   227

THIRTY-FIVE: *Not What You Think*   229

THIRTY-SIX: *A Little Sugar*   232

THIRTY-SEVEN: *Koi?*   237

THIRTY-EIGHT: *As Upset as Koi*   241

THIRTY-NINE: *Plans*   244

FORTY: *Blurry Limits*   247

FORTY-ONE: *Compromised*   251

FORTY-TWO: *Speculation*   258

FORTY-THREE: *Rattled Nerves*   267

FORTY-FOUR: *Cash Money*   270

FORTY-FIVE: *1884*   277

FORTY-SIX: *Pay to…*   283

FORTY-SEVEN: *On a Mythical Island*   285

FORTY-EIGHT: *I'm Coming*   288

FORTY-NINE: *He Began to Read*   294

FIFTY: *The Right Time*   298

FIFTY-ONE: *Pygmies!*   304

FIFTY-TWO: *Do You Know Me?*   312

FIFTY-THREE: *He's Right, You Know*   316

FIFTY-FOUR: *Man Plans and God Laughs*   323

Part III.

FIFTY-FIVE: *Pennies on the Dollar*   327

FIFTY-SIX: *Changing Perspective*   331

FIFTY-SEVEN: *As though Across a Flame*   336

FIFTY-EIGHT: *A Farce*   340

FIFTY-NINE: *Close Enough*   347

SIXTY: *Like a Bolt of Lightning*   350

SIXTY-ONE: *Not His Mind*   356

SIXTY-TWO: *His Problem*   359

SIXTY-THREE: *Notsie*   360

SIXTY-FOUR: *It won't Stop*   370

EPILOGUE   371

Cast of Characters

Robert Vesey – narrator, son of Denmark Vesey

Telemaque/Denmark Vesey – protagonist, enslaved in Africa and brought to the New World

Koi – Telemaque's childhood friend

Master Thomas – Telemaque's first European owner, fiancé of Madame Chevalier's daughter (owns the *Briel* and the *Liverpool*)

Madame Chevalier – Telemaque's new owner in the Caribbean

Adam – Jewish merchant of the Caribbean and North America, Koi's new owner (owns the *Rotterdam*, *Jupiter*, *Kameel* and *Eleanor*)

Jacob – Captain who works for Master Thomas, Madame Chevalier and others (owns the *Eclipse* and the *Vasa*)

Millie – One of Mater Thomas's slaves, hired out to Madame Chevalier

Captain Palmer – Seaman of the Caribbean (owns the *Libertas*)

Dr. Ramsay – Doctor turned preacher, writer and abolitionist (owns the *Mary*)

Seymour – American spy who works for Master Thomas as overseer of *Paradis* Plantation

Captain Vesey – Slaver, privateer, chandler and owner of Denmark Vesey (owns the *Prospect*)

ATLANTIC OCEAN

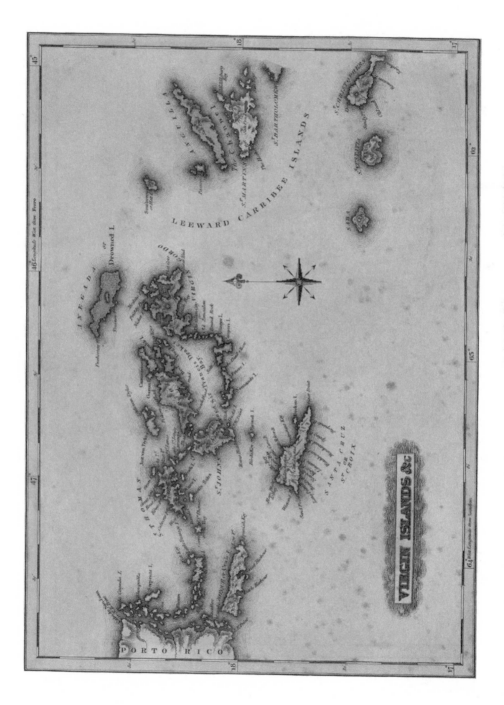

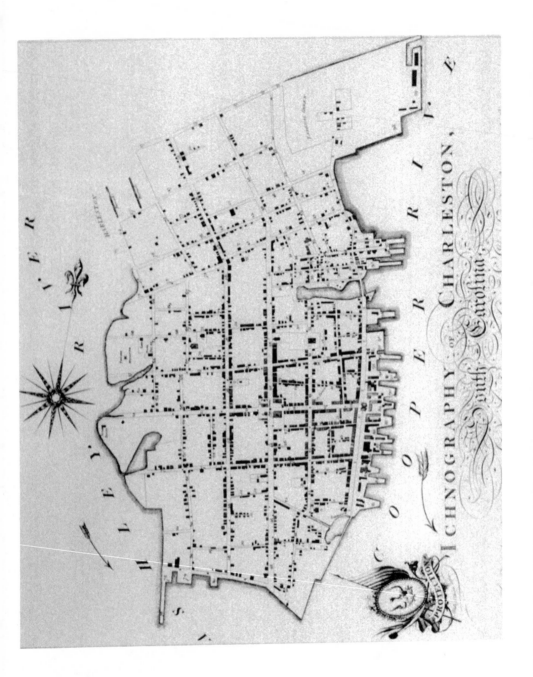

ICHNOGRAPHY of CHARLESTON, South Carolina

Due Unto

Denmark Vesey's Story

PROLOGUE

April 14, 1865
Fort Sumter, Charleston Harbor

The flag pole stood naked as people gathered round.

White men in dark suits. Women in hoop skirts with parasols and fans. Soldiers in dress uniform. Most numerous among them, the liberated in their finest. All disembarked for the island wearing faces as stiff and decorous as their attire.

Among the early arrivals to the ceremony, Robert Vesey fixed his eyes upon what he'd come for. He climbed the steps of the east parapet for a better look. To memorize. He would never again have a chance to examine the entrance to Charleston Harbor from such a unique close vantage point.

Satisfied, Robert took a moment to enjoy the panoramic view and ocean breezes at the precipice. Seeking shelter from the sun he climbed down three steps to a cobbled wooden bench shaded by the wall. Fort Sumter still lay in ruins after the Union bombardment and Confederate surrender. Aaron Barkey, a young Jew and the only Yankee reporter for the *New South Post*, climbed the east wall too and sat next to Robert in the little shade.

In solemn silence the two strangers observed the thin crowd milling about the stifling interior of the island's fortification. A brass band aboard the flotilla snaking toward the fort was hours away from leading a chorus of *The Star Spangled Banner* for the thousands of expected attendees.

When Major General John Anderson arrived, Aaron took out his pencil and recorded in his notebook that Anderson would raise the same American flag he'd lowered from Fort Sumter four years earlier.

To add intrigue to the national significance of his story Aaron turned to interview Robert, assuming he was an illiterate ex-slave. He started with, "A grand day to celebrate the Union victory, wouldn't you say?" Followed by, "I'm a reporter. I write for the *New South Post*. You know, one of those newspapers you see white folks reading."

The graying whiskered architect's quiet glare unsettled the young man. Though still new to his job, unaccustomed to conversing with war weary Charlestonian's of either race, he was determined to be a good reporter, to do his job well. Aaron swallowed through the lump in his throat and spoke again, extending his hand.

"The name's Barkey. Aaron Barkey."

After an elongated pause Robert met the young man's hand. Shaking it he said, "Vesey. Robert Vesey," before turning his attention to boats docking at the landing.

Aaron was certain he'd heard that name before.

"Vesey," he repeated the name. "Yes. I once heard Frederick Douglass speak. To a gathering of Negro soldiers. The 54th Massachusetts. Where I'm from; Massachusetts. He shouted to the colored troops…'Remember Denmark Vesey of Charleston!' Like a battle cry. I remember asking myself who he'd meant by that. Do you know? Were, are you…somehow related?"

"He's my father. Was," Robert said.

The powers that be stole his father's life many times. Time and again. But Robert believed the last vestige of his father's legacy remained—out there—buried in the shifting sands of the Charleston Bar at the harbor's entrance.

In response to this chance encounter, sensing a scoop, a hook, a sensational slant, Aaron licked the tip of his pencil and put it to his notebook.

"Can you tell me about him, your father?"

Though leery of the young white man's intentions, Robert had always wanted his father's side of the story told, again and again. Immortalized. Most of it anyway.

Wringing his hands, he said, looking through Aaron, "I'd hardly know where to begin."

A refreshing cool salt air breeze ruffled the pages of Aaron's notebook resting on his knee. Looking out at the approaching flotilla with thousands still aboard, then at the sparse crowd assembled below Aaron said, "We've plenty of time."

After the rustle of more wind between the two men, Robert paused and said, "Telemaque."

"What?" Aaron said, as perplexed by the unusual word as the answer.

"Tel-e-ma-que. His African name was Telemaque."

Part I.
1775-1776

ONE

What's the Count?

The wedding bonfire blazed against the night sky extinguishing the stars above like early dawn. Telemaque looked over his shoulder again into the surrounding darkness.

Stepping closer to his tribe dancing around the flames, his eyes met Koi's.

As shrieks of joy reached a crescendo, singing solos to a chorus, the percussion of the talking drums, resonating hard and deep, could be felt for miles. With the bride and groom long gone, in the midst of making love, everything was about to change forever.

The Dahomey king's army, half armed with guns, including a battalion of Amazons, attacked the celebration like a violent monsoon. Musket flashes cracked like lightning scattering the villagers. The warriors pursued their goal—the capture of Africans from the interior for Europeans at the coast—with precision.

"What's the count, Jamison?" Captain Christopher Warrett asked as he stood within the sliver of shade cast by the mainmast of the *Briel* anchored off West Africa; November, 1775.

"Look there, sir," First Mate Jean Michelle Jamison said as he leaned into the captain's shade.

He didn't have to be specific. Abra, Telemaque's mother—tall, slim, half naked—attracted the admiration of the officers. Ogles from the crew. She stood out on deck in line with the other captives. Her full breasts and slight distended belly, revealing her to be with child, made her all the more alluring, as did the radiant glow of her smooth skin.

The appearance of the red-tipped, primed, branding iron jolted their lust. To a man they watched Abra. Able seamen preparing to unfurl sails. The quarter master's mate standing next to the helmsman. And the bosun, now holding Abra, the next slave in line.

"I prefer white sugar," the captain said while following Abra's ordeal.

Abra held her breath at the sizzle and bubble of her flesh against hot iron. Dazed by shock and panic, the intense pain to her shoulder resumed immediately. The pasty viscous salve applied to the burn only added to her perpetual unease. It had no effect on her other, much worse, deeper wound; the gash to her psyche created by separation from loved ones, home, friends, her identity. The torture and constant threats, the confinement, forced each captive into his or her own private hell. As she rubbed her swollen belly Abra concentrated on thoughts of her son and husband, and a show of strength for her daughter, next in line.

After picking at his pants and adjusting his girth on the pitching deck the rotund captain returned to squinting through his spyglass at the *Diane*. A French ship struggling with luffing sails further offshore, among the reefs. He tilted his head and twisted the lens in an attempt to focus and ameliorate the harsh glare of sun on water. Dissatisfied, he collapsed the instrument.

Leering at Abra, Jamison's trance was broken only by the captain's insistence.

"What's the count, Jamison?"

Suspicious of the answer, Captain Warrett had kept his own tally with his spyglass from the bridge of the *Briel*. He'd focused on the skiffs and canoes as they shoved off from the pier of the slave factory at the edge of the African continent.

"One ninety-three altogether, sir."

At the coast, Telemaque was among the last put into a skiff at the fort's pier, along with Koi. A little girl from a sometimes friendly, sometimes rival Ewe clan. A point of confusion for Telemaque. He'd never known Koi's mind amid alternating political feuds and trans-clan marriage celebrations. Or just why he'd always liked to gaze upon her more than any other. The children arrived aboard the *Briel* just as Telemaque's mother and older, post pubescent sister, Sade, were branded and forced below into the hold.

Bruised and sore—punched in the face by a white man at the fortress door after he'd cried out to his mother—Telemaque dared not call out to her now. Instead, he turned to Koi, squatting next to him. Her commiseration—communicated in a sign language only the two spoke—eased the tightness in his small chest.

The task at hand of loading, branding and confining almost two hundred Africans in chains on a crowded, rocking, sweltering ship required order amid chaos. The forty-two year old captain's confident demeanor reinforced his commands barked from the bridge. His tone induced immediate compliance throughout the crew; despite his peculiar proclivity of picking at his clothes. Pulling and picking to adjust his pants.

Calls of seagulls swirling close by were drowned out by intermittent cracks of a whip and cries of pain onboard amid the clink clank of chains in use. This rhythmic cacophony set to motion continued unabated measured in time by the creaking, sway of the ship on the rolling surf.

So close to shore, the absence of wind aggravated the crew and officers alike. The stench of the hold hovered in place like the smoke of a whaler's fat boiler. Permeating every garment fiber, pore and orifice. The men struggled in the heat to hurry their routine.

Continuing his report to his captain, alluding to suitability, Jamison said, "About fourscore are of a Ewe tribe or two, I believe. Most are Akan of some sort; Asante, no Fanti, perhaps, sir. Some are from further inland, Dagomba, I imagine." Searching for eye contact, he was disappointed again.

Though seething at the suspect veracity of Jamison's report, the captain masked his emotions by saying only, "Very well, that will be all," as he returned to his spyglass.

"Aye, Captain."

For investors in the *Briel,* and her competitors as well, their timing could not have been better. King Kpengla of the Dahomey kingdom, a vassal of the Yoruba Oyo Empire, had strategically positioned his forces within the West African interior. He then ordered his commander to enslave all neighboring tribes in his army's path to the sea. Telemaque and Koi's Ewe clans were among those captured en masse as the Dahomey army swept across the landscape. The move enriched the king in his exchange of slaves for trade goods, including guns, while displaying his power to his rival Asante and Dagomba kingdoms—a fortuitous event for the *Briel*'s investors.

After the *Briel*'s surgeon applied salve to their branding wounds, Abra, Sade and the others were sent below into the reeking hull. "Seasoned" through constant use—voyage after voyage—the hold emitted a putrid, foul odor of urine, feces and vomit. It assaulted the senses at first breath. Men were corralled into one berth, women to another. Telemaque, Koi and the other children, ten and younger, were allowed some leeway.

Earlier, Telemaque's father, Mawusi, as cunning as stout, surveyed the men in line waiting to be branded in search of allies. Men he could count on to fight for their freedom and that of their wives and children. Once the slaves were chained at the ankle to shelve-like platforms stacked three high they were left to swelter lying on their backs in the dark stagnant oven-like temperatures. Telemaque's father said to the anxious man next him, "Do not fear the *toubabu*, the foreign albinos. They are weak. Remember, we are warriors. We need only wait for the right time to strike them dead to free our women and children."

The man replied as his eyes adjusted to the dark, "They will violate our women soon. I've witnessed their leers already."

Mawusi fumed at the thought and knew the man spoke of his first wife, Abra.

For the *Briel*'s prisoners, a tack across the Atlantic guaranteed a macabre collage of fear, disease, pain, misery and death while traveling for an indeterminate time to an unknown world in a strange and mysterious cavern of wood. But for the captain, officers and crew, a familiar course set from West Africa for St. Thomas in the West Indies meant wages, women and rum.

Once at sea, Captain Warrett again spotted the large French flag trailing the *Diane* as she continued to struggle along the coast. Having purchased human cargo up and down the West African coast, with 281 souls onboard, the *Diane* was overloaded. Unable to find sustaining winds to catapult her out into the orbit of trade winds and currents still farther out at sea, she languished too near the treacherous reefs.

As seen from a distance aboard the *Briel*, after spilling her sails the *Diane* listed, then careened before disappearing from sight. Captain Warrett ordered the *Briel* to come about and return to the coast in search of survivors—the code of the sea.

Maintaining enough shackles in working order throughout the Middle Passage was a constant worry for slavers. Salt air corroded and compromised parts rendering the whole an illusion of restraint and order.

The suffering, desperate slaves aboard the *Diane* had thwarted their restraints and revolted against their French captors. Though her crew had beat to quarters, it was too late.

Back at the coast again the crew of the *Briel* set about fishing the *Diane*'s survivors from the sea; three sailors, and an African girl clinging to the *Diane*'s flotsam. She was being jostled by foul air and dead bodies bubbling to the surface. Soon to be devoured by sharks lurking nearby. The bubbles included the last breath of a hundred slaves still chained by the ankle to the *Diane*, resting on her side in a hundred feet of water. Toward the shoreline two French sailors and most of the Africans who'd escaped the *Diane* were hidden from view for moments at a time by high cresting ocean swells. Telemaque, Koi and a half a dozen other slave children allowed topside, watched as Captain Warrett looked through his spyglass. He could see some African's heads bobbing, struggling in the surf like the two sailors as the rest washed ashore.

With her maritime duty fulfilled above the site of the *Diane*'s wreckage, blocked from prevailing winds by the jagged shoreline, the *Briel* too, at first, struggled to fill her sails. But soon a swooning gust just strong enough to billow her jib guided her out to sea. At the bridge, Captain Warrett ordered the unfurling of the *Briel*'s entire complement and began anew his course set for the West Indies. Below deck, in the hold, Mawusi's plan was already well underway.

"What's the count?"

TWO

The Mystic Worker

Seven weeks later the prisoners of the *Briel*, minus sixty-two, dead, were unloaded like any other cargo from all manner of ships at Charlotte Amalie, St. Thomas. Though one girl had been lost at sea in a storm, most of the dead Africans had succumbed to an outbreak of smallpox. And while still others perished from maladies of the heart and soul, some had died the death of insurrectionists, including Telemaque's father.

Telemaque's mother, Abra, his sister, Sade, and his friend Koi had cared for the sick and dying, miraculously saving many a sailor and African alike. As they now walked on wobbly legs down the gangplank chained together, and to others, seagulls called out from above the smell of days old fish. The hot sun bore down on them not unlike a day in Africa, through puffed white clouds and blue sky. The thought reminded Abra of the home life and village she missed. As a widow, she mourned her husband. As a mother, she worried about Sade and her boy, left behind aboard the *Briel*, and her unborn child who'd taken to kicking her from within the safety of her womb.

"Stay," Abra said under her breath.

"What?" Sade asked her mother, just in front of her. Only aware that her mother had spoken.

A contingent of sailors approached the captain carrying his sea trunk and those of the *Briel*'s dead sailors, including Jamison's. One sailor carried an emaciated, unconscious boy; Telemaque. He asked, "Where to, Capt'n?"

"Put them in the dray," pointing to a cart on the wharf next to a makeshift pen for the ship's goats. "Have the chests sent to the first hotel you see on Norre Gade, just below the fort, it's the only one."

Pointing to another part of the island; "Take him to the auction house with the others. Have him put in isolation, until his health improves, or doesn't," the captain said before disembarking down the *Briel*'s gangplank. He was on his way to his employer's office with a bandage on his wounded foot and the ship's logbook tucked into his armpit.

"Aye aye, Captain," they replied before carrying the chests and Telemaque ashore.

Telemaque was among the fortunate. Not only would he likely survive the pox, but being so young, his nightmares of the voyage aboard the *Briel*, including the death of his father would not ripen for some time.

The dense port town progressed up the steep grade of a dormant volcano. Stairs replaced some inclined streets for residents to climb to homes or businesses. From high upon the mountain slope Fort Christian and two stout towers guarded Charlotte Amalie below. Teaming with life ashore, the bay's blue water sparkled between a forest of swaying timber.

To capture harbor breezes and avoid the street smells and noise Master William Thomas's offices were on the second floor. His large windows overlooked his dock and Charlotte Amalie's waterfront. Captain Warrett's climb up the flight of stairs and into Master Thomas's office had posed a challenge to his still raw wound, inflicted by the rebellious slaves. His foot and head throbbed in pain leaving him flush, sweaty.

Captain Warrett was greeted at his employer's place of business by an arrogant assistant whose nostrils flared as he showed the captain into the slave trading headquarters.

Master Thomas stood behind his large desk, feeding ackee seeds to his late father's colorfully plumed macaw. The bird was perched atop a stand next to the desk. At the interruption by one of his captains, Master Thomas began to pace behind his desk. His hands clasp behind his back.

The disheveled captain, still shaken from his battle at sea, began, while at attention, by adjusting his pants. Eyes straight ahead he said, "Pleased to see you, sir," before risking a quick glance at the bird. "It's my pleasure to report the *Briel*'s safe passage. A cargo of 131 slaves for market, sir."

New beads of sweat formed on his brow as the rest rolled down his face.

Master Thomas, a short thin reed of a man in his early forties, a Brit, wore a black coat over a white shirt and a pretentious ill-fitting wig atop his little head. He alternated his attention to the floor with glances at the captain as he paced. Master Thomas ignored the view of business out in the bay as Captain Warrett studied it through the large open windows.

"Warrett, how many did you lose?"

Standing taller and straighter, "Thirty-two, sir."

"You're a liar!" the bird shrieked, looking at no one.

Master Thomas blanched at the words, gorgonized.

The bird bobbed and craned his head.

Not only surprised by the bird's power of speech, he was astonished by what the bird said. Words often spoken by his late father—to him or to anyone else his father wished to intimidate whether he'd suspected a lie or not.

Master Thomas pretended he'd not lost his composure though he continued for a moment to stare at the bird's jerky head movements, its eyes wide, looking at no one.

"Crew?"

Captain Warrett cringed in anticipation of a loud, tongue lashing. Blinking, he said, "Thirteen, sir."

At first, Master Thomas did not react. He already knew the answers to his questions; a mole onboard the *Briel*—the cook who served the captain and officers each day. But then, he turned and looked straight at the captain.

He put his hands on his desk, leaned forward, and asked, "Are you sure of your count, Captain?" (A woman had jumped to her death upon the *Briel*'s arrival; consumed by schooling sharks beneath the wharf.)

Alarmed at his own omission, a sin he'd had his First Mate Jamison flogged for, "Yes, sir. I mean, no, sir," he winced at his words. "The correct count is 130, sir." After muttering to himself, "Damned sharks," he made another furtive glance at the bird.

The notion that Master Thomas already knew everything the captain had to report before he'd even appeared finally dawned on the tired, injured captain. Coursing through the suffering man's mind between throbs of his aching foot and head were his own words: "What's the count, Jamison?" and "Damn you, Jamison, your only excuse is no excuse. You neglected to amend the ledger…your responsibility—unmet!"

"Growing feeble-minded, are you, Captain? Can't keep the savages in manacles, nor their count!"

"Yes, sir. I mean, no, sir," the captain winced again.

"Well, the one you left out, or rather let jump in, will be deducted from your remuneration."

The captain's arrangement with his employer, assuming a minimum "spoilage," was a bonus of three hand-picked slaves among the cargo once he had completed the voyage.

The captain exhaled; relieved he had not already been dismissed from service; fired. He regretted this occasion would no longer be an opportunity to request new shackles.

Master Thomas made concessions to the truth about the *Briel*'s voyage. He overstated her losses in order to decrease his per unit transportation costs. He was determined no mention of the insurrection would be documented. Insurance policies refused claims on losses incurred during a slave rebellion. As such, as a trade-off, rather than disciplining the captain, Master Thomas made the captain complicit; a corroborating account of Master Thomas's official version of events.

"That leaves you with two as your remaining bonus. Have you made your selection? What do you plan to do with them? You could sell them to me," Master Thomas said, aware of the captain's choices. Master Thomas was thinking of the Abra gossip his mole had heard circulate among the men. One crewman had overheard the captain refer to Abra as the "miracle worker," for her contribution to saving lives amid the scourge of pox. That image among the crew morphed into the "mystic worker." The captain noted the transformation as it was bantered about his ship.

The mention of, and eagerness to buy his two slaves, aroused Captain Warrett's antennae.

Master Thomas produced a fraudulent insurance document for the captain to attest to and sign. It read:

Vessel Owner: *Thomas & Company*
Particular outcome of voyage: *Slaves delivered to West Indies*
First region of slave purchase: *Bight of Benin*
Second region of slave purchase: *X*
Total slaves embarked: *199*
Total slaves disembarked: *130*
Crew at voyage outset: *22*
Crew deaths during voyage: *13*
Captain's name: *Warrett, Christopher*

Captain Warrett checked and signed the document. Master Thomas had filled in the "Total slaves embarked:" blank with "199." He then again asked about buying the two slaves.

Master Thomas had been reared among the island culture. He feared the spirit world of the islands as ardently as he ridiculed it.

Aware of Master Thomas's propensity to put great stock in all manner of superstitions, especially African mysticism, Captain Warrett referred to the two slaves he'd picked for sale, "Yes, I've chosen the wench with child. The one with 'healing powers.' And the one I understand is her daughter. She's a handsome one, the 'mystic worker' is, as is the lass."

The words "healing powers" and "mystic worker" struck their mark. Master Thomas had fantasized about finding a compromised apothecary, a ktenologist, or voodoo practitioner of potions even before his recent engagement. He is engaged to the daughter of his late father's fiercest rival in life as well as business. She is also heir to a unique, valued island.

Many times Master Thomas has imagined a successful conclusion to his scheme; to hasten the demise of his future mother-in-law, Madame Chevalier; a widow. He has in mind substituting something "exotic" for the medicine an itinerant doctor from St. Kitt, Dr. James Ramsay, prescribes for her.

Like his father before him, Master Thomas covets Madame Chevalier's Road Town businesses, yes. But even more, Master Thomas is obsessed with plans he has for Madame Chevalier's island. The island is unnamed on many maps. It was not listed in the Danish West India Company's mid-seventeenth century private sale of "the Tortola Island territory." Nor is her island listed among the current British holdings of two dozen other islands along either side of the Sir Francis Drake Channel. As such, the island remains outside the jurisdiction of any sovereign nation.

Indeed, Master Thomas sees his courtship and marriage as a path for the lifelong bachelor to take possession of the island. But each passing month, or year, represents an opportunity cost to him, a delay in profits beyond his father's wildest imagination.

Captain Warrett's wink-and-a-nod airs meant to bait Master Thomas into making an attractive offer on his slaves was successful; even masterful. Master Thomas came to believe—through his own powers of persuasion and superstition—that the African woman, Abra, possessed a knowledge of "voodoo potions." And, as such, Master Thomas felt he'd finally found a means to his end. However, as a shrewd negotiator, he attempted to remain cavalier as he spoke of the two slaves. He not only did not want to drive up the price he'd pay, he wanted to conceal the sway superstition held on his faculties.

Cautiously, Master Thomas said, "So, what's your price?"

This being among the most rare of occasions—to be on the power side of a trade with Master Thomas—Captain Warrett took a moment to savor the feeling. Not unlike when a beached ship's hull rises with the tide. However, in consideration of future employment he didn't want to seem unreasonable or exploitative. He said, "I'll take three hundred and fifty pounds for the lot. Two each at Thomas & Company's insurance value, seeing your point of view toward the voyage, and as beholdin' good will towards another voyage soon. Twenty-five for the auction house, seeing I've already placed them there. And another seventy-five, on account of the cargo's *special* properties." The last part he added with emphasis to ensure that Master Thomas felt Captain Warrett, too, believed in the slave woman's magic powers.

"Agreed," Master Thomas said as visions of owning a beautiful African conjurer exploited his imagination to arousal.

Later, at the auction house, Captain Warrett withdrew the smallpox healer and her daughter from the auction. After locating the two slaves, dressed in plain coarse cotton, and after paying the minimum commission, the captain asked the proprietors to bring them forward onto the trading floor.

Adam Wolff, a thirty-something bearded Orthodox Ashkenazi Jewish businessman dressed in black with a singular six inch curl of black hair dangling from beneath his hat on either side of his face, stood among the others as he looked for the pox healer from the *Briel*.

A man of some authority, keys dangling from his belt and a swagger of propriety, accompanied by slaves trailing behind him appeared in Adam's sight. Along with the man's two special charges near him he'd brought more slaves to the floor for customers to examine; soon to be showcased for sale from the platform erected along a wall of the room.

Other buyers approached other slavers and slaves.

Adam approached the man he had singled out, "Are you the man with the pox slave?" The mole's story of "a mystic worker" and her helpers traveled fast from the *Briel* to the auction house, taverns and brothels.

"Why, yes, as a matter of fact I am," the man said through blackened teeth as a smile materialized across his wrinkled face; Abra and Sade stood behind him with Koi close at hand.

"They're mine," Adam said, nodding toward Abra and her helper, Sade, certain he'd purchase them.

Captain Warrett approached the slaver facing Adam from behind. He put his hand on the man's shoulder as he whispered into the slaver's ear, reminding him of the two slaves he was to deliver, not sell!

"Begging your pardon, gov'nour, if you please," the man said as he walked away from Adam, coaxing the two slaves, Abra and Sade—with a kind tone and an arm on Abra's shoulder. Adam waited; Koi peered up into his eyes like a child to a stranger.

From across the cavernous room a scream and struggle ensued. The pregnant slave—the very one Adam intended to buy despite her surprising condition—attempted to refuse her new arrangement. Abra fought to get back to Koi, to insist Koi be taken too. The distress in her voice reminded Koi of her mother's, in Africa. Koi attempted to race to their side, but the handlers did their job. One of the slavers swatted Koi away with the back of his hand, propelling her back to Adam's feet.

The slaver Adam had originally approached returned to the center of the room, near enough for Adam to confront. However, as Adam questioned him the slaver simply smiled again through his black teeth, insisting with the point of his finger that Adam must voice his concerns to a desk clerk seated across the room.

While paying the amount demanded, Adam's attempt to adjust the conversation to the proper outcome was met with derision amid the clerk's words that included the name "Jacob"; summoning a large bald white whale of a man. Soon standing beside the clerk's desk, Jacob's response to Koi's crying and Adam's presence was so swift that Adam and Koi found themselves on the street outside the auction house, squinting through direct sunlight at one another having hardly ever moved their feet.

Forced to leave his dignity and his planned purchase behind, Adam mumbled to himself, *Mann tracht und Gott lacht* (Man plans and God laughs). He took the child by the hand and departed the Danish West India Company as bewildered and almost as upset as Koi.

THREE

Pigs

While Telemaque languished in isolation within the walls of the Danish West India Company prison, Abra and Sade joined a half-a-dozen young male slaves, three no more than boys, onboard a fifty-seven foot sloop, the *Eclipse*. Abra's belly ached and Sade moaned at the prospect of another confinement at sea, unsure of the duration of the voyage or their fate at their next destination.

They couldn't help but notice the captain of the vessel, Jacob, as he told his crew to prepare to set sail for *Paradis*, a plantation named for the island on which it stood; a distressed property being acquired by Master Thomas.

Before shoving off, the crew loaded livestock and hunting dogs along with barrels of salted herring, flour and rum, sacks of cornmeal, coils of hemp rope; and then a fresh side of beef hung from the rafters in the hold with the slaves.

The journey in the dark, damp, mildewed cargo hold worried Abra. Sade knew. She sensed her mother's anxiety and discomfort as they both eyed the silent young men and boys seated across the hull. Several filthy swine—loaded after three barking dogs were chained by the collar to a rib of the ship—wandered freely. Their stench trailed them as they trotted past, up and down the hold. Every ten minutes or so all eyes turned to their squeals and grunts as one or another fought the others over another rat discovered scurrying for cover in the dim light below deck.

An hour into the voyage, as the seas became rough, Abra's water broke. The eyes of the young male slaves alternately stared or were hidden from view by their arms or each other's bodies as Abra's screams, heard topside, elicited smirks from Jacob's sailors.

After two hours of labor—Sade doing all she could to comfort her mother—a baby boy was born, bloody and shriveled on the uneven wooden plank floor. Everyone marveled at the new life, waiting, willing the baby to move. Before they could pass judgment of the child's fate, he let out a cry that even the sailors thought they'd heard.

The pigs bore down on the scene immediately. Confusion ensued. The tethered dogs barked and yelped. No hysterical scream or blow could deter the swine from consuming the baby's torso in less than a minute. The constant barrage of punches kicks and shouts finally scattered the squealing, snorting beasts to opposite ends of the hold to continue devouring remnants, pieces, of the newborn in relative peace. They left a lone, tiny foot behind.

From deep within her being Abra expelled an unearthly roar of anguished fury so dense it pulsed through the hull's inhabitants silencing the hogs and hounds for two beats. Sade picked up the tiny foot and secreted it away in her coarse cotton dress pocket.

At the sound of all the commotion, and Abra's outburst, two sailors with a lantern whisked below to investigate. They shrugged in the dim light and reported nothing out of the ordinary to Jacob.

Abra stared in shock at the wet afterbirth before her; the umbilical cord still attached to her like a severed lifeline to her past, present and future. She turned to her side, hiding her face and wept. Even Sade could offer no solace.

An hour later an exhausted Abra slept, too deep to hear movement until it ceased; the sound of thuds and sailor's shouting startled her awake as the *Eclipse* tied up to the working dock of *Paradise*.

FOUR

Dangling

Koi found herself stowed aboard Adam's ship, the *Rotterdam*, bound for an unknown destination and future. Rather than climb into an empty swaying hammock suspended from the rafters Koi fashioned a bed of old sails upon the hold's plank floor. Exhausted, she tried to sleep despite the pounding of the ocean against the hull and odor of bilge water swill sloshing beneath her head.

Slaves like Koi, as well as dozens of indentured servants stooped and slept shoulder to shoulder throughout their passage from St. Thomas to Charles Town, South Carolina; a city of twelve thousand, half of them enslaved. The city was in the midst of protests and rebellion against their mistreatment, their "enslavement," by their English king.

The concussion from news of "the shot heard 'round the world" last year reverberated still, rattling the politics, economies and tranquility of half of its white populace, including Koi's new owner, Adam Wolff. Ever since the battles at Lexington and Concord, anticipation of a British military response had heightened—more battles, more rebels, more rebels, more battles—stifling many plans for the future.

The mood of Charles Town alternated between panic and resolve, not unlike three years earlier when a smallpox epidemic killed hundreds of whites and thousands of slaves. There seemed no where safe to run. Smallpox, the scourge of the century, had led to the death of millions, including the king of France, Louis XV, in 1774. Variolation, a method of inoculation, out of reach to the masses, was available, for a price, to the wealthy and to many military conscripts. Washington petitioned the Continental Congress for funds to inoculate his whole army. Slaves thought to be immune to the disease were sought after as valuable care givers.

Adam's failed attempt to acquire pox-immune slaves for a sideline variolation business did not deter him from his main mission. Beginning with his great-grandfather, Adam's family business interests—real estate, shipping, commodities—though centered in the West Indies, had prospered and grown through the generations to span the eastern seaboard of North America as well as much of the Caribbean. And now, in spite of, or because of, his family's disapproval of his bride of choice, Adam was determined to show them all, to prove himself; to surpass his grandfather's, and even his father's success. He would turn the impending crisis into his opportunity.

Among other means—through the business of, the art of, smuggling—he would not only rescue his family's business interests in the American colonies, but also capitalize as quickly as possible on the new Continental Congress' voracious appetite for war supplies ahead of all-out war. A war that Adam reasoned would not last long and would end with the colonists being crushed under the weight of the mighty British Empire.

FIVE

Que Sais-je?

Master Thomas told his fiancée, Madame's daughter, he had to travel to an acquired "farm" on a remote deserted island—save some fifty slaves—Paradise Island. And, so as to not encourage curiosity, he neglected to mention to her that the vacant plantation house, *Paradis*, was fully furnished with French luxury, and that from its perch on high, overlooking a bay, the manor house provided stunning views that included her mother's island. A perfect perch from which to watch his plans for Madame Chevalier's atoll unfold.

The previous occupant of *Paradis* held the property through his family who were French absentee owners for several generations. The plantation income had grown erratic, ruinous to the lifestyles of those dependent upon it. In the polite salon discussions of Parisian society slavery was disparaged even as coffee, tea or cocoa was served with white sugar. So the sale rid the family of an embarrassment, their slavery connection, while providing a badly needed injection of capital. None in the family knew of anyone, except *him*, who had ever visited the source of their wealth.

Master Thomas had asked the barrister who had arranged the distressed sale to meet him there. After curt salutations Master Thomas inquired about the seller, asking to meet him.

"Dead," the barrister said as he closed a heavy ledger book. "He didn't last more than a week. Mysterious. But, *que sais-je?* Men raised in Paris don't know the climate, the food, precautions."

"You're a liar! Arrr…Oo-koo," said the bird Master Thomas brought with him.

The barrister's head recoiled, surprised by the outburst, which, of course, was the calculated, intended response.

A fortune teller confirmed Master Thomas's conviction that the bird was his father reincarnated, and as such had become an integral part of Master Thomas's business acumen.

Master Thomas ignored the bird's outburst, applying one of his own.

"What *do* you know?" Master Thomas said, harsh and eager, as though oblivious to the lunacy of a bird resting on his shoulder.

He had just signed the deed in exchange for what was a paltry sum for the property, yet, still, a small fortune among the islands.

"Doctor Ramsay could find nothing wrong," the barrister offered as proof. "He's buried near the slave quarters, outside the slave graveyard. His family would not pay to sail him home." As another island lifer, the barrister was as superstitious as Master Thomas. "Do you want to see where we buried him?" he said with gruesome delight.

Though titillated, Master Thomas struck an indignant posture meant to ridicule the barrister's superstitions and mask his own morbific pleasure.

"No, I don't want to see his grave!" he said, shocked that the sudden death of his predecessor may have occurred near him he looked around. Then, slapping the head of his cane into his hand, "You might have said something before now."

"I see you're a man of business, you drive a bargain. You've seen the books," the barrister said looking for a piece of paper, as if no other explanation should be required.

"But your omission of facts is…"

Before he could finish his sentence the barrister reminded Master Thomas, "I've omitted nothing. The facts are, the man died. Nothing more," as he shuffled more papers on the library desk.

Master Thomas could see the wall being built stone by stone, word by word by the barrister. Master Thomas began again, attempting a measured polite cadence, to dispel the previous sharp exchange.

"Would you be so kind as have the overseer join us and make our introductions?" he said, with an incorrigible tinge of polite arrogance. And, he couldn't resist, "Or, is he *murdered* too?"

A silence froze the room, allowing each man to take stock. The grandfather clock standing next to them chimed, then again, then three more times, as the barrister put his remaining paperwork away into his satchel. He waited for the last chime.

"Certainly, sir. I'll hail him. He's on slave row now. But, I cannot stay. I have other business I must attend to, on Tortola."

The barrister left Master Thomas alone in the library of the plantation manor house to inform the overseer his presence was required within.

The barrister opened the door to the manor privy where he'd seen the heavy overseer go. "Seymour! The new proprietor requires your presence, immediately! And I have pressing business elsewhere," he said before releasing the door to slam shut. The barrister then walked away at a brisk pace toward the dock.

"Wait," the overseer said. He dropped the newspaper he'd been reading, an article written by a surgeon and minister, a Dr. Ramsay. The overseer shouted, "Wait!" but he was too late.

The lone remaining house slave of the deceased, Theresa, let him in.

"You asked to see me, sir," taking off his tri-corner hat. "My name is Lyman Seymour. I'm the overseer."

"Yes, Seymour, I'm sure the barrister has filled you in as to who I am. What I want to know is what have you done to this plantation? I have looked at the books, well-kept mind you, well-kept. But, you've lost slaves beyond explanation. Production and revenue are down. What do you have to say for yourself?"

"I've only just arrived. Been here a few months," Seymour said, blinking innocently and in an unruffled, plain spoken manner.

"Oh, I see. This is getting stranger by the minute," Master Thomas said turning to the window for a glimpse of the efficient barrister's backside climbing aboard a boat at the dock.

"So, who *was* running this place? And how is it you are here?"

"My friend, in Road Town, at the hotel and tavern there, the nice one near the mercantile store, he's the business manager. He introduced me to the planter, the deceased that is. Seems his overseer had deserted the plantation the day before his arrival. Expecting the worst from his new employer, I suspect, he disappeared. He hired me then."

"What are your qualifications?" Master Thomas said, beginning to pace.

With his eyes following the bird perched on Master Thomas's shoulder Seymour stated, "I've been a slaver all my life, sailing out of South Carolina, since I was a boy, almost. This is more of the same, just a different surface."

"Well," Master Thomas said, returning to the ledger books he had opened on the library desk, "Production will return to banner years with or without you. Do you get my meaning, Mr. Seymour?"

Seymour stood stunned.

After Master Thomas's pause for effect, "I've brought more slaves…"

Seymour attempted, "I know…"

But Master Thomas raised his finger to silence him.

"I've brought more slaves and I want to see these numbers," he said, pointing to an array of calculations, net profits, indicating production, at sugar cane market prices minus slave costs at market prices. All other expenses were dwarfed by the cost of replenishing slaves. Replacing an entire slave population every three years was the norm on Caribbean plantations. Almost all the slaves would die of disease or overwork within that time.

Seymour felt Master Thomas's spell on the room. A man of business, cold to the quick in contrast to the amiable Frenchman who'd hired him.

"Now, among those new slaves there's a woman. Bring her to me at 10 p.m."

"How will…"

Master Thomas raised his finger again before Seymour could finish, "I am told, you will know." He stepped to the window, turning his back on Seymour, "That will be all for now."

"Yes, sir," Seymour said. "I'll see to the woman."

Lyman Seymour, alias for Erik Saffer, was an agent of the Committee of Secret Correspondence of the Continental Congress. His tavern sponsor, its business manager, was also his Secret Committee colleague, sent to the Caribbean to keep an eye on the British.

The slave quarters consisted of a dozen huts, built to house a hundred slaves in banner years. Their designs reflected different African practices amalgamated through decades of changes and repairs with local material. Most were thatched circular huts of earthen floor. The steep path from the overseer's house meandered to and through the quarters. The huts along each side of the terraced path alternated like a thick chain. Beyond the community the path narrowed as it descended onto a plateau leading to a rocky shore at sea level with a view across the bay of Madame's island.

Upon their arrival a few days earlier Abra and Sade had poured into the makeshift village with the others from aboard the *Eclipse*. The other new arrivals, the boys and young men who'd witnesses the birth and death of Abra's boy, gravitated to the young men standing at the threshold of the second hut along the sloping lane. Abra recognized one of the slaves as having been aboard the *Briel*. They smelled of slick sweat. Abra and Sade were approached by an old woman who greeted them in a faint voice, beckoning them to come with her. Her expression grew more urgent with every step toward a sturdy hut nearby. The old woman dragged one leg, a birth defect, leaving a dirt trail like a stick dragged across the ground.

The old woman was from Jamaica, but her mother was African, and she'd learned many dialects throughout her long life. She'd also gained a reputation of shaman status among the few that remained from the date of her arrival three years ago.

"The…, oh, there's that *bomba* now, quick," motioning her guests into and away from the door of the hut.

With a whip held in his right hand, the length rolled into a circle, Moses, the *bomba* (the slave's word for driver), approached.

"Which of you is a saltwater?" he'd said.

Conversation among the young men stopped. As he drew closer Moses repeated himself in French and two African tongues he'd learned. As one of the frightened young men spoke the driver hit him with the long heavy handle of his whip, knocking him to the ground, forcing those around him back.

"That's what I'll do to you if you cross me, all of you," he said as he looked them in the eye one by one. He wiped the sweat from his brow and left, grumbling.

"That's Moses. The *bomba*. He been here, I hear, ten years. Worked for three overseers. The last one run off. They was devils together. He drives the gangs hard. Some say he do to impress the whites." She took a step, dragging her lame leg and cackled, "Some say he just miserable," as if she knew which was which.

Peering outside the old woman said, "Oh good, he gone." Turning to Abra and Sade she said, "Lord, child, you a sight, where you come from?"

From the tone of the old woman's voice Abra felt safe, and broke down into her arms, sobbing. Sade and the old woman, Selena, both attempted to soothe Abra as she sobbed in her native tongue of the travels and travails she had endured. "Is this to what end?" Abra asked in her Twi dialect. She had been strong for herself, Sade and the others, but Abra knew her boy was out there somewhere, living a fate she could and could not imagine.

Selena made and served them hot tea. The aroma of evening meals being prepared by shared fires in the lane filled the night, alive with evening conversation that ignored an occasional clink clank of chains around ankles moving in the dark. Selena prepared for three, using the fire started by her neighbor across the way. After eating and lying still and quiet inside Selena's hut she suggested they stay. Abra smiled a slight, gentle smile, a grateful smile. They all bedded down early in accordance with the rhythm of slave row, up before dawn.

The night of Master Thomas's arrival, Seymour made a show of his entrance into the sleepy village by bringing one of the dogs Master Thomas brought to the island. He tied the dog to a tree along the path outside of Selena's hut and announced himself. Selena appeared.

"I'd like to talk," he said.

"And?"

"In private."

"Come in. No one here but me understands you." She went inside her hut. Seymour stooped and entered toward the warm glow of a newly lit candle within.

"You speak English. You're from Jamaica," stating obvious conditions he learned, not the reason for his presence.

"I've a proposition you may find…unbelievable." He pulled the newspaper he had been reading from his pocket and showed her Dr. Ramsay's article, wondering if she could read. She studied the print and moved her lips as though she might be reading with them, or pretending. Whether she was hiding her ignorance or aspiring to impress, Seymour could not say.

"I want to help the slaves get away, a few at a time. I've already diverted some before the new master bought the place. But, now that won't be possible without you. Will you help?"

Selena was taken aback by the proposition, made by a white man—skeptical of his motives.

"Why?"

Struck by her candor and intellect, Seymour said, lying convincingly to the vulnerable destitute old woman, "Fair enough. Let's just say there are mutual interests at play."

"What's my interest?"

"Ah, to the point. Freedom, once the others are gone."

"All of them?"

Sensing resistance, Seymour said, "Maybe not. On other plantations, invariably, some choose to run. We could fake their deaths as though they'd died in their attempt. Others die of fatigue or of fever anyway. You just add some healthy slaves to the sick. In any event, they'll go, replaced by more and so on. We'll add empty graves to mark their passing."

"When?"

"Soon. I'll count on you, then?"

The old woman nodded.

"Then, you'll also understand that I have to *act* like an overseer *to be* an overseer."

The woman nodded again, puzzled by the statement.

"Good," he said. "Now, I'm going to take the woman with me. Look," he said, "she's not even listening. If you don't resist, she may not either."

"Are you going to free her?" Selena asked as her eyebrows rose.

Seymour grabbed Abra by the wrist, getting her attention, "No, this is the *acting* like an overseer part."

Seymour brought Abra to the manor house. Theresa brought her to the back entrances, to the terrace door, just outside Master Thomas's new office, the library.

From the clouded sky view, high above sea level, Abra noted beams of moonlight that appeared through parted clouds, painting the dark ocean with spatterings of white. In the distance across a bay she saw an island protected by a furious crescent of disturbed white water, Madame's atoll. Its hilltop aglow, Abra considered it, thinking of it as a fat bee's wax candle protruding from a pool of thick hardened wax back home.

Theresa knocked on the glass window pane and began to walk away when Master Thomas appeared at one of the French doors.

"Wait," Master Thomas said, his tone unequivocal.

Theresa stopped, slow to turn to face Master Thomas. He said, "I want you to tell her I know she has a daughter, here at *Paradis*." He leaned on the doorframe. Theresa understood. She spoke in direct terms to Abra. Abra yelled, gripping her coarse dress. Master Thomas pulled Abra in while pushing Theresa aside before closing the door in her face.

Theresa walked away quiet and fast, her head held low.

"I'm told you hold magical powers," Master Thomas said, circling Abra as he spoke. "Well, we'll see to those in due time."

Feeling complicit and dirty Theresa hung back on the walkway rather than return to the manor's grand entrance right away. Soon she heard Master Thomas's bird screeching, excited, and saw Abra's silhouette. She seemed bound by her wrists to the library's chandelier.

Further away, Sade and Selena huddled, observing the glow of light emanating from the manor's windows, observing a place Selena had seldom seen and Sade looked upon with frantic worry. A place of beauty used for brutal, unthinkable horror. Sade wanted to race to rescue her mother. Only Selena held her back. They resolved to wait without comment. Sooner than they'd feared Abra came out of the door of Master Thomas's office and down the brick walk, crying and shivering, clutching her dress at the throat, stammering towards them as yet unseen.

Sade and Selena's sudden presence out of the shadows frightened Abra. Once she realized she was safe she cringed in shame. She refused their touch and shushed their words of love and comfort.

Theresa told Selena that Master Thomas reminded her of a white boy she saw, a master's son, torturing a neighbor's tied up pet, then, him glorifying himself by squirting his jism on the animal.

Abra made Selena promise she would put Sade on duty with her, to protect her from Master Thomas and the fields. Selena made a promise to the broken woman she was not sure she could deliver. Selena worked in the mill; she supervised the children and the old and lame stoking the fire with dried sugar cane stalks that heated the vat of crushed sugar cane juice. Sade would work hard, but with some shade. Most of all, Abra felt, she'd have Selena for protection.

The next day Moses arrived early pre-dawn to gather the work gangs. He plucked the new arrivals and had the blacksmith fit them with leg irons. Though they hadn't run yet, they might, like many of the other new hands after a few days in the fields. As he lit and handed out torches Selena raised her machete. Selena's unspoken job included cutting off the arm of any slave pulled into the cane crushing wheel (to reduce the amount of blood let into the vat). She walked toward the sugar mill, signaling she was taking both Sade and Abra with her. Knowing her for years, Moses granted Selena latitude unthinkable to the other slaves. He nodded, and the decision Selena feared most was approved in an instant.

Her-two new African friends might just live, feeding stalk remnants and wood to an insatiable white hot smoky fire all day, every day, for years, or until the end of their lives, whichever came first.

SIX

Anticipation of the Unknown

After a dozen days at sea, Adam watched as the *Rotterdam* docked at Vanderhorst Wharf; the site of a fish market and Craven's Bastion on the Cooper River side of Charles Town. The bastion was being shored up and re-fitted with new cannons to repel an anticipated British naval assault. The wharf's land's end stepped into the middle of East Bay Street, a main thoroughfare for the water district.

Walking inland into the old walled city, Koi marveled at the canyons of wood and brick stacked two and three stories high while she carried almost her body weight in luggage. Adam meandered from one side to the other of streets looking into shop windows for bargains to carry away before the city was leveled in battle—feigning a blind's eye to Koi as she followed him. A slave woman on Church Street carrying her baby on her back while balancing a basket of corn on her head reminded Koi of her mother and sister.

Africans were everywhere: working the docks, sweeping a ubiquitous white dust of sand and crushed shell from storefronts back into the street, driving wagons, shoring up brick fortifications or walking the streets just like her. She wished Telemaque could see through her eyes and wondered what she might see now through his.

Adam stopped at his family's Charles Town residence. Before he made it to the top step, Augustus, the butler, opened the front door. Koi's eyes followed skyward the façade of the narrow three story brick home of Caribbean-inspired Georgian architecture.

Augustus welcomed "Master Adam" as a dotting uncle might receive a familiar face out of the weather. Taking Adam's coat Augustus asked about specific family members and friends he had not seen in years; his Caribbean lilt still discernible twenty years after being shipped first to New York to look after Adam while he attended King's College, and then to Charles Town, where he'd resided ever since.

"Who is she?" Augustus asked.

"I bought her on St. Thomas. By mistake. Well, not exactly, but...I'll explain later."

Skipping beyond the obvious question of why not leave her in the Caribbean Augustus opted for the more immediate, "What are we going to do with her?" as though, as a professional manservant, the child were no more than another piece of luggage, the same as those surrounding her bare feet.

Augustus followed with, "What do you call her?" as Adam ascended the stairs.

Koi craned her neck, looking up, up the stairwell to the ceiling of the third floor to a colorful stained-glass window making use of the morning light to great effect—yet another marvel Koi's eyes wished Telemaque could see.

"Statia," Adam answered from the top of the first flight of stairs, though he had just thought of it, having never addressed the issue before now. Upon acquiring her he had thus far successfully directed Koi with little more than a few words he knew she didn't understand and a gesture or two. Augustus knew the name well, of course, Statia—an island in the West Indies, a colony of the Netherlands. "Statia" is what the locals called their island home of St. Eustatius; Augustus's *real* home.

With Adam out of sight and thoughts of home on his mind, Augustus's demeanor changed. He stooped his tall, lanky dark frame to Koi's level, looked her in the eye and gently took her hand. A slight smile appeared on his face as his calm confidence washed over Koi like a gentle mist. The two walked to the kitchen, a close yet separate building, separate to ward off the threat of fire. The aroma of Augustus's Lowcountry cooking—oyster and shrimp stew and boiling Charleston Yellow rice—wafted the room. Augustus served Koi her first complete meal in months. The food consoled her as much as it filled her belly.

As Koi ate Augustus walked to the back of the small courtyard outside the kitchen behind the house and summoned a neighbor slave over the fence.

Within minutes an African, a rather new arrival Augustus had befriended, appeared in the kitchen. He watched Koi eat, examining her like a piece of driftwood washed ashore; a link to the mystery of his own arrival in the white man's land, a relic from Africa. Koi stared back, following the eyes of her unannounced, silent visitor.

After circling the room The African spoke, but not in a language Koi recognized. After The African tried a second language with no response, he tried another, Twi, the language of the Ewe. Koi responded in kind. The African jumped with delight to the sounds repeated to him. Smiling, she repeated them again, eliciting the same joyous jump from The African who soon disappeared. He returned moments later with his arms full of two robust women who immediately embraced and cooed over Koi like her aunts at home.

During the following days and weeks Adam would call out to Augustus that he was leaving again on another of his many errands. He would continue in this manner until he'd exhausted his list.

Closing the front door to his home off King Street he'd turn and walk down Hassle Street passing the origins of reformed Judaism in the colonies, the Beth Elohim congregation. Then, to and past Meeting Street, turning right onto East Bay he'd step from the shade of buildings into the bright sunlight and walk south toward the Exchange at the foot of Broad Street.

Beginning in 1753 with Parliament's Jewish Naturalization Bill— granting limited rights to foreign-born Jews, including land ownership—his family had acquired a great deal of South Carolina real estate. Too much. Little of it insured and none of it adequately. Their portfolio included part of the late Francis Salvador's estate, the first Jew to hold an elected office in the Americas and a hero of the recent rebellion.

After checking on his ships, the *Rotterdam*, the *Kameel* and the *Jupiter*, now at anchor in the bay, Adam walked among the serpentine ballast stone alleyways of the water district, past sail maker workshops, rope factories, chandlers, grog shops, fortune tellers and brothels. He soon emerged from the low rent district to arrive at the foot of Broad Street whose wide expanse was meant to impress visitors and citizens alike. But, rather than enter the illustrious Exchange building there, he walked into Shepherd's Tavern, up Broad Street, at the corner of Church Street, to conduct his business.

During these precarious times any and all news or rumor made the city swoon, requiring Adam to conduct himself without a whiff of panic in his manner or voice. Feigning concern, despite constant speculation of a British blockade any day, he managed to overcome the subdued usual enthusiasm of most would-be buyers and sell two buildings to Lindsay Wafford, an old classmate at King's College. One with its own wharf. He had been forced to sell both for half of what they had been worth before the news of real fighting against the king's troops. To appease his defeat he envisioned both properties burned to the ground before the war's end.

And in the time it took Adam to conduct his affairs in Charles Town, Koi assumed the beginnings of a New World persona she would wear over her African heritage for the rest of her life. Beulah and Beatrice, the two women The African had brought to lavish affection upon Koi continued their mission to help Koi adjust. They brought her clothes, a pair of shoes and fashioned her hair. Beulah's master lived in the house behind the Wolff property, along with The African and several other servants. Beulah's own child, born in Charles Town, had died of smallpox three years earlier, when she was Koi's age.

Beatrice had been Augustus's partner for twenty years, ever since they met in New York. As a free woman of color, when Adam's family moved Augustus to Charles Town she had moved too. Though short in stature, she was as steadfast as the strength of her arguments. Her fiery rhetoric dotted her command of subjects she read about or learned in a school for the poor and enslaved established by Reverend William Vesey, Rector of Trinity Church in New York. Her approach to life, all these years after the reverend's death, was to continue his work in her own way. She held and taught her own clandestine classes. Koi became the fifth student in Beatrice's schoolhouse—a shed attached to a barn at the edge of town, owned by a Jewish family she had served almost as long as Augustus's servitude to the Wolff family in Charles Town.

Augustus assigned Koi a number of light chores to keep her busy and train her to take orders. Something that, as Augustus sensed, Koi had never known. Her tribe in Africa had slaves, traded slaves; people taken in war, people reduced to slavery as punishment, or born into that station. At first, at night, he would hear her cry out in her dreams.

At Beatrice's school Koi began simple arithmetic she already knew, but she now learned the subject, and how to read and write in English. When Adam discovered Augustus's partner educating Koi, despite a law forbidding it, he insisted Beatrice add Dutch and French to Koi's curriculum. Beatrice arranged to have a slave woman from St. Maarten conduct lessons in French and Dutch. And Beatrice attended them herself alongside Koi and Beulah.

The African, short, plump and darker than a ripe plum, became Koi's court jester, making her laugh every visit. On one such visit he brought a doll he made himself; carved in mahogany with a hand-stitched dress of coarse fabric and tobacco juice stained cotton sewn as hair. Koi adopted the doll, promising The African to keep her safe, always.

As Koi walked the city guarded by the women, hand in hand, she stared in wonder at buildings and the hustle of the streets. Stepping over the occasional rubbish and avoiding horse manure Koi looked into shop doors and windows at wares she had never seen for purposes she could only imagine. Beulah, Beatrice and Koi all practiced French and Dutch with their tutor as they shopped the waterfront Fish Market among a throng of slaves and indentured servants buying dinner for the city's households, alongside poor whites, some begging. As the ladies flirted with some of the free and slave fishermen selling their latest catch, the tutor would name a variety of species in French and then translate, then repeat herself in Dutch. Her students replied in near unison while standing over the swarming flies and smelly fish.

Bolstered by news of victory to the north—at Moore's Creek Bridge, in North Carolina—enthusiasm for the war effort among the patriots soared. Charles Town's rebels soon redoubled their evisceration of the crown's representatives in print and in public: hurling crude, bold threats of violence at known Loyalists in the streets. Acts that prompted the Royal Governor to flee the city for the safety of a navy ship at anchor in the bay.

However, soon after cheers that George Washington had outmaneuvered the British in Boston Harbor—he had placed Fort Ticonderoga's cannons on Dorchester Heights—rumors began that a detachment of His Majesty's warships had sailed south, for the Carolinas.

The week after that, new reports and exclamations—that a British Navy detachment had arrived just beyond the Charles Town Bar—ratcheted up fears. Threats of imminent invasion whisked through town like the gusts of wind before a hurricane; rendered all the more omnipotent with every roll of cannon past houses and shops.

Magazines were emptied of their armaments, moved to batteries along the rivers or to the new fort being constructed on a barrier island at the mouth of the harbor; Sullivan's Island. These portents sent citizens scurrying about, their faces molded by despair, stocking up on supplies and settling their affairs in anticipation of the unknown.

SEVEN

Tabula Rasa

Though the Danish West India Company monopolized the wholesale slave trade, Thomas & Company's advertisements had elicited many small orders. One such order arrived in Charlotte Amalie from Madame Chevalier.

"*Give me that,*" Master Thomas said as he snatched the paper from his assistant's hand. He had immediately recognized the name.

Madame's correspondence requested another slave; an adult male, to purchase, to augment the management of her small island. Her part-time, on again, off again, female house servant, Millie, whom Madame hired from Thomas & Company, was incapable of taking advantage of the marine life in abundance around her island or of tending to her growing menagerie of animals.

Master Thomas took his time filling Madame Chevalier's order, but within days of his return from *Paradis* he perused the cells of the slave market prison for a suitable slave to purchase. He was careful not to divulge his knowledge of the pox outbreak aboard the *Briel*—doing so would void his contract with the monopoly because of laws forbidding the sale of diseased or defective slaves.

He found Telemaque, sunken-eyed, coughing, yet ambulatory after nearly two weeks of isolation. The fact that Telemaque had recovered from the pox and would therefore, in theory, no longer be subject to re-infection was an unfortunate trait of the boy as far as Mater Thomas was concerned. Nonetheless, he decided he had found the perfect slave to sell to Madame.

For Master Thomas, any opportunity to sabotage Madame Chevalier's designs paid homage to his father. His father's happiest moments included making his nemesis, Monsieur Henri Hebert

Chevalier, Madame's late husband, unhappy. The two men not only competed in every arena of commerce, except the slave trade, they even vied for the affections of the same whore at the best brothel in Road Town. The latter of which led to each's undoing. They had both died prematurely, senile, suffering from syphilis contracted while competing in their favorite sport.

For Telemaque, the day's sail from St. Thomas to Madame's island aboard the *Libertas*, topside, was sunny and warm. It began as a fun day. Millie, Madame's house servant, made it so. She was kind to the young boy. She shared her fruit and water with him and made him feel like, "I'm surviving. You will too." His feelings of safety and well-being made him long for his mother and sister; his little finger coiled involuntarily at the thought of Koi.

Captain William Palmer had ferried Millie to and from Madame Chevalier's island many times. As on previous voyages, on this occasion the young and handsome captain's more than casual interest in Millie's forbidden fruit formed the nexus of Millie's and Telemaque's casual bondage onboard his ship. Through her coquettish ways Millie often let Captain Palmer know she shared his desires.

While free to be a child lost in play aboard the *Libertas*, running the length of the deck, shouting out loud, calling out to the schools of dolphins paralleling the progress of the boat he heard Millie's voice. The "Stop!" Telemaque heard from a portal, from below deck, reminded him of Millie's absence.

Her unfamiliar tone alarmed him and called him to action. To save Millie from the most prevalent trait of the white man he had come to expect, savagery, Telemaque leaped to the galley hatch to go below. A crewmember playfully checked his advance, but hearing Millie's voice once more, "Oh, stop it!" (squealing with delight, in mock protestation), prompted Telemaque to disable the man by running headlong into his groin. The blow dropped the man to his knees, prompting laughter and jokes from the other sailors.

Telemaque jumped past the groaning man, skipping several rungs on the galley ladder way to quickly open the starboard cabin door, only to find a sight as singular to him as the first sight of his mother naked. Finding only speechless averted glances from the two occupants of the cabin, no longer sensing danger, Telemaque slowly backed out of the cabin and closed the door.

Puzzled as much by the snickers from the crew as by what he had seen, Telemaque wandered the deck, processing the moment.

Within a few minutes the crew grew silent at the sound of footsteps on the galley steps. With all eyes on the hatch the captain emerged and after a good stretch of his arms skyward he surveyed the landscape ashore and the activity of his sailors. He then gave the order they were anticipating, "Reef the mainsail." The crew reduced the amount of exposed canvas in preparation for the turbulent ocean winds the *Libertas* would encounter once she sailed beyond the shelter of the starboard side island, Paradise Island. Before she could enjoy the protective cay of her destination—Madame's island—the *Libertas* would be sailing the next few miles in the open, unpredictable Atlantic.

After half an hour of open water, the first mate of the *Libertas* passed along orders to come about one last time. The final tack would place the 54-foot ketch on a course around a crescent-shaped coral reef protruding a thousand feet from an island into the Atlantic. Only partially visible from the sea at low tide, the jagged rocks and dense coral protected the eastern shore of Madame's atoll like a series of stealth mines, sinking any vessel that dared venture too close.

The reef forced any boat approaching from the Atlantic to sail either the deep but narrow northern channel between neighboring islands or to tack yet again and sail clear of the impenetrable barrier through a shallow but broader southern channel.

The reef's protection also created a calm, walled bowl of ocean no more than 20 feet deep, approachable only from the beach. It provided a safe haven in which many species of marine life thrived. Spiny rock lobster and eels hid among the coral and rock crevices, while fanciful purple fin triggerfish, yellowtail snapper, black banded porkfish, colorful puffers and angelfish swam above flounder and rays buried in the sandy bottom.

The entire island consisted of an area little larger than a hectare. Its two steep scruffy hills ascended from the lagoon's considerable beach with additional tiny isolated beaches between outcroppings of rock and foliage.

From within the narrow channel just before twilight Telemaque studied every rock, every shrub and peered overboard into the water, marveling at the streaks of seabed he could see in the fading light through the clear dark blue translucence. A turtle's head and shell broke the surface, eyes seemingly fixed upon him.

"Drop the sheets, buoys out! Hanson, take the bow. Alphonse, man the stern, port side. We're going in," said the captain. The channel opened to reveal a small, beautiful harbor; large enough for a half a dozen vessels of equal tonnage to the *Libertas* to safely anchor. Telemaque's party eased in alongside the island's lone sturdy dock, opposite the *Eclipse*.

After delivering Abra, Sade and the half-dozen other slaves to neighboring Paradise Island, with his crew playing cards below deck, Jacob now stood on Madame's dock, arms folded across his barrel chest. He'd been told by Madame Chevalier to wait for the *Libertas*'s arrival before he could go. Her quasi-authority over him always made him seethe but today the delay of his departure for the big island of Tortola served to peak his outrage. He withheld any greeting to the captain's "Ahoy." Taking the line thrown to him by a crewmember, he tied it off with a grunt, securing the ketch.

"Permission to come aboard," Jacob boomed.

Before the captain could respond, the weight of Jacob's frame tipped the *Libertas* slightly toward the dock and rocked her back with Jacob on deck. "Where is he?"

At perhaps seven feet tall Jacob towered over the men. Stunned by the man's size and girth but realizing who "he" was, Captain Palmer responded by raising his index finger and motioning for the boy to be brought forward.

As the sun set behind the peak of neighboring Paradise Island, standing before the little boy the height of Jacob's head blotted out the early full moon like a lunar eclipse and his enormous physique cast a shadow the length of the deck, engulfing Telemaque within. A lone bright white spot of moonlight glistened at the crest of Jacob's silhouette.

The whites of the little boy's eyes searched for Millie.

With a weighty hand placed on Telemaque's shoulder Jacob said, "Come with me, boy."

"Wait!"

Captain Palmer stepped forward, surprising himself. He knew Telemaque was a slave. He knew what that meant. He also knew Millie was fond of the boy and didn't want to just hand him over to this brute. He also knew what that could mean. And, while Jacob's imposing physique could not escape notice and gossip among islanders, Captain Palmer had never met the man.

"Who's your master?" the captain inquired, only to realize that Jacob, as a white man, would take offense if he were not an indentured servant, and maybe even then.

"Who do you work for, I mean?" he said, before Jacob could object.

"I work for no man, or woman, without my choosin'," Jacob said. "I'm here to deliver this slave to Madame Chevalier. That's all. What's it to you?"

Moving between the men to quell the angry exchange, "I'll take him," Millie said, placing her hand on Telemaque's other shoulder. "That's why I'm here. Massa Thomas sent me to see after the boy and ask Madame is there anything she need from Charlotte Amalie."

Looking into Millie's eyes for fear, then taking in all of her, slowly; admiring the cleavage of her breasts caught in the moonlight, Jacob replied, "Come with me."

Telemaque didn't say a word, but looking back, waved a single hand to the captain and crew. The three made their way down the dock to the beach and began their ascent to the "big house." Only there was no big house. Just a small well kept open home on the top of the larger of the island's two hills.

As the trio ascended the sandy path up the hill, Telemaque began counting to himself. Taught at an early age to count, by playing Oware, he learned to inventory livestock. Now, with idiot savant-like precision, Telemaque counted everything to relieve his anxiety; to exercise some control over his new and unpredictable world.

Seventy-six steps. From the end of the dock it took Telemaque seventy-six strides up the steep sandy trail to reach the threshold of Madame Marie Rachael Locoul Chevalier's small, handsome home at the top of her atoll. The door wide open, Millie told the others to wait before going inside.

The boy and the giant stood in silence side by side. Telemaque looked up observing Jacob's blank stare at Madame's doorway. The rigid stare masked the man's arousal; his thoughts of trapping Millie alone. While Jacob's eyes looked straight ahead, for the first time the boy noticed a short, wide scar across Jacob's right cheek. Bathed in the soft glow of lantern light from the vestibule, Telemaque thought of the painted scars on the faces of the devils who had captured him in Africa. It all seemed like only days ago. Waiting to enter Madame's lair Telemaque relived the moment that night at the bonfire when his eyes met Koi's.

As the drums beat faster Telemaque had thought then, *I wonder if my father can arrange for her to be one of my wives.* Koi had broken Telemaque's stare, averting her eyes, searching for her mother's gaze.

When the Dahomey army attacked the wedding celebration, scattering the village, all those not engaged in mortal combat fled into the jungle. Telemaque lost sight of his family in the mêlée. Four male warriors and an Amazon pushed, pulled and herded Koi and her family, sweeping Telemaque and others into their grasp. Each captor screamed at their captives as the village crackled, set ablaze all around them, filling the air with a pungent odor of gun powder and burning reed rooftops.

Flames reached high into the clear starry night. Not far into the jungle surrounding the burning village, one of the king's men shot one of Telemaque's tribesmen. A young man physically resisting his captor's grasp. The musket's flash illuminated for an instant the killer's grimacing scarified painted face.

Not until deep into the jungle did the king's men stop and shine their torches on each captive to check their prizes. The slavers insisted the captives remain silent as they yelled to communicate with their allies making similar treks away from the village with other captives. Monkeys screeched in the treetops and squawking birds took flight from the smoke; antelope and buffalo rumbled the earth, stampeding in the night while Telemaque's village glowed in the distance. Big cats sauntered away from the commotion.

Captors and captives alike stood still in flickering torch light, waiting in silence. The breeze that flowed between them carried the scent of day-old elephant dung nearby. Someone's footsteps had disturbed the droppings, mixing it with the odor of burning village rooftops. Flies forced from their meal examined the interlopers closely, buzzing and landing on the war party and prisoners.

A voice of authority, an apparition approaching in the night said, "What are you doing!?"

Soon revealed by the captor's torches to be clad in a white European shirt, the man's bright teeth and eyes contrasted his dark hue that melded with the night.

"Why have you stopped? Keep moving!" the voice from the glowing white shirt boomed.

Koi spoke to her mother in a low voice.

As one of the king's men raised an old belaying pin high in his hand, about to strike Koi's whispers, instinct ruled Telemaque's actions. He fell to the ground, faking a seizure; an affliction he had seen before and knew would strike awe and idleness into any audience. Unaware of his ruse, all but Koi backed away. They watched

Telemaque shake and squirm as if experiencing an epileptic fit. His eyes rolled back into his head and saliva drooled down his cheek.

"What's happening? What's he doing?" one slaver yelled, afraid.

"It's an evil spirit, inside him!" another shouted.

The commander pulled his flint-lock pistol from the sash across his waist and cocked it before aiming at the boy thrashing on the ground.

Ceasing his gyrations Telemaque turned limp, motionless for affect, despite the flies landing on his face. He opened one eye to observe a review of his performance.

His ruse proved a success—he had captured the slaver's attention, stopped Koi from being hurt, all eyes riveted upon him, and he had learned a valuable lesson he would use again one day.

As Telemaque seemed to regain his senses the commander passed judgment. He tucked his pistol away and said, "Get him up. And keep moving!" before he disappeared in the darkness.

Millie returned to the doorway and signaled Telemaque to come to her. "Madame says 'That be all, Jacob. And tell Captain Palmer, I won't be needin' a way home.'"

Jacob's eyes menaced Telemaque before wincing at Millie, not so sure if playing messenger boy was Madame's idea or hers.

"Madame say so...Now get!" she snapped as Jacob turned to walk away with a bravado she wouldn't have displayed if she'd have had to accompany him back to the dock. Within the safety of Madame's care and needs Millie felt almost invincible.

As Millie entered the parlor, looking across the room she took comfort in her surroundings. The parlor, or great room, was open, expansive, the walls decorated with books bound in all colors. Its broad polished wood plank floors were the same as the vestibule, but mostly covered by a single beautiful burgundy Persian rug, its intricate design trimmed in dark thread. A large stone fireplace focused the sitting area while French doors opened wide to an enticing terrace, high on the hill, revealing panoramic views of the sheltered lagoon below, neighboring islands and a view to the horizon across the Atlantic; open water all the way to Africa.

Dressed in black, Madame sat alone in the great room reading in her winged backed chair next to the stone fireplace, facing the view of the water. The moon's reflection created a mosaic path of white across the waves.

Curtsying before Madame Chevalier, Millie inquired about Telemaque, standing just inside the vestibule.

Speaking in her native French as though he weren't there, Madame Chevalier told Millie to, "Send him for firewood so we can talk." Millie took two steps toward the vestibule and spoke before realizing the boy was gone.

Madame Chevalier closed her book and reached to hand it to Millie, instructing Millie which shelf and where on the shelf to return it among her vast collection that occupied most of her great room's wall space. Followed by, "Have a seat, child," motioning to the settee facing the stone fireplace.

"How's Master Thomas been treating you and the others at Charlotte Amalie? Is he treating you well?"

Madame's estranged daughter had not responded to her letters for quite some time, and living in relative isolation Madame was still unaware of the recent engagement announcement for her widowed daughter to become Mrs. Thomas.

Hesitating a moment, after slowly placing her chin into her chest Millie answered, "*Oui*, Madame." Then out of fear of retribution she continued in French, "*Merci*. Just fine. He let my Aunt Sarah jump the broom with Cicero last Sunday. We laughed and sang the day away." Millie allowed some enthusiasm in her voice, something she would never do in Master Thomas's presence. She did not mention the lashes Cicero had taken weeks before or that Sarah was pregnant with Master Thomas's child.

"That's good," Madame Chevalier replied, still suspicious of Millie's forthrightness. Master Thomas and his late father had a sadistic streak cultivated throughout the islands by public displays of cruelty. Madame wished to use this point to devalue his currency among islanders, just as her husband had done for years before his death.

Continuing in French, Madame said, "Have you seen my daughter?" Through Millie Madame learned something of her daughter's life since she'd left Madame for the more cosmopolitan life of Charlotte Amalie a couple of years before—after her daughter's husband had been lost at sea and her only child had become a sailor. Madame's grandson, Jean Michelle, had told his mother and grandmother that he sailed on a spice ship to exotic ports though he reeked like a slaver.

"*Oui*, Madame. She's fine. Happy!" Millie smiled as she repeated the line she had rehearsed with Madame's daughter. Millie improvised the smile.

Madame said with a tone reserved for when confronting a lie, however well meant, "Happy. Yet, my letters remain unanswered. You've delivered them, have you not?"

"Oh, yes, *Oui*, Madame," Millie said with a slight bow of her head. Madame drew a deep breath.

"Tell me about this boy. What do you know about him?"

Millie smiled again, a genuine smile, opening up to Madame. "He's a wonder, Madame. He was mostly dead when Master Thomas sent him to us. We thought more of where to bury him than what to do with him. We put him on a table in the corner of the kitchen, near the fireplace, and every house servant was always checking on him and feeding him leftovers from the Big House." Here Millie stopped, lowering her head. She knew that was against Master Thomas's wishes. He liked his table scraps to go to his prize hounds used for tracking down man or beast anywhere on the islands.

"Go on, child," Madame said.

"Well, within a couple of days he was sitting up and grinning at the women feeding him. Then one day, he just got up," as if to say that was the end of his illness.

"But, where's he from? Does he speak anything but African?"

"No, Madame. I don't know exactly where he's from but I recognized some of his words. His words are close to my heart. His name is Telemaque."

Madame Chevalier parroted Millie, "Tel-e-ma-que."

As if on cue, Telemaque appeared at the door, an armload of firewood weighing down his slight frame. Madame Chevalier motioned for him to come forward. Telemaque did so, placing the wood to the side of the stone fireplace on top of remnants of other logs. Then he presented himself to her. He looked her straight in the eye, something a broken slave would never do.

Madame Chevalier recognized something special in the boy's handsome face right away. He did not cower. He stood erect, respectful but not afraid. As he returned her gaze he performed a simple nod in reverence to his new mistress. He did not speak.

"He's so young. And small. Clearly *not* what I ordered. But, he'll have to do. I suppose he'll grow into his duties," Madame Chevalier finished her sentence in accented English. Motioning toward outside, Madame said, "Go and fix us some tea, will you, Millie," a command not to be misconstrued as a question. Millie curtsied again and left for the kitchen, a separate building on the lesser of the island's two hills.

Madame moved to the edge of her chair. She took Telemaque by the wrist and spoke to the boy, cognizant he could not fully comprehend his situation. Still, she felt he would, nonetheless, understand the gist of her message.

Her manner was direct but soft-spoken. "*Tu* are one of the lucky in this part of the world," pointing to him and back to herself, "to both of our advantage."

Easing back into her comfortable chair she scrutinized the boy all over again. "Tell me your name. What do they call you?" She obviously knew the answer, but she wanted to hear it from him. He had yet to speak, and she wanted to see how he presented himself, and she wanted to hear his native tongue.

The boy understood the question. He had been asked the same many times by kitchen and household servants at Master Thomas's home. One had taught him to enunciate the answer in English and in French.

Expecting a one word response in African or broken English, "*Mon nom est* Telemaque," came the response. In keeping with the modus operandi of their discussion Telemaque also pointed, to himself. The gesture was not lost on Madame. She recognized he not only picked up language skills quickly, he mimicked her hand gestures, for effect, just as she had done.

Madame sat motionless, expressionless for a few moments before taking the boy's left wrist again and telling him, "I think I'll keep you, despite Master Thomas's sanctimonious impertinence. But, from this day forth you shall answer to the name Denmark." She paused and repeated the last words, this time emphasizing the word *Denmark* as her index finger touched his chest. "You will carry that name to mark your arrival. I will inform Millie."

Contemplating the boy's demeanor and response Madame quoted in her mind one of Jean-Jacque Rousseau's principles, expressed in *Emile, or On Education*: "children are born good and it is the company they keep which corrupts."

Her thoughts carried her back to Paris, to her youth. Christened within Notre Dame in 1704, she had been raised in a family that, as minor figures of the court of King Louis XIV, enjoyed comfort. Her father was an assistant to Louis Nicolas le Tonnelier de Breteuil, the King's liaison to foreign ambassadors. As such she received an extraordinary education, sharing the same tutors as Breteuil's daughters.

One of Breteuil's daughters in particular, Gabrielle Émilie le Tonnelier de Breteuil flaunted her intellect and confounded her elders to the astonishment or delight of any audience. Madame, too, recognized in Gabrielle the brilliance others would later acclaim.

Part of Madame's friend's arranged marriage included the understanding that, amid her husband's affairs and prolonged absences, she was permitted her own. One companion was a controversial intellectual, a poet, novelist and *mauvais garçon* of his time—Voltaire.

After his return from exile to England, Gabrielle and Voltaire reveled in each other's scientific and philosophical curiosity and she welcomed him into her chateau. It was during this time she wrote *Institutions of Physics* including passages concerning mass and energy. Her published findings were accepted and validated beyond any of Madame Chevalier's wildest expectations. (Madame's friend's work verified the square root in the world's most famous equation, $E=mc^2$.)

One of Voltaire's coachmen became Madame's husband. Though her choice of husband was rejected by her father as beneath her station Madame found him irresistible. The two young lovers eloped to the Caribbean to start a new life on the promise of a job as innkeepers on Tortola, privately disappointing and publicly embarrassing Madame's family. The man the young couple put their faith in turned out to be a drunkard and a gambler, losing the inn and adjoining tavern in a game of chance.

Monsieur managed to convince the winner, the captain of a whaler, to let him buy the properties from him over time, with interest. Having no stomach for inn keeping, and a family in Nantucket, he agreed, remaining among the best customers the Chevaliers had through the years. With their profits they opened a mercantile business, exporting sugar, molasses, rum and gin while importing all manner of goods from Europe and the English colonies. They left African imports to others.

In the blink of an eye Madame was back in the Caribbean, her adopted home of over fifty years. Her gaze was once more fixed upon the small thin handsome youth before her; she thought, perhaps, her own *tabula rasa*, her own *Emile*.

Millie returned carrying a silver tray with a tea pot, cup and saucer, silverware and fresh ground brown sugar, goat's milk, butter and sliced bread. Millie placed the tray near Madame as usual.

As "Denmark" looked through and beyond the open square front window, across the secluded bay to the dark neighboring island, Paradise Island, Madame said, "Millie, I want you to begin the boy's house training right away. I've given him his new Christian name;

Denmark. He must know the routine and what's expected of him before you leave again. You may begin with the kitchen duties. See what he can do, on his own, and then fill in what's missing. Now go, child. Take Denmark with you. I'm tired. Leave me in peace. I'll ring for dinner."

Part II
1776-1800

EIGHT

Fresh Graves

Over time, whenever Master Thomas visited *Paradis*, Abra knew. She would be summoned to his library.

Each time before knocking, Abra stopped along the path to look upon the ocean; the view of the same topography was always different with new weather. She would see the small island she first admired nestled among her larger neighbors. And beyond, water that touches Africa. She'd pray for her husband, her ancestors, Sade, the soul of her baby and Koi, but most of all for her boy, wherever he may be.

On one such occasion Master Thomas requested Selena appear too with Abra. He told Selena that under good authority, he suspected Abra of voodoo. Capable of potions that harness the spirit world.

As Master Thomas said these things, circling Abra, he insinuated that Selena knew as much already. He explained to Selena he wanted Abra to adulterate, to bewitch, the contents of a bottle—an elixir he handed to her—so as to induce the immediate demise of whomever consumed the potion.

Even before the Tortola territory received regular British mail service, what had become Madame's business establishments, her hotel and tavern, had become the defacto mail drop to serve the literate residents and clientele of Road Town. Madame's mail to and from throughout the world, including her medicine prescribed by Dr. Ramsay, arrived first at Road Town before delivery to her island.

Jacob delivered the mail.

Master Thomas had intercepted Madame's medicine by instructing Jacob to stop at Paradise Island first with Madame's mail before making his delivery to Madame's island.

As Selena left Master Thomas's library with Madame's elixir Seymour stepped into Selena's path from out of the darkness, from the same hiding spot Selena had once occupied with Sade while waiting for Abra.

"At midnight, send three slaves to Steeple Point. Take this lamp." He pulled a new lamp of French design from underneath his coat. "It's small but more powerful than ten candles; when the slaves see a boat below return their light, that's the signal. We'll call them runaways that fell from the cliffs, each buried in a fresh grave," he said, smiling. Seymour had already arranged for the sale of these soon to be runaway slaves to three copper mine investors. Seymour's grand design was to profit from Master Thomas's ruin under the guise of patriotic duty.

Selena returned to her hut. She used the new lamp to examine the content of the bottle and then pick three lucky slaves.

Abra hugged Sade and Selena when she returned that night. As had become their custom, the two stayed in the hut, waiting for Abra to return from Master Thomas.

With Seymour's lamp Selena and Abra examined Madame's prescribed medicine; designed to prevent fainting spells. According to Selena's analysis and taste, the solution contained nothing more than colored sugar water. The ploy made Selena consider Seymour too might be nothing more than a hoax—should she trust him, his path to liberty?

Though still questioning Seymour's motives, his intent, the arrangement Seymour spoke of took place as planned that night. Or so it seemed; the lamp was found, still warm, next to the path to the heights of Steeple Point—a remote rock outcrop at the water's edge, the highest elevation of Paradise Island.

The earth of three fresh gravesites was turned as instructed. In the moonlight at the graveyard that night Sade produced the remains of her brother's tiny foot. She'd kept it secreted away from her mother all this time. The sight of the relic of her infant son both horrified and soothed Abra. She was horrified that she may have been responsible for bringing yet another life into this hellish existence, but relieved that the child would never know of it. Because she didn't want his soul nor his bones to occupy this cruel white man's world she asked Selena to take her to the shoreline, beyond the slave row.

At the water's edge, before casting the remains into the ocean, Abra prayed to the Ewe's Goddess, Mawu, that the soul of her son would travel the water back to Africa. Abra had given her deceased son the name Mawusi, after his father, meaning "in the hands of God." Selena said a *vodun* prayer wishing the child might make it to where Selena believed all ancestors lived; on an island beneath the sea.

That next morning before dawn, after discovering three slaves missing, Moses brought Master Thomas's dogs to the lane with his whip tied to his belt and a musket under his arm. He expected trouble from Seymour, recompense for his dereliction.

Finding Seymour already on slave row Moses said through a gratuitous smile, "Master Seymour! Good morning. As you may know I'm about to sic these hounds on some missin' field hands."

Raising his hand high for Moses to stop, "That won't be necessary," Seymour said, his own musket resting in his other arm. "They fell to their deaths, escaping, or suicide. The slaves buried them already. I let them. They were adamant about putting the corpses in the ground, facing east, laid on the right side, and so on. No harm in it."

Moses, incensed he was not consulted, struggled with the mingling hounds as they pulled on their leashes, sniffing, growling and howling at his feet. He stormed off, yanking and yelling at the hounds on his way to return them to their pen.

Moses got it into his mind that a particular young field hand knew more about the runaways than Seymour did. Anxious to prove it, he drove the young man all day cracking his whip, cursing him. During the morning's work the other field hands heard Moses yell to no one in particular, "Don't tell me nothin' about nothin' 'round here!" And later, while taking out his frustrations on the young slave he suspected of complicity, "I'll get to the bottom of this!"

At the mid-day break, before the gang's trek back to the fields, Moses interrupted the suspect slave's meal. Muttering to himself, he led the young man to a pole. Lashed him to a rope attached to a ring at the top and yanked the rope taut. Then, Moses put his whip to work.

Crack!

"One!" Moses counted, slashing into the sweat-slicked exposed target.

"Auah!" the slave screamed.

Crack!

"Two!" Moses announced to the gathering crowd; they were shocked but powerless to stop the spectacle. The youth shuddered.

Crack!

"Tree!" Moses said with more than usual exertion in his voice.

Crack!

"Auah!" the slave screamed again and began to cry. He yelled something in his native tongue when the next lash struck without warning.

Crack!

"Auah!"

Moses lashed without count till he could swing no more. He finally paused, hunched over to catch his breath. His gaze met the slaves watching in silence.

Standing taller Moses yelled at the assembled crowd, "None of you better run! Or, I'll tie you up one by one!"

Moses then pushed two of the gathered slaves a step back to carve himself a path of retreat. Wiping sweat from his brow he staggered away without another word.

The slaves did not return to the fields that day.

That afternoon, after caring for the whipped slave's wounds, Selena returned to Theresa the medicine bottle Abra was directed to conjure. But before she walked more than a few steps of the path away from *Paradis* Theresa reappeared at the doorway and said, "Wait! Master Thomas wants to see you."

Master Thomas came to the door quickly, out of breath, "What is this? This seems what I gave you!"

"Oh, no, Master Thomas," Selena said, lowering her posture but not her eyes. "The power you don't see is the gravest. You know that," she said with a forced wry smile, playing on his superstitions. She could see her effect in his posture and eyes.

Examining the small bottle anew he asked, "Is its effect immediate?" And then, to test her honesty he challenged her, "What if I were to drink it?" he asked, faking a slight struggle with the cork top.

"Oh!" Selena dropped to her knees, careful to fold her crippled leg on the way down. She looked hard at her hands clasp in her lap. "Please! No, Massa. I don warned you."

"What are you afraid of?"

Selena began to rock in place, "Even if you live, even if it don't kill you, it don't matter, the spirit world will..."

Convinced, Master Thomas turned pale. He was frightened of the potions toxicity, but enthralled by the prospect of Madame's impendent demise. He changed his grip of the bottle to two fingers of one hand and handed it to Selena. He produced a white handkerchief and wiped his hands clean. He said, "Give it to Theresa," before turning his back and slamming the door shut.

NINE

Knock and Run

The Charles Town May Day celebration was an event unlike any Koi had ever witnessed. Flowers were in abundance as were decorated houses and shop windows. Costumed revelers danced and sang around a tall maypole, with colorful streamers in hand from attached on high. The lightened mood of citizens who looked forward to this celebration every year stood in stark contrast to the weeks before when a military invasion seemed imminent.

Mischief abounded throughout neighborhoods of the city; adults as well as children relished in the merriment. As custom dictated, May Baskets—filled with sweets and flowers—were left by revelers on doorsteps, with a knock and run. If the recipient caught the basket giver in the act, a kiss was in order.

Outside of the wall of the old city, slaves, free blacks and handfuls of poor whites celebrated May Day in their own way, including a maypole of their own making. The celebration beyond town, larger than the organized festivities within, always drew weary attention from the city guard and well-to-do whites; always worried by what went on beyond their control.

The gathered mass clapped and danced to African instrumentations of popular English tunes before leading to more raucous, heart thumping, talking drums, shaking gourds, whoops and song. The aroma of cooked meats and bread wafted the air as hawkers shouted their fare. Laughter floated everywhere among the crowd of smiling faces including Koi, Augustus, Beatrice, Beulah and The African as they moved with the rhythms and dancers they encircled along with the crowd.

A young Charles Town born slave of fifteen jumped into the middle of the circle of revelry and danced the way her grandmother's grandmother taught her mother. A heartfelt recollection of the past.

Beulah clapped and danced from the circle's edge, laughing with the others. Beatrice, more reserved, enjoyed herself alongside Augustus, both clapping, as The African danced in place the way he'd learned in manhood training not long ago in Africa.

Koi was so enlivened to hear and see a familiar dance, one she'd witnessed and participated in many, many times, she smiled and jumped into the middle too, dancing with the older surprised girl, who smiled back and shook faster. Koi performed the steps the way she had done just months ago, in Africa. The older girl suggested Koi follow her lead. Koi repeated the steps and replied in her native tongue, showing her teeth as white as swans. The older girl then understood who was teaching whom and took Koi's hand to dance together to the beat.

Returning to her friends among the crowd encircling the performers, Koi practiced her English on Beatrice and Beulah. Koi said, "I like festival, very much," wondering as much at her own delight as her ability to smile. Beulah smiled wider in response and said a simple, enthusiastic "Good!" with Beatrice exclaiming, "Excellent!"

Beulah hid her pain like her past; she pretended to let it drift away like her mother's corpse at sea; thrown overboard on the slaver.

When Beulah first arrived in Charles Town, over thirty-five years ago she was Koi's age, and the city's life was not a happy time. In 1739, a saltwater slave named Jemmy had led a band of twenty runaways in rebellion. In their escape they attacked a store at the Stono River near Charles Town. They decapitated the owner and stuck his head on a pike before robbing the store of guns, powder and shot. They had hoped to reach freedom in Spanish Florida. Along the journey south their numbers swelled to a hundred or more as Jemmy's followers killed whites along the way. The procession sparked the alarm of local militia. In pitch battle at another river's edge forty-four slaves and twenty whites died. There, though some of the fugitives scattered many were captured. When a defeated slave died on the march back to captivity, the head was put on a pike at mile markers to warn other slaves against future attempts of insurrection. The response included the Negro Act of 1740, turning back allowances made through the years. The act prohibited slaves from growing their own food, assembling in groups, keeping some of their earnings when hired out by their masters and learning to read. Over time, the punitive measures of the 1740 act had faded with memories so that by the 1770s strict enforcement of the act was seldom imposed.

And yet, in early May of every year—among the tiresome old complaints against the black's unofficially sanctioned annual gathering—excuses for banning the event resurfaced. Often accompanied by punitive remedies, some trivial, many draconian.

On this May Day several groups of white men observed the black festivities from a distance, fresh from their own celebrations within taverns and brothels. One of the men from a group, as a form of entertainment, began to stir the ardor of his cabal by offering a tried and true argument for disrupting the happy occasion.

"Look at 'em," he said, "Mixing free blacks with slaves isn't good. It gives slaves ideas." Another joined in immediately, "Not to mention it's against the law, a gathering this large, outside a religious setting." A Tory dandy offered his token criticism, "holding a celebration so near their graveyard seems, well, callous. They're practically 'dancing on their graves'" he said with a laugh he'd hoped would be contagious. Laughing alone, he put his perfumed handkerchief to his nose.

The debate among these Loyalists was elevated at the mention of blacks filling the ranks of the British regulars (ignoring the large number of blacks in His Majesty's service to the Royal Navy). Another huffed, "Especially after Lord Dunmore's debacle!"

As nods of agreement were exchanged, someone in the group, thinking out loud, said, "What if the rebels arm them?"—referring to the masses of black faces stretching for as far as the eye could see. He immediately regretted the very thought. And that he had spoken it aloud.

His counterparts paled amid a protracted silence.

To shake the men from their stupor while starring at the throngs, the first to speak said, "We should have them rounded up and searched for silver spoons in their pockets. Lord knows they go missing from my household with regularity."

Just then, another man rushed to their group, an excited expression upon his face as he related his news.

"Did you hear? A child has been murdered! By a Negro! An African, I hear! The authorities are on the move to apprehend the savage. They should be here any moment!"

The men greeted the grim news with giddy enthusiasm. They moved closer to and lined up along the boundary wall for the entertainment value of a show of force.

The only evidence of culpability was circumstantial. The dead girl had been bedridden with a high fever for weeks. But, at the urging of whites insisting on arrests, the Charles Town sheriff and a posse of city guards had set out to effect an abrupt interruption of the black May Day gaiety.

The armed posse's sudden, violent appearance induced panic throughout the mass gathering.

The crowd's reaction—to flee the frightening scene—reminded Koi of that night in Africa, at the bonfire wedding celebration, of her father, her mother and sister, and of Telemaque. Within the flash of the city guard's muskets her new found joy and persona retreated as she was once again herded by devils and gunfire.

The authorities grabbed The African by his powerful arms, from behind, accosting him, ignoring other's pleas and his dismay. A small child of his master's family had been found dead; someone had to pay. The authorities looked no farther than The African, known to be attentive to young children. Koi clutched her doll and watched as guards dragged him away.

In Koi's mind her mother's shrieks—as she was dragged away by slavers on the path in Africa—mingled with The African's loud protests. During her flight from the May Day mêlée Koi recalled the sights and sounds of her shared journey with Telemaque.

Moving; always moving. The Ewe captives were pushed along through African bush country Koi knew well in the light of day. Shouts by the king's men into the night, answered by kinsmen urged the pack on. Their pace through the jungle, swift and unimpeded, did not ebb until their winded captors were forced to slow down. By then, the king's men had reached their first objective. The migration path. A path that bisected most of the Lake Volta region; north to the deserts of Timbuktu or south to the West African coast.

On the migration path the warriors of the Dahomey king's army were greeted by others binding their spoils; mostly women and children, a few old men. The surviving Ewe warriors of the village, of both captured clans, would join the other captives soon. Unbeknownst to Koi, the two Ewe chiefs—one was her father—who'd sat side by side throughout the wedding rituals and celebration were among the first to die; too old to be of much value to the whites at the slave factories along the coast and too valuable to the captured tribe's retribution if allowed to live. Koi noticed Telemaque search the faces along the path, looking for his family.

Prisoners at the path were greeted by hemp ropes for all, chains for the gamest and guns for the hopeless. The lecherous glances and crude comments made as Koi's mother was tied to a single captor were familiar to Koi. Though too young to know the meaning of the words, she knew she heard dishonor. Telemaque, Koi and her sister, were lashed together on a line around their necks and hands.

As a youth of privilege within her village and tribe, accustomed to subservience among her family's slaves, Koi bristled at her own treatment on the path. She told herself that the slaves of her household never knew the abuse she now endured. Still within a day's march, she expected her father and village warriors to save them all at any moment. Longing for salvation as a child ordered to be patient, the familiar feeling of denial, of obedient waiting in return for anticipated reward kept her calm. As solace, she assured herself that her father would deal a harsh blow to these men. Recompense for all she and the others suffered in silence. More than once she felt her father's presence nearby.

Instead of salvation, Koi and the others walked all night. At each order to stop she thought no one could go on. Lashed just in front of her, Koi knew Telemaque had risked the wrath of the unwashed aggressive captors by slowing the pace of the coffle for her. Koi's legs being shorter than his own. When the moon was low in the stars the children were at last allowed to rest; to sleep in a field at the edge of the trail for a time. Until dawn.

The warmth of the sun woke the children one by one. Each was too frightened to stir until they heard a loud emotional outburst from further up the trail. Koi heard one distinct sound, her mother, to whom she immediately called out, followed by her sister and Telemaque.

Searching the path ahead the children witnessed Koi's thrashing vocal mother being grabbed from behind by her handlers and dragged away. She called out to her children. And continued to do so even after she imagined they could no longer hear her. She called out to her ancestors too, and to Mawu, the Ewe's supreme creator, appealing for the care of her children.

The commander in the white shirt—now dirty, soaked in sweat—appeared at the site of the crying, hysterical children. In the light of day the children could see that his European shirt was augmented by his tribal attire. His necklaces and earrings swayed with his powerful moves. Now, as his troops and slaves resumed their march, he ordered the children gagged. Two henchmen warriors moved to carry out the commander's orders. One tried to calm Koi long enough to gag her mouth. With a smile the warrior lied to Koi in her native dialect, saying, "She'll be back."

At first Koi resisted—refusing the gag—shouting again for her mother. Then, whimpering through tears, signaling with her hand she asked her captor to come closer. He put his ear close to her small mouth. Once he did she bit it, tearing the skin. Her captor leaped upright yelling in pain, cursing. He jumped from his toes in place as if the motion would somehow offer relief. Angry—if he hadn't been so preoccupied with his bloody ear and humiliation he would have struck Koi.

Telemaque, though frightened, drew strength from Koi's courage. He too stood up to the men, demanding not only where but, "Why are you taking her mother?"

The largest among the slavers present responded to Telemaque's insolence by clubbing him to the ground, knowing Koi and her sister, tied to Telemaque, would follow.

Koi heard one of the commander's lieutenants standing by complain that Koi was too much trouble and that, "she cannot keep up!" Suggesting they should abandon her, leave her to be devoured by the jungle.

The commander smiled and said to his men, laughing, "I like her. She fights. She'll fetch a good price." As he walked away to follow the others down the path he shouted back over his shoulder, "Gag them. Put the little one in a sack. And keep moving!"

The largest man cut Koi's tether to Telemaque and penned her slight frame to the ground, forcing a thin broken sail slat into her mouth like a horse bridle. Two more slavers came to his aid with a large thick sack in hand. A lieutenant gagged Koi's sister.

While holding and gagging Telemaque, the others opened the sack wide enough to wrestle Koi inside before tying it shut. One of the slavers produced a long pole. Two of them then lifted and carried Koi down the path. Her memories of the next days were clouded by darkness as she squirmed and screamed through her bridle from within her pitch black, swaying, suspended threaded dungeon.

Inside the smoky Shepherd's Tavern Adam put down a newspaper article he'd come across. He had been marveling at the hypocrisy of it—a reprint of Patrick Henry's fiery...*give me liberty*...speech. Within the speech the line...*Is life so dear, or peace so sweet, as to be purchased at the price of chains and slavery?* lingered in his mind as he found what, or rather, whom, he was looking for. The man had taken a seat at a table in a corner and was soon surrounded by eager chairs, leaning in closely to hear his every word.

The men—each of them predisposed to varying degrees of patriotism and profiteering—listened for an angle to wedge a way into contracts for supplies of every imaginable nature; shipping, financing, insurance. All the while, reminded of a dearth of recruits for the Continental Navy.

These conversations about business and politics and military necessity were being served up in hushed tones with Madeira, distilled spirits or a meal throughout the American colonies.

The business class of the rebels bemoaned the Continental Congress' on again off again boycott of British goods, including British slaves. Such wavering onerous policies made dockside allegiances more treacherous to navigate and the laws of commerce malleable, rendering smuggling a veritable necessity.

As Adam approached the corner table, a man dressed in his second finest silks stood in his way. The man haughtily interrupted the Continental Congress' provincial agent and those seated around him by asking in a voice loud enough to be heard above the din, "What about privateering? I can post my commission, whatever the cost, and fit three schooners for sail tomorrow." Pausing, he said, "I'll be in the market for crew. Any takers?" As the man looked around the tavern in rapt anticipation for obvious rebels, he stated his most pointed question—the answer being his real mission—"Do you have authority to provide letter of marque?"

Others at the table stopped and turned to the expensive clothes, powdered wig and Loyalist air, the source of the voice, before their grumbling ensued and spread throughout the tavern.

The agent, Benjamin Thornton, a Quaker, raised his hands to quell the crowd. With a deliberate stare he panned the room from his chair, looking men in the eye. Once silence gave him the floor he then spoke in a slow, deliberate tone to the tavern audience as he described his knowledge and authority on the subject.

"As you know, for some, privateering has been very successful, very successful, and profitable, but dangerous; indeed for others it has proved ruinous, even fatal."

Over two thousand privateers had already converted whatever ship would float for war, swarming vulnerable prey before wounding their prizes into capitulation.

He continued, "In answer to your question, sir," looking only at the Loyalist still standing in the crowd, "Yes. But you apply. Privately. As for the business, some states have issued letters. General Washington authorized vessels to harass the British from the start. Benjamin Franklin has done the same across the Atlantic. And, as an agent of the Congress—I will do the same. But, it is arms, powder and men we need now. Sailors for the Continental Navy! We'll pay…"

"Not enough!" Someone shouted across the crowded room of tables, interrupting Agent Thornton; all presumed him to be a privateer captain himself. Many in the tavern paused at the shout and laughed at its message. Privateers paid better wages and a more hefty share of the prize loot than the Continental Navy. And with only a single voyage commitment—common knowledge among tavern patrons.

Before losing his audience again, the agent turned the conversation to a list of war supplies needed, "Blankets, tents. Food! The Congress will pay a fair price with (paper) Continentals for your goods." The agent knew the crowd of merchants knew the British would confiscate their goods—or inflation would likely drain them of their value before they could reach another buyer. (Some had already done their deal with the Quaker agent dressed as a militia officer, and were grateful to have money in their pocket, even Continentals.)

For those among them with the courage to sail and attack, a privateer's commission (a letter of marque), even at the price of two thousand pounds—the same as the lowest price of a ship—offered phenomenal rewards. Many times more than the capital required to buy, provision and lose two, or even three ships. All expenses could be recouped with the enormous profit from the capture of a single prize ship. A white sugar laden sloop, or a straggler British supply ship, or sleek merchant vessel sailing for the coast with luxury items; any of them sold at Prize Court meant a fortune to a captain and crew.

This last appeal by the agent…"Step forward men, if you please. We have a city and colony to defend," produced his intent; a shuffle of chairs, most emptying, some filling as only earnest participants replaced the merely curious or fair-weather patriot. Agent Thornton pushed the remnants of his pork, onions and rice meal further aside and began to study paperwork in front of him.

Adam approached and sat in a still warm empty chair beside him.

Agent Thornton said, as though he were finishing a point of a lengthy private conversation, "The ostentatious are often unreliable, and in these times, usually a spy," motioning with his head in the direction of the earlier questioner, inquiring about privateering authority.

Adam introduced himself without comment on the spy in an effort to focus the agent's attention on his proposal alone. Careful to not draw attention to himself, Adam produced recommendation documents signed by men of renown as the others across the table engaged in an animated conversation with conviction. He began by avoiding what he sought most. In hushed remarks Adam proceeded with his narrative of commercial activity so broad as to cease the agent's eyes from blinking.

"I was told of your firm, among others, at my appointment," Agent Thornton said, blinking again, rapidly to regain his bearings. He turned his focus to the six inch curls of black hair dangling from beneath Adam's hat. (Adam used them to great effect in negotiations, like shiny fish lures.)

"So, you are aware of the nature of my mother country's, Holland's," Adam paused, "neutral trade?"

"Yes, yes, of course. It seems your country's colony in the Caribbean is a weigh station for all the world's munitions. At a price," the agent added, regretting it.

"Our price is trade goods. We will supply what is requested, paid for in goods. We'll barter or sell them. But no Continentals. Agreed?"

The agent exhaled, audibly disheartened. He'd not met a single patriot as he'd hoped to find. Even before Agent Thornton could reply, with the words of Adam's father fresh in Adam's mind—*one plays the player, not the cards,* and Adam knew his counterpart held a weak hand—Adam said, "There is one last item."

Further disillusioning the agent—rather than offering or suggesting recruits for service in the Continental Navy—Adam continued, "On behalf of my firm, I would like to request letters of marque for two schooners, the *Kameel* and the *Jupiter,* docked quayside as we speak."

"But, your principal business is the West Indies." The agent had brought up jurisdiction, customarily limited to a specific locale.

"There are exceptions, as you know" alluding to Washington's authority. Adam continued, "We request the eastern seaboard, and as you note, the West Indies."

Forewarned as to the lackluster demand for Continentals, and charged with acquiring hard goods, urgently needed, right away, Agent Thornton had been authorized to trade with near impunity, to improvise, in order to fill muskets with shot and stomachs with rations at almost any price, to strike most any bargain.

"Agreed," the agent said without enthusiasm.

The recently commissioned agent produced a list comprising an order too large for Adam's trading company to accommodate. Adam signed the contract immediately.

The bargain struck, Adam clinked his mug with the agent's to seal the deal. And to wipe the gloom from the agent's face he offered, "Cheers!"

In a matter of minutes spent with an agent of the Continental Congress, Adam's goal of wealth beyond what his ancestors could imagine was realized. On the strength of one contract—to sell illegal arms and provisions to be smuggled north to a rebellion—the family business had become a principal supplier for the American Revolution.

In the bargain he'd made tiny St. Eustatius, Statia, and by extension, his family, a prime target of the mighty British Empire.

TEN

Metaphor in Motion

As Denmark dreamt of his family, his African enslavement and of Koi, a faint but deep sound resonated within his subconscious. The rhythm beckoned him like talking drums. In his sleep the approaching sounds—huffing, clinking sounds—seemed like the king's army the night of the bonfire raid. In his nightmare he recalled being hit again along the path for not keeping pace with the others; his finger flinched.

The blow came just before his group had stopped. The slavers halted the march once they had emerged from the jungle into an open space along the path, an egress to a substantial mud-walled village.

The children of the isolated village rushed to the wide open gate of the compound as the village guards approached the mass of travelers with faux derision and bravado to assess their peril. A fight would be senseless, devastating.

To their relief, the "travelers," a term the village guards took pains to use, wished to trade. They negotiated with the elder guard an exchange of slaves for food. Pleased to be on either side of a trade rather than an unequal fight, the village elder struck the deal for peace.

Telemaque, tied to Koi's sister, appeared before their captors followed by a screaming sack in motion suspended from a pole carried by two of the king's men.

When spilled out into the daylight among the onlookers Koi's emotions and body froze—crippled by endless darkness, confinement and vertigo. The king's men laughed. The village guards were forced to oblige. Orders were relayed from the village guards to their chief and those charged with fulfilling the agreement.

As the slavers and village guards waited, the negotiating slaver smiled a laugh, gesturing to Koi's sister.

"I should charge you double for this one. See…" With the handle of his whip he lifted her checkered kente, a loincloth of camel's hair and wool, "…she almost bleeds."

The village elder guard raised his clenched chin without looking at anyone. Within minutes the restraints were removed from the young captives and three goats stood at their feet. Flat bread and pungent palm wine arrived, offered with a tribal blessing. Anxious to conclude the trade and retreat from the continuing train of armed slavers and contraband at the path, the elder among the two village guards spoke, gesturing to the children to come inside the walled village.

Another villager assigned to the children, as wards of the tribe, treated them according to custom. Telemaque and the girls were each assigned a household in which to serve as their slave. The three children were put to work in the fields gathering end-of-season yams. Most of the entire village, all of the women and children above a certain age, set about gathering the remaining crop of buried yams nearby, just beyond the village wall.

Telemaque and Koi winced at what they discovered in harvest yams left too long underground—worms. The exposed white larvae curled, reached and squirmed, disturbed by the light of day. In these moments, wiggling their finger at one another, imitating the worms' reactions to their new environment, Telemaque and Koi created a private code, a metaphor in motion, a barometer, a register of private comment—thoughts, feelings, emotions—communicated in exiguous vigor or form; the two children had developed a subtle language all their own.

The three children experienced a routine of relative ease during their enslavement. They had a roof over their head and food to eat. They were provided with comforts if not respect, physically unfettered and unmolested (with one exception). After the first week, at dawn each morning, the night sentry took a perverted delight in waking Telemaque from his dreams with a kick to his right shin as the slave boy slept beneath the reed roof overhang outside his master's dwelling. Each morning, the same kick, the same shin. Telemaque developed a limp.

Once Denmark could stave off the approaching sounds no more—as his finger flinched and he imagined his shin in pain—his eyes opened fast, big. As though falling. He leapt from his bed to shake away the aura of his thoughts. He splashed fresh water from the cistern onto his face. Careful not to wake Millie, he took a moment to seek out the sounds he heard.

Across the bay Moses's gang of slaves had rounded the bend of neighboring mountainous Paradise Island, singing on their path to the fields. Led by a sorrowful deep low cadence, answered in chorus, the verse reached a crescendo—culminating in abrupt silence—punctuated by jingling chains and the percussion of a hundred quick steps marching in unison like an army.

He could now see the train of light from the forced procession's torches as they made their way along the shoreline. The gently sloping sugar cane fields lay ahead, where the mountain abated to the sea. From the top of Madame's island, his new home, Denmark gazed at the tall plants blanketing the coast across the bay, their long thin leaves blinking in the pre-dawn glow of fading moonlight. As dawn broke he saw smoke rise from the sugar mill where unknown to him his mother and sister toiled to feed the fire.

Over time, the slave's movements on Paradise Island, their routine to and from the fields came to demarcate his own day like clockwork. And they served as a constant reminder of another life just across the water from his isolated island sanctuary.

Denmark soaked in his new environment, following each of Millie's instructions, learning her language, a mixture of French, English and Negerhollands—Black Dutch—as she spoke. As Denmark's duties became routine he no longer required instruction or prompts. Indeed, in time, Denmark's questions became more abstract and inquisitive, to a point beyond Millie's ability to answer with confidence. To augment Millie's role, Denmark's chores soon included daily meal preparation and service for Madame; delivering her newspapers, served with coffee and brown sugar.

Each day after his afternoon chores he took the liberty to explore the island and its waters. He tread every foot of the hills. On the western side of the island he discovered several small scrub beaches abutting the rock foundations of the hills, protected from the wind. He'd become habituated to saltwater, the taste, the sting, the pleasure. In the process had become an accomplished swimmer, able to hold his breath for long dives.

He swam from beach to isolated beach admiring sea life, starfish, sponges and sea urchins among the flittering small fish as he searched the bottom for food and a treasure of man-made relics tossed or fallen overboard through the centuries. He lived in the fantasy world youth imagine: gazing upon azure water, colored by sun and depth, bound by steep neighboring islands of green foliage clinging to gray rock slopes towering skyward.

On one such occasion, as he sunbathed on a warm smooth boulder to dry off after an afternoon swim, Koi appeared through his closed eyelids. Gone in the twinkle of sunlight glare, a smile moved his lips and a finger. Soon back in the inviting water he took a deep breath, held it, and floated like a lone stalk of sugar cane drifting in the bay. Looking up, eyes to the sky, ears briefly submerged, he thought of one of his last a days in Africa; with Koi and her sister and a bevy of slaves assembled at an itinerate slave market along a river. Thoughts of his mother and sister, worry, resurfaced with his ears.

Through the months these images played over and over in his mind, sometimes triggered by the hymns of the slaves to and from the fields, the clink of a chain, the crack of a whip, or even the call of Madame.

"Denmark!" he heard Madame call. "Denmark!" she'd called again. This time with more urgency accompanied by the clang, clang, clang of a hand-bell she kept in her parlor.

That day, much to Madame's delight Denmark had discovered a field of conch, thirty-seven of them, four fathoms deep, at the bottom of the far end of the little bay. While examining a sample of his catch on her terrace, once her enthusiasm passed, Madame warned Denmark not to set foot on another shore or to obey orders from another island. To do so could mean death before rescue. His only protection against the harsh outside world was being the property of Madame Chevalier. As she considered his effort, she reconsidered some of her original opinions of Denmark. He'd just upended one—that he might be too small for his role—and reinforced another—that he was an unusually bright and observant boy.

She promised to get a small boat for him to use in the bay.

In the midst of her lecture, she decided to undertake the experiment she'd toyed with in her mind. Though Millie's reluctance to be schooled seemed to corroborate Monsieur Jean-Jacques Rousseau's thesis—that women, like Sophie, the female character in one of his most famous works, *Emile, On Education*, were incapable or disinclined to learning—Madame knew that she and her childhood friend, Gabrielle, were living contradictions to Rousseau's precept. And now, looking at Denmark, she vowed to disprove the acclaimed assertion of the philosopher and historian David Hume. In his essay *Of National Character*, Hume had stated, *I am apt to suspect the Negroes and in general all the other species of men, for there are four or five different kinds, to be naturally inferior to the whites.*

Thinking ahead Madame pictured what might be possible for Denmark in his lifetime. She smiled like a schoolgirl with a secret and thought Voltaire would be so pleased with what she envisioned.

Madame told Denmark to follow her into her parlor, her library.

But, because Madame had violated her own tenet with Millie—that beyond the rudimentary, learning must be hungered for—she chose to only point out to the boy his new masters. She would allow them each to make their acquaintance to the boy in their own good time.

"You see these," she said, spanning her hand across the room, pointing to the floor-to-ceiling bookshelves, opposite the stone fireplace, interrupted only by two doorways. "And, these," pointing to the shelves either side of the stone fireplace, "these are all yours." She couldn't help a bit of a laugh; a puzzle to Denmark that nonetheless brought a smile to his face.

"I tell you now even before you can begin to comprehend what I'm saying; what this all means. And later, I'll tell you again. And when you come of age, you will be free, mind, body and soul. Mark my words."

Denmark didn't know all of her words yet, but he knew he was going to like what his new mistress was saying, what she had in mind. Her gestures and the kindness in her face and voice told him so.

Though somewhat stooped in her old age, upright she stood almost a foot taller than the boy. Holding and leaning on Denmark's shoulder for support, Madame Chevalier used her cane to point out various works of interest to her, and hopefully, one day, to him.

"These were mostly gathered from travelers who frequented our tavern, hotel or mercantile store at Road Town. I traded for books they brought to me, and over the years, as you see," she said, lifting her light cane as an extension of her arm, "business was quite good. I've been able to amass a small library."

Pointing to a bookshelf beyond the stone fireplace and a portrait of her family above the mantel—Madame, her deceased husband, her daughter, her late son-in-law and her tall, blond grandson—she explained, "Over there are works by philosophers, scientists and mathematicians: Descartes, and also Pascal, even Leonhard Euler's *Introductio in Analysin Infinitorum*, a Swiss who had influenced both of them."

Still with cane in hand she pointed to books closer to where Denmark stood, "And here we have John Locke's *Some Thoughts Concerning Education*. And this," pointing to a slim leather bound volume next to the novels *The Vicar of Wakefield* and *The History of Rasselas, Prince of Abissinia* alongside *Mr. William Shakespeares Comedies, Histories, & Tragedies*, "is a copy of Montesquieu's *Persian Letters*. Story telling is a practical skill as well as a joy; and there, Hume's *History of Great Britain*."

Here Madame interjected, "Remind me one day to warn you about him," followed by "We've had many English guests," as though an explanation for the content of her collection was in order.

"Also, some recent additions; this one, *The Wealth of Nations*, is by Adam Smith, another Englishman. And this one, here, my most recent addition, is *Common Sense* by an anonymous Englishman, who now calls himself an American"; Madame huffed slightly at the novelty of it all. Moving toward the terrace view she said "I hope one day you will appreciate these, as gifts, as I do." Then, giving the thought a moment, "if you fall in love with Shakespeare, as I have, or Michel de Montaigne, a man who influenced all of them, maybe you will."

She then looked into the boy's patient gaze to communicate. "When you are ready," she said, "start with those," pointing to a row of nearly identical volumes of *Encyclopedie*, edited by Monsieur Diderot with contributions by Rousseau. "I just acquired the last volume not long ago."

During one of Millie's visits before Denmark's arrival, a newspaper Millie had delivered with Madame's coffee contained a note tucked between its pages. In fine cursive the note had read:

In the name of your country and the English rebels' cause, note ship movements and news from your correspondence. Place your dispatches between the covers of 1611.

Madame knew the number well. A date, referring to a book. The only local copy she knew of was in her own tavern and hotel library; an old, oversized, heavy copy of the King James Bible, printed in 1611. The book, displayed open, occupied its own lectern in a corner, seldom consulted by Madame's clientele.

She considered every possibility she could entertain, including that she may have received someone else's mail. She tried to imagine the author of the note among the known local political landscape. While the intrigue of the espionage request delighted her—taking part in making trouble for England—the mission of swaying the outcome of battles yet fought pleased her even more. And the thought that war might disrupt Master Thomas's slave trade, saving lives and costing him money, was a delicious bonus.

She responded to the request with a hand-written warning about British war plans. Her wax-sealed note was tucked inside a letter addressed to Armand Nedved, her business manager. The letter specifically told Armand to place the note *within the folds of 1611*.

On the next of Dr. Ramsay's frequent visits to her island she coyly requested he deliver the letter to her hotel after he stated his next destination was Road Town. Madame felt secure in her method and choices. She held both men in high esteem. In Madame's opinion, the doctor, a fervent, prolific critic of the inhumane treatment of slaves, kept a sane mind amid unimaginable carnage and misery all around him. And Armand, handpicked by her late husband, had earned her respect and trust by faithfully executing her every wish.

The warning dispatch was the synthesis of hints gleaned from correspondence with customers, regulars, from around the world; many of them English. It also provided observations made from her spyglass atop her atoll, including the number of English frigates and privateers spied en route to and from nearby Antigua, where the British maintained a shipyard. Among these details was the most ominous, a warning to Charles Town.

To the inhabitants of Charles Town, South Carolina: A detachment of the British Navy split from the fleet departing Boston for Halifax will soon assemble at the mouth of your harbor and deploy Royal Marines to nearby barrier islands.

Early on Denmark only indulged Madame Chevalier. Initially, he cared nothing for his new life. All he wanted was to be free, to go home, to be with his family and his people in Africa. He questioned what good learning anything more than a rudimentary understanding of Madame's language could possibly do for him or his people. This attitude was not lost on Madame. So much so that she began to question the wisdom, the motivation, of her tabula rasa experiment.

But, over time, as Denmark's language skills improved—with help he'd mastered Millie's primers in weeks—the answers to his questions revealed themselves to him in books. As he began to be able to read, first in French and then in English, his appetite for learning surprised him. And Madame found that he soon could not only contribute to, but even advance, conversations on an array of topics. He was learning not only from the books in her library—books she noticed missing and returned—in ways Millie was either disinclined to or was incapable of—but also from their discourse.

What fueled his studies were stories from ancient history. The fable of Eunus, a fire-breathing slave who organized an insurrection. A chronicle of the sacking of Henna. A biography of Spartacus, an enslaved gladiator who became a slave rebellion leader. And at Madame's insistence, the story of how Moses freed the enslaved Jews from ancient Egypt.

At any time on any day Madame would interrupt Denmark's chores, directing him to a chair in the shade on her terraced pinnacle with captivating views. If Millie were visiting at the time she'd ask her to serve them coffee.

Madame would ask him how he felt about certain topics; the opinions held by Hume, Voltaire, or others from passages she pointed out to him.

On one such occasion, after Denmark's "go to Hell-like Hume, et al." response—that he was a living rebuttal to Hume's argument regarding the Negro "species"—she asked if he could imagine what Michel de Montaigne might say about Hume's assertions. Why de Montaigne's inquisitive mind spawned debate, providing a structure for writing mimicked by others ever since. Though these were difficult themes of difficult words for Denmark he enjoyed the *repartee*. The bits of clarity these conversations bestowed upon him were like rays of sunlight between parting clouds, revealing new finds at the bottom of Madame's bay.

On one occasion like this Madame asked him about a book he'd not yet opened.

"I don't know the story yet."

"When you do read *Candide* by Voltaire, think of de Montaigne. What about Mr. Swift, have you enjoyed the adventures of *Gulliver's Travels?*" The boy nodded with a grin. The subject matter and colorful illustrations made the book his favorite.

"Do you think Lilliput-like other worlds exist?" To this Denmark stared into the abyss of Madame's lagoon below and with a slight turn of his chin, his thoughts turned to the uninhabited islands that flanked the Sir Francis Drake Channel. They were always visible from Madame's atoll. He innocently shrugged his shoulders in wonderment at the prospect.

"Which brings me to geography, or at least what we know exists today. The map has changed in the span of my life, as it will during yours." Dotted lines on Madame's maps reflected the limits of knowledge and topography of land masses as yet uncharted by Europeans. Madame pointed out to Denmark the modern powerful nations, their capitals. She spoke the names of rulers and as best she could she explained to the boy the geo-political battles raging among nations of the world.

During his own private study sessions he discovered the art and science of navigation. Madame showed him on her maps where they lived and where he and all the other Africans had been taken from across the ocean. With this in mind he'd plotted a course to Africa in his imagination with an instrument he'd seen drawings of and read about: the sextant.

Sailing the boat Madame had acquired for him within her bay, Denmark made a show of displaying his seamanship to her. And yet, confined to the bay, unable to "set foot" on the tall slopes that rimmed most of the bay, to sail beyond Madame's shores—in time, the sheer inclines of the neighboring islands appeared more like walls of his imprisonment than idyllic scenery.

Eventually Madame relented, somewhat. Instructed to always remain visible from the spyglass atop Madame's perch, she allowed Denmark to sail beyond her bay into the channel and among the neighboring islands. His time on the water became Denmark's solace. Piloting her small craft among shoals and through the swells of the deep water channel, he became an adroit sailor, able to maneuver in traffic and negotiate changing winds and currents.

One day, on an excursion beyond Madame's bay Denmark disappeared from Madame's spyglass, as though the curvature of the earth had swallowed him whole; he'd vanished.

Denmark vowed to "set foot" on one of the uninhabited islands along the Sir Francis Drake Channel, alone. He wanted to be completely alone, in a kind of no man's land. A place where no people roamed, not even Lilliputians. (Well, he conceded, maybe Lilliputians, but no one else!) He yearned for freedom and independence—what every youth, slave or free, craves even before knowing what it means.

He beached his small craft on a tiny quiet uninhabited island across the channel from Madame's. He felt free, or *thought* he did. A boyish grin of serene satisfaction appeared upon his face. But as a fatherless boy, as an African without a tribe, as a slave, he struggled with the notion.

Though these reflections sobered the boy, they also drove him to his next destination; an island not only written about in books, but spoken of at Madame's tavern. A notorious island that had once formed the nexus of local pirate lore. Madame's patrons had said Bluebeard, Captain Kidd and Black Sam Bellamy all stashed treasure there during their respective heydays of villainy. In Denmark's time, the island cultivated cane and the culture of violence Dr. Ramsay railed against and Madame feared for Denmark.

The island's beach was met by enormous smooth boulders tumbling into the sea. Some were over twenty feet tall. They all leaned against one another forming large arched openings between them. After beaching Madame's boat Denmark approached one of the many watery openings. The shadowy, cool, gentle pools of water within beckoned him.

Once inside, Denmark was comforted by daylight streaming through gaps between the resting boulders and the soft sand between his toes. He stood for a moment in ankle deep water. He waded further, soon chest deep in water that stretched contiguously throughout the entire maze of caverns. After looking back, to keep his bearings, he took a right turn at his choice of two passages, leading him to a larger chamber ahead of still deeper water.

After a brief swim he ventured back to the more shallow water, to the first fork and route he'd ignored. Following it created another set of choices, the first of which seemed to go on forever. Too frightened to confirm his suspicions Denmark turned to find his way out. Within a step his toe felt something foreign to the touch, something inanimate. Curling his toes he clawed it and brought his foot close enough to grasp the item with his hand. A ring. Not a plain band ring. It was a woman's mourning ring, decorated with a casket on either side of a jeweled setting, missing the jewel.

Excited, he carefully put the ring into his pocket while searching the sand bottom with his feet for more treasure. But after a thorough sweep he felt nothing more than shells and more soft sand between his toes.

He felt happy, but with a gnawing twinge of worry, too. He didn't know if bandits might still favor the place, perhaps lurking deep within the cavern he'd shunned. And, he knew the longer he was away the more trouble Madame would have in store for him.

Nevertheless, back in the sunlight once more he couldn't resist exploring more of the island. He traversed the beach where he discovered a path worn into the scrub, wind-blown vegetation. His fantasy of pirates and buried treasure soon returned as he followed the path into the interior.

Through a short thicket and up and over a small hill the island vegetation gave way to an immense sloping field of scraggly gray rocks. The wind smelled of fresh dirt and sweat. The hands, shovels and pick axes of a gang of slaves worked the earth. Unbeknownst to Denmark, his presence attracted the attention of three white men off to the side of the works.

They didn't give chase. Instead, they began hysterical gestures. The man whose attention they sought—the man who'd sold them the slaves and now oversaw their labor—finally responded. Setting his eyes upon the interloper, Seymour ran straight away for Denmark.

Very soon, what the copper investors had so urgently encouraged now seemed hasty. With the slave's overseer absent—chasing a boy— the three pasty men felt vulnerable; exposed. Naked to the whims of shovels, pick axes and grudges in idle hands. A silent exchange of glances between the slaves set the investors into motion. They jockeyed for position to be the first in flight. They bumped and stumbled into one another while running and calling out to Seymour on the narrow trail to the beach.

With the advantage of a head start, Denmark was able to shove off, raise his sails and put a hundred feet of water between him and his pursuer. By the time the three copper mine investors reached the beach, colliding into one another in an abrupt stop, they saw Denmark gliding away. Their protector was bent over at the waist, gasping for air after his run.

Still heaving, still bent at the waist and holding his fat belly Seymour shook his finger at Denmark as he declared, "I know who you belong to!"

ELEVEN

There's Always Trouble

The day of Denmark's disappearance Dr. Ramsay arrived for a visit with Madame. He found her distraught. Not with Denmark's disappearance, for she concealed that unhappy circumstance.

She was crushed by new news. She'd just learned through her correspondence that the heir of her husband's nemesis was not only the new owner of the plantation across the bay from her island, but that he was also engaged to marry her daughter. Madame decided to use the opportunity of the good doctor's visit to insist he make an unannounced visit to *Paradis*.

She wished to at least discredit Master Thomas, or if she could, ruin him, before confronting her estranged, widowed daughter regarding the wisdom of her choice.

Considering the doctor's writing on the subject of inhumane treatment of Negroes she wanted to create a sense of urgency in the doctor. Ostensibly for his own good as well as the slaves, while using him to further her own designs. She wanted to stress that given the new owner's history—his and his father's reputation for cruelty to slaves—the doctor might not only uncover harsh treatment during a visit there, an unannounced visit could correct or prevent future mistreatment. And, as an additional enticement, Madame stressed that the visit might also provide material for the book she knew he planned to write; a synthesis all of his published work.

"I have a chapter for your book! And it's just across the water from where you sit; awful, filthy conditions, mortality beyond the usual horrendous numbers. You should investigate! I've heard of more and more slaves landing, to replenish the dead."

Sitting up straight in his seat, "Who owns the estate?"

"William Thomas of Charlotte Amalie. His family's been in the slave trade since it's amounted to trade in the Indies." She knew the historical, generational connection, adding up to countless slaves shipped, abused and killed would stir his blood.

"Well, that does sound promising." Looking around he said before taking another sip of Madame's brandy, "Could I interview your slave boy, Denmark? I recall you mentioning his past. It could be tragic."

"There'll be plenty of opportunity for that later," she said without divulging Denmark's unaccounted for absence.

Leaving his ship, the *Mary*, anchored off Madame's island Dr. Ramsay boated across the bay to Paradise Island. Nestor, Dr. Ramsay's African slave, unloaded Dr. Ramsay's bag first then helped the doctor disembark for *Paradis*. (Nestor had informed Dr. Ramsay about smallpox inoculation, a technique that had been in practice for generations in parts of Africa).

Because no one on the island came out to greet him, the doctor and Nestor wandered the island rather than present themselves at the manor door. They soon came upon the slave cemetery, with three fresh graves. The space stood out in contrast to the dense scrub growth along its perimeter. So did a tomb of coral rock opposite so many plain weathered unmarked graves. The rock tomb's only distinguishing characteristic was its age; relatively new.

They reached the slave quarters as the *Paradis* slaves arrived for the mid-day break and meal. Having lived, preached and practiced medicine among the island culture for years, Dr. Ramsay knew the routine as well as the brutalities.

Wearing a black wide-brimmed hat to ward off the sun and his clergy collar to ward off threats of any sort Dr. Ramsay approached Moses, the man with the whip.

"I understand there's been some trouble," is all he said, because on slave plantations, one could always assume there was, or had been, trouble.

After looking over the unknown, unannounced visitor and his manservant, the driver rolled his immense shoulders, asking himself if word of the lashing traveled that fast, or if the reverend was asking about the dead runaways, or maybe the multiple smallpox deaths, earlier.

"What trouble?" he said to play dumb.

"I want to see your sick slaves. Any pox patients?" he asked, searching Moses's eyes for an answer.

Selena spoke up from the entrance to her hut, "No, sir. Abra and I buried the last one." Abra nodded, wearing a red kerchief she'd taken off the head of the last young dead man. The same young man she'd recognized from the Middle Passage; that first day at *Paradis*. He had removed it from a pox victim, a sailor, buried at sea aboard the *Briel*.

Dr. Ramsay preached, "Pox outbreaks can run as wild as brush fires, consuming an entire plantation if not snuffed-out quickly."

The *Paradis* field hands stood as silent as a choir listening to the pulpit.

"Well," Dr. Ramsay said, "have the sick that can manage it to sit on their stoop and I'll be around. Where are the ones that cannot walk?"

"Here," Selena said, motioning the doctor to her door. Selena kept the lamp hidden.

"I can't see enough in there. Have them brought out," Dr. Ramsay said to Moses, expecting to be obeyed.

Exasperated, Moses said, "They're not even sick, just lazy. Some need a lash now and then. They just don want to work."

"Where's your boss?"

"Master Seymour? I don know. He don tell me nut'ting," Moses said.

After Moses and Nestor carried the young slave Moses had whipped over to Dr. Ramsay, Moses said, "Yesterday, he did say som'ting about seeing a barrister."

This comment unnerved the doctor as he considered the prospect of being sued in court, or worse. Though his Caribbean island circuit crossed an area almost the size of England, the roads (as the sea lanes were called) connecting the settlements he frequented made them seem as close to one another as distant villages of the English countryside. So, his controversial views were well known throughout the islands—and because of his published work—even beyond. His life and well-being had been threatened many times.

Just in case of trouble he carried a pistol with his Bible, both in his medical bag.

Sunlight in the lane revealed the extent of the slave's wounds. The breeze thankfully lessened the odor of the decaying and damaged flesh as Dr. Ramsay examined him.

"This man's half dead!" the doctor said.

"Wait! You'll see!" Moses ran back into Selena's hut and retrieved another slave, lifting and carrying him all by himself. He rolled him from his shoulders onto the dirt next to the slave with lash wounds and said, "See!"

Dr. Ramsay's examination of the new patient became more acute the longer it lasted, until, in surprise but not shock, the doctor said, "This man *is* dead, you idiot."

"No! No! Wake up!" Moses said, shaking the man who'd died of exhaustion. Selena and Abra had been nursing the man only minutes before Moses exhibited him.

"I'm going to report you to the authorities, and in print! I'll see to it you reform your treatment of God's creatures before Judgment Day!"

"No! No! Don't" Selena broke in, "He's a good *bomba*, he didn't mean it." She took Moses by the arm as she spoke. She wanted, needed, to protect the status quo, to let Seymour continue freeing slaves from Paradise Island. Moses smiled wide to mask his astonishment and relief at Selena's (disingenuous) kind words as he questioned Selena's motives.

"I've read your work," Selena said. Dr. Ramsay's vanity cast a new spell on the moment. The flattery so unbalanced the doctor that he ignored his shock that Selena could read.

To quell Selena's fervent plea, to reassure her, however falsely, he insinuated he would defer any complaint "out of respect for your wishes."

That night, Seymour appeared at the threshold of Selena's hut after meeting with the barrister that handled the sale of *Paradis* and three copper mining investors.

Each of them was eager to keep the exploration a secret. And they were willing to be generous to buy not only Seymour's silence but his allegiance. Thus, they hoped, to close the loop of secrecy while securing a reliable flow of *Paradis* runaways to work the mine.

"I have good news. I've made another arrangement. We're set to free three more. Can you have three more ready for the next new moon?"

"Yes," Selena said. She did not know how or whom, but she would never say no to freedom.

"Good. And, there's something else," he said studying her.

She felt his hesitation, but waited for his request to come to her like a Venus flytrap waits for a bug.

"I need a favor."

"Yes," she said.

"I need a messenger. Someone to meet someone; a friend. The friend will have a piece of paper. Just bring it to me. Simple."

"Where is this simple person goin' be?" Selena asked, lowering her chin, but not her gaze.

"Right down this path. All the way to the ocean. You've been here a long time. You're bound to have meandered down there some time or another," he said, goading her. He knew of her belief, common in the islands, that the spirit world is said to be strongest where the path meets the sea.

"What's this person look like?"

Seymour hadn't answered that question to his own satisfaction yet. He chose his words, "I can't say. That is, it will be dark, the encounter brief, simple. No need to be certain of who so much as where. The idea is to pass the dis...the paper, unnoticed, as in, at night."

"All right, all right, I understand," she said with the swipe of her hand in the air around his uneasiness.

"So, same plan. Don't forget the graves," Seymour said to her.

"As if I need reminding. We had a death today, a real death," she said as she reached for the lamp, followed by, "Just one 'ting."

The tone of retribution he most feared visited Selena's voice earlier than he had planned.

"Yes," he said, hoping to seem sanguine.

"You have to take Abra and Sade as two of the 'tree."

Seymour started to complain, "I thought we had an understanding, three males at a time," but sensing her determination, he corrected his tone, and tried again.

"But, of course, yes. This is no place for a mother and child," he said, imitating what he imagined Dr. Ramsay might say, from reading his writings. Seymour now knew what to plan for. He told Selena to then have five slaves ready to be picked up from Steeple Point.

"Abra is in a bad way," she almost finished her sentence with, *with Master Thomas*, but she didn't. She didn't want to pit one white against another if there were no benefit in it. The two men already worked at opposite ends. "As for Sade…" she didn't say, *someday she would replace her mother's visits to Master Thomas*. She did say, "…freedom anywhere is what's best for her." As she spoke those words, she added another face to Seymour's five.

TWELVE

We?

Several sailors travelled quick-step down the dock from the tide stink at the Cooper River seawall. Adam's two schooners were loading the Continental Congress' barter goods onboard and making ready to get underway.

The men delivered the message of a new round-up, a sweep not unlike the disturbance at the black's May Day celebration. People had been arrested. This one however targeted known white Loyalist and random blacks on the streets—a response to rumors of British Regulars in the area. Promised their freedom in return for their service many slaves had joined the ranks of Lord Dunmore in Virginia six months ago.

Adam was standing on deck with both captains aboard the *Kameel* discussing the latest rumors of British fleet positions. After the messenger's interruption, Adam said, "You gentlemen have your instructions. Be sure to meet the *Rotterdam* before the Charles Town Bar with the tide."

"Aye aye," the officers answered. The two captains of the schooners were rivals in life—not just for prize money, but for glory in battle.

"Well, then. I'll be on my way," he said as he departed, anxious to find Augustus and the others safe at his family's Charles Town home.

Despite Adam's contracts to supply the rebellion, he knew that mobs of inebriated rebels roaming the streets were capable of all manner of violent miscalculations. He worried for his own safety as well as theirs. He told the driver to hurry, promising him a fine tip.

Adam found Augustus and Beatrice seated with Koi beneath the chandelier over the Wolff family dining room table, glum. Koi was scared and watery-eyed but quiet. Beatrice wrung her hands.

No one rose from their chair. With the heavy dining room curtains drawn the room smelled of wax from a lone candelabra. Its light reflected from a mirror on the fireplace mantle. Standing at the head of the table Adam waited to speak. When he did he said, "Augustus, you must know by now of the events to come, of a fight, a war seen from this very stoop."

Augustus nodded the obvious and asked, "What are you going to do?" Meaning—*what is it you have in mind for us?*

Augustus would not hold to a scenario that separated him from Beatrice. Though a matter of logistics for him; Adam's decision was a defining moment for the others.

Beatrice put her hand in Augustus's beneath the table. Adam pulled up a chair and sat with the others before speaking again.

He began, "Well, though the main theater of war has been well north until now, it is due to arrive any moment. I propose we sail to St. Eustatius, Statia. Home. There's much to do there."

After a few ponderous moments, leaning toward Adam as punctuation, Augustus asked, "We?"

Beatrice and Koi, both paralyzed with anticipation, leaned forward too. They all waited for any hint of clarification. All else hinged on Adam's meaning of the word "We."

Adam began again, "News of the British evacuation of Boston emboldened the rebels. But, now, now the question is where has the fleet sailed? Rumors are they will strike Charles Town next. That their troops have already landed on the coastal islands."

Silence pervaded the room, except for an occasional sniffle from Koi clutching her doll. As his audience continued its vigil, waiting, Adam came to realize that the only word of any consequence to them was the word "We."

"I suppose I could let you decide, Augustus," Adam said. He felt the relief in Augustus's posture.

To abridge his definition he said, "Of course, I'll take Statia (Koi) with me. She can make herself useful."

The air grew thin. No one had heard that name in months. They called her Koi. The only remnant of identity, of family she had. To hear her slave name, "Statia," was noise to their ears.

"But, she's so young! How did you come by this girl?" Beatrice said with deliberate impertinence.

As a free person of color she was still angry at all whites for the recent turn of events that had affected her friends. She, like Augustus and Koi, had grown fond of The African and had hoped to help him somehow. And their friend Beulah continued to be confined within her master's home, a home still in mourning. And now the rebel's increasing virulence threatened everyone in their path.

Adam stood and walked the perimeter of the long table.

"I bought her by mistake. But, as I said, everyone must earn their keep. I have plans for her in the field of medicine. I have a physician in mind, Dr. Ramsay, with whom she may apprentice. We could use more medical practitioners on Statia. With over five thousand souls on our island at any given time we need the ability to combat pox outbreaks and the like," Adam said. Too defensively this time, he knew. With a slight bob of his head he admitted, "I also had a smallpox variolation business in mind. It pays handsomely. I have reason to believe Statia is immune. She survived a pox voyage!"

The couple did not try to disguise their displeasure with Adam's plans for Koi.

Adam shook his head at the thought of the words he'd used to refer to the scared little girl in front of him now; *I bought her, by mistake.*

He stood and began to describe the transaction he'd sought.

"I thought I'd bought the two females standing in front of me. A woman, and her young daughter, so I'd heard. Statia, I remember, was standing behind them. But at the clerk's desk he charged me only fifty pounds, for one young female. I corrected him, and he attempted to correct me according to his books. There were multiple bids going on the floor, highly irregular. The agent who I'd understood sold me a mother and daughter disavowed me with the wave of his hand. The clerk looked me in the eye as though the transaction was square and proper, as ordered. His obtuse response of 'come again' to my questioning left me with a scene to make, or Statia. And before I could argue another word a brute the size of a beached whale had put us both out, into the street. I was left with Statia."

Augustus and Beatrice contemplated the story, and Adam's role in it.

Adam tried to renew the urgency he'd come to the house to instill. "We can't stay, Augustus."

The fact was not lost on Beatrice or Augustus. The future of Charles Town was frightening. Beatrice offered a "maybe you should go too," to Augustus, not wishing him to suffer to protect her. The reply she was hoping for was instantaneous.

An unequivocal, "What!" from Augustus closed the subject.

Grasping the back of a dining room chair Adam interrupted their exchange, "We could all go."

Augustus and Beatrice whispered worried looks at one another.

Unsure of what it meant, Adam asked, "Is it decided then? We all go?" wondering about the nature of their continued discontent.

Augustus turned to Adam, "Beatrice," he started, then corrected himself, "We," he hesitated, "We're thinking of Beulah."

"Ah…" Adam remembered her around the house, along with The African.

He considered the overwhelming demands he faced amid scarce labor once ensconced on St. Eustatius. In addition to Augustus, and now Beatrice, he reasoned he could always use a hand. Adam considered that Beulah's owner may well indeed wish to be rid of her. Under the circumstances—her ties with a child murderer, The African—at a discount.

"Well, I'll go and have a word with my neighbor."

Beatrice cried out and embraced Augustus then Koi who began jumping in place, smiling now. Koi understood enough of what had just transpired. Though not looking forward to another ship, she was comforted by the idea of sailing with her Charles Town friends.

"Augustus, you drag those trunks out of the garret and pack our things. I'll go and purchase Beulah!" he paused recognizing the nature of his transgression. Clearing his throat he said in a less boisterous tone, "I'll send a wagon round. From the *Rotterdam*. For all of you, and the trunks. How about that?"

"Fine, Master Adam. That will be fine," Augustus said.

Once Adam had closed the front door Beatrice grabbed Augustus by the shirtsleeve and said "We've got to get The African out. Now. And, I know how."

The notion took Augustus's breath away. He clasped her by the arm with alarm in his grip. But the first thing he said was, "What do you have in mind?"

While the powerful were busy debating the defense of the city or its British occupation, The African had been beaten for weeks on end. Over and over. And told again and again he would hang. Told and beaten enough times to finally satiate his interrogators and the grieving father. As a practical man of business, the father had tried to sell The African rather than forfeit his value. But amid the turmoil of the revolution, all business, even the slave trade, had been retarded.

The African was being held in a cell at the Work House—a public prison for punishing slaves and holding runaways. A place where the guards were paid by plantation owners to whip their slaves. A place with a specific room set aside for that sole purpose. It was soundproofed by sand-filled walls so as to not disturb the neighborhood.

Two weary guards stood at the entrance to the prison.

Augustus, Beatrice and Koi arrived in a private carriage she had managed to barrow from her employer. Ostensibly to avoid the unruly gangs of rebels roaming the streets accosting blacks they feared would join the British. Beatrice had bribed their "Augustus of the house" to be their coachman.

Leaving Koi in the enclosed coach, Beatrice and Augustus approached the prison guards without hesitation. Augustus handed the guards a "supper pass" forged by Beatrice, a basket of food in hand. Plausible and customary enough, the guards opened the prison and the iron door to The African's cell. The African remained curled in a corner, bloody, motionless and quiet.

As Beatrice moved to enter the cell Augustus pulled a pistol from beneath Beatrice's frock. He cocked the flint lock while shouting, "Stand back!" with as much ferocity as he could muster. Shocked by the display, the guard's threw up their hands, dropping their weapons to the floor. They shouted back, "Don't shoot! Don't shoot, old man!"

Beatrice shook The African to rouse him. The beatings had rendered him barely conscious. She spoke loud and clear into his ear, "Rise! Get up! Get up, now! Get up! Your life depends upon it!" She kept repeating herself even as he rose and shook off his daze, "Get up, man! Get up!"

Augustus locked the guards in The African's cell and threw the keys into an adjacent occupied cell, to cheers from within. Other prisoners who'd witnessed the events, thrilled at the prospect of liberation too, roared with jubilation.

The coachman and rig waiting at the prison gates drew the attention of a city guard walking his beat, just down the street. He decided to walk closer. As he did, Augustus, Beatrice and The African, limping and covered by a shawl Beatrice brought for this purpose, approached the other side of the waiting enclosed coach.

As the guard touched the bridle of one of the horses, the coach shifted under their weight as the three entered on the other side. The coach door quietly closed as the guard first spoke.

With no good response committed to memory, the coachman slapped his reigns in the face of questioning. Held by their collar, the horses didn't move. The coachman's silence, taken as insolence, became the guard's mission to address. With another snap of the coachman's reins and still no response the guard started to climb the coach—but a Boom! shook the settled evening. Augustus had fired the flintlock pistol into the air. A flintlock pistol that had been in his possession for some twenty years. It had remained hidden from view all this time. To be used only for safety against intruders. To his knowledge it had never been fired before.

The horses responded immediately, hysterically bumping against one another before they took off running, knocking the angry guard to the sandy crushed shell street. The coachman regained control and coaxed the horses around the block, out of sight, and on their way home.

The guard's wounded pride sprang into action, alerting others long before he learned he'd held The African's life by the reins but let him slip away. A city wide search was ordered for all the escaped prisoners. A special envoy was sent to The African's owner's address.

Once the wagon Adam sent from the *Rotterdam* arrived to carry the trunks, the wagon driver and Augustus struggled together to load a large, heavy one. Augustus then helped Beatrice into the wagon seats and lifted Koi to her as the child clamored up the steep sideboards. The street was so quiet they heard the city guard's envoy and entourage depart from the house behind them—their horses clomping the hard packed street as they hurried along, toward Shepherd's Tavern.

The wagon driver noticed his charges' keen interest in the sounds of the authorities.

"I'm no fool, you know," he said, smiling at the others with a foolish grin on his twenty-two year old plump baby face.

Augustus and Beatrice froze. Their thoughts raced. Their hearts pounded. Both assumed the young man was insinuating something about the weight, or contents, of the large, heavy trunk.

"My orders are to avoid the delay of needless questioning, at all costs. They went that way, so we best take our leave this way, to the *Rotterdam*!" he said as he snapped the reins. The wagon jerked forward and rambled down the street, toward East Bay Street and Vanderhorst's Wharf.

From the bridge of the *Rotterdam* Captain Mathew McGreevy looked upon the group with suspicion. He'd been made aware of a sailor ordered to carry wagon trunks from ashore, but he had no other word. Augustus looked down the wharf and noticed the officer's interest in their arrival. And with Adam nowhere to be seen he could be anywhere in the city.

A large prison wagon approached the wharf down East Bay Street and creaked to a halt in front of them. The driver swung open the cage door and each shackled slave, man, woman and child in various states of dress, climbed down the wagon step with care and took a place among the others. In single file they walked the wharf in silence, as though prepared by a whip for this moment. Condemned to a fate they could only ponder; an early death in the cane fields of the West Indies as likely as any other.

Koi held her doll tight and thought of The African hiding in the trunk in the wagon.

A fast carriage driver brought his charging horses to a pin stop at the wharf's landing. Adam had arrived. After accepting a generous tip, the driver moseyed his bread winners over to a water trough next to a tree.

"Good! You're all here," Adam said. Realizing his mistake, he muted his enthusiasm.

Handing the wagoner sailor a tip he said, "Have the trunks stowed in my cabin at once." The sailor left to recruit more muscle.

As the prison wagon rolled away, past the carriage drinking from the trough, Adam broke the bad news.

"Beulah, she's… I couldn't get her. The authorities have her. The African somehow managed an escape from the Work House. They're questioning her now about him," Adam said. The news shattered their much anticipated future together, replacing the joy of the moment with sorrow and numbing disbelief.

Beatrice spoke first, "Well, we can't go. Not now. Not without her, she'll be…"

Augustus said, "We'll stay. And get Beulah, later," nodding his head to soothe Beatrice.

"You can't stay! What will you do?" Adam pleaded with Augustus.

"We have folk we can stay with in the Lowcountry, the Sea Islands. Things will change with the British," Augustus said, speaking from his experience dealing with them in the first half of his life, in the Caribbean. "They'll have different priorities than this witch hunt. So, soon we'll get back into the city, see about Beulah, the house, and see you when the fighting quits."

Adam asked Augustus which side would occupy the city then.

Augustus said, "Who do you think!" as an expletive. They were of the same mind—that within a year's time the British Empire will crush the delusional colonists and hang hundreds of them.

Beatrice consoled Koi with thoughts of the future and with meeting again when the war is over. "Soon. It's not safe here for a child." But Koi could not restrain herself. She held Beatrice tight, sobbing, clutching her doll.

The sailors the wagoner recruited arrived and carried Adam's trunks to the *Rotterdam*.

Looking up at Beatrice between tears Koi said in perfect English, "What about The African?"

"Well, I'm sure he's miles away and safe by now," Adam said to calm the child.

Augustus looked at Beatrice, then at Koi. He then turned his back on them. Taking and turning Adam's shoulder he walked a few steps with Adam.

"Master Adam."

He paused.

"Master Adam, Beatrice and me. We set The African free."

At first Adam thought what Augustus had said must be in jest, perhaps metaphorical. Then, reading Augustus, Adam knew Augustus was serious.

As the scheme sank in, recognizing the success, Adam came to view the result as a clever prank on the authority figures he viewed with disdain. As if a schoolmate had pulled one over on an overbearing headmaster. A private joke that made him laugh and kept him laughing as the shock wore off.

"There's more," Augustus said while Adam was still enjoying the moment, "He's onboard now."

"What?" Adam exclaimed, no longer laughing. Suddenly alarmed.

"In one of those trunks," Augustus said, motioning his head toward the *Rotterdam*. "Almost in your quarters by now, I imagine."

Adam's posture turned stiff.

"We had to get him out. He didn't do those things," Augustus said. "He's a good man. Who will serve you well. I spoke to him. About what this means. About you."

Adam wanted to be angry, but he knew he'd have done the same thing for a friend, especially one condemned without trial. And, he had to admire the daring of the old man and his feisty Beatrice.

But Adam could not hide the reluctance in his acceptance. He took a deep breath and said, "Very well," as and let it out.

The distinct sound of troop movement, guards on foot and officers on horseback quickened everyone's pulse. They could hear the approach racing down the street towards the waterfront

Adam put his hand on Augustus's shoulder and wished him and Beatrice well as he said in Yiddish, "*Mann tracht und Gott lacht* (Man plans and God laughs)."

Koi hugged them both as "See you in a few months" and good-byes were exchanged. Adam and Koi hurried down the dock as Augustus and Beatrice slipped into the city.

"Permission to come aboard, Captain McGreevy?" Adam said, smiling with Koi at his side.

The captain nodded, less inclined than usual to indulge Adam's good nature.

"The British are here."

Astonished at the repercussions, Adam said, "Exactly, what do you mean?"

"The marines landed troops on a sea island, Long Island. I suspect to cross over at low tide to Sullivan's Island where the rebels are constructing a fort at the mouth of the harbor."

"Well, as soon as we meet the others and sail past the Bar, everything will be fine. Shove off." Then, adding, "Oh, have you seen my valet?" to give his captain something other than war to think about.

"Who? Oh, why, no. Where is he?"

"In my quarters, no doubt. Will you excuse us? Come along, Statia," Adam said directing Koi to follow him.

Adam followed the galley way of private quarters to his, next to the one he'd reserved for Augustus, Beatrice and Koi.

Inside his quarters were four trunks, one quite large. Koi opened it without asking. The short plump man popped up from within—initially wide-eyed, in fear. But when he saw Koi and Adam, his fear disappeared into his smile as he enunciated his gratitude, "Yello."

"He doesn't say much. Not proper English," Koi said, looking up at Adam. "Well," Adam said, "we'll have to change that. Ask him to get out, and then let's find something more suitable for him to wear." At a loss as to what had been packed in which trunk he said, "Where is Augustus when we need him?"

They all felt the *Rotterdam* move, and begin to sway in the Cooper River as the pilot boats towed her into the harbor. Adam left them in his quarters to catch a last glimpse of the busy wharf and town. And to see to it that the yeomen pulling his ship were careful and well tipped as their reward. To his delight, a crew of workmen, patriot militia and Continentals were busy tearing down his old warehouse (the one he'd sold) among others, placing as many cannons as possible in their place.

Once the *Rotterdam*'s sails were unfurled Adam soon spied the *Kameel* and *Jupiter* in route to the rendezvous point at the harbor's opening to the Atlantic. As the three ships maneuvered in boat traffic and winds, the optimistic mood aboard all three ships disappeared instantly at of the sight and sudden—BOOM!—sound of a solitary signal shot from a British man-o-war maneuvering at the Charles Town Bar.

THIRTEEN

Prince of Abissinia

When Denmark returned to Madame's island he went straight to the source of pleasure for Madame, the conch field he'd discovered long ago. He proceeded to gather enough for a fresh meal. As Denmark returned from his crustacean harvest he saw a boat tying up to Madame's dock.

As the investors' arrived to register their trespassing complaint, Madame was getting organized, anticipating re-supply. Madame had asked Millie to make ready too. Millie was to sail back to Charlotte Amalie with her lover on his next circuit and in her mind's eye she was already experiencing the time she and Captain Palmer would enjoy together in his berth.

Hoping to postpone Madame's railing against his disappearance Denmark managed to slip into the kitchen and begin preparing Madame's dinner. He also hoped he could please her enough to at least mitigate her anger at his disappearance.

As Denmark was finishing his dinner preparations he spied from the kitchen window the bumbling copper investors' departure. He recognized them by the manner in which they attempted to board their vessel; all at once.

Minutes later Denmark was surprised to find Madame at the threshold of the kitchen. Denmark paused at the sight of her there but returned to his chore as she began.

"Why did you do it? Haven't you been warned enough? Do you not remember what it's like, the reality that exists for you beyond these shores?"

Denmark glanced at the bay and Madame's dock.

"The wind shifted and blew me off course," he insisted rather than attempt to explain his motives.

In a determined yet shaky tone Madame spoke of the limits to his liberty on, and safety off, her island.

Though Denmark could hear the terror in her voice and see the hurt in her eyes he felt more like a rebellious boy arguing with his grandmother than a slave sassing a master. He talked back to her for being hard on him while he was toiling away to make her dinner.

Millie could hear the conversation from the little garden outside the kitchen where she pretended to gather vegetables so she could eavesdrop.

Hearing the words coming from Denmark's mouth sent shivers through her being as she replayed the whipping Madame had ordered for her mother one sunny morning on Tortola. Madame had taken out her anger—her pain and disgust over her husband's dalliance with a whore—on Millie's mother. Millie had stood close enough to the whipping to feel the drops of her mother's warm blood spatter her little feet. Feeling her mother's screams once again reverberate through her chest, Millie rushed to tamp down the fiery temper she'd witnessed that day.

"The boat remains ashore, *indéfiniment!*" were Madame's final words as she departed the kitchen, brushing through Millie's approach.

Despite Millie's love for this boy she'd helped along, the first words out of her mouth were, "Boy, don't you got no sense? You don't watch out," slapping her side, she said, "She'll put you in her pocket!"

Continuing his work, puzzled, Denmark strained to produce a devil-may-care grin; to which Millie's voice became more shrill, "All she hasta do is say the word. She'll sell you, put the money in her pocket and Master Thomas 'll put you in the fields, or sell you off to anywhere!"

Though he felt a kinship with the men of the gangs he witnessed every day, the horror of life among them across the bay or elsewhere hit the boy hard. He considered that he would have to escape from any form of bondage beyond Madame's shores. This reminded him of his attempted escape with Koi and her sister, in Africa.

The casual slavery the three children experienced in Africa after being traded for goats along the path, presented opportunities for them to gather together in the afternoon after their chores. Free to explore the village and its perimeter. During this leisure his mind began to wander, and to plan an escape. Late one afternoon, after regaling the legendary story of the Ewe diaspora—of how the Ewe people had escaped from the walled city of Notsie—he told Koi and her sister of his plan. Rather than use well water to splash, splash and splash again to compromise and punch through a mud wall to escape, as the Ewe had done in their escape, his plan was more brazen.

"Tomorrow we meet at the well at first light. We'll join the young boys leaving with the goats for grazing. Beyond the wall, down the path, we'll run into the bush and follow the morning sun home." The direction home he reckoned as they had been led to this place. No thought was given to what they may find when they reached their homes. If they made it that far. The allure of yesterdays, of home, is all any slave of any age considers.

Leaving their master's huts before dawn to gather wood and water for the morning routine was customary for him and all the other village slaves. Meeting at the well simply meant loitering until Koi and her sister were present too.

As was the goat-herding boys' custom, they gathered around the base of an enormous silk cotton tree, a kapok tree, at the center of the compound. A tree whose roots dated to the founding of the village. Each boy minded his respective herd of several goats.

Nervous—as the sisters meandered—he counted the goats. As the herd and young boys walked past, he mingled at first. Then the three merely continued walking with the boys, right through the open village gates past the inattentive guards. Twenty paces beyond the gate they dared not look back. Trading eye contact, they thought they would be stopped any moment.

No one stopped them.

He remembers shouting, "Run!"

He took off, running with a limp, startling jungle life in his path. Koi and her sister soon passed him but slowed to keep him in sight behind them. The three moved nonstop all day as though home were more in focus with every stride. Monkeys screeched and followed the children's progress from the safety of the treetops.

The children did not stop until they reached an opening in the tree canopy at sunset. Comforted by the sight of stars and exhausted by the long trek, he volunteered to stay awake so that Koi and her sister could sleep. Later, he could keep them open no more.

His eyes opened wide as he heard, "Denmark! Denmark! Are you listening to me?"

Millie stood at the threshold to the kitchen, exasperated.

Jolted from his recollection, Denmark nodded a response and hurried his dinner preparations as Millie turned to leave for Madame's house.

The next day, Denmark considered Madame's hint. She'd left a lone book out on the terrace where he could not miss it: *Rasselas, Prince of Abissinia* by Samuel Johnson. A fable about a young African prince, Rasselas, who travels with his teacher—on a journey of self-discovery—to understand the truth of happiness.

FOURTEEN

A Pugilistic Battle: My name is Koi

The British fleet's signal shot from the Charles Town Bar sent her contingent of Royal Marines into motion from a sea island adjacent to the rebel's island fort. The Admiral's pincer move, by land and sea, was designed to send the patriot rabble fleeing for their lives, away from their guns trained on the mouth of Charles Town Harbor.

Instead, the Royal Marine subterfuge, attacking from the rear, failed—the tidal gap between the two sea islands coupled with a small but determined contingent of waiting rebels proved too formidable— and at sea, the only navigable course over the Charles Town Bar proved so narrow and close to land that His Majesty's ships were forced to sail by the fortification one at a time; to fight a pugilistic battle. The inability to deploy all of the fleet's guns simultaneously, over 250 cannons, rendered the fleet's superior firepower moot. One after another, the British man-'o-war ships swung wildly with all their might as the rebels held up their guard, hunkered down behind spongy palmetto log walls that easily absorbed the enemy's blows. One on one, blow for blow the British threw everything they had against the rebels' concentrated and well protected 31 cannons ashore.

Civilian ships, including the *Rotterdam, Kameel* and *Jupiter* sailed away from the action, but not all sailed back to port. Many witnessed the engagement with as much wonderment as fear. The booming, flying, crashing British shells would seem to obliterate their target, but to the surprise of the fleet and spectators the little fort returned accurate barrages of its own. The spectacle continued all day. The smell of salt air was replaced by that of acrid gunpowder smoke. At one point, the rebel flag dipped, knocked down by a shell, but it soon stood tall again amidst the sand cloud dust enveloping the little fort.

The explosive broadside force of the 50 gun *Bristol*, followed by the 50 gun *Experiment*, then the 50 of the *Solebay*, and the *Syren*, then the *Actaeon*'s 28 guns, the *Friendship*'s 26, the *Active*'s and *Sphinx*'s 20, the *Thunder*'s mortars—all failed to cower the rebels within. The rebels own hard straight blows to the bridge of the *Bristol* wounded officers and dignitaries alike, tearing away the backside of the Admiral's uniform with splinters from the *Bristol*'s railing. Other British ships also suffered damage from direct hits. In time the fleet's riggings and sails were in tatters. English casualties mounted—one hundred dead and wounded, then two hundred, then finally over three hundred dead and injured sailors lay strewn across the fleet's decks. During the action the *Actaeon* ran aground and remained mired in the mud. By the end of the confrontation the *Actaeon* was abandoned and set ablaze where she'd floundered to deny the rebels her military value.

Shouts of victory aboard private spectator ships called out at the sight of the British fleet retreating, and the hardscrabble fort erupted in celebration from within. The *Bristol* led her squadron north to retrieve the disheveled Royal Marines stranded on Long Island adjacent to Sullivan's Island.

A flotilla of private craft sailed the harbor to get a glimpse of, and for some, a parting cannon shot at, the mauled ships of the line sailing away. As curiosity seekers ventured close to the *Actaeon*, watching her burn to the waterline, the *Rotterdam*, escorted by the *Kameel* and *Jupiter*, sailed by her too. Adam's convoy then continued on, across the Charles Town Bar before tacking south for the Caribbean, St. Eustatius, Statia. Home.

Once the *Rotterdam* was in open waters Adam returned to his cabin, leaving command of his ship to her captain at the bridge. As he walked, the charges against The African came to mind. He'd left Koi alone with the man. But he soon rejected the notion because of Augustus's word and their earlier exchange on the topic. Opening his cabin door Adam found Koi on her knees before The African. She was sewing a length of breeches retrieved from a trunk. Clothes befitting a gentleman's valet interested the now stoic African.

"Well, splendid," Adam said to Koi, followed by, "Statia, can I rely on you to instruct your friend as to his duties as you have observed Augustus?"

"My name is Koi."

Befuddled by the child's impertinence he soon judged the blunt, honest language not as disrespectful, but rather as the child's expression of pride.

Adam said, "Well, I was thinking of Statia. It's such a well-known name in and among the islands…" his voice trailed off, losing his enthusiasm as he witnessed Koi's transformation before his eyes. The touch of Beatrice in her face and a tinge of Beulah in her posture clearly insinuated—*I know why you picked it, but*. Koi repeated, "My name is Koi."

Adam waited, thinking. He could tell by Koi's stubborn resistance that his attempts—regardless of the force attached to any name— would meet no more success than the English broadsides against the little fort at Charleston Harbor. So he said, "And, what a lovely name it is." Relieved that Koi was relieved, "Your cabin is next door. I'll leave you to your chores. I have my own. Food is served on the galley below us. Help yourselves. Don't be bashful. You have free rein aboard, just stay out of the way of the sailors, and be mindful of the slaves when they're brought on deck for exercise. Some can be dangerous." Koi and The African looked at him the way Augustus and Beatrice looked at him when he made such comments.

"All right then, I'll be on my way," he said, exiting his quarters for fresh air and sight of his privateers either side of the *Rotterdam*, miles at sea, sailing south, following the coastline.

Adam stood on the wind-blown deck surveying the orchestration, the movement, of his investment strategy, on land and sea. Critiquing his performance in Charles Town and pondering the fate of his family, and his island home, he considered how exposed each was to the rolling tide of war.

He recalled a more recent, mundane yet important omission. He'd forgotten to ask "Koi" to name The African. The moment had passed, and under the circumstances he was not looking forward to the prickly subject in the future. He would nonetheless paint the chore as part of the façade of a proper valet.

Adam also gave some thought to The African's future on Statia as the pull of his home grew stronger the closer he sailed to her. The African, an unexpected addition, stout, young and strong, brought capabilities neither Augustus or Beatrice nor Beulah possessed. And Koi, though too young for medicine—Beatrice was right about that—she could in time, he hoped, become a medical resource on the island. And if her work—administering smallpox voliation treatments for the well-to-do—pays more than her upkeep, all the better.

One day—a week into the voyage—as Koi wandered the deck with her doll the captain invited the privileged passenger to the bridge. The day was beautiful: puffs of white clouds and blue sky and still bluer water of small swells topped in white. Koi allowed herself a moment of ease as she leaned on the bridge railing, watching the seamen work together, hoisting a line, letting out a sail to catch more wind to sail still faster. She spied two dolphin jump, jump, and jump again as they followed the *Rotterdam*, traveling at six knots.

Crack, came the sound of a whip from the main deck below, audible above the ruffling wind, and the unmistakable clink of chains. Koi smelled them before laying eyes on the group. Two dozen slaves walked on deck. The men in shackles. All eyes squinted and turned away from the sunlight. Crack! The sailor with the whip wanted the slaves to dance, all of them. His fellow jailers encircled the scared, dirty group. Men, women and even children were being shipped to the West Indies for resale where prices were higher than in the warring colonies. Holding the bridge railing with one arm Koi slid to a crouching position. Watching between the railings, hiding; she was troubled by her feelings. She felt empathy for the plight of the hovel living as she once did, and guilt for her relative comfort. She held her doll tight in her other arm. Soon the handlers were satisfied with the slave's performances and wished to be rid of them, to lock them away again.

As the captives filed by beneath the bridge Koi stood and leaned over the railing for a more clear view of her past. She spied a little girl, disconsolate and scared, walking with an old woman. As she peered farther over the railing for a closer look Koi's doll slipped from her grasp, falling to the feet of the little girl. She stopped to pick her up, and then looked up for the source. Her eyes meet Koi's. The eyes of both girls welled up, just beginning to tear. Koi communicated first. She nodded. The little girl waved amid the crowd walking past. One of ship's crew pushed the little girl to move on, back into the hold with the stacks of lumber and barrels of rice marked Charles Town Yellow. The little girl shot a smile at Koi and hurried on, clutching The African's doll as tight as a mother's arm. The African will understand thought Koi.

After listening to the incessant burst of shells all day long back in Charles Town Harbor, the silence of sea at night, with only the rush of wind and the ocean parting against the *Rotterdam*'s hull felt strange to Koi, as though not to be trusted. Free to roam the ship topside with The African, Koi's star gazing brought to mind the stars she'd seen through an opening in the jungle canopy the night of her escape in Africa with her sister and Telemaque.

After star gazing and then sleeping deeply through the night, Koi didn't hear the voices or the footsteps the next morning.

The sun bore down hard onto the floor of the jungle.

Telemaque's instinct, to wake the girls, got them noticed. Hearing the girl's rustling awake within the foliage stopped the men along the trail. They focused their attention on the three children, now staring back at them.

The children's escape route had been flanked on either side by trails to nearby villages. Talking drums had alerted the area to the three slave's flight and called for their return.

The familiar village elder did not punish them.

Instead, within a few days he shepherded them untethered to an itinerant market one-half days walk away, to a wide river's edge. Rather than vegetables, produce, or wares for sale, at this market there were only slaves, of all ages. Eyeing a pod of manatee swimming upriver, flamingos searched the shallows and monkeys watched them all from the water's edge. The slavers put out armed spotters and encouraged the slaves to wade into the water to refresh their vitality and appear sharp while the traders haggled prices.

Entering the cool dark water Denmark, Koi and her sister each marveled at the sight. None had ever seen so many people in one place. Hoards of slaves, driven into the river like so many herds of cattle to drink.

The children scanned faces looking for the familiar.

As those on the far bank reached the others in the middle of the slow-moving chest-high river, silent stares gave way to greetings, condolences and woe. The three children migrated toward a group of women near some reeds for comfort and cover. The slave women were gracious enough to pretend a bond of kinship to lift the children's spirits.

Splashing in the water of that river became an indelible memory for the three children. Ears submerged—no sound, looking skyward, like they'd experienced swimming with their family and villagers—each in their own way day-dreamed that they would someday be free again.

Beating drums and blowing gourds called everyone out of the water. But it was a musket's fire that drew everyone's attention, including stragglers like the children. Sorted into groups of women, children and men on the riverbank, the slaves were on display for the coastal traders to walk among selecting several from each category. The traders paid for each with sums of the local currency, cowrie shells and bars of iron as well as rum, knives and guns—confident in the knowledge that a more handsome price awaited them at the European sea shore fortresses.

When Telemaque turned to commiserate with Koi and her sister a trader approached with purpose.

"You! You there!" he said. "Yes, you!" he said as he walked closer, taking her sister by the arm with such certainty one could believe he'd recognized her in the crowd. Alarmed at her fate, she resisted. The stranger grunted, then pulled, then skipped the twelve-year-old's feet away from the others as she screamed, cried, and shrank from his grasp. He managed to hold her almost erect by elevating her wrist while ignoring her continued pleas.

Those remaining were left to watch the scene unfold. Koi's sister was dragged down to the river and into her captor's canoe loaded with twenty more slaves. The canoe soon shoved off for the confluence of the river's end and the ocean's beginning.

Koi was next, plucked from among the remaining children. Telemaque instantly challenged the trader. But he was struck in the head with the butt of a musket, knocked almost unconscious. The last time she saw him he was face down on the sandy riverbank shore, immobile. He could hear her scream for him. "Telemaque, Telemaque!"

Another musket boomed as a warning to the hysterical captives.

The African's grasp onto Koi's arm—not unlike the slaver who'd selected her from the riverbank—shook Koi from her Africa memory. He pointed to the orange flashes in the distance. A moment passed before more thunder from the source arrived; cannons aboard ships off the coast of Spanish Florida.

Ordered by signal flag from the *Rotterdam* to remain on course, the captains of the *Kameel* and *Jupiter* were jealous of the fight at hand. Though reassured more opportunities for prize ships lay ahead, in the West Indies, the captains could well imagine the action taking place; a lone merchant ship headed north, a flotilla of privateers hugging the coast sailing south.

Privateers seldom sailed alone. They'd nip and snap at their prey, cut and harass her until they sensed weakness, then move in like piranhas. Thousands and thousands of these commissioned privateers plied the shipping lanes of world commerce—more every year of war—from the American east coast to the West Indies and beyond to distant continents. While in hot pursuit of prize money, riches far beyond normal means, they thought nothing of stealing the property of others under the guise of liberty and equality.

The *Rotterdam* and her escorts sailed on, making good time enjoying fair weather through the Bahamas and past Hispaniola before being lashed by a severe storm south of Puerto Rico. The storm slowed the convoy then forced it to seek shelter. The three damaged ships eventually dropped anchor at Soper's Hole, an inviting bay of the island of Tortola along the Sir Francis Drake Channel.

The next morning revealed flattened shanties and downed trees ashore.

Among Adam's convoy, two masts, the mainmast of the *Kameel* and the mizzenmast of the *Rotterdam* lay at right angles. Indiscriminate clumps of flotsam were strewn about the creaking hulls. The *Jupiter* was taking on water at a rate beyond the bilge pump's capacity to remove it.

For two weeks Adam and his captains relied on repairs made by the skilled labor of shipwrights and maritime supplies from Madame's mercantile store at Road Town.

Spirits were lifted with the erection of the repaired masts. As Adam's convoy set sail at dawn, east, through the Sir Francis Drake Channel toward the Atlantic even the normally taciturn Captain McGreevy smiled at their good fortune. They'd not only navigated a storm to safe harbor at night, a scenario that had doomed many a vessel to a watery grave, they'd repaired their damage to good order. And now, maneuvering through a calm channel in fair wind one could forgive the whims of Mother Nature.

Joining the captain on the bridge Koi gazed upon the channel with curiosity as she took a deep breath of fresh salty air. Thoughts of her loved ones came to mind, and with them, her mother's voice; a refrain of the prayer her mother had called out, for all to hear, in Africa. Her mother had prayed that other adults would care for her daughters and her prayer had been answered. Koi thought of Abra, Beulah, Beatrice, Augustus and The African. Even Adam. And hoped her sister had met a kind fate. She hoped that someday they might all be reunited. Koi smiled as her finger twitched at the thought of Telemaque out there somewhere looking at the same sky she admired.

A town, Road Town, appeared port side. And a string of smaller uninhabited islands, starboard. They dotted the convoy's course to the Atlantic. The last island before open water stood out among the rest. Between its huge boulders spilling into the sea from the beach, hundreds it seemed, she could see dark cavernous recesses between them.

Just before sailing into the great wide open expanse ahead—as the convoy left the protection of the channel for winds that had traveled uninterrupted for thousands of miles across the Atlantic—Koi looked back. She studied the islands in the *Rotterdam's* wake. Another island, a "new" island curiously appeared as though it had morphed into being, having split from its larger neighbors. Though tucked in close the tiny island stood apart, separated by water and posture. An almost imperceptible roofline appeared along its peak. Koi was looking at Madame's home atop her atoll. And beyond Madame's island, still higher, high atop one of the neighboring islands stood a white columned gray stone mansion: *Paradis.*

While admiring the last tips of land before the open Atlantic, a ship appeared from around the end of Paradise Island flying the British Union Jack. She'd taken on a small cargo of slaves in the night off Steeple Point and had set sail soon after dawn. It was the *Eclipse,* Jacob at the helm, secretly hired by Seymour.

Flag signals were sent and answered between the *Rotterdam* and the privateer captains. The *Kameel,* starboard of the *Rotterdam,* and the

Jupiter, port side, peeled off for the kill. The *Kameel* lost the wind in her sails so she set a course behind the *Rotterdam*, hoping to gain enough speed to participate in the attack. To merit an equal share in the prize with the *Jupiter*. Each crew prepared to fire.

The *Rotterdam* sailed on.

Once the *Jupiter* changed her course her prey responded in kind to seek shelter within the bay of Madame's island. However, the *Eclipse*, slow to regain the wind, faltered. With her momentum and logistical advantage stalled she would soon be overtaken by the *Jupiter*. The *Kameel* was gaining on the scene. With a shot across *Eclipse*'s bow from the *Jupiter*, Jacob envisioned his fate. The crew and captains aboard the *Jupiter* and the *Eclipse* began to stare at one another from the closing distance.

As faces drew ever closer, more defined, a single shot fired by a greenhorn privateer set off an unordered fusillade of blasts. The close range broadside of 10 pounder cannon shot rendered concomitant swivel guns and musket balls moot. The *Eclipse* began to sink. As the gunpowder smoke cleared shouts from survivors were met with disbelief.

Sade, Selena and one other slave shouted to the *Jupiter*'s crew for rescue as Abra and the other slave, a young man, plunged to the bottom within the hold of the smoldering *Eclipse*.

Having witnessed the carnage and its aftermath the captain and crew of the *Kameel* yelled and waved from her deck as she turned back to catch up with and escort the mother ship, the *Rotterdam*.

The *Jupiter* put the lone white large bald survivor of the *Eclipse* ashore on the neighboring island, Paradise Island. But they kept the other survivors of the attack—three of the five slaves from aboard the *Eclipse*—as their prize.

FIFTEEN

Our Little Speck

The conflict was too far away for Madame to identify the sinking ship, the *Eclipse*. But the cannon blasts were close enough to rattle her windows during breakfast.

"What's happened?" Denmark and Millie asked as they both rushed to Madame's side. Stepping back from her spyglass Madame said, "I think the rebel's war for independence has found its way to our little speck on the globe."

"Why? What've we to do with it?" Denmark asked.

"Are you sure it's not the *Libertas*?" Millie said, twisting the strings of her apron.

"I can't be sure of anything. But, we'll discuss that later. For now, you two do your chores," she said, hoping the trouble would remain beyond the reach of her spyglass.

SIXTEEN

The First Salute

Soon after the skirmish at sea near Madame's island Adam's convoy was reunited in the waters off Saba Island, just seven miles north of their destination, St. Eustatius. The lookout in the *Rotterdam*'s crow's nest shouted, "Land, ho!" at the sight of Saba Island. Then, within minutes, he shouted again, this time with alarm rather than joy in his voice, "Enemy colors, dead ahead!"

Adam had his signalman direct the *Kameel* and *Jupiter* to sail ahead and seize her.

Both the *Kameel* and *Jupiter* spied the enemy's silhouette along the thin ocean horizon; a lone brigantine under full sail—tough to catch. But following orders, the two crews threw more sail to the wind, wet their sails to make them more rigid, less pourus, increasing their speed, and checked their weapons. After adjusting their sails more than once to take advantage of favorable winds Adam's two schooners were gaining on their prey.

The brigantine's colors waved in a smooth light rhythm over the water beyond the stern as she pressed on, aware of the attention she'd drawn. To thwart her pursuers she made a heady tack on a brisk wind and strong current, putting more distance between her and the privateers.

The chase ended where Adam's mission had begun, St. Eustatius. The ship Adam's raiders could not catch was an American Navy warship, the *Andrew Doria*.

Adam and his captains had made a common error. The American Grand Union flag, "Congress' colours," the nascent country's first— thirteen red and white strips with a Union Jack in the corner—was often mistaken for the British Union Jack, especially from a great distance. In fact, the British thought General Washington had surrendered when he raised it above Prospect Hill, in Cambridge, during the struggle for Boston.

When the *Andrew Doria* arrived in Oranjestad Bay, St. Eustatius's port, she tipped her new colors, and in her exchange of cannon salutes with Fort Oranje, set off a worldwide diplomatic firestorm. Holland had become the first country in the world to recognize "America" as she would any other sovereign nation. Adam heard the cannons fire from across the water.

When told of the gun salute King George III was not amused.

SEVENTEEN

Life, Liberty...

"*Condamner!*" Madame cursed as she stepped away from her spyglass secured atop its tripod. She'd been following the approach of a sloop. A confiscated American privateer ship Master Thomas had re-christened the *Vasa* before selling her to Jacob for two times what he'd paid.

"Millie!" Denmark could hear her shout. "It's Jacob at the helm." Millie's heart sank.

"Hold your tongue while he's here, child. I wasn't quite prepared for him. Take Denmark and get those crates, empty them of goods if you have to, and take them and those bags down to the dock; give them to Jacob's crew for supplies. Don't even look Jacob's way. We don't need any trouble today."

Jacob's commands scattered all life forms in Madame's bay. Sea turtles plopped their heads underwater, birds took flight voicing their protests.

Denmark and Millie grew more afraid with every gravelly bark heard across the water as Jacob drew near. They were close enough to see his crew's hunched backs, scurrying away from Jacob along the deck as he chastised their every move. With nowhere to hide on the dock Denmark and Millie would have to endure Jacob's special talent for inducing fear, vulnerable to whatever terror was in store for them.

As the boat glided to rest, Jacob sneered at the two slaves from the helm while studying the curves of Millie's dress thinking, *someday.* Following their prior instructions, the deck hands dumped the bags of goods—flour, corn meal, sugar and an entire wooden barrel of rice marked Charles Town Yellow—onto the dock. The deck hands returned the slaves' somber greetings with menacing glances while mumbling words of derision. In short order all the supplies were ashore and Madame's crates and heavy empty bags were aboard the *Eclipse* for replenishment.

Relieved that Jacob and his crew had shoved off without incident, Denmark and Millie dared to question the enigma that had appeared—though as conspicuous as barking dogs—unnoticed before them. There, resting atop large bags of food stacked into a pile sat two wrapped presents. A cake and a scroll, each tied with a colorful ribbon and bow. They turned to one another laughing at the surprise and their good fortune.

The sacked goods he could manage, the barrel, however, stood immutable. Denmark managed to transfer the rice to sacks. Thirteen trips later, Denmark had counted each step; requiring only sixty-three strides of his growing legs. By the time he was done the heavy barrel stood in place alone, as empty as the dock.

Carrying the last bag of rice, once he'd made it up the hill but not quite to Madame's yet, he heard it—the slave song. Torches lit the dusk as the slaves marched double-time out of the fields, back to their homemade roofs over their homemade families, fashioned from other families an ocean away from their plantation prison-farm existence.

With Denmark's last few strides up the hill his trained ear could tell the songs were making the turn. Soon the cadence would be muffled then silenced by distance and topography. Indeed, by the time he laid eyes on his refuge at the top of Madame's island the songs were lost to strong winds buffeting his ears at the crest of the hill.

Millie had already laid out the cake and was about to light a candle. Madame doted over the sight as though she herself had baked the cake and presented it fresh from the oven. She called Denmark into the house as he walked toward the kitchen. The three gathered around the sugar cane cake to recite a simple prayer. One they'd repeated with Madame often enough to know by heart.

"Dans le nom de Jésus
Nous rassemblons autour de la table
Pour donner merci pour nos bénédictions

Dans le nom de Jésus
Amen."

Madame blew out the candle Millie had lit. Amid the smell of wax
and fresh ground white sugar Madame tried to capture Denmark's
imagination, to usurp his absent gaze across the water by seeking,
finding and retrieving the prize hidden inside.

"Found it!" she said.

Denmark's attention returned. Millie had expected more based on
Madame's excited anticipation.

"It's a painted cylinder. Oh, and it opens!" Madame said handing
the tiny vessel to Millie but retaining the small coded message rolled up
inside. A private message to her, intended to be kept that way.

Madame improvised the content of the rolled up message, "It says
'Enjoy your cane cake and present.' Well, then, let's have a look at the
scroll, shall we," Madame said, reaching for it next to the cake.

She pulled the red, white and blue striped ribbon from around the
large furled document whose dramatic opening, *When in the Course of
human events*…demanded the attention of all who read it.

Madame read more of the document aloud, then to herself,
mumbling. She'd not gotten far before, flummoxed, she had to pause,
to rest, to ponder the change, the magnitude. Fathoming the
declaration she then laughed, thinking of the English, scurrying about
to put out rebel fires, and now this, a declaration of independence!

Denmark wanted to hear more.

Madame said, "It says to enjoy your cake," as she peered over the
document at the boy.

Denmark knew the tone in her voice was not to be trifled with.
Madame picked up her fork and took another bite before reading more
of the rebel's declaration.

Returning his attention to across the water, lingering in his mind
were the words Madame had read aloud, *Life, Liberty and the pursuit of
Happiness…* as he sat eating his cake, cognizant of his brethren across
the water eating slave fare. As he learned where to put a salad fork, to
serve from the left, to put his napkin in his lap, they learned how to cut

and stack sugar cane with just two strokes and how to apply
homemade balm to heal wounds from the lash.

EIGHTEEN

Statia

"**B**oys, wait," Adam said to two of his three boys after disembarking from the *Rotterdam*.

"Koi!" he shouted, "Come along, and bring your friends."

The *Rotterdam* had docked near Adam's warehouse on Statia. Adam's middle son, Avi, jumped aboard to greet his father as Adam's eldest, James, helped the dock workers tie the ship fast. Ezra, the youngest, remained at home with their mother, Sara.

Koi watched from the bridge of the *Rotterdam* as father and sons laughed and hugged, thinking of her own loved ones. In one hand she held everything Augustus, Beatrice and Beulah had given her in a traveling bag. With the other hand she held the little slave girl's as she clutched Koi's doll. Koi had asked Adam to grant the little orphaned girl leeway aboard the *Rotterdam* and Adam had gone even further, suggesting that she move in with Koi and The African. The little one's outlook changed overnight.

As the two girls watched their fellow slaves disembark the little girl felt Koi's grasp tighten for the instant she mistook a boy for Telemaque.

The African stood at the gangplank, stoic in his buffoonish valet attire. He passed along a reverent, solemn acknowledgement to each departing slave.

Adam made awkward introductions at the dock and led the band ashore.

From aboard the *Jupiter*, Sade, Selena and the other survivor of the *Eclipse*'s sinking were soon rowed ashore along with Adam's other slave cargo. Then the *Kameel* and *Jupiter* slipped through the forest of masts in Orjanestad Bay for the open sea to resume their real work, privateering.

Though St. Eustatius had changed sovereignty over twenty times since Columbus first sighted her, she'd been Dutch for more than a hundred years.

She was prized now, as ever, as a weigh station for colonial, European and African trade. Nicknamed "The Golden Rock"—not for her precious metals but for her prodigious commerce—she was a gold mine in profits. St. Eustatius, already the richest island in the Caribbean, was getting richer by the day selling all manner of contraband at war prices.

On the north side of the small island stood two dormant volcanoes and to the south another much larger one called The Quill. Rising to two thousand feet, The Quill dominated the skyline. The two mountainous ranges were separated by a plain where the town of Oranjestad was crowded by Fort Oranje; both perched along the ledge of a monstrous sheer cliff falling off to the warehouse district and harbor below. Several hundred thin one story warehouses lined the nearly mile-long stretch of Bay Road, each jutting out to meet the sea.

As seen from a distance, Statia's docks, warehouses and roads resembled an ant colony in motion, moving cargo—most of it illegal— to and from a hundred ships at anchor. After an eighty year war of independence from Spain, the Dutch (though in league with England) had declared their neutrality, choosing to smuggle goods other nations required rather than fight for them.

Merchants of every nationality shipped at least some of their goods through Statia—sold to the highest bidder rather than priced and taxed by a monarch's trading monopoly. European Heads of State seethed at Statia's trade. And yet, in times of war, they all turned to the little island they despised for their military necessities, enriching the islanders at every turn.

The amount of sugar, cotton and tobacco imported into and exported from Statia's weigh-house dwarfed the amounts actually grown on the little island. Trade remained not only her primary source of wealth, but her best defense. Her value lay in her status as an untouchable depot, a veritable cornucopia of the world's goods, from spices, fine porcelain, furniture, rum, wine, coffee, sugar, cheese, gunpowder and guns stacked next to silks, next to casks of pork and beef stacked next to crates of tea obscuring crates of hats, boots, blankets, and uniforms bound for America. Linen dyed with indigo sat next to barrels of the liquid dye itself. Goods spilled out onto the shoreline road where huts, shacks, booths and tents appeared, tucked in with inventory and a makeshift lumber yard. Traders competed for loads of cargo that sometimes required three or four languages and currencies to transact.

All these goods came from thousands of French, Danish, Irish, Spanish, Russian, Swedish, American and even English smugglers. To disguise their sales, British merchants sold arms to the rebels by shipping them first to Holland, then on to Statia for transshipment to America.

The day Koi arrived the islanders were jubilant. All of them; the little trading post was a frisson of activity. Workmen of every ilk stepped a little livelier as they shuffled and shuttled commodities overflowing from warehouses.

As Adam's entourage passed his family business, a stone warehouse fitted with office space, he glanced into the cool, dark interior and was happy to see James join the workers there without comment.

Avi held the waiting horses as Adam mounted, then helped Koi and the little girl up onto his yellow mare, Sophia. The African jumped astride the other horse, a white gelding named Spark as though he owned him. Avi, helped onto Spark by The African, shrugged his shoulders rather than reply to his father's look of surprise.

The horseback riders rode high above the heads of wave and counter wave of seamen, stevedores, carters and slaves in the lane of Lower Town. Next they climbed up the steep, steep cliff, up Baypath to Upper Town. Following Avi's directions, The African demonstrated his horsemanship by navigating the crowd, easing the gelding through the revelry in the streets, clearing a path for Adam and the girls.

Sara recognized her husband atop his horse from far down the dusty narrow road as Adam approached. She traded her housework for a looking glass, European makeup, perfume and a fresh dress.

Ezra ran into the road, jumping in place at Sophia's side, shouting "Papa, Papa!"

Sara leaned on the threshold in the shade of the vestibule, waiting for the touch, the sound, the scent of her man. Six feet tall, she was the daughter of an African Amazon and their New World master in Jamaica. Adam bought her on sight.

From atop Sophia, Koi could see well beyond Adam's modest two story home of rock, homemade brick and mortar to the patches of cotton, tobacco, corn and then, sugar cane fields that stretched to the end of the sloping horizon.

Once their extended embrace ended Sara kissed the love of her life, as did he.

Sara then asked, "From which place did ya gadder dis menagerie, deary?"

"Well, it's just as you're insinuating, I know. I've somehow brought home more strays. Again. But, they fell into my lap. What else am I to do? Anyway, it's why I have you," he pulled her close, "and I think, why you love me; for my compassion."

"What are their names?" Sara asked looking over the new arrivals, all now watching them.

"This is Sta...I mean, Koi," Adam said. "And her little friend...What is your name?" he said stooping to her eye level.

"Statia," the little girl answered to everyone's surprise. Including Koi who'd told the little girl her story about insisting on keeping her African name.

"Smart little ting, dat one," Sara said with a smile. Adam smiled too.

"And this, this hulk of a man, Augustus and the rest simply call 'The African' though I've encouraged a new Christian name for him."

The African looked to Sara then Adam and bowed a cordial greeting. His gratitude showed through his expressive eyes.

Satisfied with introductions the couple walked hand in hand into their home.

With the exception of an occasional appearance to be sure the children were fed, the Mr. and Mrs. remained behind closed doors for two days. The African looked after the horses, sometimes with Avi watching, while the children played and roamed the farm. James stayed busy working at the family warehouse in Lower Town.

Each morning, before the rooster crowed, while tree toads still croaked in the night, Koi heard the murmurs of hired slave gangs move into the fields beyond the house.

Gradually life on Adam's property put Koi at ease. Each day became an adventure, a pleasure; the pleasure of being a child among an accepting loving family. Laughs with Avi, Ezra and Statia—whether playing games inside or picking wild fruit from trees near the farm, or chasing one another, running through the rain forest in the shadow of The Quill—were soon taken for granted.

Trained to care for the cavalry of a Yoruba chief in his homeland, The African had displayed his skills by caring for the Wolff's horses and repairing the broken farm implements piled at the base of the forge and anvil. He soon adopted the responsibility as his own and slept next to the work.

James, tall and mature beyond his sixteen years, took charge at the warehouse. He coordinated and motivated men from all walks of dock life to move heavy cargo with care and efficiency, noting the goods in Adam's ledger. This allowed Adam to turn to correspondence with the company's best new customer, Hortalez & Company, a shell company in Paris, a rebel ruse, run by Benjamin Franklin.

NINETEEN

No Man's Land

Throughout the years of the American Revolution Millie continued to help Madame and Denmark. And Denmark continued to deliver Madame's coded war dispatches across the bay. Madame would watch him from on high through her spyglass, following the faint white sails against the dark water from start to finish.

One new moon evening the stars were masked by thin low white clouds flowing counter to their usual movement. Denmark needed only to raise his jib to tack across the bay.

The silent secretive sentinel who'd accepted the dispatches in the past had been replaced by a conspicuous heavy white man. Denmark recognized him as the man who had chased him away from the copper dig site years before. The man's routine was always the same. He'd make disingenuous compliments to secure the dispatch from Denmark's hand, but then follow them with veiled threats to Denmark's freedom once delivered. Denmark missed the camouflaged sentinel with a lame leg.

Over time Madame's lessons had become more rigorous and structured. No longer content with elementary reading and writing— taking dictation for her correspondence, devising her coded messages or reading the news to her—she began to demand more of Denmark. She insisted he present an adolescent version of oral arguments and attempt short essays. She would have him argue both pro and con on an array of ancient and contemporary topics such as the fall of the Roman Empire, Charlemagne, the Norman invasion of England, Joan of Arc and even the origins of England's clash with her colonists. She demanded he defend why the colonies should fight to separate from their king and country.

As part of his education Madame also brought Denmark with her on business trips to Tortola. To expose him to what he seemed so curious about, the larger world. Yes. But also to educate him as to what he should be wary of beyond their cloistered sanctuary. These trips, she reasoned, might help prepare him for his future employment and career. And she was correct. The experiences never failed to leave the desired impression upon him.

One sunny Sunday on her island, feeling energetic, Madame pronounced the day particularly ideal for learning; *magnifique*. The two settled in on the terrace with books, ink and paper at hand. Some books doubled as paperweights over unfurled maps.

She asked Millie, recently returned from St. Thomas with Captain Palmer, to make lunch so she and Denmark could continue to work.

"Denmark, how do you feel about delivering my dispatches?"

Though accustomed to Madame's candor, he was nevertheless unprepared for her question. Keeping Millie's admonishments in mind as well as the restrictions he'd endured years ago after his disappearance, Denmark was hesitant to speak. For many months after his disappearance Madame had stipulated that the boat be used only for dispatches—as punishment.

Now, torn between the understanding he and Madame nurtured and the threat of sudden reprisal Millie assured him rested just beneath the veneer of Madame's benevolence, he remained silent for a time gazing at her to gauge which persona had asked the question.

When he felt she could wait no longer he said, "Well, they got me back into the boat, so I suppose they're a good thing," searching for a banal, acceptable answer while avoiding the real question, *the danger and consequences involved*. Nor did he point out that delivering the messages required him to violate Madame's tenet to never "set foot" on a neighboring island. He knew the observation could ignite what Denmark wished to avoid—the dark behavior Millie warned him about.

Though he did not doubt Millie's account of her mother's experience at the hands of Madame—and he himself, after all, had experienced firsthand a measure of her temper—he, however, had never experienced more than a tongue lashing. Madame's island, indeed Madame, had saved him from the life he witnessed each day across the bay and on Tortola. Though only thirteen he was both mindful of and grateful for his good fortune. Believing her intentions were good, he in turn wanted to please Madame. To conform to her wishes, though they sometimes ran counter to his own.

"Oh, I'd forgotten about that episode," she said like a parent applying balm to an exposed wound.

"Do you know why the information is important? How what you do is so important? How our help, in small ways, your help, helps effect big changes? You recall the coded Vigenere ciphers as well as I. And, you've read of the consequences played out months after each dispatch."

Denmark thought of the victories the dispatches helped create. Washington's surprise attack at Trenton, a British surrender at a place called Saratoga—a defeat so shocking it had encouraged the French to join the war.

"Yes, I've read of the consequences, but I'm not sure I understand them. Why is Madame, France, your native country, so interested in this place, America?" he asked, pointing to a map of the world. "France is here."

"*Oui*, however, once we laid claim to all of this," she said, passing her hand over much of eastern North America, "but the English stole it!"

Denmark looked upon the boundaries of geography—the European known world—and the empty space beyond outlines demarcating the shorelines and frontier rivers of North America, South America, the islands of the Caribbean and the continent of Africa.

Moving that map aside and replacing it with another Madame asked, "How about this map. Notice anything…missing?" accentuating the last word.

Denmark studied the map of the islands he'd explored along the Sir Francis Drake Channel. He followed the water home with his finger. But home was nowhere to be found. Where Madame's island should appear, next to Paradise Island, the map showed only water.

His raised eyebrows told her he had grasped her point, and appreciated the surprise.

"More than a century ago, when the Danes won the day—and the region's islands—their cartographer in Copenhagen failed to note this tiny island in his inventory. The same error was repeated when private hands purchased the islands. And again, with their sale to the English. No one in London noticed our little sanctuary from thousands of miles away." And then she said with a smile, "That's one reason why my husband welcomed the opportunity to own her. No sovereign power claims, nor rules, the sand beneath our feet; she's our own little piece of no man's land."

From the geography and world history he'd learned, thanks to Madame, and even the likes of David Hume, Denmark understood how unusual, if not how fortuitous, these turns of events were.

"The advantage, of course, is we have no oppressors, because we have no alliances. The disadvantage is that because we have no alliances, we have no protectors either. Someday, as I have said before, I intend for you to apprentice and then one day run my affairs at Road Town, as a free man. And, when my eyes cease to open, this island will be yours. Shared in ownership with my daughter and grandson, of course, like my business interests, but yours nonetheless. Remember well the advantages and disadvantages I speak of today. I fear that one day they will mean everything to you."

The two stood silent for a moment over the map, both contemplating Madame's words.

Her remarks had their intended effect upon him. Among them, the words "...as a free man... this island will be yours...no man's land," opened his eyes to a future. He realized at that moment that on Madame's island he'd found what he'd been searching for all along out in the channel; freedom.

Once his excitement had passed Madame asked to look at Denmark's recent work, his essay assignments. He handed them to her and opened a book.

"What's this? I didn't," she paused, correcting the spelling of the titles aloud, before reading the content. One read *Due unto Others*, and another *The Golden Stool*.

"It's d-O, and that's the 'Golden Rule.'"

"No. They're correct," he said. "They're homonyms, puns." The revelation was as remarkable to Madame as if Denmark had defied gravity before her very eyes. Madame burst into laughter. She'd underestimated her growing charge once again. She caught her breath and ended the thought with a few more chuckles.

"Before I read them, tell me what they're about."

"Well, the first one, *Due unto Others*, as you see I've only begun. The other, *The Golden Stool* is about a revered symbol. A real stool made of gold, conjured by Komfu Anotchi, a shaman of the Asante Kingdom. It fell from the sky to forever unite the stateless chiefs far and wide as Asante. No one has ever sat on the stool. Each new ruler is held over it as ceremony. It's too sacred. Attempts to steal it means war against all Asante."

Pondering the imagery in Africa, Madame said, "Oh, how pagan. Do you really believe it just fell from the sky, made of gold?"

"Do you believe Moses parted the sea? Or, in the power of the American declaration to unite the rebels?" He said. "How is the Asante story different? But, then, *que sais-je?* (what do I know)," quoting Michel de Montaigne's famous motto.

After a long silence, smiling, she suggested he ask the Reverend, Dr. Ramsay.

"I understand he's back now, from his sojourn in London. The threats of violence and lawsuits, he hopes, have subsided. His book idea seems to be progressing; he's calling it *An Essay on the Treatment and Conversion of African Slaves in the British Sugar Colonies*.

Denmark let Madame's dodge lag and die without resuscitation. Madame let this Sunday's lessons end there.

Observed through Madame's spyglass, the next ship to approach her island was the now familiar *Vasa*.

Madame gathered her wax-sealed letters and business correspondence and stacked them on her dining table in anticipation of Jacob's arrival. Millie tried to temper her disappointment. The best response Millie could manage to Madame's hurried instructions was an ill-at-ease but evenhanded, "*Oui*, Madame."

Madame's next words came slowly. Madame's speech slurred and she faltered where she stood. She took hold of Millie's arm before slumping into a velvet-backed chair.

Only because of Millie's familiarity with Madame could she translate: "Send for the doctor. Tell my daughter. She'll know to send Dr. Ramsay."

"But, Madame…I can't go…I'm staying. Let me send word with Jacob." Madame uttered "No! Now," as partial paralysis affecting the left side of her body garbled her speech. "He'll loiter. Get the doctor." Her right hand grasped and tightened then released Millie's arm.

"*Oui*, Madame, now."

Millie eased Madame into the chair to make sure she could sit upright on her own and ran from the house down and over to the kitchen to summon Denmark. Hearing of Madame's condition, he ran to her side. The two helped Madame to her room and Millie put her to bed.

As Millie bid Denmark farewell at the dock, she did something she'd never done before. She kissed Denmark on the cheek as she said good-bye. Her gesture lingered cool and wet on his cheek as the wind carried the *Vasa* away.

"Come on, Missy, plant me one, right here," the first mate of the *Vasa* mocked once they had secured the lines for a long tack.

"But, we want some of that captain kissing," another sailor said as he drew close, testing Millie, and Jacob at the helm. Neither said a word. So the first mate stepped closer still, grasping her arm to direct her below deck. She screamed, yanking her arm free to Jacob's retort, "Mind your manners and you won't get hurt," nodding to his crew as they held her mouth and forced her below.

TWENTY

Macabre Seascape

While Denmark waited with Madame, Jacob emerged from his cabin aboard the *Vasa*.

Millie lay there naked with her eyes wide open as though still surprised by her fate. Her face was disfigured by a ballast stone to the head. Blood stains spattered the walls of his berth; evidence of a brutal, senseless murder. During the next hour the crew earned their turns with Millie by carrying out Jacob's orders to clean up the mess amid the stench of death and mildew that hung in the air.

Two crew members struggled to dispose of Millie's body. They swung her by her wrists and ankles, rocking her back and forth until momentum carried her aloft, higher than the boat's stanchions. Then—they just let go. Her corpse, as black as the night water, would be viewed as just the spoilage of a slaver, set adrift in the sea lane.

A plausible explanation perhaps, but what puzzled Captain Palmer aboard the *Libertas* at dawn was the number. Only one. When he'd seen signs of slavers dumping "spoiled cargo" in these waters before, there'd been half a dozen or more at a time, all bloated, drifting together as though in commiseration. With the lone corpse bobbing dead ahead, Captain Palmer signaled to his first mate to take the helm and keep her course steady. He moved forward, port side, to take a closer look.

What struck him at first was the freshness of the specimen, as if this slave had just died. He searched the water for another boat.

The morning seas were calm, the rising sun cast a long low line along the horizon, a kaleidoscope of color, ribbons of orange and yellow hues upon plump smooth swells. The lone corpse bobbing cork-like was the centerpiece of a macabre seascape; as beautiful and serene as gruesome.

When the bow of the *Libertas* passed the body, the sunlight's contrasts and distortions vanished in the shade of the hull. Even face down in the water, he knew. Captain Palmer saw his lover's face in his mind. Wrenching, he murmured in denial, "No, no." But Millie's thin neck and the beautiful arch of her back were unmistakable. The Captain ran the entire length of the deck to stay near her, and when he reached the stern of the *Libertas* he dove overboard rather than risk losing sight of her.

At the Charlotte Amalie wharf, Captain Palmer hired a wagon and placed Millie's shrouded body inside the bay, to wait. He sent a slave to walk over two piers and bring a casket back from those stacked there for transport, knowing such things to be out of Millie's mother's meager reach. He then lifted Millie into the casket himself as half of Master Thomas's slave dock hands watched in idle reverent silence.

Alerted to the spectacle of a work stoppage on his wharf, Master Thomas learned of the slave girl's death, and that she was one of his, a house servant. But not just any house servant. The dead girl was the one that took care of his future mother-in-law on her little island.

Master Thomas saw her death as a managerial embarrassment and a serious inconvenience. One that jeopardized his tranquility while picking his pocket. He ordered his clerk to account for the loss in the company ledger as he left the office to restore productivity on his wharf.

As with other "inconvenient" deaths in Jacob's past, Master Thomas didn't have to look far to see what had taken place. This sort of deduction was amortized as a cost of doing business, but Master Thomas's inability to control Jacob would be seen as a sign of weakness by the other slavers (and a disappointment, for they fared no better in their attempts to curb Jacob's behavior). Master Thomas vowed to avenge this latest slight, to challenge Jacob, and Jacob knew it.

TWENTY-ONE

For God's Sake

As The African rode Spark with Koi perched behind him the two witnessed fresh roars and puffs of gun smoke out in the glistening sea. They were leading Sophia behind them on their way to deliver a message from Sara to Adam at his warehouse office.

Sara let Koi, now looking every bit a young lady, ride with The African on these errands so Koi could see the sights of town and Sara could get at least one less responsibility from underfoot. Koi admired the simple colorful one story homes along the sloping curvy paved streets that lay open to the sun, and enjoyed the fragrant gardenias and ocean breezes. Vocal macaws perched roadside implored residents on porches and spare lawns to look at the pair riding the familiar white gelding.

The sound of cannons at sea grabbed the attention of everyone on Statia and nearby St. Kitts. Even after the booms died away the distinct smell of gun powder lingered in the air. The approach to Adam's warehouse teemed with excitement. The conflict had taken place within firing range of Statia's Fort Oranje.

The *Baltimore Hero*, from Maryland, had broadsided a British merchant ship, the *May*, in full view of neighboring St. Kitts, for all to see—including the British government and military authorities stationed there. The *Baltimore Hero* had then sailed her prize into Oranjestad Bay to celebrate. The vicarious thrill of booty come ashore was enough to elicit toasts and cheers from sailors, dock workers and draymen alike.

At Lower Town a crowd had assembled around a new attraction that blocked Spark's passage to Adam's warehouse, though within sight of it. The African held the horses still as he pondered his options. A momentary break in the crowd's ring allowed Koi and The African a glimpse of the proceedings—a slave auction. Thirty slaves altogether cowered in the street in front of Adam's warehouse door. Sade was among them. Koi immediately recognized her though four years in the fields of Statia had aged her beyond her years.

An auctioneer rose atop a barrel and began to shout for everyone's attention. The crowd encircling the slaves grew still. Voices lowered as he proceeded.

"You've had a look. Now, we'll begin the bidding with her lot!" Cat calls, whoops and shouts accompanied Sade, bare breasted, as she and a young man were pushed from the others by handlers holding coiled whips.

Sade kept her head bowed. The sound of the crowd animated Sade's recollection of the night of the bonfire, the devil slavers who'd ended her joy, her way of life. She felt dead inside; a rigamortis of her soul crept through her, slowly choking the flow of thought the farther away in time and space she was from her mother, brother and father.

Koi stared at Sade from atop Spark, willing Sade to raise her eyes from the ground in front of her—to see Koi on the gelding. She shouted Sade's name but the crowd's voices had erupted, drowning out her own. The buyers in the crowd bid and counter bid one another in rapid succession until, "Sold!"

From the periphery Master Thomas stepped forward. He lifted his cane to the auctioneer, as in "that's right," acknowledging the sale to him amid snickers and raised eyebrows at a bird adroitly navigating Master Thomas's shoulder as he moved.

Master Thomas was determined to further his plans of competing with the waning fortunes of the Danish West India Company's monopoly—a plan in which the unique status of Madame's island played a crucial role. So he plied the island roads for bargains from captured prizes, estate sales and other unusual, or illegal, cargoes of slaves. He sought to build inventory while replenishing his dwindling stock decimated by runaways, brutality, and apparently, another outbreak of the pox at *Paradis*.

The report to Master Thomas of more smallpox deaths was a lie employed by Seymour to account for more graves.

Sade and the other slave disappeared from the auction.

"Next, we have a fine old mamie. Step lively, woman."

Selena stepped forward, head held low.

"Let 'em see your face."

When Selena lifted her eyes to the auctioneer he said, "No! Look at them, not at me!"

As the auctioneer started the bidding, Master Thomas's first glance became a stare. He stepped from the crowd. He approached Selena and walked a half circled around her. Then he stood very close to the old woman. Shaking his finger in her face he said, "You're supposed to be dead! You and that *quack*! I have graves to prove it!" The crowd took notice of the surprising exchange. Some laughed, others "oooh-ed," intimating the status of a runaway. Selena averted her eyes to the bird.

Master Thomas wanted to berate the old woman. He wanted to demand an explanation of *Why Madame Chevalier still lived! Why the African beauty's magic had failed!* But doing so would reveal his plot to murder the old lady and the hold superstition had upon him as well.

One man among the crowd, a black man, wiped his welled eyes dry with a handkerchief as he followed the spectacle. Dressed as any Jamaican mulatto gentleman, he composed himself and bid much higher than her perceived value, quieting the crowd and the other buyers. Koi witnessed the scene in awe; a black person buying another. Her mother, her sister, everyone she knew...she jumped from Spark without a word and raced to Adam's door before The African could stop her.

Once inside she stopped to stare at the sight. A deep dark cavern; goods stacked from the cool floor to the high ceiling. The workmen stopped too, to stare back at her. Adam and another man, a customer, appeared from behind the closed door to his office. And as the two men walked, talking over one another to make their point, James cajoled the warehouse crew back to work. Koi followed Adam and his customer toward the door to the street.

Adam opened the door to find others vying for his attention, Master Thomas among them. Adam could also see The African some distance away waving a piece of paper in his hand.

Adam continued the debate, arguing for his point of view with his customer, Captain Brown, who was also his friend and his shipper. Adam insisted that his cargo and the proceeds from the slave sale, both intended for a Jewish trader in Charles Town, should supersede the captain's own personal shopping list. Each man wanted to take the remaining space in the hold where munitions—shipped at the Continental Congress' expense—were already loaded.

"Mr. Wolff, I presume," Master Thomas interrupted, extending his index finger until it almost touched Adam's chest. Responding to Adam's irritated glance at it Master Thomas withdrew the gesture.

Koi tugged on Adam's sleeve to no avail. She waited. Speaking with her eyes she stared up at his, hoping for a glimpse of his attention. Then she shook her wrists for a moment as impatient children sometimes do. Patiently impatient, dissatisfied, she indulged a look at the bird.

Reacting to Master Thomas's rudeness Adam said, "And who are you, please?" Without waiting for Master Thomas's response Adam shouted to The African, "Walk the horses away from the crowd. Wait there."

The bird moved closer to Master Thomas's head in response to Adam's outburst.

Looking Master Thomas over, then at the bird, Adam said, "Koi, go and get whatever it is," pointing to The African by Spark.

The captain resumed his case, claiming neither had called dibs on the extra space in the hold. He began to explain his route to Charles Town and his arrival date.

Within a few moments of slithering through the crowd of men, to and away from The African, Koi handed Adam the message from his wife. After reading it Adam tucked the paper into his pocket. He felt Koi standing next to him, peering up at him, again, as the sea captain tried to slip away by saying good-bye.

"No, wait!" Adam said to the captain.

Koi tugged Adam's sleeve again.

Master Thomas bristled at what he perceived to be a child's impertinence. To check his own impatience he smacked the handle of his cane into the palm of his hand as his nostrils flared.

Bending at the knees from his perch the auctioneer complained to the quorum, "Could you men be quiet!"

To Master Thomas the auctioneer said, "Just pay the man if you must go now," nodding his head toward Adam before resuming the auction.

"William Thomas of Thomas & Company, Charlotte Amalie," Master Thomas said, trying again to interject himself onto the mix.

Ignoring Master Thomas's introduction, the captain said to Adam, "I tell you what. Her sister ship is in the road. She'll be loading soon. Put your load in with hers and I'll see to it myself that it's all delivered. Fair enough?"

"Good, yes, thank you. *Shalom*," Adam said shaking hands with Captain Brown as he departed.

Though anxious to flee the scene the well-dressed mulatto waited on the periphery, trying to appear nonchalant.

Master Thomas interjected loudly in a tone of defiance, "You've sold my stolen property!"

Acknowledging the comment, "I beg your pardon," Adam said, squinting at Master Thomas. Adam had taken an instant disliking to the man—and his bird. "What does that even mean? I've…"

Master Thomas interrupted him, raising his finger high, back and forth until assured of Adam's yielding. Koi took the lull as her opportunity. She again yanked on Adam's sleeve.

"Wait, Koi!" Adam said, looking down at her.

Master Thomas struck Koi, hard, with his cane. Her eyes watered as a welt rose on her arm.

Adam punched Master Thomas in the face, knocking him to the ground. The bird landed on the ground too, near Master Thomas. The violence riveted the crowd. They turned their attention to the dirt at the auctioneer's feet. Many laughed. More than one yelled, "Fight!" ignoring the auctioneer's cadence as it trailed off.

Dusting himself off, after lifting the bird to his shoulder, Master Thomas smiled through his red stained teeth and pain and wiped the blood from his lips with his handkerchief. A sycophant handed him his wig and cane. Placing it on his head he approached Adam.

"So, I see you are fond of your nigras. But I also note you're a Jew, and as such I surmise you're even more fond of making money. I'll tell you what. I'll drop the subject of theft, for now. You just sell me the lot of them in the road and we'll be done with it. I happen to know the auctioneer too. You'll get a fair price."

"You're a liar!" the bird squawked as it moved down Master Thomas's shoulder.

Eager to be rid of the man and collect on the sale all at once Adam said, "Done." The men concluded the deal with a nod, not a handshake. Cognizant of the negotiations, the auctioneer called off the bidding.

The crowd complained and began to disperse, returning to work.

Summoning his courage the mulatto stepped forward, "Wait!" All eyes turned to him. After a breath to allow his unequivocal tone to dissipate, "I bought her," he said; "The woman," nodding to Selena next to the auctioneer holding his money. "She's mine." Desperate to maintain his composure, he adjusted his vest and averted his eyes to his attire.

Koi and the men looked to Master Thomas.

"She's not for sale. She's a runaway."

The auctioneer denied he knew she was a runaway, leaving out details of her arrival and inclusion in the auction.

Adam asked the mulatto to step inside, through the doorway to his warehouse. "I'll be a moment," Adam said to the others.

As soon as the two were alone the mulatto said stone-faced, "She's my mother," insinuating *for God's sake*.

The weight of his words lifted Adam's mood.

He smiled and placed a hand on the desperate man's shoulder while looking him in the eye. Thinking of Sara, he said in Hebrew, "*Tzedek* (Justice)." Go in peace and enjoy your life," he said, shaking the man's hand firmly while patting him on the back.

Back at the threshold of his warehouse the mulatto slipped behind Adam and took his mother's arm as Adam nodded to the auctioneer.

"Bugger off, the old woman's already sold," Adam said to Master Thomas. "And you agreed to the rest before the subject. Done is done," he said folding his arms across his chest. "Pay the man," Adam said, cocking his head, signaling the auctioneer. James and a few warehouse workers came to the door and stood behind Adam as Master Thomas twitched his nose and rapped his cane in his hand. Thinking aloud he said, "She's not worth it," and turned his attention to the auctioneer. James and the others disappeared from view.

Koi pulled on Adam's sleeve again.

"Good heavens, child, *what is it?*"

As Sade and the other slaves at auction were put in irons Koi said, "I want to be sick. I want to be given the pox, like you said."

"Why the urgency, child? We discussed it, yes, but in the future."

"No. Now. And, I want to buy a slave. That one," she said, pointing into the distance at Sade boarding a transport to Thomas & Company's slave ship in the bay.

"What?"

Adam was as astonished as intrigued by what the child wanted to devote her future, meager earnings to. Dr. Ramsay had convinced him Koi was not necessarily immune, though she'd evaded the pox during an outbreak.

Nevertheless, he said, "You can't buy any of them any more than I can. They've been sold," leaving out 'to that repugnant little man over there,' as he eyed Master Thomas boarding a tender for his ship.

"But, she's my friend. Sade, she's my friend!"

"Why didn't you say something before now?"

Koi gave him a Beatrice and Beulah look.

Exasperated at his inability to do anything about Koi's revelation and anxious to see Sara after he read her love note, he could offer little comfort to Koi. "There's nothing to be done I'm afraid. I cannot save the world…*Mann tracht und Gott lacht* (Man plans and God laughs)," he said aloud, as much to Sara as to Koi, and, to himself—as he did a dozen times more on the way home, once again, almost as upset as Koi.

TWENTY-TWO

The Red Kerchief

Madame's health slowly returned, though Millie had not. It had been over two weeks since she'd left with Jacob aboard the *Vasa* to summons Dr. Ramsay.

Madame was now well enough to sit up and read, with a fresh cup of coffee at her side. Denmark spoke of taking out the boat—out to see the sunken wreck; the victim of a privateer battle four years earlier that had rattled Madame's windowpanes and brought the American war to her "little speck on the globe."

Madame lowered her spectacles, stalling; though out at the limits of her ability to observe through her spyglass, she reluctantly relented. Perhaps in gratitude for him not sailing off when he could while she was incapacitated. In turn, he checked on her three more times, just to be sure she didn't need anything before he shoved off.

The weather only partially cooperated. A few black clouds called attention to the bright spots of sun on the otherwise dark waves rolling toward Madame's island. Great gusts of wind among the gathering clouds made for fast sailing but the choppy waters tempered Denmark's speed. Peering through her spyglass, beyond the range of focus, the wreck site was as fuzzy now as ever. Denmark imagined the day as a chance to scour every underwater detail he'd only been able to imagine until then.

Sailing over the site, to his surprise, he saw two hulls resting on the uneven bottom. At about five and eight fathoms, respectively. The more shallow ship tittered on the edge of a ledge twenty feet from the channel's true bottom. The more shallow wreck had been protected from the path of the deep strong current flowing out to sea. Her severed mainmast almost protruded the choppy surface. The other, deeper ship, what remained of her, was strewn across the ocean floor in pieces. Long ago she'd been rigged to explode by Seymour's guerrillas. They had anticipated, correctly, that once abandoned she'd be boarded by a British patrol. The gunpowder killed or maimed many of the enemy. The exposed ribs of the mined decoy ship were charred at the tips where the explosion and subsequent fire had burned her to the water line.

In order to dive a site of more than twenty-five feet and stay for any amount of time Denmark knew from experience he must begin right above it. Though his anchor would reach the ledge, he didn't trust it in that weather. Instead he dove in and tied off a bow line to the broken mainmast of the decaying wreck to keep Madame's boat moored in place. As he did so he got a better look at the ship.

Seen through the distorted lens of fathoms of water, despite the degrading effects of four years of salt water and worms had had on her she seemed remarkably intact. Inviting; as though just resting, settled in place, she was waiting to be resurrected.

On his first dive the amount of sunlight changed as he reached the sunken ship. Looking up to the floating moored sailboat above him he saw a dark cloud pass over before scaling the rocky slope of the neighboring island.

When he reached the ship she appeared to be buried to her gun ports in silt and rock. Fish of all stripes swam about the wreck. Large grouper meandered with tuna, snapper and jellyfish. A sea turtle lumbered past menacing barracuda and sharks lurking in the depths. The well-preserved deck seemed eerily familiar. He kicked hard for the surface, for air.

At the surface he considered his next dive. He remembered seeing a hatch. *Was it locked?* He took a deep breath and dove in. He immediately grabbed the line that tethered Madame's sailboat to the sunken ship. Following the line he pulled himself down, down, down, fast. The strategy propelled him through the depth until he arrived flatfooted on the deck of the *Eclipse*. Once he did he recognized her. Recalling the bald white whale, Jacob, and his crew, he envisioned them there now, on deck, laughing at him. He looked to the forward hatch door, closed and locked. He surfaced again.

While climbing into Madame's boat to retrieve some tools he thought he remembered an aft hatch as well aboard the *Eclipse*—she'd come to rest uneven, meaning her stern, and the aft hatch, lay still deeper than her bow, closer to the edge of the watery cliff.

On his third dive, Denmark dove in from the deck of Madame's boat with tools in hand, plunging deeper faster by their weight. When the tools he held hit the *Eclipse*'s deck he'd arrived in half the time as before. He'd landed next to the wide open aft hatch. He peered in, still holding the tools to control his buoyancy. Too dark to see much, he grabbed a timber inside the hold and pulled himself in. The hold became darker still the further inside he went. His free hand felt barrels, floating. Beyond them he reached with his other hand. The tools suddenly felt heavier. Air. He'd found, air!

Treading water he took a deep breath. A tinge of the odor of gun smoke and fire lingered in the trapped air. Once he'd found an unidentifiable crate to cling to for buoyancy he moved further to explore the boundary of the air pocket. His kicking and stroking of the water shifted the harmony of silt—and the remains of those who'd drowned—undisturbed for years till now.

Denmark did not know that his presence, his disturbance of a delicate balance had removed silt deposits from cracks in the hull. His pocket of air was shrinking. Air that, at first, only seeped through the cracks had become a torrent of bubbles streaming to the surface. The shifting weight and loss of air within the hull forced the *Eclipse* to slide ever closer to the perilous ledge.

As he continued to feel his way in the dark he soon found the limits of his haven. He wanted to try to bring the floating crate in his hand to the surface as his prize. He took another deep breath and plunged to swim to the hatch, but something enveloped him!—the outstretched arms of his mother, Abra. It felt like bone to the touch.

The shock, his frightful scream, decreased his air supply as he broke free of the spindly embrace. He dropped his tools as he pushed away and instinctively grabbed hold of cloth to the touch—the red kerchief from around Abra's skull. The one she'd removed from the last *Paradis* pox victim. He fled for the surface.

He hoped he was swimming in the right direction. Toward the open hatch. As he struggled he hit his head, hard, on a rafter. He saw only purple in his mind. His chest deflated, he gulped. He'd almost exhausted his air.

He saw a light, far ahead, as though at the end of a tunnel, or thought he had—then—complete darkness again. *Had the hatch closed?*

It was not until he felt rain pelting his face, salt water waves choking his airway and stinging his eyes that he realize where he was; that he'd made it out alive. He had no idea how he'd reached the surface.

Once he climbed aboard Madame's rocking sailboat, he found her listing port side with her bow almost submerged. His head throbbed. The line he'd attached to the *Eclipse*'s mainmast was taut. For all these years the *Eclipse* had been spared the ravages of the bottom of the channel. But with her equilibrium compromised—the loss of her buoyancy—the *Eclipse* conceded her ultimate descent. Sliding ever closer to the ledge she threatened to pull Madame's boat to the bottom with her on her plunged to the deep.

Suddenly the wind grew stronger. A large wave crashed over Madame's boat and a belch of air bubbles erupted above the *Eclipse*, jostling the water. The sequence momentarily eased the tension in the line creating enough slack for Denmark to untie Madame's boat and throw the line away like a hissing bomb.

Among the debris that surfaced with the bubbles was the red kerchief he once held in his hand; a shiver struck him. He fished the kerchief from the water and hurried for home, thankful to be alive.

TWENTY-THREE

A Surreal Mark of Time

The worst storm in the history of the Caribbean hit the next day. It killed more than 20,000 people in the Lesser Antilles from Tobago to Tortola. Countless more were severely injured.

The storm's 200 knot winds reduced Upper Town to shambles and pummeled Fort Oranje as huge waves swept out to sea or tore to pieces the warehouses of Lower Town.

After digging out from beneath the rubble, the survivors on St. Eustatius set about digging enough graves to accommodate all the dead.

"Trade! Trade must go on. There's a war on, you know!"

"Which one?"

"Take your pick!" was the common refrain said in jest to keep from crying as the islanders struggled to comprehend their world.

Indeed, in addition to the conflict in North America, Britain was engaged in challenges or alliances with half the world for dominance. From Europe to the Caribbean and South America to North Africa, the Indian subcontinent and the Pacific; the world was at war. And St. Eustatius was being prodded—gently after the known extent of her devastation—to get back to business; the business of military supply.

Among the munitions orders passing through Adam's hands to and from all corners of the globe were the private correspondence of Benjamin Franklin, John Adams and Silas Dean. All agents of Hortalez & Company.

France's entry into the American war meant shuttering the French island of Martinique. The island had once served as an alternative privateer base and weigh station, but with France officially a combatant the island was too vulnerable to British attack.

From then on Hortalez & Company relied more and more of little Statia. She was asked to fill a role disproportionate to her size. To supply ninety percent of all the materiel required to maintain a revolution. A revolution against the most powerful empire in the world, no less. And to do it from a thousand miles away.

In addition to a stockpile of goods and hard currency any head of state would envy, the carrot of becoming one of the richest places on earth was dangled before her as her reward.

Beatrice and Beulah arrived with Augustus while St. Eustatius was still in the throes of rebuilding. Augustus kissed the ground at the end of the wharf. The remnants of a hundred damaged warehouses for as far as his eye could see looked more like oyster middens along the shores of Charleston Harbor.

After giving up on ever finding The African the Charles Town authorities had released Beulah. She'd run away from her master straight into the arms of Beatrice and Augustus hiding in the Sea Islands of South Carolina.

After the successful siege of Charles Town, Augustus's ability to survey the town was made all the more precarious. On the last occasion he walked the city's streets he'd seen Adam's home commandeered as quarters for British officers.

On that same last day in Charles Town Augustus had a chance encounter with a privateer on East Bay Street. That serendipitous meeting led to him book passage for himself, Beatrice and Beulah on the *Prospect.* A ship anchored along dunes north of town to avoid the Charles Town blockade. There, in a low voice the captain had ordered his crew to make way for another run to the Caribbean. Despite her heavy load of lumber and Charles Town Yellow rice, the hull stank worse than a whaler. But thanks to Captain Joseph Vesey, they had at last arrived at Augustus's nirvana, Statia.

Beatrice gripped his arm tight amid the destruction and the hustle of rough characters working Lower Town. After catching their breath from the trek up the steep Baypath road Augustus led the way to Adam's farm through familiar lanes edged by few familiar landmarks.

Their arrival at Adam's farm was timely. Between tending to the injured on the island Dr. Ramsay had inoculated Koi by violation so she could serve as nursemaid to future smallpox victims. These weeks later she still suffered the consequences. Enduring a persistent high fever, discomforting pustules and vomit between muscle spasms. Sara had put Koi on the terrace in a shaded hammock to catch cool ocean breezes while sleeping away her infection.

At the stoop to Adam's farmhouse Augustus explained who they were, producing a smile on Sara's face. She'd heard about all of them, especially Augustus.

"Please, Come in. We been expecting you, someday," she lied to make her guests feel at ease.

Sara wrote a quick note and gave it to Statia, saying "Statia, deary, give dis to de The African. Tell him to take it to de warehouse. Tell him Koi's still too sick to join him for de ride down."

The trio's eyes brightened at hearing the familiar names. After they inquired with concern about Koi's condition Sara walked them to the terrace saying, "She was asleep, and burning hot with de fever so I put her in a hammock in de shade out cher, to let her rest in de cool breezes."

Recalling Koi's harrowing story of her capture and confinement, in a sack in Africa, and her adamant refusal to sleep in a swaying hammock aboard the *Rotterdam*, all three looked at one another with an alarm that perplexed Sara.

"Oh, Lord," Beulah said, as if watching a master retrieve a whip.

"Oh, my," Beatrice said. "Think. We have to think."

"Tink," Sara said. "What's to tink 'bout," annoyed by her guests reaction to her care for a girl she'd come to see as one of her own.

Hearing familiar voices, Koi thought she was dreaming. She felt herself swaying—as if her dream of her Charles Town friends was happening while traveling in her dark swaying fabric dungeon in Africa.

But when she opened her eyes, the panic at her movement was instantly relieved by surprise, confusion and joy at the sight of Beatrice, Beulah and Augustus standing next to Sara. She spilled onto the terraced floor to escape the swaying. Beatrice, Beulah and Augustus clapped, smiled and laughed at the sight of Koi's smile, and her height.

Decorations of the holy season were usually a staple on St. Eustatius during the month of December. But this year was different. Ethnic and island foods, a Nativity scene, Hanukkah Menorahs, fir trees, sweets from St. Lucia, a Boxing Day parade and a Grandfather Frost celebration on New Year's Eve were muted or absent altogether this year.

This year the still dazed, battered, islanders walked befuddled through the motions of the season's rituals. Many lived in squalor amid the material fortunes of abundant trade goods. The few homes that did manage a haphazardly display of their decorations for the holidays did so from bare rafters and walls of construction sites.

Like other islanders, Adam's work load since the storm doubled as he struggled to fill war orders while rebuilding his home and warehouse. The wrath left by the 1780 storm, later named *San Calixto II*, transformed the holiday season into a surreal mark of time.

TWENTY-FOUR

Living State of Dead

"**G**ood morning, Madame. *Joyeux Noel,*" Denmark said.

Recalling happier Christmas mornings he felt this Christmas was still—despite the devastating aftermath of the storm—a cause for celebration; of life. Given the hurricane's strength, it was a wonder neither of them had been killed.

While checking on Madame at the storm's onset Denmark had been struck in the head by flying debris. When he woke, during the lull of the storm, he frantically tried to dig Madame from beneath the rubble of her home. Part of her roof had been blown away and the rest had fallen in on top of her.

She was injured and unconscious when he found her. He put a piece of broken glass close to her face. The moisture it collected relieved him. But her condition left him bereft. As the high winds and rain returned he fashioned an A frame against a sagging wall over Madame's bed from which the two could ride out the remaining terror.

With the storm's passage the rain subsided. Though she remained unconscious Denmark made Madame as comfortable as possible. He bandaged her injured head and sat next her, thinking.

He could see across the bay through where a wall once stood. The songs of the slave gangs were silent. He considered the state of slave row on Paradise Island as he recalled an article he'd read years ago in *The Royal Danish American Gazette* chronicling a hurricane. Written by a young man on St. Croix, Alexander Hamilton, the article described the slaves' reactions during the storm's lull—an eerie desolate calm—and the chaos amid the storm's return and aftermath; no whips, no masters. Just dazed survivors.

Now, Madame's island was quiet. Too quiet. Her home smelled like smoke and dampness. A fire started by a candle had been drowned out by the rain that soaked the books that had not already burned. He felt almost as though he were all alone. And he had to imagine that might be the case soon.

Sound. The pounding surf on the reef. Macaws and gulls. Clucking chickens and baying goats. All sound seemed amplified as he walked the premises several times. All the while his head snapped every time he thought he might have heard Madame's call. But each time was the same as before. No change in Madame's living state of dead.

Over the next few days he planned to run away. Many times, each day. He packed a bundle for that purpose. But he couldn't leave Madame. He couldn't help her, yet he couldn't go. Even if she'd wanted him to go. Told him to go. Where in the world would he go?

His hands shook like a sober drunk's as he opened a soggy map he'd retrieved from the rubble. He glanced at the waters around the island as he studied his quivering fingers. In his mind's eye he could see from the tiller of Madame's little sailboat the horrors of Paradise Island, Road Town, and the hordes of privateers sailing those waters.

And he knew that crossing the Atlantic in Madame's tiny craft would not only be scary as hell, it would be suicidal for even the best of mariners. Remembering bits and pieces of his Middle Passage experience, he recalled the thirty, forty, fifty foot swells of the ocean and the face of the little girl washed overboard in the storm. He thought of his family, Koi and Millie. *Where could they be?*

The field hands on Paradise Island soon resumed their low songs on the way to and from the sugar cane. They'd been put back to work harvesting what could be salvaged and replanted for a new sugar cane crop.

Master Thomas had replenished Paradise Island with the purchase of slaves on St. Eustatius and elsewhere. Denmark's sister, Sade, among them. Sade found herself back at the sugarhouse without her mother or Selena, but with Selena's machete in *her* hand. Within days of the storm Denmark watched the sugar cane vat fire smoke rise high into the sky across the bay.

As on Sunday's before the storm, Denmark heard the dogs of *Paradis* wail and bark, excited, as though on the trail of runaways. Even after convincing Master Thomas of his innocence; that he'd had no role in the "fresh grave" scheme—Seymour had said he was as shocked as Master Thomas by the shallow empty graves and he'd portrayed the escapee Selena as the mastermind behind it all—Seymour continued to secret away slaves to sell to the copper miners or to distant plantations. During the week, Moses would torment, interrogate or whip the men, trying to break their silent conspiracy. But every Sunday he chased phantom "runaways." He was convinced that all he had to do to please his masters, to win a reward, was find them.

By the time commercial activity of nearby Beef Island at Trellis Bay had come back to life Madame had too. Early one morning Denmark's first glance at Madame shocked him.

Madame's eyes were wide open, unblinking, fixed on an object in midair. A look Denmark thought meant death had surprised her in the night. Then she blinked, and turned her gaze to his eyes. She followed him as he moved toward the foot of her bed.

She tried to make a smile, but her heart had attacked her again; this time in her sleep. She felt a tingling feeling in her left arm and experienced some paralysis. She moved her right wrist, and stopped. She did so again and Denmark got her message. He brought ink and brittle paper he'd salvaged. Madame scribbled, *"Merci."* She took a deep breath and slept till noon. Though Madame opened her eyes later in the day and took sips of water Denmark offered she remained in critical condition, unable to help him plot their future.

About the time sea lane traffic resumed in earnest on the outskirts of Madame's island she felt well enough to stand for short intervals. She resumed her observations at her spyglass amid the ruins of her home, but with enthusiasm. Her strength returned only slowly as Denmark made the best of their limited supplies and reduced circumstances.

They were expecting help. Millie. Re-supply. And mail.

She'd been absent far too long. But they held out hope that she'd return soon, safely, and with Dr. Ramsay.

At the next new moon, though he carried no dispatch, Denmark sailed to the shore of Paradise Island as he had many times. Desperate, he went this time to ask for help. But there was no one there.

A day later Madame sent Denmark back, hoping her secret espionage ally would be there. And this time the American spy was there. But the fat man offered no aid. Instead, he berated Denmark for seeking his help. He castigated him for not bringing new intelligence. Cursed him. Then he warned Denmark that after the war was over he would have no more use for him, or Madame. He swore he would seek revenge. Revenge for Denmark's trespass—revealing the secret copper dig site.

TWENTY-FIVE

As for the State-less Rabble

On Saturday, February 3, 1781 while still rebuilding, St. Eustatius faced complete and utter destruction—again.

Unbeknownst to the world, yet, as Christmas carolers sang in the streets of London, parliament declared war on Holland, including Statia. Especially little Statia. They used as their pretext the capture of Henry Laurens at sea. Henry Laurens was the former President of the Continental Congress. And as American envoy, he carried with him a seemingly unsinkable dossier—thrown overboard. In it was a treaty with Holland...*to conclude a loan for the use of the persons calling themselves the United States of America.*

Upon the fleet's arrival at St. Eustatius the British Admiral wrote in a dispatch sent ashore that it was his intent...*to leave St. Eustatius as barren as the day it erupted from the sea...instead of the greatest emporium on earth, it will be a mere desert, known only by report.* The *Sandwich*, the expeditionary force's flagship—at 90 guns—surpassed the entire strength of Fort Oranje. She was accompanied by nine other ships of the line of 74 guns each. And half a dozen more ships from 64 to 28 guns each as well as fire ships, mortar ships and troop transports. Altogether, more than 600 cannons and over ten thousand men stood at the ready in Statia's harbor waiting to be noticed.

Governor Johannes de Graaff's voice trailed off as he read aloud the last line of the Admiral's dispatch: *If any resistance is made, you must abide by the consequences.*

Though a small crowd had gathered at the Governor's mansion to hear what they already knew, the rest of the town stayed indoors. Taverns closed, lodgings filled and a steady train of refugees walked past Adam's farm. They were fleeing into the sloping rain forest, up to the crest of The Quill to hide their valuables and evade capture.

Adam's office window looked at the remnants of the wall of the neighboring warehouse. Hearing unfamiliar activity outside his door he soon found what all the commotion was about and charged into action.

"Come with me," Adam said to James without taking his eyes off the navy ships.

Inside his office, Adam quickly opened his safe and took out a heavy saddle bag of coins. He also retrieved documents containing the most egregious examples of smuggling and placed them inside it.

"Take this. Do not stop for anyone. Give it to your mother. Tell her I'll be along soon. Ask her to let you bury it in the southeast corner of the cane field, at my request. Then take everyone to the cave at the base of The Quill. The one I showed you when you were a boy. Do you remember? Can you find your way there, leading the others?"

"Of course. I've been there lots of times since then," he said, smiling at the fact his father didn't know. Despite his father's mood, and the ominous threat offshore, the boy's youth and optimism—swelled by a cloistered life on a secluded island—rendered him fearless. "But, shouldn't we wait for you?"

"No. Though I hope to arrive by the time you've gathered everyone for the journey, do not wait. And take Sophia with you. Your mother can ride her."

After a farewell hug, Adam said, "Now go; hurry!"

Outside Adam's office, hats in hand, stood Adam's entire warehouse crew. One man stepped forward to ask permission to do what Adam knew they would all do—climb The Quill. Adam merely nodded to wish them well.

Next, Adam returned to the office and retrieved other sensitive paperwork from his safe and threw it into a barrel in the warehouse and lit it on fire. After dousing the burnt remains he secured the premises with a lock. He observed other warehouse merchants hurry to do the same as he began his trek home, on foot.

At Upper Town weary platoons of Royal Marines moved slowly after their long steep climb up the Baypath road. Wearing heavy red wool uniforms amid the island heat exhausted the troops. Some marched slowly over the open drawbridge to occupy the fort while still others fanned out into the narrow lanes of the shuttered town. One company headed straight for The Quill's jungle slope.

In addition to complete submission, a sort of doomsday report was ordered among the first of 38 written Proclamations. It insisted on a *full and just account* to be compiled by the townspeople. An inventory of the entire island. Her assets—for looting purposes—and her people's nationalities—with an eye toward diplomacy.

The French and Dutch, as enemy civilians, were allowed to take their household furnishings into exile with them. The exception being Governor de Graaff, who would be tried in London for, among other offenses, being…*the first man who insulted the British flag by taking up the salute of a pirate and a rebel.* And yet, he was provided an entire ship to transport his household, family and servants. The Americans and British—if they survived the voyage aboard a prison ship—were to be, likewise, tried in London. But likely hanged as traitors. Other nationalities were allowed to scatter to the wind.

The ordered inventory of households and businesses—required to be written in English—came up short in the Admiral's estimation. He felt sure the townspeople were holding back. A number of anonymous informants seeking privilege, leniency, or revenge confirmed his suspicions. And although he questioned the veracity of one rather dubious source, the Admiral added to a dispatch to the General ashore: *PS – a Rascal Jew has hid a chest in a cane patch—a Negro will shew the place, upon a promise of Freedom and reward…my officer will tell you the whole affair.*

Beatrice passed away. She'd died of a heart attack at the sight of the fleet in the harbor. Sara and the others couldn't leave her, so they all remained until Adam arrived home. By then, British soldiers had blocked the road beyond his farm leading to The Quill.

Though reform had taken root, by choosing Sara over synagogue, where blacks were still shunned, Adam had put himself at odds with all his Jewish brethren—on the island and in Charles Town. That is why, like on any other Saturday, Adam was working at the warehouse while observant Jews were gathered at Honem Dalim (She who is Charitable to the Poor). A synagogue his grandfather and father had helped build on the island in 1739.

Now, in keeping with Adam's unorthodox view of Judaism, he determined he would defy the rabbi and the entire Honem Dalin congregation. He would bury Beatrice, a black *goy*, in their hallowed ground alongside his parents and grandparents. He ordered Beatrice to be washed and wrapped in a *tachrichim* (shroud) in accordance with tradition.

Caskets had been scarce since the hurricane so Adam and The African crafted one from boards off his barn. Then Adam escorted Sara and the boys, Augustus and Beulah, Koi and Statia to the cemetery. The African trailed behind in the neighbor's wagon holding Beatrice's makeshift coffin. The menagerie of mourners were a spectacle as they trudged through the lanes.

The General ashore wrote to Admiral Rodney aboard the *Sandwich* that in the name of diplomacy, to avoid international repercussions, he had to adjust his patrols to accommodate a spate of processions. Funerals at the Reformed Dutch Church and the Jewish synagogue. The Admiral dropped the dispatch to his desk and immediately called out, "Lieutenant!"

On the deck of the *Sandwich* the navy lieutenant passed along the Admiral's orders to his marine sergeant. Incredulous, the sergeant complained about the order to another, "What about the diplomacy the officer's 'ave been preaching to us about…Are we now to be grave robbers, digging up some old Jew's mum?"

Laughing at his friend's distress the other said, "Blimey, mate! There's the beauty in it. There's no one to answer to. Not for them. They're a state-less rabble, with no nation of their own to retaliate!"

At the Jewish cemetery a patrol of British soldiers could be heard marching toward the gate as Adam finished his prayers over the open grave.

"Halt!" the officer bellowed to his troops on the dusty road.

The Royal Marine Sergeant followed the advice of his friend as to how to behave and what to say. "You, there…," pointing to Adam, "step aside. All of you, back!"

Two of the soldiers who accompanied the sergeant from the street flipped open the coffin lid.

"Get her up, out!" the sergeant ordered.

Beneath Beatrice's body lay coins of every denomination as well as jewelry Adam had given to Sara—his mother's things. The satisfied sergeant secured the loot in a marine's knapsack.

"You," the sergeant said, pointing to Adam, "Come with me."

The Royal Marine Sergeant personally delivered Adam to Admiral Rodney's quarters aboard the *Sandwich* where a number of officers conferred. The Admiral, informed of the events ashore, took the floor.

"What's your name?" the Admiral said above the din.

Utter silence ensued, all eyes turned toward Adam.

"Adam Wolff," Adam said with a slow rise of his chin.

"Lived here long?"

"All my life. As have generations before me."

The Admiral paused to further take stock of the man.

"You've lived a life of luxury and plenty all your days then, have you?" he said, thinking of his own hardscrabble background. A life at sea by twelve. The recent humiliation he is only now, with this prize money, to recover from. To retire on as a wealthy man among the landed gentry. Though leader of His Majesty's fleet in the southern oceans after many years of Service, he'd lived three years in exile, in

Paris. The fruits of high living, he'd fled his gambling debts and Jewish creditors in England. He'd only been able to return to London, and to Service, after a wealthy benefactor came to his rescue.

By the time Admiral Rodney was interrogating Adam, another squadron of marines had already dug up a chest in which James had placed the saddlebag.

The Admiral continued "And, at the expense of the lives of His Majesty's forces...You're a Jew aren't you? Am I right?"—as though the fact alone represented an indictment.

"Y-e-s..." Adam said, drawing out his answer to question the Admiral's point.

The ship groaned at the ensuing silence; the assembled officers grumbled or averted their eyes.

Finally, the Admiral said, "This is the point of my confusion..."

Looking around the large cabin of officers, "Captain Wafford, would you be so kind..." the Admiral said, motioning for Lindsay Wafford, a Charles Town Loyalist volunteer to step forward.

"Admiral," he said, saluting. "At your service, sir."

"Captain Wafford, didn't you tell me you recognized this man's name as that of an old classmate, from your British colony? A Briton from whom you purchased property." Admiral Rodney gingerly ignored the fact that Jewish property ownership rights had been revoked years ago.

"Yes, sir. In Charles Town," the nervous green officer replied to the Admiral.

"Thank you, captain. That will be all."

Captain Wafford avoided making eye contact with Adam as he stepped back to blend in with the other junior officers.

"So, you see..." the Admiral paused to look at a document, "So, you see Wolff. I don't know whether to hang you as an Englishman, a traitor, or as a pirate for your ships pillaging at sea, or to treat you as a Dutch enemy combatant, or a prisoner of war. Each carries its own..." he paused, "ramifications."

He sat on the charts blanketing the desk in his quarters and pondered Adam, making him wait.

Among the audience of young officers, in one's aside to another he whispered through a crease of a smile, imitating Admiral Rodney, "But, as a Jew…well, who's to fuss."

Adam stood a little straighter waiting for his verdict.

A rap on the cabin door brought a messenger who whispered into Admiral Rodney's ear. After which the Admiral squared his shoulders and resumed.

"Tell me, Wolff…have you any more booty buried? In the cemetery, perhaps?"

"No," Adam said without hesitation.

"No saddlebag buried in a sugarcane field?"

Adam's chin fell for a moment. After a deep breath, he raised it again, reestablishing his composure.

"What of my family?" he asked, masking his terror with resolve in his voice.

The young messenger answered, out of turn, "All we found was a house full of niggers!" eliciting low laughs.

The Admiral said, "Your family, as it were, shall fare much better than you, I dare say. They will be sold as inventory with the other slaves. Some 1600 of them on the island at last count. Save one." The Admiral did not elaborate. He turned to the paperwork on his desk and shouted to the officers present, "Now, get him out of here! Dismissed. All of you."

The next dispatch to shore had soldiers rounding up offenders all over the island. A squadron of Royal Marines was sent to scale the heights of The Quill. Boarding houses, lodgings, taverns and warehouses were scoured for loot to confiscate. Islanders were herded to deport or imprison. A special order decreed that all Jews were to be corralled quayside, immediately. The Jewish men were separated from their families. Brought into a warehouse where they were stripped of their clothing. Each garment was searched for hidden valuables.

Meanwhile, emboldened by Adam's cashe, British soldiers inspected every burial since the hurricane. They dug up grave after grave after grave till satisfied they'd left only bones in the island's cemeteries. The soldiers then burned the synagogue and many Jewish homes on their return to base.

Given one day to settle their affairs, the Jewish women and children did not see their men again. Shipped away without family or property, the Jewish men were exiled to neighboring islands or still farther afield. Adam and his son James, along with the British and Americans, were labeled English traitors and loaded onto prison ships in shackles for the long hard voyage to Great Britain.

Master Thomas bought Beulah, Augustus, Koi, Sara and her other two boys at Admiral Rodney's quayside auction. He loaded them onto a confiscated ship bound for St. Thomas.

But The African and Statia were missing.

Adam had told Sara about the accusations against The African. Told as part of the story of Adam's hasty departure from Charles Town. She now quizzed Augustus and Beulah who averted their eyes. No one spoke of anything but other explanations for their absence, together. Though worried, they tried to imagine his capture from the horse barn, along with Statia; loaded onto one of the other ships transporting slaves.

They all searched faces upon their arrival at Charlotte Amalie, St. Thomas. Hoping, in vain, for Statia or The African to disembark from one of the other slave ships. They also scanned the faces of Statia's exiles, looking for Adam or James, but neither was among them.

As they marched to the prison and auction house Koi spoke of what was in store for them.

TWENTY-SIX

Treasure

Denmark's outlook darkened as his worst fears about the future returned.

Of late, Madame's mood had changed too. From placid to stern. A frown of wrinkles often appeared on her brow as though she were contemplating a question she'd rather not answer.

One morning he awoke briefly to a faint mispronunciation of his name. Thinking he must be dreaming he closed his eyes.

"Den-mark!" Madame soon said again. This time emptying her lungs in the effort.

He jumped to his feet to find that Madame had bumped her head on a roof beam of the makeshift A frame above her bed. She'd re-opened her old head wound sustained during the storm. She sat hunched on the edge of her bed, bleeding.

"Coffee. Breakfast. And, another bandage."

"*Oui*, Madame," Denmark said, responding to the hint of her real speaking voice. To stop the bleeding, he wrapped around her head the red kerchief he'd fished from the sea above the sunken *Eclipse*.

Soon, Madame began to repeat things she had said through the years. Things he was to remember when she was gone—dead. Denmark tried to reassure her she was going nowhere, help was on the way. But he knew her condition was beyond his means to judge. And he wanted to hear what she had to say. Some of it anyway.

She spoke of how she had planned to install him as her business manager of the tavern, inn and mercantile store as a free man, when he came "of age." Denmark wasn't sure what "of age" meant. He had no reference. He'd been deprived of his tribal indoctrination, signaling demarcation into manhood. But he knew from his trips to Road Town that the time was not now. Not yet.

"These are hard words to speak, Denmark. But, I must. If my plans, my life, were more certain, I would know what to tell you. What to expect. But, if the end comes sooner I will no longer be able to protect you, to guide you. Nor leave you here, on this island as your sanctuary. You would not be safe here. If I die before Millie returns— and I think by now something must have happened. If she'd been only weeks delayed," Madame waved her hand by way of explanation, "but, well, it's been over two months now—if I die before help arrives, bury me here, on my island."

Denmark looked down, contemplating what either or both realities might mean.

"You are to go to Road Town. Armand at the inn is a good man. He'll care for you. Put you to work. And, in time, according to my will, despite my daughter's challenges you will share in the management and prosperity of the businesses along with her and my grandson."

Madame picked up documents taken from her nightstand and motioned for Denmark to take them from her.

Madame could see Road Town in her mind. The Chevalier tavern and inn was one of the oldest and most impressive buildings of the little ramshackle town. It sat some distance from the main road along the shore.

She also recalled a rampart of several cannons placed high on a hill overlooking Road Harbor. One couldn't see the guns from the water's approach to the town. The clever location put the small garrison out of reach of enemy fire. Too high for a ship's cannon's trajectory. Yet, from the tiny perch the twelve pounders could aim with precision, raining down shells on a chosen adversary. And the jail. Madame closed her eyes before going on.

Handing Denmark the documents she said, "Take the boat to Half Moon Bay. Beach her there and travel overland to the inn. Do not enter Road Harbor under sail. Do you understand?"

"*Oui*, Madame." He did not challenge her emphatic instructions. He paced a moment then stood still.

"Madame, these are hard words to speak," he began, parroting her, not unlike their very first meeting. "Why have you helped me all these years? Why are you helping me now?"

His questions enlivened her. The puny African boy she'd kept and nurtured, body, mind and soul was now speaking like the articulate, thoughtful, erudite (and strapping) young man she'd hoped he'd become.

Clearing her throat, Madame began, "Well, I know something of discrimination. I've experienced it in my life. Not like you, of course. But, in my own way. As a woman. And, as a woman shunned for her choices in life. And, I know something of the outside world. How harsh it can be, especially for..." here she paused. "Someone like yourself. One day, long ago, someone, a whaler from Nantucket, who became a dear friend, a best customer, helped my husband and I when we needed help the most. I promised him that one day, if I could make a difference in another's life, I would. For you, Denmark, from the beginning, I felt I could do that for you, and therefore I should, as he had done for us...." Her voice trailed off.

"Due unto," Denmark said.

Madame nodded a slight smile remembering the pun. She scratched at the scab beneath the red kerchief and wiped away a tear forming in her eye.

She thought of all the times Denmark could have run away. And the time she thought he had.

"Why didn't you run, Denmark? You had opportunities?"

Denmark considered the question. Of course, in truth he had run, many times, in his mind. The honest answer came to him just then, "Because, *I love you.*"

Madame choked at the words a moment.

"I love you, too."

The odd pair let the words span the feelings between them.

After a time, Denmark began to pace again. He had another question to ask. And if he did not ask it now he never would.

"Madame, what about Millie's mother. What happened?"

Madame stiffened at the thought and stared at the wind as though the scene were replaying before her eyes.

"I was wrong to order what I did," she said without elaborating on the horror. "I made a mistake. I've often asked Millie's mother for forgiveness. In my mind. I've even thought, tried, to speak to Millie about the subject," she said as she began to cry. Wiping the tears away she cleared her throat again and said to the wind, "I will when Millie returns. I promise." A promise made more to Millie's mother and Millie than to Denmark.

Breaking his concentration, Madame said, "Please, stop pacing!" in her new somewhat slurred vernacular. Signaling with her one good arm she said, "Sit down," motioning to a chair near her bed. Denmark sat down.

"One more thing."

Feeling faint again, she wanted to explain to him where her money was. What to do with it. She pointed to where her armoire and dresser stood, now hidden from view beneath the roof debris. But the words would not come. After several fruitless attempts, she threw the word "*trésor*" at him with the desired effect.

"Top drawer," she finally slurred, pointing to where the dresser should be. "Put those in," referring to the two documents she had handed to him; a letter to her daughter and her will.

"What's there is for you." Denmark got up from his chair a walked a tingling few steps to the dresser and brushed away the debris obscuring it. The fantasy of—*what had she called it?*—treasure, heightened his anticipation. He reached inside the deep drawer as Madame motioned again for him to continue.

She attempted to say, "In the back." He had to rely on her gestures this time because he didn't catch a word. Madame attempted more gestures before saying a lispy, "*Le sac.*" The drawer smelled of perfume and leather. Mixed in with boxed jewelry were unboxed necklaces, bracelets and rings throughout the drawer. In the back corner of the deep drawer sat a substantial leather bag with drawstrings. Denmark turned to Madame, amazed and unsure of what she might ask him to do next. Of surprising weight, he put the heavy purse on the bed next to Madame. She opened it with her good hand and took out a few coins. Her small, delicate fingers grasped francs, pieces of eight, pounds, gilders and moved her hand toward him.

Denmark cupped his hands and she dropped the coins in.

Then, pointing, she said, "Put those back."

He put the money into the dresser drawer. Once he'd returned to her side, she said, "Again," holding another handful of the heavy metal.

After sprinkling more atop the jewels he then carefully stacked a number of the coins in the corner of the drawer and returned to her bedside.

"*Vous*," Madame annunciated almost as clearly as ever. She pushed the bag in his direction, as to hand it to him. And she handed him a note she had just scribbled. It said, *faux fond, la poitrine est pour ma fille* (false bottom, the chest is for my daughter).

She pointed to where her armoire should stand.

Leaving her bedside he brushed aside debris hiding the armoire. Madame nodded. He swung both doors open. She nodded again. He removed shoes until he noticed the anomaly along the inside bottom of the furniture. An indentation into opposite edges allowed his fingers to remove it, revealing the hidden compartment inside. There laid a closed Jonathan Swift-like strongbox, askew on the true bottom. He removed the heavy chest and placed it in the chair next to her bed. She pointed outside. She'd written another note. This one read: *Hide it under your rock.*

"All of it, now!" she said.

He was surprised she knew his hiding place.

It was one of the most important moments in his life and he knew he was not prepared. He whispered under the weight of the heavy load, "*Merci beaucoup.*" His eyes translated the rest before she hurried him along, waving her good arm.

Denmark dug beneath his hiding spot. A huge rock jutting out toward the edge of the cliff that overlooked the lagoon and the coral reef barrier that formed it. In the process he found items he'd stowed away there through the years. Among them a hand-made sextant he'd fashioned from an illustration in a book. A rusty hilt found at the bottom of Madame's bay. A tin box of toy soldiers Madame had given him one Christmas. Inside it was the mourning ring.

Then he dug the hole deeper. He placed the sack of coins inside the chest and covered the fortune with dirt. Next, he placed the remnants of his childhood on top of the dirt before covering them up as well. The shallow placement of his toys, at the beginning of the hole, he reasoned, he hoped, would deter further exploration. If anyone ever disturbed the dirt they might arrive at the same conclusion he hoped for—that they'd discovered nothing more than a child's treasure trove.

TWENTY-SEVEN

My Juliet

Madame's strength soon seemed to return, but her behavior became more erratic by the day. At times she was morose, then giddy, loving then petty. When Denmark informed her that he had used the last of her sugar in her coffee she just laughed at the irony of it. Pointing to the smoke rising where Sade minded the fire, Madame said, "Think of it, an abundance of the sweet granules is being skimmed and cooled as we speak, just out of reach across the bay!"

The next morning when Denmark served a breakfast of fresh eggs to Madame she tossed the plate to the ground, "Why can't you cook like Millie!" The episode and what Millie would say about it reminded him of her absence.

Though Denmark had confirmed Millie's story about Madame and her mother, he felt there was something more to Madame's behavior—something more at play than an ailing heart or her natural temperament—she seemed to be losing her mind.

Two days later a familiar ship rounded the tip of Paradise Island sailing for Madame's. The *Libertas*. She rode deep in the waves on a slow but direct course. Denmark told Madame of Captain Palmer's boat as he followed her approach through Madame's spyglass.

After all this time of enduring the circumstances mother nature had left them in; after Madame's plea for help from her spy cohort had been dismissed, even scorned, their future threatened by him; the two rejoiced at the prospect of Millie's return with Captain Palmer, perhaps with Dr. Ramsay aboard, and material relief too! At last.

Captain Palmer and his crew waved to the boy as Denmark bound down the path from Madame's perch in excited leaps. As they secured the *Libertas* to Madame's dock they unloaded a young slave girl; put her ashore aside a barrel of Charles Town Yellow rice. As Denmark reached the end of the dock, she stood with her back to him alongside the other supplies, watching the sailors work.

Denmark approached with curiosity as he admired her slender physique and proud stature. When she turned around at the sound of his approach Denmark stopped. His eyes met hers like across the bonfire the night of the king's raid.

He allowed the distance between them to say—it couldn't be— while his heart insisted—it is!

Her own disbelieving gaze never left the eyes of the boy walking toward her.

Just feet apart, their eyes revealed themselves to the other, defying five years of growth and absence. Saying each other's name:

"Telemaque!"

"Koi!"

They embraced. Their hearts soared as they jumped in place, still holding the other tight. Then, hand-in-hand, the children danced in a circle around and around, squealing and laughing with delight as though they were sharing the moment together in Africa.

The storm damaged dock compensated, thumping and creaking in time as the astonished captain and crew of the *Libertas* watched. Amazed at the odds that saltwater slaves, once parted, could ever, would ever, be reunited.

Clang, clang, clang! They all heard the bell ringing from up the hill: Madame calling.

As they walked Denmark and Koi excitedly spoke their native language, Twi. Asking each other, "What are you doing here?" Even more astonished than the sailors, they were in shock.

"I can't believe it!" they repeated as they hiked up the path hand-in-hand.

"You live here?" Koi asked as they walked.

Koi realized of how often she had thought of Telemaque since their odyssey together so long ago.

"With Madame," he said, pointing to the top of the hill. "I'll introduce you. She's no longer as stern these days, not since the storm," he told himself as much as Koi, thinking of their conversations and recent events. He omitted the facts of this week. He couldn't explain them away to his own satisfaction yet. "She treats me well. Where have you been? Who is your master? Have you seen any of your family? Or mine? My mother, or Sade? Was my mother's baby a boy or girl?"

"Yes, I have seen them…"

She paused to consider her words, glad to be interrupted by the top of the hill and Madame.

"Who is this?" Madame said, clearly irritated at the presence of a stranger—a black girl walking with Denmark hand-in-hand—not Millie. Still wearing the red kerchief over her head wound, she stood with her cane, holding on to the only column that remained to support the roof over the threshold of her wrecked house.

Reminded of Madame's ephemeral scary bents, her squinted stare and sharp tone worried Denmark.

Trying to appease her he said, "Madame, please allow me to introduce *Mademoiselle Koi*," he said in perfect French, with a courtier's bow.

"Who? What?" Madame said.

In an attempt to make his feelings for Koi clear to Madame, to stress the importance of the moment to him, to her—though the reason for his feeling's hold on him remained as opaque now as when he was a boy in Africa he said, "She's like my sister, Madame."

"Your *sister*!"

The mention of Denmark's family agitated Madame even more. She reverted to a state of confusion that had come and gone this past week, since the bump to her head and her last heart attack.

Denmark mustered the courage of another analogy, "She's my Juliet," he said with another bow as he presented Koi anew.

Koi averted her eyes from Madame's disapproving gaze. Madame's mouth opened, but at first she did not speak.

Then, moments later, she quizzed Koi about Millie, as though she ought to know.

Koi's puzzled look revealed her innocence.

Just then Captain Palmer arrived having ascended Madame's path to deliver the bad news. He told them of finding Millie in the channel. Retelling the ordeal brought him and then everyone to tears. All were silent as the reality sunk in and speculation began.

Finally, Madame said, "*Condamner,* Jacob!"

Captain Palmer said with revenge and determination in his voice that he'd been hunting the white whale ever since.

Asked about Dr. Ramsay, Captain Palmer had more bad news. Dr. Ramsay had been forced to flee back to England following one too many death threats. And Armand had disappeared. A friend of his had replaced him. His name was Seymour. Madame was dismayed Armand had not sent word somehow of his sudden departure.

Then Captain Palmer handed Madame a bill of sale for Koi. Made aware of Millie's death, Master Thomas had picked Koi out among the slaves who'd arrived from St. Eustatius. Rather than own her himself, rather than hiring her out to Madame, as with Millie, he'd charged Madame the full market price of an adult slave.

An hour later, Denmark escorted Madame to the kitchen to see, after months of worry and privation, all the food Koi had helped him and the crew haul up from the dock, including brown sugar. Madame hugged Denmark and Koi like favorite relatives at a party.

And Captain Palmer's *Libertas* had sailed slow and low in the water for a reason. She'd brought lumber to rebuild Madame's home. Grateful, Madame removed the red kerchief from her almost healed head wound and privately asked Denmark to place a generous sum of coins in it from his hiding place. She then invited the captain and his entire crew to her home for dinner.

Over their meal Madame asked Captain Palmer again about her new employee, "What did you say his name was?"

"Seymour. Lyman Seymour."

"Well one day soon, after the house is repaired and it's convenient for you you'll have to come by again and take Denmark and I to meet him. Won't you?"

"I'd be happy to," the captain said. "How about next month."

"That would be excellent, *splendide*! *Magnifique*!"

Over the next two weeks the captain and crew set about making repairs and reestablishing order to Madame's hilltop perch. While Denmark helped with the boisterous work, Koi's introduction into Madame's routine took place in cool silence. Many of Madame's requests and preferences were indicated to Koi through Madame's eye contact and facial expression—until, during one such day of reconstruction Madame asked Koi to sit.

As with Denmark, she offered Koi a cup of the coffee Koi had just served and inquired about the girl's relationship to Denmark. Over the course of this and other conversations with Koi Madame perceived the deficiencies in Beatrice's academic resources, but admired the effort. The results of Beatrice's work inspired Madame to also see a future for Denmark. Madame began to see an equal partner to balance Denmark's life once she was gone.

Looking at Koi through the eyes of the young man Denmark had become, tried as he might, he was unable to stop staring at his childhood friend—her small pert breasts and slim figure. He now looked at Koi in a way different from the way he had back in Africa. To his mind's eye she'd become a sensuous young woman. Though Koi shied from his seemingly unending gaze she enjoyed his enthralled attention. Each day he looked forward to the completion of their afternoon chores so he could ask her to go swimming with him. The beaches became their time alone.

Koi told him about what had happened to her since parting with Denmark's mother and sister, at Charlotte Amalie, and her most recent sighting of Sade. As Denmark digested the horror the two pondered the predicament of each's family; how much they had lost and suffered since the village bonfire.

In an attempt to enliven the moment, Koi told Denmark about all the places she'd been and the people she'd met who had taken care of her.

But after speaking at length of her journey to Madame's island, Koi grew silent and still. Her eyes wide, searching, like a lone lost gazelle in Africa.

Denmark sensed what she was feeling, and thinking. He knew too well the uncertainty that follows sudden and profound loss. Once experienced, one never forgets what it's like. What it means to have your family, your life, stolen from you, forever.

While contemplating their future he tried to reassure her, and himself.

"We have a future here. With Madame, now that she is better. And, for years to come, and someday…well, I'll be free. When I am 'of age.' She told me I will be her business manager."

"What do you mean?" she asked, eager to see a new future.

"Come with me," he said. He led her up to the top of the hill to his hiding place, anxious to show her.

TWENTY-EIGHT

To Survive

Madame's bell delayed Denmark's surprise for Koi. The two set about making and serving Madame's dinner with such efficacy and grace they brought a smile to Madame's lips. While cleaning the kitchen the two watched light from the portholes of the *Libertas* dance and listened to the sailor's jokes skip across the calm water.

Denmark put his finger to his lips as he motioned for Koi to follow him. He led her back to the rock outcrop. As he began to dig Koi was drawn to the moonlit view from atop the cliff down to Madame's lagoon below. She moved closer to Denmark.

"Close your eyes," Denmark said.

She dutifully complied. The smell of fresh dirt overpowered the salt air, heightening her anticipation.

"OK, now you can look."

Koi opened her eyes to a scene she'd only read about in story books. Next to the scattered toys of a child she saw an opened chest. Inside was a leather sack overflowing with coins. Jewelry was spread across still more loose gold and silver coins scattered atop Spanish gold bars gleaming in the moonlight.

Koi let out a cry that Denmark staunched, putting his hand to her mouth.

"The chest is for Madame's daughter. But the sack is for us. When I am free and a partner in Madame's business. When I am 'of age.'"

Koi put her own hand to her mouth lest she call out again. She touched the items and when Denmark did not object she picked up a handful of coins to feel their weight. She let them fall between her fingers. She then picked up and held a necklace to her neck and put it back, just so. Next she struggled to pick up a gold bar, but left the heft inside the strongbox.

"She gave this to *you*?" Koi asked, still astonished at the sight.

"To us," he said.

"There's more. One more thing. From me." He produced a ring. The mourning ring. He slipped it onto her finger. She could see tiny identical patterns on either side of the center of the ring but didn't recognize them as skulls in the dim light.

The two then sat together in silence shoulder to shoulder thinking of the strange place they now occupied. They both gazed eastward— toward their homeland—across the vast ocean they'd traveled years before.

Each felt that at least now, now, they had a secure place in which to be together again. They had one another. And a sack full of what this strange new jungle required to survive.

Koi's solace drifted to visions of her recent past. She'd been moved time and again. Her seemingly secure life full of adult benefactors had been obliterated. And her recent return to Charlotte Amalie's auction house reminded her that despite her education and previous relative privilege she was still, after all, just a slave in another alien village.

"What if Madame doesn't live that long? What if her daughter and grandson challenge Madame's will, to set you free? What then? Should we leave before we have to find out? My friend spoke of a place called the 'Sea Islands,' at the coast near Charles Town."

The sight in each other's mind's eye of sailing to North America appeared. The image of huge ocean swells, storms, sickness and death induced a shared stupor. Each relived a recollection at sea. Koi thought about the little girl rescued in Africa from the *Diane*.

During the first storm encountered at sea, Denmark, Koi and a handful of other children, including the lucky slave girl rescued from the *Diane*, watched with horror and amazement at the dexterity of the *Briel's* nimble able seaman, Gideon Williams. He seemed so small against a backdrop of black clouds as he climbed the rat lines and scurried across the yardarm to tie off the mainsail, flapping loosely fifty-five feet above the deck. Amid the high winds and first raindrops his mates had shouted him on.

"Go on!" yelled one, waving a red kerchief he'd untied from around his neck, revealing tiny red pustules forming there.

"Give it your best!" said another.

"Don't stop now, Williams. You're almost there, boy!" an old timer yelled, cupping his hands around his open mouth to direct his voice.

If Williams failed, the captain was sure to send one of them next, high up into the mainmast.

After making his way through the twist of lines and flapping canvas, Williams secured the mainsail to cheers from below. Just then, a rogue wave hit. The full force of the wave rocked and rolled the ship, breaking Williams's grip. He plunged to the deck like a windswept errant line. Even as everyone grabbed for anything to hold on to, his splash onto the water covered deck chilled them all.

The giant wave sloshed and rearranged everything in its path as it rushed to resume its place in the sea. All across the deck anything not tied down—the dead sailor, barrels, buoys, rope, and the little girl from the *Diane*—all swished to the ship's scuppers and railing before spilling overboard with the power of an immense waterfall.

On deck, Koi, Denmark and the other children were swept from their feet. Swirled and tossed around like so much debris. Yet all the rest were able to hang on until the wave disappeared and the *Briel* righted herself.

Within moments all the children realized the loss among them. The absence of their new friend frightened them as the taste of salt water and rain dripped from their lips.

Denmark and Koi heard a faint cry through the fury of the wind and rain and roar of the disturbed ocean. Looking at one another then the ocean, they peered over the railing into the trailing wake of the ship. Both of them saw her face out at sea. The little girl held up her thin arm, up high, and waved it when she knew they'd seen her.

"We have to go back! We have to turn around!" Koi yelled to a sailor who didn't understand a word she'd said. He ignored her pointing overboard at the raging sea.

Denmark rushed to another sailor, the only free black on deck. But as Denmark approached the man the intermittent rain turned into a torrent and another wave, less violent yet still formidable, crashed onboard between them. The sailor was gone.

Denmark quickly returned to Koi at the railing. But there was no trace of the little girl where she once bobbed; cold, afraid, alone.

Koi tried not to think of the sharks.

Shaking the image from her mind she blurted out unanswerable questions about their future, snapping Denmark from his own voyage recollection—his mother's branding.

He tried to reassure her, and himself, "Madame will live. She's better." Wrestling with the alternatives, he said, "She has to."

Both began thinking the same thing. There's only one way off Madame's island.

Koi said, "What do you call her, your boat? What's her name?"

Denmark, still troubled by the notion of leaving Madame alone offered, "She wouldn't get us far…"

Though he had been so proud to defend it at the time he had announced the name to Madame and Millie, he now felt shy about revealing his choice.

"*Koi*. I christened her, the *Koi*."

They spent the next few moments looking into one another's eyes.

As she'd done the night of the bonfire, she broke their gaze.

A moment later she looked into his eyes again for another long while before she said, "I have something I need to tell you."

Taken by her serious tone, he nodded and waited.

"Madame's sick."

"But, she's better now. Since the storm."

"No. It's not her wound, or her heart, or her mind."

"What then? What do you mean?"

"She has the pox. I don't know how…maybe from some blanket or such."

In Koi's mind she saw her first image of Madame, clinging to the lone remaining column at the entrance to her home, the red kerchief wrapped around her head wound. She didn't know the history of the red kerchief but she knew that under certain conditions, the smallpox virus can survive for years if not decades.

"But, she has it. I've seen the symptoms. Not only on you but many others since. I've been trained to spot the disease, early. By Dr. Ramsay. Madame's Dr. Ramsay. I've seen the signs."

It occurred to Denmark that he'd seen some tiny red marks on her face and hands but he'd attributed them to the heat. To the conditions they'd lived in of late. He finally said, "But, even if you are right, she'll survive. I did. You'll make her well. Won't you?"

"I'll do my best, of course. But, she's old, and feeble," Koi said without looking away. She had to make him understand. To make him think of the consequences if she couldn't.

TWENTY-NINE

One Eye Open

The day Captain Palmer and his crew departed everyone was in good spirits. Though Madame's supplies were diminished from feeding an entire crew, the house and kitchen were in good repair and life had returned to almost normal for the first time since the terrible storm.

But as soon as the *Libertas* tacked once again to round the corner of Beef Island and sail into the Sir Francis Drake Channel, Madame spied trouble through her lens. Two schooners—the *Kameel* and the *Jupiter*—fired upon the *Libertas*. Having learned her lesson from attacking the *Eclipse*, the *Jupiter* trained her guns on the masts and riggings, as did the *Kameel*, to avoid damaging the hull. To prevent their prize from sinking.

Captain Palmer and his crew were raked by the grapeshot. Most died the instant of the first barrage. The next barrage came not from the schooners but from a British squadron of warships sailing from the channel. The British struck all three ships in focus of Madame's spyglass. Out-gunned and out-manned, the *Kameel* and *Jupiter* attempted an escape from the British warships by hoisting more canvas. Madame watched the schooners emerge from the gun smoke and then disappear behind the tip of Paradise Island. The British Navy pursued them.

The quiet, immobile *Libertas* bobbed in the swells. All onboard were dead by the time Denmark and Koi tied up alongside her. The captain was nowhere to be found.

Seeing that the *Libertas* was in danger of being washed onto Madame's reef Denmark dropped the shredded sails. Found and hoisted an old jib, and sailed her into Madame's bay. Her dead remained strewn across her deck as he anchored the *Libertas* right where she'd spent the last two weeks.

Denmark and Koi found where Captain Palmer had stowed the red kerchief of coins in his cabin and then sailed the *Koi* ashore to the leeward secluded beach, where Denmark kept her. When they met Madame in her house she had just completed her notations of the conflict, recorded in her leather book. She was locking it away in her desk drawer. The three stood together sharing a solemn moment.

"Madame, there's no sign of Captain Palmer. I'm sorry," Denmark said with a bow of his head.

"*Oui*. He was a fine man." She raised her head and face up high as though issuing forth a silent prayer. A moment later she asked, "What of the crew?"

"Three dead onboard, as we speak…"

"Good heavens. Get them off of there. We'll put them in the little clearing, down the hill from the vegetable garden."

As they were leaving she asked, "Do you think you can handle it? Shall we send for help?"

"NO!" they said, too fast, in time, and too forcefully for the occasion. They didn't want others to commandeer the *Libertas* as their own. Denmark, more settled, repeated, "No, we can handle it."

The two looked at each other knowing the others' thoughts; *A boat to get off this island (someday)*.

Grim reality came soon enough. They started digging graves.

"No. The head must be facing east," Koi insisted.

"But, you don't know what religion, if any, these men practiced."

Koi's Beatrice and Beulah persona appeared, inducing Denmark's silent obedience, conceded with a sigh.

The deed done, exhausted by the affair, the whole island seemed to slumber like iguanas—with one eye open. That evening, with Madame settled for the night the two secreted themselves down to alongside the *Koi*. The gently palling water led their eyes to the dark, quiet *Libertas*, rocking at anchor in the moonlight.

"We'll have to repair her sails, somehow. When I lowered them they were shreds in my hands," Denmark said.

"We could use the *Koi*'s, and patch them!" she said.

"That could work."

Musing over his words, and forming his next, he said, "We could only put some sails to the wind at a time anyway, undermanned as we are. She normally sails with at least a few sailors, and Captain Palmer."

"Where are we going to go? The Sea Islands?" Koi's words were a blend of excitement and fear.

Denmark said, "I'd like to look for our families; I wish we had some friends," picturing the captain, and Millie, Armand at Madame's inn, and the old, shrouded woman across the bay who'd accepted Madame's first dispatches. He could see them all plainly.

"I want to find my mother and sister," Koi said staring straight ahead, thinking of the last time she had seen either; in Africa.

"We should look here. We are here. You've seen my mother and Sade. Your family is bound to be here too. They're all here, somewhere. Besides, we'd never make it to Africa, not without some help." He almost said "home," but Africa felt less like home as the years passed. And with his father dead, and his mother and sister known to be on this side of the Atlantic, Africa seemed a world away; beyond reality.

"We could recruit Africans to come back with us," she said, trying to imagine it.

The two sat on the sand, their backs together, thinking.

Koi said, "Once all else is in place, do we wait until…"

He could feel her cock her head toward Madame's house, to let Denmark finish her sentence.

Madame's smallpox freckles had advanced. Some had become inflamed blotches of red.

He heard the question but he was silently preoccupied by his libido. He hoped to make Koi his wife. He had decided to attempt to become a man with her. In the absence of tribal teachings he hoped for divine intervention to guide him.

Inspired by the moonlight he turned around and leaned in close to her as he was thinking, "I'm going to… "

"Denmark!"

Madame repeated his name, "Denmark!" as she—clang, clang, clang—rang her bell.

THIRTY

Dashed!

Late one afternoon Denmark spotted two vessels on course for Madame's island. One would arrive soon. When he and Madame looked through the spyglass she too recognized the closer of the two from her frequent visits to Paradise Island; it was Master Thomas's ship, the *Liverpool.*

"Maybe, he won't disembark. Maybe he's only stopping," Madame said, unconvincingly.

The expression of doubt on Denmark's face elicited from Madame, "All right, all right; wishful thinking perhaps. You go down to meet him at the dock. And you," she said, pointing to Koi, "stay in the kitchen unless called. Do you understand?"

"*Oui*, Madame," Koi said with a slight curtsy before disappearing from sight.

His visit to Madame's today was of a definitive sort—intended to finally begin his long awaited designs for Madame's island. Master Thomas reasoned he could conclude his business in short order. Then take this opportunity to enjoy a drunken romp through Road Town's brothels to celebrate before passing out in his four poster bed at *Paradis* Plantation. *No one would be the wiser*, he thought, well satisfied with his plan.

A storm was pushing its way ashore. Denmark stood at the end of the dock by the time Master Thomas's private ketch passed the *Libertas*, rocking high in the *Liverpool*'s wake. The weather had picked up—

gusting through the channel, buffeting the hulls with small white-caps and whisking the dock. Cool damp wind from the Atlantic, a precursor, made its presence felt.

Taking the lines thrown to him, Denmark tied them off with the help of a deckhand from the polished craft. Its gleaming brass fittings reflected distorted moving mirror images of life in the fading light of day.

On deck two well-dressed identical mulattos held a curious small chest between them as they stared at Denmark. The deckhands went about their tasks. All waited for Master Thomas who soon emerged topside wearing his customary black and a colorful bird perched on his shoulder.

As Master Thomas and his twin escorts descended the gangplank Denmark stepped into their path.

"Master Thomas, sir."

Unaccustomed to young slave boys approaching him unless summoned, he said, "Nigra, what's your name, your Christian name?"

"Denmark," followed too long afterwards with, "sir."

"How is your Madame?" he asked.

Denmark lied well.

"In her bed, sick," he said, spoken as though Master Thomas should already know of her illness. Denmark glanced at the curious bird.

"Where's the doctor? Did you not bring a doctor with you?" Denmark asked with a little too much force.

Master Thomas struck Denmark across the face with the back of his hand instead of his cane. The bird croaked. "On her death bed is she? Well, fortunately I have just the remedy for that," he said through a wily sardonic smile.

Then, standing more erect he rubbed his hand before reaching into his coat pocket to tap a small bottle of adulterated liquid. This new concoction was brewed by a genuine ktenologist. Whisked from the Tower of London to the docks of the Thames and on to a ship bound for America. He joined hundreds of other criminals on the voyage. Part of the fifty-thousand England dumped in America through the decades. His crime? Grave robbing. For cadavers. For medical research. The good doctor assured Master Thomas the elixir was fatal. But because Master Thomas had been fooled before, just in case, he also felt the length of hemp rope he'd placed in his pocket too—plan B.

Taken aback, still recovering from the blow, still within range of a second, Denmark nevertheless stood his ground.

"Sir, Millie was sent with Jacob to fetch a doctor," he said, rubbing his cheek, "That's why I asked." Insinuating that the murderer Jacob knew of Madame's plight and by extension, as an employer, so should Master Thomas; followed up quickly with, "Sir."

Denmark snuck another glance at the bird that seemed to stare at him.

Recognizing the *Libertas* at anchor, Master Thomas asked, "Where is Captain Palmer? Visiting Madame's bed side?"

"Dead, sir," Denmark said, though in truth Denmark didn't know.

Eyes fixed upon the *Libertas*, Master Thomas said aloud, to himself, "Well, I'll be towing her when I leave."

Master Thomas pushed past Denmark and started up the hill to Madame's home. The mulattos followed with the chest.

Denmark dashed to an alternative trail he'd blazed through the years. It took him past the small beach of tiny rocks and sand where the *Koi* was beached, then up the island's lesser hill, winding through brush and trees, past the sailor's graves, and the garden and up past the side wall of the kitchen. He waved to Koi through the window. Then he put a finger close to his lips to urge her silence. He continued on to the house, arriving ahead of the others.

At the crest of Madame's island Master Thomas and his retinue were greeted by expected gusts of wind but also an unexpected sight; Denmark. That surprise was accompanied by another. Bursts of sustained high wind swirled atop the island. Reminiscent of the onset of the recent great hurricane. A solid band of black rain clouds advanced across the horizon like a curtain drawn across a stage.

Holding his white wig in place, Master Thomas and his entourage barged past Denmark smirking at the vestibule.

"Madame Chevalier!"

Master Thomas was surprised to soon see her standing before him in her parlor—not in bed. He noted with caution the red blotches on her skin. Some had formed into yellowing pustules.

He had announced himself to her with his back to the twins making it clear no other introductions were necessary. No one spoke through an extended silence in which the wind's low whistle and the rustle of palm fronds outside were the only sounds in the room.

Madame wrinkled her nose at the sight of the bird and looked over the mulatto twins with suspicion. The bird cocked and craned its head as though attempting a better view of Madame.

"Boy! I'll have a brandy," Master Thomas said without turning his eyes from Madame's.

Denmark entered from the vestibule where he'd held back, listening. At the liquor cabinet he spit into a glass in a way only Madame could see and poured the brandy. While serving it on a silver platter, Denmark winked at Madame. She masked her appreciative laugh with a faux cough, sharing in the juvenile defiance.

Madame had allowed herself to hope, up until the last moment, that the first words she'd hear would be, "Momma, I'm home!"

"How is my daughter? Have you a letter for me?"

Master Thomas waited to respond. A tactic practiced by his father—meant to toy with an adversary. Madame, waiting…unable to look at her despised son-in-law…alternated her attention between the bird and the chest carried by the identical strangers.

Master Thomas took another sip of brandy and through a silly grin relented, "Funny you should ask. As a matter of fact I do, that is…" he snapped his fingers and the mulattoes walked forward with the chest, pouring the contents onto Madame's dining table.

"It's your lucky day. As you can see, I have many…"

Unopened letters, fifty or more addressed to and from Madame's daughter spilled out onto the table. Madame picked one up, then another and another.

"What's the meaning of this!" she said, outraged, looking at random at the wax-sealed letters, never opened. Madame felt the flutter of her heart, then a fainting sensation.

"That's part of why I'm here today. I'm afraid there's more."

"More? What more?" Madame said looking aghast across the table of letters.

"She's dead. Your daughter. And, him too," pointing to Madame's grandson, Jamison, in the family portrait hanging again above the stone fireplace.

"You mightened have warned me about her addiction," he said as though Madame had sold him a diseased slave.

Many years ago Madame had treated her daughter's cough with laudanum. The cough went away, but her daughter's laudanum use remained. It became the source of the long riff between mother and daughter.

"But in the last letter I received from my daughter she seemed well. She said she'd broken the last bottle."

"Apparently not. The servants found her in her room, in bed, quite dead. An overdose, I suppose."

He did not admit his role as supplier. He'd had Seymour, his *Paradis* overseer, pose as a doctor. Seymour eagerly accommodated Master Thomas. He'd assured Madame's daughter her opiate usage was not only necessary, but essential to her well-being; guaranteeing the addict an uninterrupted supply to refill the cold empty bottle she held tight to her bosom.

Nodding this time toward Madame's family portrait, "And your grandson died at sea. A thief. One of my captains ordered him flogged for stealing. He expired strapped to the mainmast of one of my ships. Didn't live to steal from me again. Serves him right, I should say."

Madame stood in shock, her mind and heart reeling.

Jacob's *Vasa*, the other boat Denmark had sighted earlier, sailed into Madame's bay.

As Madame and Master Thomas spoke, the mulattos walked throughout the parlor, hands clasped behind their back. One perused the diminished but repaired library, while the other admired the view from Madame's French doors.

The house seemed to inhale with every gust of moist salt air. The pungent aroma filled the room. It began to rain outside. Only intermittent at first, but the drops where the size of thimbles. One of the twins closed the terrace doors.

While telling Madame about her daughter's demise—without mentioning the sight of Jacob's *Vasa*—Master Thomas summoned the browsing brother with the tip of his finger. He whispered something into the man's ear.

Denmark had retreated to the vestibule, listening to the conversation from where he could see the other boat. There was no mistaking Jacob at the helm. As the *Vasa* docked opposite the *Liverpool* Denmark could hear Jacob's rough commands to his crew.

Denmark ran to and past the kitchen again, this time touching Koi's outstretched hand as he passed her. He ran down past the garden and graves, reversing his path to the water's edge, peeling off clothes as he scampered and leaped whole sections of the trail in his descent. He stopped to put his clothes beneath the *Koi* and pick up one of the many tools he kept there. Tools he'd recovered from wrecks strewn across the ocean floor at the perimeter of Madame's reef. He slipped into the rain splattered water as quietly as the white-capped waves lapping ashore.

With the *Vasa* tied fast, her crew went below to escape the intermittent rain before Jacob even stepped onto the dock. The new dock shuddered under the enormous weight of his over four hundred pound frame. Much to the surprise and worry of the lone sailor left standing watch over the *Liverpool*. His captain and crewmates were below, enjoying a rowdy game of cards.

At first Jacob turned to the sentry, but something about the wide-eyed look on the slight, sun-dried Portuguese sailor told him the little man wouldn't understand a word he said.

Frustrated, Jacob was about to set off down the dock toward the sandy path up the hill but, slapping his thigh, thought better of it. He wasn't sure what he was supposed to be doing. Master Thomas's instructions didn't say what this was about. He suspected that his summons and Master Thomas's arrival had something to do with Millie's screams about the old lady. That Millie's revenge was at last catching up to him. About to make life hard for him, at least for a while.

He paced in front of his boat, rubbing sprinkles of rain from his bald head.

Denmark observed Jacob from afar. As he swam closer to the *Vasa* the sun began to disappear behind the tip of Paradise Island. He took a deep breath before diving for his target. Rusty wrench in hand, Denmark worked his underwater magic on the *Vasa*, first. Her rudder wouldn't answer much longer. After taking another deep breath, moments later, neither would the *Liverpool*'s.

In a hurry to make his way back up the path, putting on his dry clothes along the way, Denmark could hear some words spoken along the main path but he did not dally to listen. Instead, he raced back to Madame's side, to his alibi, should anyone survive.

The brothers argued as they walked to the dock.

"I don't know. I don't trust him," the disconsolate of the twins said in French. His hand over Koi's mouth to keep her quiet. In a vain attempt to free herself Koi struggled and scratched and kicked.

As the second sons of a wealthy French St. Domingo planter and his slave concubine, they'd roamed for months in search of a way of life suitable for abandoned aristocrats of color and leisure.

"What choice do we have?" the schemer of the two said. "Despite his cruel nature, we simply do as he asks…take the boy, after…" he paused rather than continue the thought aloud, "and for our trouble we are rewarded. Then we will find ourselves in the good graces of a powerful white ally in the region. Besides, we need the money to make our start. Here."

"Well, I'm not going through with it. None of it!" his brother said. He was referring to the killing of Madame, the sabotage of the *Vasa* and taking Denmark prisoner. Not part of the deal, the girl had been added into the mix later. "I don't even want to touch that old lady!"

Within minutes the twins were face to face with Jacob at the dock.

They informed him of their errand. And of a message from Master Thomas.

"Be sure she doesn't meet the same end as the last one."

The brothers were ignorant as to what exactly that meant, but they could imagine.

The characteristically obstinate Jacob sassed their insinuation. He denied any involvement in the death of that last slave girl, Millie. His intense sneering and the tone of his order to take Koi below so unnerved the brothers that the schemer abandoned any thought of sabotage. The two disembarked as quickly as possible to remove themselves from Jacob's hostile purview.

Walking back to Madame's the brothers renewed their argument.

The schemer said, "At home, we've had slaves wait on us hand and foot all our lives, growing up. Spying on their women in the fields, bending over...remember?" he said, chuckling to lighten his brother's countenance. To have him lower his guard long enough to receive his next blow.

The schemer's tone changed as he delivered it, "Well, if you don't want to end up like them, a field hand, a slave, you better listen up! With this, and maybe more, he might let us manage that tavern and inn, or that mercantile store of his at Road Town, like he said."

His disconsolate brother, no longer smirking at the childhood memory, replied, "...like he said, hah! Well...you're telling him we failed. Where did he get the idea we even knew how to do such a thing?"

Their conversation was cut short by, as if on cue, the slave gang's song traveling across the bay on their return from the fields. A reminder of the schemer brother's foreboding words.

The next time up the hill Denmark did not see Koi at the kitchen window. After stopping to search the empty kitchen he thought Madame must have called her, so he continued on to the house.

While waiting for his hired help to return Master Thomas paced the length of Madame's table making subtle jabs at the reputation of Madame's deceased husband. He tapped the small bottle in his pocket again and fingered the rope there as he paced.

All that was required was to subdue the old woman. That was the plan; that's what the brothers were here for. He'd do the rest; to be sure it was done and done properly. But with the twins having yet to return from the dock, a new idea brewed amid Master Thomas's prattle. Maybe we could drown her in the cistern and toss her into the bay. He turned his back for a moment, thinking.

Thump, THUMP!

Master Thomas turned to see Madame's lifeless body on the floor. Her chest had tightened before her heart burst. She had hit her head on the corner of the table before the floor.

"Splendid! Oh, how convenient!"

Unable to contain himself, Master Thomas broke into a maniacal laugh. The bird croaked as Master Thomas pranced in place.

But his gaiety was cut short.

"What are you looking at?" Master Thomas shouted at the dumbfounded twins, just returned from the dock. As they stood in horror he rebuked them, "I should cut your pay, now that half your work is done here!"

He soon regained his senses and composure. These men were to play other roles in his plan. He still needed them.

Gently at first he said, "Now, don't be daft, lads. I didn't hurt anyone. She was an old woman. She had wrinkles on her wrinkles, if you like. Think of it as if she died of a broken heart. What's a more suitable ending than that? Poetry it is. In any event, it saves us from the most troublesome task." He then sharpened his tongue to his usual self.

"Now, get her up! And into bed, like she expired there."

Instead of going in through the front door Denmark knocked and then entered the back door—to Madame's room—the way he was accustomed to bringing her breakfast. He walked into an alarming sight. Madame's dresser drawers were all open, ransacked. There stood Master Thomas. He'd found what he was looking for—money. The money Madame had asked Denmark to put there—to be found.

His slight smile disappeared as did the coins, replaced by an indignant scowl. The man was angry he'd been caught rummaging through the old woman's things, stealing her money, and he was disappointed there was so little of it.

Like an exhibit he held up Madame's will, found alongside the money.

"You didn't have to kill the old lady..." he said, followed quickly through a sinister laugh, "She freed you in her will." Using his anglicized phonics—as though Denmark's African name were comical—he drew out the consonants, "Tel-e-ma-que." Ever the one for the drama of inflicting pain, he added, pointing to the bottom of the page, "And there's even a codicil to free the girl too. Koi, is her name, eh?"

The twin's ears perked up.

"You know you'll pay for this. Killing your popular owner. The locals will hang you!"

"You're a liar," the bird screeched taking flight. It landed on the shoulder of the somber twin at Madame's bedside. Master Thomas cocked his eye at the bird.

Turning to Madame, Denmark was sorry she had passed alone—with Master Thomas in the room. He hadn't yet considered murder.

He rushed to place Madame's hand mirror to her face, waiting—nothing.

"Where is Koi?"

The possible answers to his question raced through his mind.

"Oh, no. Oh, dear Mawu! No!" invoking the Ewe goddess while deducing the worst answer.

For fun Master Thomas pushed on the downtrodden boy with a laugh.

"I put the girl onboard the *Vasa*. Like Millie before her, she's in Jacob's hands now."

Here Master Thomas paused to glare at the brothers, questioning whether they had *fixed* Jacob's rig as ordered. Though disappointed by their lack of affirmation he let it go, for now.

"Cover her!" Master Thomas told Denmark in response to Madame's deadpan stare at him. Denmark covered Madame with slow deliberate speed, pausing for a moment of respect and reflection.

"She'll keep until tomorrow," Master Thomas muttered.

Threatening Denmark with the point of his finger, "If anyone ever asks, she died tomorrow!" To Denmark's quizzical expression he reinforced his assertion with, "Do you understand me, boy?" Impatient for a verbal acknowledgement he yelled, "Do you?" Denmark winced at the spittled shout and managed a, "Yes," to appease the flushed man.

Denmark looked out the window to search the water.

The sprinkling rain had become a torrent prompting both Denmark and Master Thomas to look toward the pounding sound on the new roof, recalling the recent storm. They then looked uneasily at each other before turning their attention to the watery landscape.

At Jacob's command the *Vasa*'s crew cast off from Madame's pier.

The minute they departed the winds started to howl, blowing even stronger than before as a sheet of rain began. Jacob sailed out through the broad southern channel into Trellis Bay. Menaced by Madame's coral reef, port side, he set a course for the eastern reaches of Beef Island with the mainsail up and the jib full.

Soon Jacob turned the helm wheel starboard to compensate for the hard abeam winds forcing the *Vasa*'s glide to port.

No response. He tried port, then starboard, then port again. Giving the wheel handles all his strength, the rudder line snapped. The helm wheel spun with ease, like the wheel of an overturned wagon— spinning, spinning and spinning on its own.

Seeing and feeling his boat adrift, drifting ever closer to the reef, Jacob called out to the first mate, "Throw out the anchor and pull in the jib." He ordered the other sailors to lower the mainsail. Frantic with their duties, racing against time, hindered by rain and wind, they could hear the encroaching roar of waves slamming against the protruding reef rocks.

From Madame's parlor, while responding to Master Thomas's command to pour him another brandy, Denmark watched the *Vasa* underway. She was listing to port at high speed until her sails were lowered. He sensed that the *Vasa* now sailed rudderless, at the mercy of the wind and waves threatening to dash her onto the reef. Denmark ceased pouring.

Master Thomas snatched the glass. They both drew closer to the French doors to watch the drama unfolding below. At the tip of the reef, where the currents were strongest, the remnants of several wrecks waited for company at the bottom.

Even through the howling wind and rain, the crashing waves and the ship's cracking ribs and masts, Denmark could hear Koi's piercing screams just as he had, barely conscious, at the African riverbank.

At the snap of the mainmast the first mate was thrown overboard with it, kicking and crying out as he struggled. He punched at his canvas shroud like a cat in a bag. Jacob died instantly. Thrown to the rocks face first. The jagged surface perforated his skull. As he lay impaled on sharp coral atop the breaker, buffeted by waves, from a distance, his lifeless dangling arm gave the impression he was flailing. No one from below deck appeared to have surfaced.

Standing next to Denmark, after downing the last swig of brandy, Master Thomas detected guilt within Denmark's heartache. He turned to the twins as the *Vasa* went down. The schemer twin shrugged his shoulders and said, "We were powerless. Jacob watched us like a one of his deckhands."

Master Thomas returned his gaze to Denmark and began to laugh. "Oh, that *is* rich! Oh, my! 'Tis you who had a hand in this misfortune! Hah, hah, hah, hah."

After a few moments of amusement, "And here I sacrificed a slave to absolve myself. So that no magistrate would question my involvement. After all, I'd be the one injured in the mishap…out the price of a slave."

Circling Denmark Master Thomas toyed with the boy, "But you, you my clever nigra…I underestimated your devotion to Millie and your capacity for revenge! Good thing you had no idea about the girl. Had I known about your cunning plan I would have spared her. No need to waste inventory! Especially inventory as pretty as she, eh boys?" Master Thomas said with a laugh and a wink, meant as a comment on Koi's potential as a whore. A high priced concubine at auction.

Master Thomas again produced Madame's will. This time he lit it on fire—a sight to behold—he let the cinders fall to the floor.

The somber twin shuddered at his complicity.

And yet, after a nod from Master Thomas—with Denmark still mesmerized by the sight of the fluttering ashes—the twins seized the boy. Each brother held one of his arms, tight.

Just before sunrise, with his hands bound to the *Liverpool*'s windlass— by new shackles intended for Captain Warrett's next voyage— Denmark followed the slave gang's song, and their torches, as they marched double-quick to the fields. He felt the wrench of captivity course through his veins. He had tried to identify with the slave gangs before, admiring their stoic dignity from afar. But his vision for the future never included joining their ranks.

He yanked again on the chains restraining him.

Having lost everything, *why go on?* he asked himself. His father. Millie. Captain Palmer. Madame. All dead. Koi…he shuddered…likely. Where is his mother? His sister, Sade?

Koi hadn't the chance to tell him she'd recognized Master Thomas as Sade's new owner.

He told himself he did not fear death. Better *there* than alone. At least *there* he would be with loved ones. He imaged meeting the dark skinned European clad "commander" at the feet of the goddess Mawu. He'd ask the African slaver, *Who had instigated this nightmarish odyssey? What was your reward for our lives? What could you ever offer as recompense?*

He shivered in the chill of the cool dark wind. It raised goose bumps on his skin. Well, *it will all be over soon*, he thought. The *Liverpool* too will soon meet the same fate as the *Vasa*.

As the sun rose above the horizon he attempted to shield his eyes from its reflections as he looked again and again, searching the watery landscape for some clue about Koi to emerge. In his mind's eye he saw Koi's eyes just as they appeared across the glow of the wedding celebration bonfire. Then he imagined the terror in those eyes. Water rushing in all around her. The pounding surf and rain. The ship breaking apart before sinking. He blanched.

He could hear the goats baying and the birds in the trees, including Master Thomas's macaw. The bird had fled from the somber twins' shoulder. He watched smoke rise from the sugar house.

That Master Thomas would not honor Madame's will—to free Denmark and Koi—did not surprise him. That Jacob died like a beached whale did not bother him. But the idea that his quest for revenge was responsible for Koi's death felt like a torment only his own death could end. He waited to hear the *Liverpool*'s anchor chain rise.

THIRTY-ONE

The Other Half

Before weighing anchor the captain of the *Liverpool* recognized a problem at the helm. He and his crew abandoned ship for Beef Island and Tortola. Angered by the news, Master Thomas knew Denmark was responsible. He ordered the twins to transfer Denmark to the *Libertas* and sail her to St. Thomas.

Leading the twins, "You do still seek employment, at Road Town, do you not?" Master Thomas asked from behind his desk in the library at *Paradis*.

"Oh, yes sir, Master Thomas," the jovial schemer said with faux enthusiasm.

The somber one sulked as he witnessed his brother's groveling.

"Well, then, sail the boy on the *Libertas* to St. Thomas. When you arrive, deliver him to that slaver…there…" pointing to the *Prospect* anchored below in neighboring Trellis Bay. I'll be aboard her soon. The captain, Captain Vesey, will give you your reward then," he said through a sly grin.

"The boy will be my fare, my compliments, for passage to St. Thomas."

Master Thomas viewed this mode of transportation as an inconvenience, yes, but also as an opportunity. An opportunity to discuss new business with the young captain. New business made possible by his new acquisition—Madame's island.

After their meeting with Master Thomas the somber brother demanded, "What did you go and do that for? We can't sail! We've only been on a boat a few times. What other lies have you told that evil little man?" With the back of his hand he slapped his brother's breast as they walked down to the bay. "Now what?" he asked in dismay.

After transferring Denmark from the *Liverpool* and shackling him to the *Libertas*'s railing the schemer tried to explain how their predicament had come about.

"You see, my dear brother," he began, but stopped. He grabbed hold of a stanchion to steady himself as the deck shifted beneath his feet. "You see, earlier, at the Road Town tavern, to seal Master Thomas's proposition, while you were visiting the privy, I intimated an understanding of ships. He was keen we possess such knowledge before he would agree to take us on, as it were."

The exasperated somber brother surveyed the lines on the swaying deck as his brother tried to maintain his balance.

In an attempt to reassure his disconsolate brother the schemer said with an unintended desperation in his voice, "I'll get us there, somehow."

A gust of wind pushed the hull like a sail causing the schemer to lose his balance. He fell to his knees on the deck, grasping for anything to hold on to. Determined to make a success of his scheme he offered, as he examined, then reexamined the riggings, lines and sails, "It can't be that difficult!"

Breaking the tension, Denmark said, "I'll get you there. I'll sail her for you."

"You?" the two said in unison.

"Yes, so long you as you both help."

The brother's angst suddenly morphed into something like hope.

To brighten his scheming brother's mood, signaling the acceptance of an apology not offered, the somber brother said, "I'll wager my half of our reward he'll get us to St. Thomas without incident." Nothing motivated his scheming twin more than a bet.

"You're on. Release him," the schemer said as he reached into his silk vest pocket. "Here's the key."

To Denmark, sailing was uplifting—a hull and sails again responding to his touch. The act of dominating the sea raised him from the depths of his despair. The patched sails he and Koi had yet to test held against the pressure of the wind and made him think he might just hold up too. But not as a slave. No. At some point he would have to run to improve his condition. Then, he'd come back to Madame's island to search for Koi. And dig up Madame's treasure.

Denmark found the two grown men's earnest obedience to his authority from the helm intoxicating. Sailing through the channel for St. Thomas he asked them to do unnecessary tasks as well as the essential. While sailing among familiar shoals it occurred to Denmark that he could sink the *Libertas*. His captors, the twins, would likely drown, but he could swim. But, to where?

He sailed on.

When they arrived that night the twinkling lantern lights of Charlotte Amalie sparkled against the dark sixteen hundred foot heights of St. Thomas Island.

To recover from his lost bet the scheming brother doubled down as the twins debated a new bet; whether or not Denmark would run once they reached dry land.

The schemer ventured, "I wager he stays put, with us. He's been raised a gentleman, you can tell. Just look at his clothes. Modest, but fashionable."

"A gentleman! Hah! He's a houseboy. Anyhow, gentleman or houseboy, he'll run. What's your wager?"

"My other half of the reward, of course."

The schemer scurried away to act upon Denmark's command— "Drop the anchor, now"—leaving his somber brother to ponder his riddle.

The waterfront district of Charlotte Amalie was always busy, often especially at night. And that night she was busier than most.

Drunken sailors exploded into the streets like blasts of music from the taverns. British Royal Marines of a fleet escorting prize ships—loot confiscated from St. Eustatius bound for London—swarmed the town.

With their eyes bloodshot from drink and their pockets swollen with coins they besieged the locals, who, bent on exploitation, spared nothing and overcharged for everything.

At first glance, from the water, the youth was dazzled by the raucous spectacle ashore. At the pier the brothers simply walked away from Denmark without providing instructions or direction. Denmark followed them just as the schemer had predicted.

However, the closer to the end of the pier Denmark walked the more a vague haunting memory of the place came into focus. Denmark continued to follow the men along the boardwalk perpendicular to the wharfs. Far enough behind them to feel detached but close enough to seem associated. He was considering his options as he trailed the brothers.

As a reminder, as evidence that they'd landed at the epicenter of the Caribbean slave trade, a caravan of humans appeared. The coffles walked in single file from the prison and auction house towards a waiting slave ship, the *Prospect*. Denmark followed their movement across the street, scanning their faces.

The few hundred households in town along with the hundred or more farms and plantations scattered throughout the island's countryside depended on the labor of four thousand slaves, yes. But, the engine of the local economy was not agriculture. It was human trafficking. The value of slaves bought and sold on the island far exceeded the value of all other trade goods—sugar, rum, gin, molasses—combined.

That night epitomized what Madame had warned Denmark about. She'd warned him that if he ever "set foot" on another island his fate was beyond her control. Denmark now understood better than ever the fate she'd feared. He knew he would have to make his own way to freedom. Even so, glimpses of the lively gritty atmosphere distracted him, spoiling opportunities he might have taken to peel off from the brothers—to escape.

It was not until the three neared the *Prospect* that Denmark realized the gravity of his delay. Almost too late, Denmark shook off the sudden grasp of the brothers who had anticipated his resistance.

He stepped back and away from them.

The schemer yelled at Denmark as though he were a welcher in some grand bargain. Seeing his brother's verbal abuse fail, the somber brother appealed to the youth in kind tones. With outstretched arms he beckoned Denmark to come closer as though appealing to a reluctant pet.

Denmark remained just beyond arm's reach.

Next, the schemer tried lying while also imploring Denmark to come closer, his arms now also extended. He twisted the storyline, suggesting that Denmark was indeed *lucky* to sail with, "What's his name?" he asked his brother.

"Vesey. Master Thomas distinctly said, Captain Vesey of the *Prospect*. And, here she is."

Denmark jumped into the street, brushing aside all in his way. Madame's voice, freedom, beckoned over the sounds of chains all around him. The shouts of "Stop! Stop that boy!" propelled him onward. He ran as fast as he could.

But he was soon tripped by a stranger.

Denmark immediately smelled the close scent of manure against his nose and tasted blood from his split lip. He saw one of his teeth on the ballast stone pavement as he was forcibly erected from a prone position. The brothers now put a firm hold on him. A splitting headache and aching mouth clouded Denmark's thoughts.

From the bridge of the *Prospect* Captain Vesey watched the advance of the well-dressed mulattos and noted their present trouble with their charge. As the brothers approached again, this time rushing forward with the large Negro child firmly clenched between them, Captain Vesey stopped what he was doing to follow their progress up the gangway.

At thirty-four, Captain Joseph Vesey was already a veteran of the slave trade having shipped out of Bermuda at age twenty. In part to escape his sister's mothering, but also to make room for her growing family. Joseph's parents had both died young. When he was a boy of eleven his father died from a kick to the head by a stubborn mule. When he was thirteen his mother passed away too, the victim of some wasting disease, an undiagnosed cancer. His two sisters had stepped in to raise their handsome brother.

In 1767 the then sociable lad had signed on to a trade schooner, the *Rebecca*, based in Charles Town. As an ordinary seaman shipping rice to Europe and rum to Africa he witnessed the unvarnished truths of slave trading first hand. Through the years, despite most of his time spent at sea, Charles Town became his home.

During the American Revolution Captain Vesey joined the struggle for independence as a rebel privateer. With letters of marque from different ports of call he had an obligation to disrupt and pillage British shipping wherever he found it for the good of the cause. As for himself, he and his crew were eager to keep most of the proceeds as prize money.

By now, word of Washington's victory at Yorktown offered Captain Vesey hope that the British occupation of his city would soon end. Charles Town's large open port had always made her vulnerable and the city had finally succumbed to a siege the year before, in May of 1780.

Captain Vesey had been forced to leave behind his new, second wife, Kezia, in the care of friends from Virginia. His first love and wife, a poor immigrant from England he had met in Charles Town as a young man had died of consumption during one of his many long absences at sea. He longed to be reunited with Kezia before Christmas.

Master Thomas's mulattos soon stood silently at attention on either side of Denmark aboard the *Prospect* waiting to be addressed. They thought they were to be expected. To be rewarded for their specific delivery.

They now stared straight ahead. Dressed in silk, at attention, they looked like toy soldiers.

At first, they made the mistake of assuming the state of their damaged goods was the reason for their cool reception. Clearing his throat the schemer said, "Captain Vesey, sir, this is the lad. The slave that Master Thomas spoke of, sir…" imploring the captain's recollection.

Beginning with "What?" the captain then said, "Oh, yes," acknowledging the name. What he recalled was the constant drink-induced chatter of Master Thomas. The little man had strained Captain Vesey's patience with his pompous yet wimpy demeanor and constant banter.

Master Thomas had said something about an incorrigible Negro boy he was including in their business of 390 slaves bound for French St. Domingo. The man had promised that two more "troublesome, high minded" mulattos would arrive with said Negro before he sailed. But none, till now, had materialized, and Captain Vesey was not in a waiting mood, especially not just for them.

"This is the incorrigible?" he asked, referring to Master Thomas's business proposition. "This well dressed child is too much for you to handle, eh?"

Initiating a perfunctory inspection of the merchandise, not admitting witnessing the street commotion, the captain said, "What happened to his face?"

Cognizant that once aboard a slaver they could be cast below and chained to the hull at any moment the twins were suddenly very uncomfortable with their reception. Once at sea there would be nothing to save them. For a long moment, neither twin spoke. Their eyes flitted back and forth to one another. Thoughts of reward gone, each now feared they were on a fool's errand.

The schemer finally spoke, eyes straight ahead.

"The boy tried to escape. He ran. But fell in the attempt."

"Fell, huh?" Captain Vesey said, "Is that the way it happened?" addressing Denmark for the first time. "Is that the way it happened, boy?" the captain repeated.

Not knowing where this line of questioning may lead, Denmark wanted to quell the rising tension on deck. He suspected cruelty within Captain Vesey's voice. All hands on deck ceased to move during their captain's loud humiliation of his visitors.

Seeing no penalty in the twins account and no gain in the truth Denmark stood taller and said in a calm even tone, "Yes, sir. I fell." The few words lingered. They fixed Denmark's standing on deck.

Reverting to French, the somber twin insisted on his reward, more to regain his self-respect than in expectation of money.

The other quickly entreated, in English, without mention of money, "Now that we've discharged our duty, we'll be getting out of your way, Captain," as light-hearted and confident as he could muster while tugging on his brother's coat sleeve.

The captain had crossed his arms in faux suspense, listening, stalling, waiting to catch the eye of his bosun. After a casual nod, Captain Vesey ignored the somber brother's French, and instead addressed the schemer. In a cordial tone, with a gentle bow and the wave of his hand, he said to his bosun, "Albert, escort these gentlemen…below. And, put them in irons!" The threatening nature in his voice sent all aboard into a frenzy of work. Then, to the captain's quip of, "After you strip them of their silks," the crew broke into laughter as the twins were seized.

THIRTY-TWO

If I were a Slave

Captain Vesey summoned the ship's surgeon to examine Denmark's wounds and escort him from the bridge for treatment. Denmark's path took him close enough to the hatch to feel the heat and smell the punch of the stench rising from the hold. He gagged as he walked, contemplating his fate.

The surgeon led Denmark into the ship's mess. Two sailors were leaving the kitchen deck as the surgeon and Denmark entered. The one closest to Denmark recoiled at the sight of the boy's cut, swollen and discolored face; elbowing his mate he cackled, "We've signed a bloody prune, mate!" producing snorts of laughter from two other crew members, seated, eating their gruel.

"Whoa, what hap'n to you, matey?" one of them howled.

"Oh, leave him be, men," the respected surgeon said. "I need his attention."

Being held by the chin, Denmark's aches made him seem uncooperative. Feelings of dejection led him to the verge of shock. Nothing penetrated his own concentration. What saved him were thoughts of ways of staying above deck. That, and counting the number of seamen aboard.

"Hold still." The surgeon's mild mannered demands were designed to be taken in stride. "You'll need a little sewing up. Have you eaten today?"

Realizing he hadn't, a "No" was all Denmark dared say. The surgeon left him saying, "I'll be back, lad." Denmark sat in silence, with his back to the crew.

"Who are you, matey?" one asked Denmark's back.

"What's your name?" another tried, back and forth, again and again the sailors badgered until the captain walked in. Their bench skidded across the mess floor, moved as the sailors rose to attention and tipped their hand in salute.

"At ease, men. At ease," Captain Vesey said. He turned his attention to Denmark. "Where's my surgeon?"

"Here, sir, here," came the winded, harried reply of the ship's last hold on life. "I needed some bandages."

Leaning over, so only the surgeon could hear, the captain told him to take the slave to the officer's quarters and see to him there. He wished to have a word with the boy away from the men. The "Aye, sir," said with a salute was all the sailors knew of the exchange.

The walls and the door the Captain walked through were constructed moments ahead of him, retrieved, unfolded, and put up across the beam expanse of the vessel. The captain's quarters had been disassembled and stowed before as a matter of course, to leave the deck space free for other duty. Manned by an oversized crew of sixty men to administer twelve light swivel cannons, many set to swivel inward, and with almost four hundred slaves below, the *Prospect* rode deep in the water.

Cast off and underway, the ship swayed and creaked as Denmark was led to the Captain's quarters and seated in a chair that materialized before his eyes. As Denmark sat down he caught a glimpse of the docks from windows stretching almost the expanse of the captain's cabin.

At first the room was silent as the captain poured a drink and by a tilt of his head induced the surgeon to join him. After a brief contemplation of the harbor and the night lights of the city climbing from its shoreline the captain spoke. "Why are you here?"

The question surprised Denmark. Questions requiring more than a few words were seldom asked of slaves.

"I've been told you've killed four or five people," the captain said slowly pacing in front of the table to which Denmark's chair had been pushed to by the doctor. Talking to himself more than anyone else he added, "Now, *that* behavior would qualify you as an incorrigible, to say the least..." without finishing his sentence, he turned and looked to Denmark, implying he was waiting for Denmark to answer for his presence.

Denmark at first stumbled, "Well, I..." not certain how frank he was allowed to be with these white people. "Those people, the ones you're...someone's...talking about..."

Captain Vesey interrupted, "Well, you're in good hands now."

Denmark ignored the ambiguous statement. To keep the conversation alive, to learn more about his captivity, Denmark asked, "What's our destination?"

"Our next port of call is Cape François. Do you know it?" the captain asked Denmark.

"I know of it, sir," Denmark replied in a manner that insinuated a knowledge of the island's wicked history—one of the deadliest places on earth to be a slave. The island economy was struggling to import more than their usual twenty-five thousand replacement slaves a year. The mortality rate was on the rise as expectations from investors piqued, taxing the tiny French colony's resources to their limit.

The island's four hundred thousand slaves cut and stacked, ground and boiled, packaged and hauled sugar cane or sugar from some seven hundred plantations, producing almost double the yield of its British neighbor, Jamaica. A value that represented one third of France's total foreign income. Income she needed more than ever to pay for her aid to the American rebels fighting her arch enemy, England.

Denmark imagined the horrors that awaited him once he left this state room. If he were ever to reach some accommodation with the captain, he would have to speak his piece. Now.

Before he could get the words out the captain spoke.

The captain had witnessed the boy's ordeal ashore as he had attempted his escape. He admired the way the boy had resisted becoming a rat as he shielded the brothers from the consequences of their lying. It reminded the captain of his days as an ordinary seaman—

of how, even among rivals, lowly sailors stuck together to shield one another from officers threats over minor infractions.

"I'll tell you what, boy. You behave yourself, don't kill anybody, and you can help the cook. Escape the hold."

Stunned by his good fortune Denmark managed to mumble an, "Aye, sir." He stood and saluted as he'd seen the others do.

The second in command knocked and with permission granted entered the cabin to report the ship's course, sailing schedule and duty roster. "Very well, Master Thornhill. Just a moment."

The captain turned to the surgeon, "Doctor, if you please, take the boy with you. Bandage him up and serve him to the cook." Lifting his hand in Denmark's direction Captain Vesey said to the ship's first mate, "Meet our new cabin boy."

To which the amiable Brit said, "Oh, and what's this one called?"

Denmark's voice answered, pronouncing his name with a smile.

Denmark was taken to the surgeon's quarters where the doctor feigned exasperation with, "Finally." Looking around for something specific, the doctor followed with "Sit."

As the bandages went on in the relative quiet of the tiny cabin, Denmark could hear bits and pieces of the slave's wails and cries. But he also heard a low melody. Like the slave song heard on Madame's island that had, like clock-work, demarked his daily routine.

Mornings came early to a ship at sea. And earlier still for a ship's cook of four hundred and fifty. After the officers, the ordinary seamen are fed, followed by multiple vats of slave fare.

The cook ordered Denmark to take the fat-laden swill to guards of the watch and to help them at feeding times. The misery upon the faces of the slaves knows no time of day. Denmark ignored the pitiful expressions the twins cast upon him as he performed his duties. The guilt Denmark felt at the privilege of his station was distorted by the ammonia from the hold's waste that flared his nostrils and watered his eyes.

Once he'd reached topside, by the time he'd traversed the entire boat stem to stern, unmolested, Denmark felt a measure of freedom he hadn't expected when the mulattos first dragged him aboard. In their free time cliques of sailors staked out choice spots on deck to loiter, mostly to gossip about fellow crewmen and officers, or superstitions at sea. But amid these easy hours were those sailors who would cut another's throat at the slightest hint of disrespect or gain in it.

The evening the *Prospect* approached French St. Domingo was rainy, with a chill in the air. Reason enough for the more than usual number of officers to congregate in the captain's quarters. Some lingered after dinner. Others joined them to escape the weather and warm their belly with Caribbean rum.

They began a lively debate about the disposition of the spoils of war now that, with Cornwallis's defeat, the British war effort in North America seemed mortally wounded. The subject of slaves came up; specifically the slaves that had fought for the British in exchange for a promise of freedom. The wisdom of such a turn of events became the hotly debated topic of the evening.

One officer, Jones, the second mate, from Wales, asked Denmark, "What do you think, boy?" as Denmark served more rum to the men gathered around the captain's table.

"Me?" he said, surprised to be asked. He waited for an officer to retrieve a glass from his tray before saying, "Well, free is free, no matter how it comes about. If I were a slave, I'd fight like hell for my freedom." Drawing jeers as well as pats on the back. Second Mate Jones furrowed his brow, regretting that he'd ask the boy's opinion. His captain's reaction to the boy's answer seemed all too predictable.

From his seat behind the table, Captain Vesey said, "That will be all, boy!" loud enough to be heard above all others. Denmark acknowledged the order by taking his leave of the captain's stateroom.

Once the ship was tied off and secured, the slaves were unloaded for their new owner, a factor who would sell them in lots of thirty-five to large plantations miles inland first; the twin's father's plantation among the buyers. The remainder would be offered to small farms along the way back to the bay. Denmark was assigned by Captain Vesey to a detail of sailors dousing the slaves with seawater, much to the slave's surprise as they exited the hatch.

Second Mate Jones supervised the process. As he tallied the headcount, a fight broke out among the slaves. One of two men chained together took a water bucket from a sailor and swung it as a weapon at the others. Clearing a path to the side of the ship they made an awkward but successful leap overboard.

The seconds of silence—the length of time of the fall before the splash—prolonged and heightened the drama. The other slaves took advantage of it. Sensing their opportunity to break free, an uninterrupted flow of slaves from the hold scattered once on deck. Running in all directions, some made it to the dock. Others fled toward the bow, more to the stern, creating havoc both onboard and off.

Jones couldn't keep track of them in all the commotion. Coming to his aid, Denmark helped him sort out the stragglers from onshore, including the twins, and confirm his count; 380. Twelve slaves had died in route to St. Domingo.

For his thanks, Denmark was clasped in irons on command of Captain Vesey.

"But, why?" his voice struggled as he stood still while being shackled. "Haven't I helped you in every way?" the boy pleaded.

Captain Vesey—responding to Second Mate Jones's shock as much as Denmark's—said, "A slave that doesn't know he's a slave is of no use to me." Waving Denmark off, Captain Vesey commanded the deckhands holding him to include the boy with the others being led away.

The boy cried out, wailing and cursing, in French, until his voice faded with the distance. Captain Vesey sailed the *Prospect* back to St. Thomas with money in hand and an order for more slaves—each, like Denmark, destined for one of St. Domingo's early graves.

THIRTY-THREE

Grand Mal

Denmark was sold as part of the first lot let go by the factor. He and his cohorts were divided from the twins and the hundreds of other slaves at a fork in the road, inland. The brothers were later separated. Sold to different plantations where they each died. One within weeks and the other in months. Just miles, only several ridge lines, from where they'd been raised as princes.

After a short walk the crack of a whip could be heard in the cane fields cultivated in every direction. Denmark saw a single black head pop out from around the tall rows of stalks—gazing at the pack of new arrivals—and heard the slave pay for her moment of idleness. Her shrieks from the pain of an old wound, re-opened, traveled the sloping fields on either side of the rugged dirt road.

Before Denmark's group was led to their quarters they made a brief appearance on the lawn of the big house. Denmark could see the white owner, who insisted on being addressed as "Seigneur," as he stood on the veranda some one hundred feet away. With his hand extended, he moved it across the group, counting heads with his finger.

The plantation slave street was comprised of eight barracks, four to a side of the rutted lane dividing them. Each dwelling housed twenty or more slaves. Most were young to middle-aged men. Few had lived there long.

Soon the younger slaves of the group, Denmark's age and younger, were being picked over. Either taken to the big house or deemed strong enough for the fields. Denmark felt sure of his own selection for big house duty.

The white overseer said, pointing to Denmark, "*Tu, là-bas! Venir ici!* (You, over there! Come here!)" Denmark stepped toward the man with the whip in his hand trying to not reveal his relief. His hopes vanished with the next order, given to a Negro driver, "*Sangler dans à la poste*. (Tie him to the post.)"

Although he'd rather be brave, not give them the satisfaction of knowing his fear, he screamed like a banshee, recalling Millie's story of her mother. And he remembered his trips to Tortola with Madame. They had witness many wretched souls whipped along the road during their carriage rides through Road Town.

The smelly sweaty *bomba* grabbed Denmark and held him tight. He pushed him toward the lashing post, fitted with chains connected to a rope atop an erect wooden rail. Once his hands were secured the *bomba* tore at Denmark's shirt like a starving man stripping an ear of corn, exposing Denmark's young unblemished back. The driver then pulled tight the rope attached to Denmark's hands, stretching him until he was forced to balance on his toes.

The lashes were fast and deep. His exposed muscle emitted a putrid odor that lingered. Cuts on cuts, one after another, until his back was on fire and his blood soaked his breeches. Pain from the first lashes deadened his senses. So much so that subsequent strikes provided an instant of relief of pain, a sadistic respite from the worst of the burning, throbbing ache. Mercifully he passed out.

The overseer always beat half to death one of the new arrivals in each group, as a lesson to the others. Denmark did not at the time realize how fortunate he was to have been chosen to suffer for his lot.

A doctor who roved the plantations of St. Domingo offering his service—keeping field hands alive for another day's labor—was visiting. The French doctor had begun his career in the slave trade, working with and following in the footsteps of his father. His family had arrived in the Caribbean in 1750, as part of a wave of French Huguenots who'd fled France following the Act of Revocation.

The irony of his prejudice, honed by living the island culture, was lost on him. The barbarity of his world was mundane, brutality banal.

Denmark was brought to him, unconscious. The doctor was asked to make him well enough to work in the fields within days. Often faced with impossible tasks, requiring heroics beyond his ability, he took one look at Denmark's condition and made no promises. Experiences like these, and the attitudes of his forbearers, led him to believe that his work amounted to little more than that of an animal doctor.

The doctor's temporary headquarters was a circular hut of crushed shell walls and a thatched roof near the big house, but closer to the kitchen than the house. As Denmark lay on a filthy wooden table his blood seeped through the cracks of the boards and formed small pools on the dirt floor.

When Denmark regained consciousness—quickly re-acclimated to fear all white men—he flinched then screamed as his skin, glued to the table by his dried blood, ripped open his coagulated wounds. He remained prone along the table, looking up.

The doctor was sitting alone on a wooden chair. Except for the table on which Denmark rested, the chair was the only other furniture in the hut. The stale air in the dark windowless room, moist and cool, was a world apart from the hot, blazing, humid air outside. In the sugar cane fields the heat was powerful enough to be an accessory to murder. The only light in the room was a hole in the roof to accommodate the now cold and empty fire pit.

Talking to himself, as though speaking to the Seigneur, the doctor stood and walked toward Denmark. He asked, "Why should I mend this boy—to have him worked to death in a matter of weeks, or days?"

"Why, indeed?" came the poignant answer, spoken as if said by Seigneur himself. The voice continued as Denmark sat up, "You must need help from time to time, what with disease and beatings and the heat killing off the field hands with regularity."

In addition to Denmark's miraculous resurrection, now seated erect, looking into the doctor's eyes, this insight, coming from a dark skinned slave who spoke like a Frenchman—not of the docks, but of the salons—surprised the doctor.

And what of his clothes? The slave wore breeches and stockings, as fine as his own.

Denmark recognized the doctor's perplexed visage. He had seen it before whenever islanders caught themselves conversing with Denmark as though he were a peer. White islanders were accustomed to addressing slaves as though they were speaking to a trained animal, expecting a nod of the head response and little else.

"Well," replied the doctor, still awed. "No, actually. I get along just fine by myself, *merci*." Moving closer, arms folded across his chest he asked, "And so, from what academy in the sky did you fall? Where did you come from?"

"*Je m'appelle Danemark*," he said. Continuing in French, "I was the property of Madame Marie Rachael Locoul Chevalier. I lived on her island near Tortola. She is responsible for my education."

"*Tu?*" the doctor challenged. He knew, or had met, both Monsieur and Madame Chevalier several times at their Road Town inn and tavern, as a child, on excursions to visit relatives among the islands. The doctor's father would bring Madame books and she in turn would make special meals for him and his son.

While still testing how well his memories had aged, the doctor pictured her and asked, "You say 'lived.' Is she not well?"

"No. She died. I was her servant for seven years. But I'm not anymore. She freed me in her will." Denmark spoke the simple truth in simple language so as to leave no hint of ambiguity.

The complete message nevertheless was obscured by the doctor's preoccupation with the words "died." Madame's death triggered memories of better days, long gone. He saw her smile as she brought out dessert for him alone, in a room full of other patrons. The gesture had made the boy feel special. He could still see the kindness in her face.

Suspicious, and a little jealous, he sat down and interrogated Denmark about how she died, probing Denmark's feelings toward Madame; a childhood hero to the doctor.

Denmark sensed the doctor's inquiry was personal. He asked him, "Did you know her?"

The doctor nodded solemnly.

"Yes. I should say, I met her a few times. Always a pleasure. My father would make a point of visiting her establishment on our travels to Tortola. Madame always remembered my name and my favorite food. Dessert."

Despite the somber nature of the discussion, Denmark was thrilled to know someone else who knew something of what he felt for Madame. Quoting Voltaire's oft-repeated assessment of du Châtelet, Denmark said Madame was, "*Un grand homme dont le seul défaut était femme* (a great man whose only fault was being a woman)."

Both grinned knowingly at the quote.

And, to both his horror and delight, in the span of minutes, the doctor's life changed.

As if in a dream, a fairy tale, the livestock before him had morphed into human form before his very eyes. The reality of Denmark forced the doctor to confront his prejudice. The maltreatment he had witnessed and not prevented over the years. He now saw in the boy what Madame had intended for all to see: humanity; his as well as that of all the other slaves.

The disparity between this young man's obvious education and his circumstances, the doctor felt, must be a mystery to Seigneur—and must remain so. Seigneur would see the boy for what he was in the plantation culture, a freak, an anomaly, a virus that must be eradicated. Seigneur would have him destroyed rather than infect his fields with intelligence.

Standing again, the doctor began to walk in a circle around the chair combing his hands through his hair, unable to map a path for the boy that didn't lead to certain death.

The doctor finally said, "I don't know how or why Madame chose to make you exist, but I can tell you this, there is no place for you on this island. There are some free blacks, yes, but those not the offspring of men like Seigneur, especially darkies like you, lead hard, often short lives."

"But there are so many," the boy entreated, referring to the huge majority of slaves on the island—over 400,000 slaves subjugated by less than 30,000 white people and their confederates.

The doctor rushed Denmark and shook his finger at the boy, "*Do not*...ever speak like that again!" The boy was already proving to be too insightful, and therefore, too dangerous for his own good.

Denmark felt the goodwill built early in their conversation begin to erode.

"And yet," the doctor said as though once again addressing himself as he walked the dirt floor, "there is a way." Denmark waited for some indication of what the man was thinking.

The doctor continued, "There is a seldom used law that guarantees planters quality slaves, money back if the goods are certified as defective."

"I've got it! I'll fake a *grand mal* and you'll attest to its authenticity. Captain Vesey will have to take me back! You're brilliant!" Denmark said to flatter the man. He was relieved to have help escaping the prospect of a short life in the cane fields.

"You know of this? These episodes...you think you can pretend?"

"I've done it before," Denmark said with a wry smile.

Faking an illness could be a difficult performance in and of itself, but feigning gratitude, now, for his return to slaver Vesey, the man who'd left him here to die, felt queer. And for the doctor, contemplating a fraud that maneuvered the boy into the hands of the slaver from whence he'd come was like returning him to the Bastille from the gallows. Still, it was Denmark's best hope.

Questioning his own motives the doctor convinced himself that this one act of altruism began his rehabilitation. It would make up for some of the abuse, rather than care, he had administered to his patients. And he knew it would please Madame. Selfishly, it would also serve as revenge of sorts.

The ruler of the plantation, Seigneur, had refused the doctor's proposal of marriage to his daughter. He'd been told the reason was not his profession or prospects, but his Protestant religion.

The doctor settled for an amalgamation of motives. He would do this for Madame as well as for Denmark and himself.

The doctor admonished the youth, "Despite Madame's wishes, you mustn't proclaim your freedom to anyone." Seeing Denmark's response, the doctor seized on the moment, "Ah, so you know of which I speak. Those who hold you as a slave will accept nothing less from you than displays of subservience."

Telling Seigneur he found Denmark to be in very poor health, and not well suited for field work sowed the doctor's seeds of deception to be harvested later. Explaining that the boy might be dead tomorrow if worked in the sun, the doctor asked if he could hire out the boy. The boy would help him with his rounds to the other plantations, arguing that he would return him in better shape than he found him. The Seigneur agreed on the condition he not be charged for "saving the slave's life."

After months of hearing of the doctor's work among his neighbors, but not seeing him on his plantation, Seigneur sought him out. He found the doctor treating slaves on the property adjacent to his. However, Seigneur was unprepared for what came next. The doctor lit into Seigneur like a gamecock eager to fight, accusing Seigneur of prior knowledge of Denmark's affliction. Complaining that the slave had been more of a burden than an assistant, the doctor demanded a payment of ten francs.

The ploy worked. Seigneur was so full of angst, not only at the doctor's accusation, but of his announcement of it in front of his neighbor that he behaved in a manner more gracious and generous than he would have otherwise.

Proclaiming his innocence, Seigneur said the doctor could keep the boy if he wished, or, if the doctor would return the boy to the factor or dishonest slaver, Seigneur would not only pay him for his trouble he would reward him with ten francs for recouping his investment.

One day, a week later, word arrived that slavers soon would lay in wait in the Cape Francois harbor. So the doctor took his charge to the docks in search of a ship out.

There they bumped into Seigneur as he was in discussions with the very factor who bought Denmark from Captain Vesey. Their appearance reminded the two men of the purchase in question. And, unbeknownst to Denmark or the doctor, Captain Vesey's *Prospect* was among the slavers anchored in the harbor.

As the men argued, doubting Denmark's affliction, the boy reprised his act. He fell to the pier. He began to quiver and shake, wriggling in fits and spurts. The unusual sight amid the foot traffic attracted an instant crowd, among them Captain Vesey.

As they had rehearsed, the doctor set about comforting and administering to the spasmodic youth, putting a leather-bound stick into Denmark's mouth. Denmark bit down hard, just as they had practiced, and the crowd held its collective breath.

In a few moments, the fake *grand mal* subsided and men began to return to their work. Seigneur exclaimed, "He's diseased! I told you! I demand his price be returned!"

Another man shouted, "Shoot him!"

As one man reached for his pistol the others close to the action stepped back.

"Don't! Stop! Put that thing away," came a voice before the execution could take place. It was Captain Vesey. "I'll take the boy back," Captain Vesey said. The doctor followed the crowd away from the spectacle.

Captain Vesey pointed to the boy at the men's feet, signaling to Second Mate Jones to collect him. Jones picked up Denmark from the pier timbers, and when he was close, face-to-face with Denmark, the second mate winked his approval of the boy's performance.

Captain Vesey stepped forward to join the remaining gentlemen in a little business. He agreed to settle for the sale of the boy. Then, as though no disagreement had transpired, he discussed with the gentlemen on the dock their demand for still more slaves. His question of "Who would be interested in a cargo of saltwater blacks?" elicited the response he'd hoped for. All was cordial again. He concluded with, "Gentlemen, I'll be back in port soon."

THIRTY-FOUR

Newly Christened

Determined to stay topside, out of the hold, Denmark sought to demonstrate his value to Captain Vesey.

Within a week of his reprieve from the threat of premature death on a St. Domingo plantation Denmark achieved his objective. During a slave purchase on the island of Martinique, an estate sale, Denmark detected a counting error—related in French—an error worth several times his own price on a slave auction block.

As his reward Denmark found that as long as he did what he was told, without mention of his freedom, he was allowed a certain measure of it. Free to roam the deck while not on duty, his greatest solace came from another new privilege as cabin boy; access to books stowed in the captain's quarters; a privilege normally reserved for officers of the *Prospect*. However, Denmark's proximity to the hold's hatch served as a constant reminder to the young man of his precarious status—apart from his brethren chained to the hull.

In time, Denmark managed to learn more about life on Captain Vesey's ship including its subtle and not-so-subtle rules of conduct. He became an accepted fixture among the crew.

Denmark gravitated to the free black sailors onboard. They offered him tips and advice for comfort and survival. Like how to ward off rat bites in the night by wrapping himself just so in the canvas of his hammock. To soak hardtack in his daily ration of grog; softening the rock hard bread into a malleable mush. Or, to hold his nose while eating spoiled beef and— in contrast to Madame's orders—to chew with his mouth open.

During the *Prospect*'s many months at sea, the American war with England came to an end. On that news, and news of peace talks,

Captain Vesey set the *Prospect*'s course for his hometown, newly christened "Charleston."

THIRTY-FIVE

Not What You Think

At the Charleston Bar, the captain's dream of home put his mind at ease. But when the *Prospect* arrived at the wharfs, reality unnerved the battle hardened veteran. A flotilla of British flags hugged the shoreline of the liberated port. Ships of all sizes commissioned by His Majesty's navy were preparing to carry away from Charleston all those still loyal to the crown.

Among those boarding or waiting to board were thousands of blacks, many of whom had flocked to the British lines during the siege and occupation of Charleston. All attracted by a promise of freedom in return for their service. Denmark was entranced by the sight of them. As Second Mate Jones recounted their story to him as Denmark scanned their faces, as always, looking for the familiar.

Denmark's longing, his constant search, forced his mind into a double-take that snapped his head. There, at the bow of a ship, he could have sworn, just for a moment, that he had seen his mother and sister. *They just hadn't seen him*, he thought. His conjecture was as confounding as absolute knowledge. The thought that he'll never know, or that he couldn't be sure, increased his anxiety as the British ship moved away. Though Koi had told Denmark of seeing Sade, on St. Eustatius, without his mother, Denmark continued to hope that someday he would find them. At that very moment he fantasized about rounding a Charleston corner to find himself face to face with them, Koi on their arm. His finger twitched.

The crowd ashore booed loud and cheered louder still, all waving, all excited at the sights and sounds of the British departure. Along the docks and East Bay Street, among throngs of jeering crowds heckling the Loyalists waiting to board was the second Mrs. Captain Joseph

Vesey, Kezia. When the *Prospect* glided to rest at Gadsden's Wharf along the Cooper River Mr. Christopher Gadsden himself was among the crowd. The space at his wharf was available only because Mr. Gadsden had denied the British navy's request to dock there.

In the early years of the revolution, William Henry Drayton, head of the Continental Congress' Committee of Secret Correspondence—and the South Carolina provincial government in waiting—asked Captain Vesey, already a noted privateer, to retrieve Gadsden and other delegates from the 1774 Continental Congress in Philadelphia. During their return voyage, well north of Charles Town, the British man-o-war *Syren* intercepted the ship assigned to Captain Vesey, a lightly armed brigantine, the *Hawke*.

Rather than risk an engagement, and the capture of his rebel elite, Captain Vesey beached the *Hawke* and led the delegates and his crew to safety on foot. Gadsden never forgot the cool headed young captain. And Captain Vesey accepted Gadsden's aid and influence thereafter. Indeed he would capitalize on the association at every opportunity he could for the rest of his life.

Post-revolution, Gadsden wasn't about to grant privileges to those who had threatened him at every turn and had imprisoned him for almost a year after the capitulation of Charleston.

Captain Vesey disembarked at the touch of the *Prospect*'s gangplank to the wharf into the arms of his wife and that of his wife's friend from Norfolk. Denmark watched as the happy couple rode away in a carriage driven by a well-dressed Negro.

Second Mate Jones and the *Prospect*'s crew immediately set sail again. Their destination was nearby Sullivan's Island to unload the *Prospect*'s cargo. The island held a quarantine pen for large shipments of newly arrived slaves. There they would remain for weeks to prevent outbreaks of disease. They would be fed, cleaned and clothed before their eventual sale at auction in Charleston.

Although Captain Vesey had given Jones an address and directions intended for Denmark—a new assignment and station within Captain Vesey's dealings—given his duties as acting captain, Jones had neglected to inform Denmark of it before the *Prospect* set sail again. As the ship approached, drawing ever closer to the isthmus of Sullivan's Island, Denmark could smell the encampment long before it came into close view. The bay's salt air began to reek like the belly of the *Prospect*'s hold.

With no instructions from Captain Vesey, indeed without a word as to his fate, Denmark could not be sure he was not meant to join the cargo of slaves, again, just as on St. Domingo. Standing on the bridge with Second Mate Jones, Denmark sprung into frantic action determined to not be led ashore in chains. He ran to and manned a swivel gun, pointing it inward toward the helm where Jones stood.

"Denmark! Get away from that! This instant! Calm down," Jones said realizing his error, what was happening, what must be going through the boy's mind.

"I'm not going ashore! I can't!" Denmark shouted.

Moving toward Denmark's perch behind the un-primed, harmless gun the second mate held his palms out, his arms wide, as he continued to move closer. "Denmark, it's not what you think," he said as he walked closer. He looked cautiously to see who else besides the helmsman might be watching. He wanted to end the scene before others became aware of it.

Denmark's thoughts, his fear, of jumping overboard before the ship could make landfall ended when Jones's hand reached the boy's arm. He handed Denmark a piece of paper with Captain Vesey's order to report to an address written on it. The paper detailed a crude map of the city's streets. Relieved, weak-kneed, a wave of calm pulsed Denmark's body as his senses returned to him; horrified at how close he'd come to an act of desperation.

THIRTY-SIX

A Little Sugar

Denmark remained onboard for the short return sail across the harbor to Charleston. The order to appear in his pocket reminded him he was still not free.

"Where is this place, Master Jones?" Denmark asked.

"Near as I can tell from the map it's on the same road as all of the docks. It's called East Bay Street. It shouldn't be hard to find."

"And what about you? Where are you staying? What's to become of you, and the crew?" Denmark demurred, realizing the finality of their conversation.

"Staying? Why, laddie, I won't be staying. Me, and all the crew, are to find new arrangements. A new ship and a new captain. Captain Vesey intends to retire from the sea, here in Charleston, with you as his right-hand man," Jones said with an avuncular smile.

After the remaining cargo of sugar and molasses was ashore, the crew were paid and said their goodbyes, all headed to many of the same back-alley taverns, brothels and boarding houses that accommodated the waterfront district.

Denmark had never seen a port the size of Charleston; two, three and four story buildings, one after another extending as far as his eyes could see, with church spires reaching skyward. Alone, he made his way off the wharf past a contingent of American soldiers marching in formation on the parade grounds of the Federal Green outpost.

The stark white streets of sand and crushed seashells, refracting the afternoon sun, proved blinding in spots as the boy walked past the smell and smoke of distilleries whose whiffs of gin and rum mixed with the odor of low tide and manure, creating a stench the affluent citizens of Charleston managed to avoid, mostly.

The freedom enjoyed by the black Brits did not escape the attention of the enslaved working the docks, nor Denmark. The boy considered trying to blend in with a group of the Loyalist blacks boarding a ship, bound for freedom. But British sentries and a scrum of white Charleston hecklers, eager to hurl their parting insults, checked Denmark's idea.

Further down East Bay Street, crossing Governor's Bridge, on the inland side, Denmark watched money changing hands—between black hands—at makeshift stands of oranges from Spanish Florida, pineapples and bananas from Cuba, melons from the countryside, reed baskets. All manner of goods on display lined each side of the malodorous tide pool that flowed beneath the bridge he walked. Some stands had temporary roofs to shade the goods. At others the seller simply spread out wares on blankets on the ground.

Once across the bridge, keeping to the route marked by Captain Vesey, Denmark walked straight ahead. The docks and warehouses receding from view gave way to storefronts with apartments above. Ahead stood a busy harness shop and stable, a grocer sweeping a stoop, a woman fetching water from a public well. As he walked Denmark was catching up to a slow walking man in the road hunched over carrying a full burlap sack of oysters on his back. Three wagon loads of rice and indigo in a hurry passed by Denmark destined for the docks. A carriage manned and occupied by well-dressed Negroes also passed by the hunched man and Denmark. Its passing raised a fine dust and the quiet ire of the rest among the streetscape—all Negroes. In fact, everyone Denmark laid eyes on since leaving the hecklers was black. Even fashionably dressed pedestrians were as dark or light as the rings of a tree. Denmark marveled at the sight: a black city, just as Koi had described.

The neighborhood improved with every step Denmark took, paper in hand. With church bells peeling the late afternoon hour the most magnificent public building Denmark had ever seen came into view, the Exchange & Customs House. Built by slaves at the head of a deliberate display of largesse, Broad Street, the Exchange was a location sure to figure prominently in Denmark's future.

At the corner of Broad and East Bay while alternating his attention from the sights to his hand drawn directions, Denmark bumped into the first white man he'd seen away from the docks. The encounter so startled Denmark he dropped the paper map.

The man's curious appearance flummoxed him. The bearded man was dressed all in black. A long black curl of hair dangled on either side of his face from beneath his hat. His curls bounced against his graying black beard as he reached, unsuccessfully, to retrieve Denmark's paper from the sidewalk. A gust of bay wind swept it away, into and down the street.

When the man had reached for the paper his coat sleeves rode up his arms and Denmark recognized the scars on the man's wrists. Scars left by shackles worn too long. The man noticed Denmark's keen observation.

Once Adam stood erect, to break the awkward silence he said, "Well, hello, young man. Was it important?"

"My directions. To my master's shop. I'm new to town," Denmark managed to say before remembering his manners. "Sorry, I bumped into you that way. I wasn't looking where I was going."

"That's all right. What's your master's name? What manner of business is he engaged in?" the stranger asked.

"Captain Vesey, sir. Truth be told, sir, I don't know. He's been a slaver. His second mate said he'd decided to retire from the sea, here in Charleston."

"Well, *Mann tracht und Gott lacht*," the stranger chuckled as much to himself as to put Denmark at ease. "Tell you what…you're walking in the direction of a number of new business establishments, on this street, just the other side of Broad," he said, pointing for Denmark's benefit. "You keep walking and you'll likely find your way soon enough. All right?"

"Yes, sir. Thank you, sir. Good day to you."

"And to you," the man said continuing his gaze into Denmark's eyes as he walked away in the opposite direction down East Bay Street.

Denmark continued his trek, following the strange stranger's directions. At a row of colorful three story buildings in the next block he spied an address number close to the one he thought he remembered from the paper. Across the street he spied a more modest, vacant structure on the corner of a ballast stone alleyway to the waterfront. Denmark looked into the large storefront window and saw a candle being lit inside the empty building. The candle illuminated Captain Vesey's familiar silhouette. Denmark crossed the street.

"Ah, there you are. Right on time, young man," the captain said. While using the one candle to light others in the front room, the captain went on, "This is my new engine of commerce, conveniently vacated by Loyalists. From here I'll trade in goods from the Indies, taking advantage of my contacts there. This colony, this state, will see a post-war boom. I'm sure of it. And I aim to do my part to profit from it."

Denmark picked up a broom without instruction and began sweeping the day's accumulation of Charleston's peculiar dust from the floor. The captain's new occupation as maritime merchant meant Denmark too had a new role, that of urban slave.

Satisfied with his new shop and anxious to return to his son and his wife (who'd be dead in a year's time) the captain escorted Denmark up Broad Street toward 281 King Street where the captain had ensconced his household.

As the two walked Denmark thought what he dared not speak; that *in a city of Negroes, they should not tolerate the harsh rule of whites*. The bell towers tolled as the late autumn evening sun began to set on the horizon.

As Captain Vesey and Denmark walked past St. Michael's church, Denmark realized why the Negroes seemed so compliant and industrious without supervision. The barrel of a musket protruded from the church's spire, held by a sentry whose face was concealed within the bell's shadow. Then, a sound akin to the talking drums of

Denmark's childhood reverberated throughout the streets and alleyways.

"What's that?" Denmark asked.

A city guard patrol of six rounded the corner to Broad from Meeting Street. Captain Vesey's serene expression changed. Just yards away from them, the guards accosted the hunched over man Denmark had pasted earlier carrying his heavy burlap burden of oysters.

Toward the end of the man's journey from the wharfs to his master's dwelling he had stopped to rest his weary back in the glow of dusk—the very moment the drums sounded each day reminding all slaves to be off the streets by sundown. The beat scored the limits of a slave's discretion in Charleston.

The six man patrol—not professional soldiers or even militia but poor whites working for wages—took pleasure in their work and made sport of their discovery. The man's explanation that the load he carried for his master was to blame engendered hysterical laughter from the patrol rather than sympathy, and a taunt; a promise to the man of "a little sugar" as his solace—a symbol of their power.

To this the man screamed, "No! God, no!" as though the men had threatened to murder a loved one. He began to run, but was overtaken before he could make his escape.

The "sugar" euphemism referred to a trip to the Work House. An old warehouse where no work, except that of a whip, took place. The building had been altered for effect and utility. A façade of towers and bars provided the desired effect. And a single room equipped with walls full of sand, insulation to muffle the cries day and night, provided the utility. Getting "a little sugar" meant getting a whipping at an old sugar warehouse.

While witnessing the encounter in the street Captain Vesey shoved Denmark and commanded, "Move on," as though Denmark too might otherwise have "a little sugar" in store for him.

THIRTY-SEVEN

Koi?

Before the revolution, though not the largest city by population, Charles Town was by far the richest per capita of any of His Majesty's North American colonial outposts. Or so it seemed. Her purported wealth—a fiction measured by the value of her slaves, bought in large part on credit—exceeded that of all of the other leading cities combined. She dominated the slave trade of North America as St. Thomas dominated it in the Caribbean.

Post-revolution—after years of war without productive commerce, crippled by rampant inflation and debt, bereft of basic necessities—as part of a new state, a new Republic, even one reeling from privation, white Charlestonians were overjoyed with their new reality. They were finally free of redcoats and the yoke of royal decree. An air of the possible pervaded every white citizen's thoughts and actions.

The fortunes of the enslaved were tied to the fortunes of their masters as much as to the local and national economies.

Captain Vesey soon sold the *Prospect* and within a few months had expanded his new business venture, moving from being not only a wholesaler but a retailer as well. On the 24th of September, 1783, he advertised 104 slaves for sale in the *South Carolina Gazette*. Slaves that had been imported aboard two ships, the *Polly* and the *Eagle*, were auctioned off at the Widow Dewee's 43 Queen Street establishment.

Charleston, indeed the entire new nation, witnessed a population boom throughout the decade of the 1780s unequaled in American history. Waves of immigrants and immigrant families arrived among trade goods delivered from abroad and with them came a demand for still more trade goods to sustain them.

To augment their income, all along the eastern seaboard, but especially in urban settings like Charleston, slave owners engaged in a rather peculiar though well-established custom; that of hiring out one's slaves to others for wages. In Charleston, among other occupations, these slaves worked the docks and rope factories, in stables and hotels, as carpenters and artisans as well as in the brickyards, lumberyards and saw mills. The slaves gave the bulk of their wages to their owners, but were allowed to keep a small portion of their hard earned income. Captain Vesey himself participated; he too was the absentee owner of four slaves that did not dwell at his domicile but whose labor nonetheless lined his pockets.

For the next several years Denmark shared a room with Caesar—Mrs. Vesey's friend's slave—above the kitchen, located across the backyard from the privy. Another two slaves, Nell and Ambrosia, slept in the home's garret. While Denmark worked as his master's assistant at the shop on East Bay Street by day and as Captain Vesey's manservant by night, Caesar hired-out his time to the city, cleaning manure and other refuse from streets. Bringing his wages home to his mistress. Working away from a master's watchful eye, with coins in their pocket, the hired-out slaves of Charleston and other cities created an underground economy and a social network not possible in the countryside.

By the mid-1780s, amid an abundance of available labor the demand for slaves waned, leading to hushed conversations that broached the question of slavery's demise. Manumissions were on the rise—often the result of a slave buying his or her freedom with money they had saved. So too were manumission societies from New York to North Carolina that advocated for and even fostered the practice.

Life on Sundays in Charleston was like no other time of the week. As was the custom all over America, on the Christian Sabbath, slaves were allowed to roam freely on their own accord, like Denmark on Madame's island. The more industrious slaves, especially those not able to hire themselves out during the week sought employment that day, while the rest took advantage of the freedom to shop, rest and play. Hundreds, sometimes thousands of slaves descended on Charleston from all directions of the surrounding countryside. They came in long canoes from the Sea Islands, on foot from inland farms and plantations, and on ferries from across the Cooper and Ashley rivers. Among those busy offering their goods for sale, most would just congregate, mingle and enjoy a day of measured, pseudo freedom.

One summer Sunday in 1787—on Denmark's one day of rest— Captain Vesey made Denmark perform what had become the most disheartening duty required of him.

"Denmark, I have a special shipment arriving today at Prioleau's Wharf, down from the shop, near the Fish Market. I need you to go and fetch some Negroes I've purchased."

Despite market changes the captain had continued his old ways, albeit on a smaller scale, buying and selling slaves like cases of nails, kegs of rum or other cargo. It was Denmark's responsibility to keep tabs on his inventory and transact some business in the captain's absence.

On this errand for Captain Vesey, Denmark walked through the heart of the slave's Sunday revelry near the water's edge at Governor's Bridge like an undertaker on duty. Again he would have to witness the look on a chained slave's face, a look he himself had projected—the gaze of a slave upon an approaching master. Only now, he was the one they feared on sight. Now, he was the one who seemingly held their fate in his hands.

At the end of Prioleau's Wharf, among the barrels and crates stood two slaves, both with their backs to Denmark's approach. One was a boy dressed in rags, no older than Denmark was five years ago when he was brought to this unique black city run like an ornate bacaroon. The value of the boy's labor made opulence and extravagance the norm; the value of the young woman standing next to the boy—barefoot in a torn evening dress—provided one of the concomitant perversions of such wealth. A perversion Captain Vesey's concubine cargo was meant to capitalize on.

At the sound of Denmark's footsteps on the wharf the boy turned around. As his chains clinked he puffed his chest like a rooster and stood stoically waiting for Denmark's reaction to the brand on his face: "R" for runaway. The young woman, less eager to face her next oppressor remained looking out at the placid tepid bay as she placed her hand on the boy's shoulder to calm him.

"Where...did you get that?" Denmark said at the sight of the ring on her finger—the mourning ring he'd given Koi.

"Telemaque?" The young woman said, questioning her hearing as she snapped her face Denmark's way. He'd not heard his name, his African name, in many years.

"Koi?" Denmark said with a look on his face as though he'd seen a ghost, or a dream come true. He looked through her swollen cheek, through the years, to see once again the most beautiful creature on earth. Koi hid her black eye with her hand—put there by a white wife, fed up with her husband's dalliances.

She rushed to embrace him. She held him as tight as the piece of flotsam that had saved her from the sinking *Vasa*. The length of chain she wore couldn't restrain her emotions nor the flow of tears that began to pour down her cheeks.

Not another word was spoken as the two held each other. Their silent embrace continued for minutes on end as the two melted into one another's consciousness, leaving the bewildered boy to his jealous gaze and thoughts of running while he had the chance.

THIRTY-EIGHT

As Upset as Koi

Fished from the sea at Madame's island, at first Koi had been sent to Master Thomas's kitchen where she was watched over and nurtured by some of the same house maids that had once nursed Denmark back to health after his precarious arrival in the New World.

As she grew into a noticeably beautiful woman, Master Thomas christened her "Cleopatra," and sold her at the same auction house where Adam had purchased her over a decade earlier. She'd then been traded from one plantation to another like a prized mare. Though traded often she was always careful to conceal her mourning ring, her only tangible reminder that Denmark and a previous life once existed. The ring was her only tie to her former self. To a life she had once dreamed could be theirs. Now, while still in Denmark's arms, she dared dream again.

As the two swayed, a subtle sway, in gentle love, Denmark held Koi's warm embrace with a strength equal to her reluctance to let go. He was dumbfounded that the woman—the dead woman—of his dreams now derived comfort in his arms.

He hadn't spoken her name in years. Even now as he tried to accept the impossible, he questioned reality again, aloud.

"Koi? I can't believe my senses."

"Yes, Telemaque. It's me."

She'd learned tidbits of his fate from the gossip of kitchen maids of Master Thomas. She realized he couldn't know she'd survived the sinking of the *Vasa*.

"How can it be?" he said, still astonished but now more light-hearted even as a tear ran down his cheek.

"Fishermen pulled me from the wreckage after the ship went down. I been," she hesitated, "around the world! Hoping I'd see you again." Koi never forgot the plans they'd made. Or Madame Chevalier. She had felt as crushed by Madame's death that day as by the sea. She knew nothing in her new world would be as pure as what she'd witnessed and desired on that little island. Now that handsome boy stood before her, a strong, tall, broad shouldered man.

Once the two disentangled from one another Koi said, "This here's Isaac. He's from Norfolk. Where we just come from. You're looking all grown up, Telemaque. What are you doing here? Who's your master? Is he good to you?" she was firing questions faster than could be answered to keep from addressing his.

Nodding in recognition of Isaac, the young boy did not return the gesture, aware that Denmark, like all he encountered, was examining the brand on his cheek.

Koi smiled, wiping away her tears. She took Denmark by the arm and began walking down the wharf as though eager to see the sights of Charleston again, albeit through one swollen eye, trying to ignore her bracelet of chains. The boy followed, with Denmark peering over his shoulder every chance he could.

Denmark took them across the street from the wharf to a blacksmith's shop to remove Koi's chains. Koi looked into Denmark's heart when it was the boy's turn. After a moment's doubt, recalling the last time he'd worn shackles, Denmark ordered the boy's removed too.

The three walked down East Bay Street, across the malodorous tide pool beneath Governor's bridge, then inland on Hassel Street toward King, a route Koi seemed to direct more than Denmark. After passing the site of the new Jewish synagogue, when they reached King Street Koi begged Denmark to let them walk in the opposite direction of Captain Vesey's house. Denmark could not say no to Koi. He glanced again over his shoulder to see the boy obediently follow as they walked toward Adam's family home just off King—Koi's tie to a previous life in Charleston.

Absent Augustus to greet him, Adam was opening the front door himself to enter the house when Koi, Denmark and the boy approached. Koi immediately recognized her old master and called out to him. When he turned to the sound of his name Denmark recognized Adam's face as the strange man he'd bumped into the day he landed in Charleston. Seeing Koi, even through the years, Adam dropped his groceries from the market. He ran to embrace her—the embodiment of his past, his family—this time, as upset as Koi.

Then, "Where have you been?" both seemed to ask at once. Adam asked about his family. Koi about Augustus and Beulah, The African and Statia. As each offered explanations, Adam's eyes met Denmark's. Koi broke their excited exchange to introduce Adam to Denmark.

"We've met," Adam said, also recalling their brief encounter. Denmark nodded and said, "Yes, sir" as the two shook hands. Koi was, of course, surprised, but pleased. Adam turned with concerned attention to Koi's state, her bruised face, her dirty dress in tatters. Koi noticed the scars on Adam's wrists. Denmark looked to the boy.

"He's gone!" he said, interrupting Koi and Adam mid-sentence. In agitated distress, he exclaimed again "The boy's gone!" addressing himself as much as anyone.

Denmark began a frantic search, running all the way down to the street corner and back, returning breathless and sweaty. Bent over, exhausted, with his hands on his knees, heaving, he shrieked in anguish, as much for the boy as for himself. Denmark knew the punishment in store for them both, as did Koi and Adam.

Denmark insisted and the others agreed they must look for him immediately in hopes of finding him before the city guard. Adam walked in the opposite direction of Denmark and Koi who hurried down King Street in the direction of Captain Vesey's house.

THIRTY-NINE

Plans

Denmark and Koi found Captain Vesey at the front door of his home, talking to a slave patrol ready to begin their evening routine before the sound of the drums, the boy in hand.

"You're lucky I was outside, and alert. The patrol picked him up right away. A slave boy running through the streets with an R branded into his cheek never gets far. I saw them grab him and inquired" the captain said. "His scar should have warned you of his reputation. Anyhow, the Work House will keep him until tomorrow," Captain Vesey said without anger to settle the matter, and to reassure Denmark he would not be subjected to the boy's fate.

"Yes, sir," Denmark said, head down, looking at the sidewalk as the guard marched the youth to be whipped and imprisoned. Captain Vesey took the opportunity to ogle Koi before clearing his throat and commanding Denmark to take "the girl" to Nell and Ambrosia, out back, in the kitchen.

"Yes, sir."

Late that night Captain Vesey awoke for no reason, he thought. As he stood to urinate into a chamber pot he peered through his bedroom window and watched as Denmark led Koi by the hand across the home's small backyard, in the direction of Denmark's room above the kitchen. Denmark had the room to himself ever since the day Caesar had been allowed to use his wages to rent a room "abroad," in town, but away from his owner.

As a veteran of the sea, once a young man in port himself, he let it go, thinking *let him have his turn for free.*

That night Koi asked Denmark to jump the broom with her. And he did.

The next day Denmark woke in a bliss he'd never known.

But his bliss turned to fear the moment he realized he was alone.

"Koi?"

Denmark asked Nell and Ambrosia about Koi when they arrived to cook breakfast, but they knew nothing. He approached Captain Vesey at first light, determined to alter the day—what he feared. Although he knew the Captain's ways—buy low and sell high, immediately—he told Captain Vesey of his love for Koi. That he wanted her as his wife. That she was his "Juliet." He made it plain to Captain Vesey he would do anything for Koi. He said he had made plans for them, as a couple, without mention of the night before.

The captain deemed Denmark's "plans" remark dangerous and all the more reason to be rid of the young beauty. No slave of his, be he shop assistant, manservant or cabin boy was to assert any rights or control of his own destiny. No "plans." Apparently Denmark, the captain judged, must re-learn the captain's practices and his place, to know it, once and for all.

The captain flattered himself that Denmark's "presumptions" were the captain's own fault. That, because of his own magnanimity, the easy life he'd allowed his property to enjoy, the young man had gone astray. Besides, the captain surmised that—without knowledge of Denmark and Koi's long shared history—Denmark's behavior was just that of a precocious young man, nothing more. A passing fancy to be forgotten no sooner than he'd laid eyes on some new, prettier young slave girl. The captain didn't understand, couldn't understand, did not want to understand, the life changing consequences of his actions.

At the Widow Dewee's all the slaves were herded into a pen behind the auction block. Standing shoulder to shoulder, the men were shackled and bare-chested. The women were unfettered in all manner of dress. Some searched the eyes of the white men around them for clues as to the scale of their leanings; misanthropic, harsh or benevolent. Others averted their eyes in shame or fright.

The men examined every aspect of a slave's body and bid accordingly. Men of a certain age commanded hundreds, women a little less. A beauty, especially a high-yellow or a dark African queen, elicited shouts of sometimes thousands.

Denmark got there in time for them to see each other again. Koi atop of the small stage, Denmark at the front doorway of the cavernous hall. When the bidding for Koi started Denmark's heart rose into his throat, seeing the love of his life, his lover, his wife, being traded like Sea Island cotton and thinking of how she must feel just now.

"Sold! Fifteen hundred dollars. You may claim your prize," the auctioneer said to hoots, hollers and flailing arms.

A man dressed in fine silk and linen escorted Koi through an arched side doorway to a waiting carriage. She'd not seen Denmark in the crowded hall. Or, if she had, she pretended well, ignoring him for his own good.

In the span of but a few minutes Koi was gone, again.

On foot, Denmark followed the carriage down Queen Street and then to the docks. He watched from a distance as Koi and her new master boarded a ship flying a British flag. As he walked closer a feeling of the familiar struck him. Closer still he could see the name of the ship emblazoned across her bow. Koi had been put aboard the *Libertas*.

FORTY

Blurry Limits

The next morning at breakfast Nell and Ambrosia told Denmark a man had come by the afternoon before, asking about Koi.

"He wanted to buy her," Ambrosia said with conviction.

"A Jew," Nell said.

As she returned to rolling more biscuit dough, Ambrosia said, "He sho' was peculiar."

Denmark set out for Adam's house.

Adam answered Denmark's knock and invited him inside. The entryway was bathed in light streaming through the tinted glass skylight Denmark observed high above through three stairwells. Just as Koi had described. There was a musty scent in the air.

Beyond the vestibule the house was dark. In part because the day was rainy, but more so because all the curtains were drawn. Even in poor light anyone could walk freely throughout the almost empty house. It was devoid of furniture. All carted away onto ships by retreating British officers at the wars end, before they evacuated the city. Adam directed Denmark to two wingbacked chairs facing one another at the hearth of the parlor fireplace. It smelled of wet ashes.

"She's gone," Denmark began.

Adam sat up, to the edge of his chair, his mouth opened at the news, but he didn't respond except to shrink back and bury his shoulders deep into the chair. After a few moments passed Adam said, "I came by." Instinctively, almost adding, "to buy her," but his lessons learned from Augustus, Beatrice, Beulah and Koi stopped him.

"I know. Thank you for trying. That's what I came for. To tell you and to thank you."

Adam just nodded. The two men sat in silent commiseration in the near dark for some time, each reflecting on their own private misery that slowly coalesced.

"What are you going to do?" Adam asked.

"What can I do?"

Adam nodded again, acknowledging the answer he hoped for. Hoping the young man was not planning something…foolish.

From Koi Denmark had heard so much about the man sitting across from him. About his family and his cadre of attendant Negroes. He couldn't resist asking him a few questions. Denmark started with the obvious.

"Where did you get those scars?"

Adam, taken aback at first, thought Denmark's question to be fair enough.

"They're from shackles, as you know," he said looking into Denmark's eyes even through the poor light. "I suppose Koi has told you the story of our island. Of being overrun by the British. My boy and I," here his voice cracked; he had to stop, to pause. "My oldest, James, and I were shipped to England. My boy died en route, along with many others. I don't know why I survived the voyage. As we approached the British Isles our convoy was attacked by the French. The prize ships were confiscated but the prison ships were not. I remained in the squalor of a prison ship at anchor in the Thames for months on end. Intended for transfer to Fleet or Newgate prison, I suspect. And a hanging from the Tyburn Tree."

Mesmerized, Denmark, ever a student of escape, asked, "How did you get away?"

"God only knows, *Mann tracht und Gott lacht*," Adam said. He continued, "One night the guards unchained me and took me topside. For what, to this day, I cannot fathom. I took the liberty to jump ship. I'll never forget the sound of musket balls hitting the water all around me. But I made it to shore and walked almost straight into the arms of a rebel's family. The widow and companions of Francis Salvador, a Jew of some notoriety in these parts. He was hailed a hero by American Patriots for his role in their revolution. Well, anyway, they cared for me, nursed me back to health and smuggled me out of London on a ship bound for Charleston, no less. So, here I am. All alone and almost penniless. I've survived. I've been trying to regain my footing on the small commission from the sale of another of Francis Salvador's property, in the frontier district. And the sale of a shoddy warehouse I'd tried to sell before the war, and some paltry rents I collect on my other few remaining Charleston properties. I sent the real estate sale money to his family back in London, of course. The other day, when I approached your master's house, I didn't have the kind of money..." Adam's voice trailed off. He knew from his lessons better than to finish the thought.

Denmark raised his chin a little, knowing the rest of the sentence he didn't want voiced either.

"I was going to offer a promissory note to the captain, if he would only wait for the money..." again, Adam had learned when to stop. Adam didn't mention his intent to revive his variolation scheme. A business venture he reasoned would endure beyond Koi's beauty.

Denmark looked at Adam and saw another Madame Chevalier or Captain Palmer.

In the months to come, Denmark found little solace in the consoling words of his Charleston friends. One such friend, Jack Pritchard, known as Gullah Jack—a shaman of Obeah he met at the Sunday market—vowed incantations to hex Koi's new master; a spell to ensure the master derived no pleasure from his purchase. "Like vinegar to a baker's palate," he'd said.

Another friend, Monday Gell, an African Ibo who worked the public stable a few blocks from Captain Vesey's home, attempted to lift Denmark's spirits with a promise of better days to come. His best friend, Peter Poyas, who lived in the opposite direction on King Street told Denmark, "Your day will come."

Denmark could no longer reconcile his master's easy countenance towards him with the twisted Christian logic he applied to slavery. Captain Vesey noted the change in Denmark. His once affable African slave grew morose, sullen, even insolent to some. Endangering not only himself, but the captain as well.

An inventory error demarked the transformation. Ostensibly in a haze, not able to concentrate, "thinking again of Koi's fate," Denmark had said, he miscounted the amount of Captain Vesey's goods in stock and in transit. As punishment, and to shake up Denmark, the captain put Denmark to work as a hired out laborer with Caesar, to work for the city. Among other civic projects, they were put to work filling in the tidal pool lowlands that flowed inland beneath Governor's Bridge.

Denmark's hard labor "punishment" proved to be nourishment to his soul. He began to save his meager share of Captain Vesey's hired out earnings with an eye toward buying his freedom someday. And his required commute in and around the city afforded Denmark opportunities he'd never known in Charleston; and a feeling of freedom akin to flirting with the blurry limits of Madame's spyglass.

FORTY-ONE

Compromised

Through the years, "free" to roam the streets of Charleston during the week, Denmark noticed things about the town he'd missed all those years of being mostly confined to working in the captain's shop and home. Soon, house slaves recognized him and subtly greeted Denmark as he passed by on the sidewalk. Slaves working storefronts and hotels, though busying themselves under the watchful eye of their masters, managed to acknowledge his now familiar face.

On his way to work Denmark sometimes took detours through the back alleys behind newspapers, bookstores, and government buildings; places he had, on occasion, visited in the past, on business for Captain Vesey, delivering advertisements of goods, including slaves for sale, registering ship manifests or paying customs duties. *The Charleston Courier*, the *Times*, the *South Carolina Gazette*, the *Evening Gazette* and all three of the French newspapers became his window unto the larger world.

Though teaching a slave to read was against the law, Charleston commerce required a semi-literate workforce, both free and bonded. Apprentices of all professions were the backbone of trade. An unintended consequence was that many slaves could read. Slave apprentices at printing presses inked hundreds of extra copies of all things of interests to their brethren. They were distributed along the docks, in the market and as far away as the slave streets of plantations, forming an underground flow of information.

Within the pages of dated newspapers Denmark read about a new revolution taking place across the Atlantic. One wrought, it was said, by the liberties won in America. A French revolution. He also read an account of America's new constitution. It replaced the old Articles of

Confederation. Though he was intrigued by Article 1 Section 9, which stated that the slave trade would only be protected for twenty years (he saw the measure as a ticking clock) he was then dismayed—no—horrified, outraged by the language of the 3/5th's clause. The clause stated that each slave—for the purposes of proportioned representation within the U.S. House of Representatives—would be counted as 3/5th of a human being; 100 southern slaves equal 60 whites in calculating congressional apportionment.

The more he read the more disgusted and agitated he became. If Madame, and he, had only known that the nation responsible for...*all men are created equal*...would become a nation of David Humes, she wouldn't have been so eager for Denmark to deliver her espionage dispatches; and he wouldn't have been so willing to comply.

Whereas news of the French Revolution provoked sharp debate in parlors and dining rooms, mention of insurrection killed conversation. Condemnation of the black's revolt off the cost of Spanish Florida, in French St. Domingo was unanimous among Charleston's elite. The pert loathing of the revolt's leader, Toussaint L'Ouverture, masked the white's genuine fear.

At the wharfs, in the streets, and in conversation over fences and among the slaves working in the fields little else was discussed so enthusiastically.

And among the more progressive minded white Charlestonians every bit of news of the Negro rebellion served as a frame of reference with which to gauge one's neighbor's sentiments.

During that year's Fourth of July festivities, in an effort to control the flow of information about the black revolt, the Charleston authorities, fed up with "too much democracy," shuttered the print shop of a Swiss immigrant named James Negin and arrested him. His crime? Printing a translated memoir entitled *A Particular Account of the Insurrection of the Negroes of St. Domingo*, written by a French Lieutenant involved in the initial campaign to put down the uprising.

Though accounts of Toussaint L'Ouverture had been printed in many newspapers and were therefore hardly a secret, by printing a book of the Negro rebellion the newcomer had misjudged the city official's appetite for the propagation of information about slave insurrections. Still, the authority's intervention proved as futile as trying to gather water beyond the dam.

Just like Denmark, every slave clamored for any news of revolution, insurrection, manumission and abolition. Well known among the enslaved, including the masses of illiterates, was a pamphlet published by the New York Manumission Society, calling for a gradual emancipation of slaves in New York. And to Denmark's surprise, among other noteworthy signatories, it was endorsed by the same man that, as a boy, had captured Denmark's attention with his description of a hurricane on St. Croix. Alexander Hamilton.

One day, on display in the window of a lending library owned by a brave and commercially powerful English émigré, Denmark saw another work that took him back many years to Madame's island. The book cover read *Essay on the Treatment and Conversion of African Slaves in the British Sugar Colonies* by Reverend and former surgeon aboard His Majesty's *Arundul*, James Ramsay.

Denmark also read about a curious new American ally with a peculiar name. A Native American Chief of the Creek Nation and confederacy named Alexander McGillivray.

The Creek nation occupied a vast territory along the nation's southwestern frontier. A territory Denmark identified from previous newspaper accounts as "Yazoo" country. The Creek confederacy ruled a twenty four million acre tract of land that the Georgia legislature had just recently authorized for sale through three private "Yazoo Companies." Land speculators had already begun selling off some of the Creek territory. The son of a wealthy Scotsman and a mixed blood mother, half French half Creek, McGillivray was deemed Chief because of the Creek's matrilineal society and the prominence of his mother's lineage.

The Secretary of War in George Washington's administration, General Henry Knox, had convinced President Washington that an accommodation with Native Americans was consistent with the creed of the American Revolution. He wrote in a report to Congress that... *The principle of the Indian right to the lands they possess being thus conceded, the dignity and interest of the nation will be advanced by making it the basis of the future administration of justice toward the Indian tribes...*

Chief McGillivray was invited by George Washington to the American capital to sign a peace treaty between the two nations.

The Chief and his band of warriors paraded through celebrations in the cities of Charleston, Richmond, Baltimore and Philadelphia en route to New York. The size of the crowd flanking the bandstand for a view of the pale, gaunt Indian leader raised a ruckus and cloud of Charleston dust that exceeded the clamor over President Washington's visit the following year.

However, as Denmark had suspected, within months of the lavish New York gala and ceremonial peace signing, land speculators in Georgia had rendered the peace treaty worthless as "Yazoo deeds" continued to sell the dream of vast riches ripe for the pickings in the western territory. By the time of McGillivray's death in 1793 over three million acres of the Creek confederacy land had been sold to the highest bidder.

Again, Denmark thought of what Madame might make of her infatuation with the rebel's new government now. What might Madame now think of the words she'd read in awe...*But when a long train of abuses and usurpations...*Denmark could almost hear her agree with him that the revolution she'd put so much trust in had actually produced a nation of Master Thomases. For his part, Denmark recalled a quote from *Rasselas*, the book she'd left on her terrace to be noticed. *Be not too hasty...to trust or to admire, the teachers of morality: they discourse like angels, but they live like men.*

Despite everything Denmark had witnessed and read he had managed to become sanguine about the future. With a slave revolt to the south, calls for abolition to the north, a waning demand for slaves—indeed a ticking clock on the slave trades' protection—and a growing cache of money in his bureau drawer, he kept his dream alive. A dream that began in Africa. A dream of one day, once again, his ears submerged in water, looking skyward, free again, at last.

One Sunday, like most summer Sundays since Denmark had begun saving his money, he traveled to the Ashley River waterfront to buy melons wholesale from a wily country woman. Denmark would then cart the melons to the Sunday market on the Cooper River and sell them to a kind, blind, grateful old woman who'd been turned loose from the plantation to fend for herself in the city; and for whom, consequently, every day was a Sunday. The arrangement worked well for all three, time and again.

The market, as a black domain, teamed with exotic life and languages. Dialects of African tribes and European nations became so inseparable, a whole new language emerged; Gullah.

Spoken by few outside the confines of Charleston and the barrier Sea Islands, Gullah served as a common denominator, a form of shorthand. A secret code among slaves beyond and within earshot of white masters. There, among the slaves sent to the market to stock the kitchens of their masters Beck spied Denmark transacting his business.

Her obvious poise and beauty set her apart from the crowd. Beck held in her arm a large, heavy copy of the Swiss printer's banned book. Intrigued and mindful of her attention, Denmark moved closer. He had now been lonely for Koi for over six years.

The aroma of fresh cut summer flowers melded with the scent of cooking meats as Denmark drew near the young woman standing in front of an itinerate stall tended by an old woman. The stall stood on infill ground Denmark, Caesar and countless other slaves had labored to put atop of the damp low ground and melodious tide waters.

With her back to Beck, the old woman continued to cook cuts of meat hung from the racks of her stall.

Beck, aware of the closeness of the handsome man whose eye she'd caught, greeted the old woman with a simple, "Hello," to get her attention.

Once the old woman turned to acknowledge Beck, she said, "How much is your pork?" Followed by "…is the meat sweet?" said with a smile in jest. While reaching for her purse Beck struggled with the heavy book.

The old woman cackled and laughed at the sound of language more like a master's than a slave's. "Chil', dey buckruh' hogmeat flabuh me mout' 'tell uh done fuhgit uh hab sin fuhkill'um."

"Uh, oh…"

Beck thought of resorting to hand gestures before Denmark stepped forward to intervene, having learned Gullah on the docks.

The old woman's answer brought a smile to Denmark's face.

"She said, 'the white man's pork flavored my mouth so, that I forgot the sin I committed in killing the hog.'" With a chuckle he explained, "Her comments were meant to proclaim the quality of the cuts, and provide a hint as to the meats' origin. Stolen. From her master, no doubt."

Though she attempted to hide her blush, Beck took an instant liking to her handsome, erudite translator. Once he'd concluded the negotiations on her behalf, the couple waved and smiled to the woman's farewell, "Eenjy."

The two explored the rest of the goods on display as they strolled the market, soon arm in arm.

Within a month's time Denmark and Beck jumped the broom together.

From Beck's copy of the banned book Denmark read with pleasure an account of the demise of his former owner on St. Domingo, Seigneur, on the *Plaine du Nord*. He'd been hacked to death by a hoard of rebel Negroes. But Denmark also feared for the French doctor who had helped him stage his *grand mal* performance to escape the island.

In 1794 a brief article appeared in a Charleston newspaper that Denmark and most others, both free and enslaved, failed to grasp the significance of. Indeed the story was written with such editorial hyperbole that it was derided and scorned among those who bothered to read or discuss it. The reporter wrote that a new invention he had witnessed in use would "not only revolutionize cotton agriculture, and modern society, but the entire world!" The young man interviewed for the story, Eli Whitney, called his new-fangled machine a "cotton 'gin."

FORTY-TWO

Speculation

Like most enslave families, husband and wife and often their children lived apart from one another in separate households. Familial interaction was restricted to Sundays and the whims of masters. And so, Beck continued to live with her child, Sarah, in her master's home on Broad Street and Denmark at Captain Vesey's on King. And yet, despite only occasional, brief encounters during the week and visits every Sunday, within a few years' time the couple had two sons. First Sandy, then Polydore. Denmark recalibrated his dreams of freedom and the amount of money he'd need to save accordingly.

To accommodate the influx of French planter refugees from the St. Domingo revolt—and their slaves—St. Philip's Church asked members of the civic commission, Captain Vesey among them, to assist with efforts to assimilate the new arrivals. The commission managed to settle many on uncultivated lands along the Santee River, well north of the city wall. Their numbers swelled the ranks of an already vibrant, burgeoning French community.

More surprising than an influx of white French refugees were their mulatto slave owning counterparts. The first sons of St. Domingo's white aristocracy. These mulatto masters dressed in the height of fashion, frequented city shops, taverns and Anglo as well as French theaters. Much to the consternation of polite white society.

Denmark once caught Beck eyeing a French mulatto planter who held the extended, mutual, admiring gaze.

Competing with the social changes wrought by the St. Domingo revolt and the French Revolution were the changes in agriculture, industry and banking. These changes were just beginning to transform the landscape, the fortunes and the politics of both Charleston and the nascent nation.

Through it all, Adam won and lost money seemingly overnight as a speculator in real estate, bank shares, canal shares and as a factor in commodity trading; financial instruments beyond the purview of most.

Adam's interest in businesses beyond shipping and real estate began with a letter he received from an old classmate at King's College. His friend bragged of a potential windfall on Continental dollars he'd bought up at four pence each. Throughout the war years the Continental dollar had depreciated dramatically. So much so that what once cost only one Continental dollar in 1775 cost forty times that by 1779. And by peacetime, the same purchase cost 179 times its original price.

Trusting the power of assumption—Alexander Hamilton's chief argument for the establishment of the Bank of the United States—Adam's classmate had purchased all the Continentals he could find with the idea of redeeming them later; once the new country had made good on all of the states' war debts. Thomas Jefferson wrote to James Madison advising him that the state of Virginia should discreetly do the same.

In good times Adam hired Denmark, Caesar and a carpenter friend to work every Sunday on the construction of a portico addition to his family home. When times were lean the work would stop for a time.

On one Sunday of no work for Denmark and his friends, when questioned, Adam attempted to qualify his financial exploits to Denmark.

"Stability deprives the markets of margins, and therefore room for profit."

To which Denmark complained that among his savings of American paper and coins, Spanish reales, German johannes, Portuguese moidores, Bengal rupees and even English pounds he never knew on any given day what his savings were worth.

"Any commodity—including money—silver, gold, copper, tin, what-have-you is only worth what someone else is willing to pay," Adam explained.

Within a couple years the Bank of the United States offered $8 million in shares to the public. Adam—as an agent of his old classmate, now a New York "Buttonwood" broker—regularly speculated in these bank shares. He subscribed at low prices, then, capitalizing on favorable price fluctuations, sold them in Charleston for a handsome profit. He repeated the process over and over. These profits, among other "bets," paid for his portico and other endeavors. While Adam and his fellow stock-jobbers debated valuations of commodities and shares, Denmark and Caesar spoke of the price of slaves on the Charleston market at any given time.

As he explained the finer points of his investment strategy Adam invited Denmark to join him as he attended to business at the taverns and street level establishments of residences in and near the water district. The clientele leaned to the middling sort of speculators, gamblers really, and therefore to French allegiances—especially since the outbreak of renewed hostilities between England and France in 1793.

"Go get your nest egg and meet me in an hour."

With Denmark at his side Adam soon found what he sought; a gamble. A game of poque—boisterous and flush—taking place in the opposite corner of the tavern they'd entered together. Their senses were instantly assaulted by tobacco smoke and the rancid smell of old spilt beer. One man rose from his seat at the card table. Adam seized the opportunity. He directed Denmark to "Follow me," without further explanation. After brief introductions, Adam was invited to join the gamblers. Denmark stood behind Adam as he took his seat, as though, despite his dated, slightly threadbare Sunday attire, he was Adam's valet.

Adam placed his and Denmark's money on the table before him. He stacked the currencies of like denominations until the modest sum of paper and coins—including almost all of Denmark's savings— formed a semicircle around his hands at rest on the table. After counting Denmark's contribution, Adam wagered an amount meant to engage the participant's attention. Denmark gulped.

Adam lost two hands in rapid succession. Denmark could hardly check his alarm. Adam didn't say much, nor would the others until they'd satisfied their curiosity. Cards laid, Adam won the third hand; a pot larger than the previous two combined.

He put Denmark's original sum into Denmark's hand and offered a proposal; an enterprise for which Denmark was to audition for this very moment. Handing Denmark a stack of bank share subscriptions taken from his pocket Adam suggested that Denmark sell them. Now. The shares had peaked in value at $400 per share, but had since settled back down to around $60. Adam had reason to believe—ahead of the next publication date of current prices—that the par value per share would drop precipitously.

"You are to keep ten percent of the share price," Adam said the last into Denmark's ear. Denmark stood erect without speaking. His eyes darted the room.

"What business did you say your family's in?" one of the players asked.

"Shipping," Adam said with a polite smile.

"I dare say, you should consider a gaming hall," came a good-natured comment from a losing better, seasoned to insinuate. The players laughed and relaxed as before the caste had changed. Adam was welcome, but envied from the start.

Recognizing an air of goodwill Adam brought up the sale of bank shares he was just discussing with Denmark.

"Well, I am dabbling in a new venture," he said, teasing the conversation. The men cleared their throat or shuffled themselves to feign interest. "As an agent, authorized to deal in Bank of the United States shares I have a number available at $65 per share. Increasing in value by the day I'm told, concomitant with the height of the new branch being built in town. But, I'm a prudent investor, looking to diversify to avoid putting all my eggs in one basket. I..."

"Hey!" Someone standing within earshot said, "This bloke is trading shares at seventy!" pointing to Denmark who retreated to Adam's side.

The men paused the game, lighting cigars and ordering more drinks from the help.

"Good work," Adam said into Denmark's ear, recognizing the entrepreneur in Denmark. "Now, get back at it."

Across the room someone was shouting the availability of Yazoo land deeds and Santee Canal Company stock.

It was Thaddeus Ball, a mustee acting as an agent for an elite of Charleston, privy to knowledge that the U.S. Congress had introduced legislation that would render the Georgia state legislature's award of Yazoo lands null and void.

Once upon a time Thaddeus had been one Denmark's closest friends. They'd met on one of Denmark's first days in Charleston. Of late, Thaddeus had become one of Denmark's worst enemies. The son of a wealthy white master, Thaddeus turned on Denmark and all those he'd known in the slave community when he had been freed by his master's will and left a small fortune. With his new found stature as a high-yellow of means, and at the encouragement of his old master's friends, Thaddeus helped organize a new distinctive, discriminating, social club; The Brown Fellowship Society.

Ostensibly set up to foster the welfare of the entire black community, through the years the fifty dollar dues they charged had in fact served only their members—the mulatto elite—and the white's desire to segregate and placate the middle ground. Over time the white elite used The Brown Fellowship Society to buffet their hold on power, just as the "Society" used their kinship to the white power structure to do the same.

Thaddeus shouted, "I've plenty of Georgia Mississippi Company Yazoo acres at 20 per deed! And Santee Canal shares at 20 as well. Make your bid before they're all gone!"

After the break for refreshments new cards were dealt.

The man who had bought a derelict warehouse and Salvador property from Adam wagered an initial bet beyond the comfort level of most of the players. Some hands folded. Adam held a losing hand.

Turning his attention to the man Adam asked the table, "Gentlemen, what's the bet?"

The man who'd asked about his family business said with sarcasm, "Well, I think it's very generous, almost patriotic of you to invest in America's bank. A foreigner at that."

Adam said, nodding toward Thaddeus, "I see competing investment options have materialized across the room."

Adam increased the cash bet by twenty English pounds; a move meant to goad his real estate adversary just enough to keep him in the hand. Another man folded, tossing in his cards.

To up the ante, feeling smug about his clout in the room, the new owner of the Salvador property offered it as an even bet for bank shares. Adam agreed, betting the sum of 28 shares to get what he wanted; his opponent's commitment; and an enormous bump in the value of the pot.

As the hand proceeded, whispers of the huge wager and the thrill of scarcity set in; the bank shares went up. Someone away from the table, speaking for a poor cabal, said his group would accept the subscription price of 70 Denmark had offered. He wanted to seal a position before there were none to be had at that price. At 70 dollars per share few below the middling sort could gamble on even a single share all alone.

Soon thereafter, Denmark, hands held high, counting paper for all to see, announced the 70 dollar shares were sold out. He said he had more shares at 73. A flustered man with another group at a table across the tavern shouted to Denmark they'd have five shares at 73!

Offering what Thaddeus asked, a successful buyer scurried away from Thaddeus and announced to the room his triumph, "$20 for a piece of Yazoo gold! Huzzah!"

Offered cards, Adam took two. His opponent took only one.

Adam drew an ace, but also a deuce.

The words of Adam's father, *one plays the player, not the cards*, raced through his mind.

His opponent had made real estate and bank shares currency.

The real estate man offered three newly acquired blacks, "bought at auction yesterday," as his bet.

Adam said, "I never acquire chattel I cannot first inspect."

The man shrugged his shoulders and pushed all his money into the pot—an amount exceeding Adam's cash count in front of him. A move meant to convince Adam of his hand's invincibility and induce Adam to fold. Adam reconsidered his hand.

Instead of attempting to see the bet by borrowing money from Denmark and then calling, Adam raised the stakes. He cocked his head, knowing his dangling black curls would distract his opponent, and wagered 60 more bank shares for the pot. The man hesitated—another man shouted from the crowd, "We'll take two at $73!" A roar in the background meant another sale. Still another man claimed his stake in Yazoo for $21 per deed, outbidding a rival standing next to him. After which yet another offered and bought more Santee Canal Company shares for $22. "Sold!" Thaddeus shouted so as to be heard above the den of tavern cacophony.

Taken aback by the lightening turn of events, all eyes on him, the real estate man felt his throat swell. He had already wagered his Salvador property and his cash. There was no getting them back without risking still more.

With cotton prices rising, no doubt, and the Santee Canal scheduled for completion next year, the man was not willing to part with a warehouse, even a dilapidated one. No longer confident in his hand, the thought of losing sobered him. Waking from the intoxication of attention, mistaken for respect, he folded.

Adam dropped his cards and the large crowd now standing around the card table roared!

Always eager to put time and distance between the conclusion of a deal, Adam stood and announced he had an appointment. Adam thanked his fellow gamblers and bid them farewell. Pulling Denmark aside he said, "Time to go!"

Outside, the afternoon sun warmed the chill of sweat rolling down each man's neck. The scent of fresh manure in the street wafted the air. While collecting the cash and remaining bank subscriptions from Denmark, Adam suggested that if Denmark were willing to gamble— to speculate his commission on the shares—if he were willing to invest in Yazoo deeds, the value of his commission could multiply over time.

"I know you have an eye toward manumission. And you know how long you'll have to dig or shovel manure for the city to get there. If ever." Adam regretted the last remark, though there was a sincere measure of truth in it.

Denmark considered the proposition. He had read about the dubious nature of the land grab, but he'd also witnessed the enthusiasm for Yazoo tracts. Besides, Denmark also knew that his station in life limited his prospects and that his focus on manumission distorted his vision of the world around him. Not unlike the days when his thoughts more often than not turned to freedom among the chain of islands beyond Madame's, Denmark depended on Adam's world view, like Madame's, as a means of stepping back from his myopic lens—to see the broader landscape. He knew little of Adam's world of speculative finance, but, like Madame, he trusted Adam—to a point.

"How about five dollars, now, to show Beck, and you invest the rest."

Adam gave Denmark $10 and explained that he planned to either invest in Yazoo deeds through brokers he knew in New York, or, with luck, invest them in another venture he had in mind. Adam promised to keep Denmark apprised of the disposition of his investment.

Denmark walked away a little befuddled as to what exactly had transpired but happy to have added to the savings in his pocket. He walked in the opposite direction of Adam. Toward the market to meet Beck. To try to explain his windfall. How much closer he was to buying their family's freedom.

When Denmark approached the edge of the market he saw Beck about to step into a carriage. Then he saw a hand reach out to help her aboard. He called out to her. Two faces turned; Beck's and Thaddeus's.

At the carriage Denmark began to explain the money, but Beck interrupted him. She scolded him for gambling his savings and said she didn't want to see him again. She said that while Denmark would never be able to afford the price of their manumissions, Thaddeus, as an agent of the white elite, could, and would, someday buy her freedom and that of all *her* children.

"Besides, I like the way he moves his hips!" she said, smiling as she boarded his one-horse carriage.

Sand and shell dust flakes kicked up by the parting carriage were illuminated to pink and orange by the late summer sun as they settled at Denmark's feet. As he stood alone he felt Koi's phantom hand slide into his before his finger twitched.

FORTY-THREE

Rattled Nerves

The *Mal Majeur* wagon in front of St. Michael's church greeted Sunday worshipers like the portrait of a brown Jesus—another truth ignored.

Inside the five by ten foot rolling cage were two men. The white one, as white as the sandy shell streets, wore a torn wedding gown, chest bare. The other, black as tar, cowered naked in the opposite corner. Both were sweaty in the sweltering direct August morning sunlight.

On display, a handwritten sign affixed to the padlocked door read:

If a man also lie with mankind, as he lieth with a woman, both of them have committed an abomination: they shall surely be put to death. Their blood shall be upon them.
LEVITICUS 20:13

Though some mothers led their children away, the crowd continued to grow. Soon it was large enough to stop carriage traffic past the church entrance. Jeers and finger pointing rose when the frightened black man voided his bladder and bowels through the cage floor. His stream of waste mixed with a deposit left earlier by the horse that delivered the *Mal Majeur* to St. Michael's door.

Denmark, unaccustomed to seeing congregations so large as to block traffic approached the spectacle from blocks away. Once he determined the nature of the gathering he turned away in disgust.

He resumed his walk to the new buildings being erected atop the infill he had shoveled into place with Caesar years ago to accommodate the growing market. The same marketplace where he had first met Beck.

Amid the activity of new market construction—proper buildings to replace the itinerate stalls—hundreds of slaves bought and sold items destined for dinner tables throughout the city. Snickers and hoots about the *Mal Majeur*'s contents reached the market ahead of Denmark.

Captain Vesey, as a member of the construction oversight committee—still trading on his Gadsden social connections—hired out Denmark to be part of the construction crew. The oversight committee had authorized the use of the dismantled Governor's Bridge as foundation material. Six market buildings were being erected to span the distance from Meeting Street to East Bay.

Changes to the market landscape paled in comparison to the other changes in and around Charleston. Changes wrought by an agricultural revolution. In the countryside—and indeed throughout the American southwest, including the contentious Yazoo lands—experiments with cotton cultivation boomed. Use of Eli Whitney's cotton gin—without consent or royalty payments—made middling planters rich, almost overnight, and the elite of Charleston super-rich. The city became a cauldron of wealth and power again, fueled by the beginning of another unsettling revolution, an industrial revolution. Cotton was becoming King and Charleston a Crown Jewel.

Fortunes in goods flowed down the Ashley and Cooper rivers to be loaded onto ships arriving from as far away as Liverpool, Rio de Janerio, Amsterdam, Milan and Calcutta; also Philadelphia, New York and Boston, and as near as Savannah and Georgetown. All of these ships in turn brought trade goods whose value filled the coffers of Charleston commerce before reaching the hands of civic improvement, education and the arts.

A wellspring of new housing, made necessary to shelter the waves of immigrants and new business transformed the city as much as cotton transformed the countryside. Once conventional lots sold out, dwellings were constructed on infilled swampland, projecting the town out into the rivers. Homes as opulent and graceful as on Meeting Street were erected on the White Point landfill. The prosperous city was soon awash in cash, activity and more slaves.

Though the city had added more than three thousand new free white residents, and the ranks of free blacks had swelled beyond a thousand, the already out-numbered free citizens also witnessed three times as many new slaves marching through the streets. The most frightening among them were "saltwater blacks"; slaves of African descent deemed dangerous because they harbored memories of life as free men.

As the number of slaves imported exploded to meet the demand for cotton cultivation, the city's support system—meant to prop up the tenuous hold on the subjugated masses—began to sag under its own weight. By the late 1790s—including the earlier wave of French slaves brought from St. Domingo—almost seventy percent of the Charleston district was enslaved. Most of them, single males like Denmark. Their sheer numbers rattled nerves.

FORTY-FOUR

Cash Money

"**W**hy have bank shares dropped? How did you know they would? And, why not invest in the Santee Canal Company? You know what's going on up there. They'll be finished soon," Denmark asked, clearly dismayed and frustrated.

"One question at a time. Take off your shirt."

Denmark looked to Caesar to gauge his opinion before he took off his sweat soaked cotton shirt and held it in his hand.

"Now, close your eyes."

Denmark again looked at Caesar before complying.

Adam picked up a sawed board and put it in Denmark's other hand.

The smell of freshly cut wood intermingling with the odor of sweat along with the weight differentials struck Denmark's senses simultaneously.

"What do you feel? Which one is heavier?"

Opening his eyes, though he understood Adam's rhetorical antics Denmark still answered, "So?"

"So, the Santee canal became obsolete the day Mr. Whitney conceived of his ingenious cotton cultivation machine. Soon the heavier agricultural goods meant to flow through the canal and down the Santee to the Cooper River will be replaced by the lightweight crop. Cotton is so light it does not require water transport. It can be easily maneuvered overland. Everything from corn, wheat and tobacco to lumber is being set aside to grow more and more cotton. Cotton to be feed into Mr. Whitey's gin and then textile factories. As for the bank, well, there's been a conspiracy of sorts perpetrated by a Mr. William

Duer, an ex-associate of Mr. Hamilton. Mr. Duer and his Six Per Cent Club has attempted to manipulate prices by cornering the market."

"What? What does that mean?" Denmark asked.

"Never mind. The point is, couple that crisis of confidence in the financial markets with the election coming up. An election that President Adams will not win—not with his unpopular stance against war with France; a position I applaud as prudent, though I'm in the minority. And especially because of that *act* he signed against newspapers. Jailing anyone who criticizes the government."

Adam could tell his political explanation was wearing thin with Denmark.

"The point is, the answer to your question is…the bank's shares have dropped and will likely continue to drop because of its political opponents. Chief among them Vice President Thomas Jefferson. So, thanks to Adams being so unpopular Jefferson will win. And Jefferson is against the bank. The bank will lose its charter."

"But, there are so many now," Denmark meant the statement as a question.

"Yes, true enough. There are many. Sixty or seventy banks by now. And more to come. Many more. But those are private banks you speak of—granted charters by their respective states because the new constitution forbids states from printing their own currency again. A reaction to the inflationary havoc Rhode Island dollars fomented? Do you remember? They were everywhere. So numerous they were considered worthless."

Here Adam paused, seeking confirmation of Denmark's recollection.

"So, states cannot ever print money again, nor own banks. But they can license others to do so. So, they've licensed private companies to do both. And Mr. Jefferson stated publicly that he would favor an amendment to the Constitution. He said he intended 'to take from the federal government their power of borrowing.'"

Adam tried to make a more simple argument, "He is taking direct aim at Alexander Hamilton, and the so-called 'Federalists' as much as the Bank of the United States."

Here Denmark's ears perked at the mention of Hamilton.

"The irony is that the Republican followers, the poor and middling sort—against the wishes of the Federalists, generally the most prosperous of the country—have been clamoring for the proliferation of paper money to grease the wheels of commerce. It's been the Federalists, led by Hamilton, that have been preaching the soundness of hard money policy; a more strict control on the amount of money in circulation."

Caesar put a hand in his pocket, running his fingers through the coins and bills Adam had given him as wages.

"Well, what of our Yazoo deeds? Has the value changed in our favor?"

"Yes, as a matter of fact it has. The price of Yazoo deeds has doubled, at least, I'd say. The trend is in our favor. You've seen the droves of new captives marched through Charleston's streets."

Denmark remained silent. Adam regretted personifying his assessment with that anecdote, even though it was the most apt, the most observable evidence.

"I see things you do not, as you know," Adam said. "And you see things I do not," he offered. "What do you make of their…their disposition, Denmark?"

"Scared. I see it in their eyes when their masters aren't watching."

Adam considered the slave's lot. "The whites, they're scared too. I hear it in their voices when they discuss the numbers; the large increase we've seen lately."

Though he too was uncomfortable with the topic, Adam continued. "Those…" He didn't say slaves, "…they're headed for the Yazoo territory. It's easier to send them through Charleston to the territory than through Spanish New Orleans. Not to mention the increased demand here. Planters of all stripes are clear cutting the Piedmont for cotton fields. Poor Mr. Whitney. His machine is so simple others are replicating it without any regard for him and his patent. He should have just given it to mankind, like old Ben Franklin and his lightning rod."

"So, when do we get our money?"

Caesar's ears perked up. Though little of the conversation made much sense to him, he knew it made sense to Denmark. And he had the feeling that Denmark might be on to something, something big.

"Well, I want to discuss that with you. You see, I've an idea, an investment idea. Not my own. A group of us that congregate at Clarke's Exchange Coffee House are of a mind to create a sort of exchange of our own. I've sold them a number of Yazoo deeds. We all plan to use them as collateral."

Here Denmark gave Adam a look of some surprise.

"Yes Denmark, I've acquired a great many more deeds through my New York connections," Adam said raising his eyebrows as if to say, *additional deeds that have nothing to do with you.*

"As I said, I've sold them to my fellow investors, the members of this cabal I'm telling you about. They are Yazoo deeds issued by the New England Mississippi Company. In any event, we plan to pool the appreciating amount to create an exchange that will honor all species at face value.

Thinking of all the crazy machinations one has go through to decipher a currency's fair market value, Denmark was instantly intrigued.

"Old state bank notes we'll keep discounting according to published valuations. But we'll honor all newly chartered bills at face value. All like denominations will be treated the same. As I say we'll still have to consult the weekly newspaper lists for the exchange rates of old bills. Comparing them to one another and to foreign currency— to get the New York value of a bill we'll still have to compare them to a Georgia state note, for example…one has to add $1/16^{th}$ and divide by 2, or for a South Carolina note exchanged for a Pennsylvania bill of like denomination, multiply by 45 and divide by 28; etcetera, etcetera. But for newly charted bank notes we'll treat each denomination the same, whether from close by, like North Carolina or from far away, say, Massachusetts."

Caesar again fingered the money in his pocket. He crumpled a bill in his hand, thinking.

Denmark followed the calculations.

"We plan to eliminate the banker's hold on the exchange rates. Their argument is that the farther one travels away from a bill's origin the less the note should be worth. *That!* That is what we'll change. That notion of distance will become a thing of the past. By honoring each bill 'as is.' Every business in town from the grocer to the tavern to the rope manufacturer, even the whorehouses will come to us instead of the banks. We'll make loans, at reasonable rates of interest, of course. The point is, we, our exchange, will be doing the business instead of the banks. What do you think? Are you in?"

Speculating had always been foreign ground to Denmark. He'd only gone as far as investing in Yazoo deeds on account of Adam. But this was different. This made perfect sense. Adam's scheme would make wages plain and simple. Although Adam's proposition would entail even more risk, Denmark realized that amassing the kind of money he needed for manumissions could take forever on wages alone.

"I'm in…" Denmark said, extending his hand to seal the deal. Caesar was as dumbfounded as jealous.

On this late fall Sunday in 1799, whether it was the thrill of speculation, or sheer desperation, Denmark didn't know. But regardless of which it was, he took another chance on his way home. He gambled the small amount of money in his pocket, six dollars, on the chance of winning more money than he would ever see from a lifetime of slave wages. He played the outlandish odds of the East Bay Lottery; he bought ticket number 1884, and regretted it immediately.

When he arrived at Captain Vesey's back yard he was surprised by the appearance of a slim, youthful woman stranger. Mary. A stranger stranger than Adam. Of East Indian descent, Mary was darker than Denmark.

Mary's family had immigrated to the United Sates before the war. First they had established themselves in Savannah as Sea Island cotton merchants. Over time the family became Anglicized, adopting English names as the family's fortunes grew and branched out. The patriarch of the family had purchased properties—mostly those of fleeing Loyalists—for his children and thriving business. In 1791 he acquired The Grove plantation just beyond the Boundary Line along the Ashley River. Mary had moved into the property to monitor her family's business interests in Charleston. After Captain Vesey's second wife, Kezia, died, the captain was smitten at first sight by the exotic dark complexioned beauty.

Mary looked upon the captain's filthy workman with charity through her beautiful dark eyes. Gesturing for Denmark to wait at the back door, she soon brought a basin of clean cool fresh water for him to wash and refresh his oily, sweaty face. The two were entranced by the other's pleasant features. As he washed, the two told one another their story—of how each had become residents of Charleston. The tranquil moments shared between the two dark souls was abruptly interrupted by the appearance of Captain Vesey at the door. Mary disappeared inside.

"Denmark, I need you to travel to Dorchester, across and up the Ashley to help erect a barn there."

Denmark tried to look beyond the captain, wishing for another glimpse of the beautiful, dark, kind woman.

Waking from his senses Denmark reminded the captain, "I'll need a pass. How long you reckon I'll be gone?"

"Here," Captain Vesey said handing Denmark the handwritten note he'd prepared, ignoring Denmark's question. "You'll leave in the morning. The pass has the name of the property owner written on it for the patrol to see."

Denmark read the familiar property name. The Johnson plantation at Dorchester, north of Parker's Ferry. While doubting that most of the poor patrollers could read Denmark regretted that he may be gone quite some time. His abrupt departure meant that he would not have an opportunity to tell Beck to tell his boys about his absence. Nor would he be able to hear any news from Adam about his investments. And he'd likely miss the lottery drawing, not that he harbored much hope of winning. In fact, he wished he still had that six dollars in his pocket.

FORTY-FIVE

1884

Denmark returned late in the afternoon on a Sunday from the Dorchester barn he helped build. He found Captain Vesey's house quiet, deserted. Nell and Ambrosia were away on their day off. With not much of the Sunday sun left on the horizon and tired from traveling on foot all day Denmark laid his weary bones down to rest.

The next day started strange, and got even stranger.

There was no smell of biscuits in the morning. Nell and Ambrosia were not, as usual, in the kitchen making breakfast for the captain's household when he descended the stairs from his room above. Denmark left to report for work with the city.

Sent to shovel manure in the streets with Caesar, their work brought them within the vicinity of the East Bay Lottery office. But they could not get near the place. A crowd of a hundred men, twenty, even thirty heads deep surrounded the lottery door keeping them at bay. Denmark did not tell Caesar or anyone else about his impulse buy. He went about his work with only an occasional glance over at the raucous crowd eagerly awaiting the announcement of the lottery's winning number. Aside from muttering to himself—enumerating the ways the powers that be would deny him the money anyway—he tried not to think about his error in judgment. But he was reminded of it when Caesar asked him where and how they might procure a noontime meal. Denmark had no money. And he had left the captain's house without breakfast.

At the end of the workday, as the glow of dusk approached, Caesar and Denmark parted ways, each destined for home. On his way Denmark was quick about making a short detour that would allow him to pass by the lottery office before the sentinel drums sounded—the time all slaves had to be off the streets. The crowd was gone. The street near empty. As he walked closer and closer his countenance stiffened as he read the distant message and numbers written on a slate board displayed on the wall outside the front door of the office.

Prize Unclaimed. $1500. Winning Ticket Number 1884.

Denmark rushed to the sign and stood on the sidewalk in front of it staring at the winning numbers. Within half a moment he emitted a spontaneous loud yell of joy as he leaped into the air. His hands held high above his head, he turned in circles, clapping then shaking his fists in triumph. His outburst was heard up and down East Bay Street drawing the unwanted attention of passersby and sending clerks and slaves to the windowpanes of offices and storefronts. The owner of the lottery hurried outside to confront the black man on the sidewalk. He insisted Denmark move along before he called the authorities. The warning forced Denmark to regain his composure. Despite his euphoria he recognized this was the wrong time and place to wage his battle. Denmark excused himself from the lottery chief with a slight bow of obedience, but he couldn't contain the wry smile his lips left affixed upon his face.

Walking as fast as he could without raising suspicious stares he made his way home. All the while hoping he had not seen things that were not there. That he had not somehow mistaken the numbers in his desperation for a change to his circumstances. After opening the drawer at his bedside bureau he checked the numbers he had committed to memory. He checked them again, and then again and again.

Denmark shouted within the privacy of his room above the kitchen. He stomped the floor with both feet and then leaped once more into the air. He then collapsed to the floor and pounded the wood shouting, "I won! I won! I won!" Rising to his knees, he cried out "Damn! God, Mawu, Allah, Jesus, God! Thank you, God, whoever you are!"

Once he had calmed himself enough to begin to think ahead he noticed the light of day fading—fast. The drums had not yet sounded, but he knew they would any moment. Denmark raced down the stairs to the kitchen, skipping stairs in his path. Leaping like he was descending the slope of Madame's island. His mind was set on reaching Adam's house before the drums sounded.

On the street, only a block from Captain Vesey's house he heard the first note. The first concussion reverberated down King Street. He started running. His heart pounding, he could feel the lashes being laid across his back in St. Domingo. Whack! Slash!

At the sight of a disapproving stare, from a lone man on his way home for the cocktail hour before dinner, Denmark ran harder. He was hoping to reach the safety of Adam's house ahead of the alarm his running would raise. When he reached two women walking side by side on the sidewalk he took to the street, but brushed against one who'd made a movement to part from her companion.

"Oh, oh, my Lord!" the woman exclaimed. The other made some comment Denmark could not make out from the distance of another two strides he'd already made toward the slight left turn of King Street while crossing Beaufain.

He then heard but did not see the sound of voices, men's voices. Denmark ducked into the deep recess of the doorway to a store on King Street, almost to the turn to Adam's house. It was the patrol heading his way. The men crossed the street to check the lock on a darkened doorstep. Denmark hunched down low. He could hear but not quite follow the joke one man was relating to his fellow patrollers. Denmark knew they would next cross back over across the street to the very door where he lay crouched.

What if Adam isn't even home? Like Captain Vesey, Adam could be anywhere, out wheeling and dealing, having dinner, gambling…anywhere. The patrollers laughed at their compatriots' punch line and started to cross the street. A loud bang up the street followed by another and a dog barking at the disturbance demanded their attention, toward Beaufain Street. The six men followed the noise to investigate. Denmark didn't realize he had been holding his breath. He took a deep breath and sighed. When he was convinced the street was clear he took off running again. When he reached Adam's door he knocked continuously until the door opened and Adam stood before him.

"Denmark! Whatever are you doing? It's after dark. Come in! Come in!" he commanded, eager to have the man inside, out of view from his neighbors. "Have you lost your mind? What is it? Why are you here at this hour?" Adam was incensed by the danger—to both of them.

Denmark, catching his breath, handed the ticket to Adam while apologizing for the intrusion and asked for his help to claim the prize—now. Denmark was surprised by Adam's reaction. There was little. Without a word Adam got his coat and hat and walked to the front door with the ticket in his hand. Denmark followed.

As the two made their way to the East Bay Lottery office Denmark did all the talking. Adam had put the ticket in his pocket.

"What are you going to say? How will they pay me? What will I do with the money? I mean, I need to put it in a safe place. And then buy my family, and myself. I can't believe it!" Denmark repeated some version of each question over and over as the men walked briskly down East Bay Street. Adam said nothing.

"Wait here," Adam said at the lottery office door.

Denmark suddenly felt vulnerable. He was standing alone outside on the sidewalk, in the dark, after curfew. And his winning ticket was no longer in his possession. The guard could come along any minute and whisk him away. Even if Adam noticed and attempted his rescue, it could be too late. Denmark could almost hear a guardsman promising him "a little sugar."

Though it made him look all the more suspicious, Denmark moved to spy through the curtains of the window. In the lamplight of the office Denmark saw Adam talking across a counter with the man who'd previously yelled at Denmark to "move along, or I'll call the authorities."

"Hello, Mr., uh Mr.," Adam said, greeting the wire-thin old man.

"Hammer. Hammer's the name. What can I do for you?"

"My name is Adam Wolff, and," reaching into his pocket Adam retrieved the winning ticket "I have the missing winning lottery ticket, number 1884," he said, holding it so the man could plainly see the numbers.

"Ah, oh, there it is! Didn't want the world to know I suppose," the man said smiling, offering an explanation Adam chose to not refute. Mr. Hammer reached beneath the counter and retrieved the bank ledger checkbook. He removed one check and proceeded to fill out the date and amount.

Adam glanced over his shoulder as Denmark peeked through the window.

Then he noticed a copy of the evening edition of a local newspaper, *The Charleston Courier*, on the counter. The headline read **Yazoo Deeds a Hoax!** Adam had read the story mentioning his name. In fact he'd heard the news before it became public information. The subscriptions he had sold for New England Mississippi Company Yazoo deeds had been part of 11 million acres the company bought from the Georgia Mississippi Company for $1.4 million. The newspaper article quoted claims that the deeds were invalid, as in *thin air*. Nonexistent tracts of land, or land that had been sold over and over many times, or both. The article went on to describe them as *worthless*…in the same sentence that mentioned Adam as the chief Charleston purveyor.

Looking up for a moment as he wrote the old man said, "I'll need that ticket, of course."

"Oh, yes, of course" Adam said, setting the winning ticket down on the counter at the man's elbow.

After writing in long hand *Fifteen Hundred Dollars and zero/xx* and signing his name he asked, "How do you spell your last name? One 'F' or…"

Before Adam could answer the man stopped, pen in hand, and raised his voice, "Hey! I know that name! You're that feller that's been selling them Yazoo deeds. My brother-in-law bought some!"

Denmark walked inside the office. He'd become afraid of standing outside alone any longer and nervous about the man's suddenly confrontational tone with Adam. He said, "Did you get my money?" A mistake Denmark immediately realized. The words just came out.

"Your money!" Mr. Hammer yelled. Recognizing Denmark from earlier that day, "Hey, I know you too!" Mad as hell, the angry old man dropped his pen and reached for the flint lock pistol he kept beneath the counter next to the bank ledger book. Adam snatched the check and the ticket and yelled "Run!"

As the two struggled out the door a shot rang out. The office window's glass shattered to pieces onto the sidewalk moments before another patrol rounded the corner to East Bay from Queen Street.

FORTY-SIX

Pay to…

Denmark and Adam ran a short way down East Bay Street and ducked into an alley before the patrollers saw them. They were still close enough to hear the men.

Responding to where the shot and sound of shattering glass came from the patrol's attention turned to the old wiry, angry man, standing on the sidewalk in front of the lottery office with a smoldering pistol in his hand.

"Which way did they go?" the old man asked the patrollers.

"Who?" the sergeant asked.

"That old thieving Jew and his nigger, that's who!"

Adam grasped Denmark's clothing and pulled him into the alleyway's dark shadows.

"Shush…" Adam said, holding a finger to his mouth, afraid. The sour smell of rotten rubbish wafted between them. Denmark stood close enough to see a bead of sweat roll down Adam's face in the moonlight. The streets were quiet enough for them to hear the sergeant command his patrol to split up, and then their boot steps running in opposite directions. In a few moments half the contingent ran past the alley entrance and continued down East Bay.

Denmark whispered, "Did you get it?"

Adam nodded and reached into his coat pockets. He handed to Denmark first the ticket and then he slowly produced the check.

Denmark held the check up to the moonlight, reading the printed, then the hand written words, *Fifteen Hundred Dollars and zero/xx.*' He stared at it in silence for a long time, examining the life changing paper like the shaman's first glimpse of the Golden Stool, fallen from the sky.

Coming to his senses, "The name! Pay to… It's blank. He didn't fill it in," Denmark said, worried.

"Shush…" Adam reminded Denmark. "That's just as well," Adam said in a whisper, relieved and disappointed all at once—the temptation to steal from Denmark removed.

"What do you mean?"

"Well, now, somehow, your name will appear there. That old man sure wasn't going to place it there. Do you want me to put my name there and take it to the bank?" The temptation was creeping back up Adam's throat like vomit.

"No!" Denmark said with too much force he thought. He didn't want to insult Adam, but the old man's comment, "thieving Jew," reminded him of anti-Semitic comments he'd heard, not only just now, but throughout his life. By and large, Adam only enjoyed relative acceptance in Charleston because of the size of the community, the largest Jewish population in the America. (The original Carolina colony charter written by John Locke in 1669 called for religious tolerance of "Jews, heathens, and dissenters.") And while Jews had been assimilated into every stratum of society, and some, like Salvador, were not only honored, but revered, anti-Semitism among most Charlestonians lay just beneath the surface of social discourse.

"I want to buy my freedom, and my children's freedom, and their mother's. I'll need Captain Vesey for that. I'll ask for his help to make a bank deposit and pay him, and for the others," Denmark said by way of explanation.

Adam was relieved because not only was temptation once more removed, he was still coming to terms with his own predicament and was loath to discuss it.

Denmark finally spoke the words both men were thinking, "Will they let a slave win the lottery?"

FORTY-SEVEN

On a Mythical Island

St. Michael's bell tolled loud and fast. The furious clanging rippled throughout the quiet city like a bolder plunged into a still pond. Denmark and Adam looked at one another wide-eyed. Soon more church bells rang out too. St. Philip's, followed by the French Huguenot church and then the First Baptist. Then still more. The fire signal!

"That's good!" Adam said. "Soon the city will be upended with fire companies and bucket brigades on the move. The patrollers will have to join in."

Denmark thought of the chaos of Alexander Hamilton's youthful rendition of the St. Croix hurricane.

Thinking ahead, as Madame had trained him to do, Denmark began, "I have another matter I'd like to discuss with you."

Adam was afraid of this conversation. Denmark always asked about the status of his investments. Adam was about to say *now is not the time* and suggest they depart, separately.

Wringing his hands, Denmark was trying to decide where to begin...

"A journey."

Adam was as relieved as intrigued. "What do you have in mind?"

"Your business has improved. I've heard you speak of a boat."

"Yes. The *Eleanor.* She's helped me slowly rebuild my connections in the West Indies. Recapture some of the trade that was once my family's mainstay. But with the outbreak of war between France and England trade has slowed and sent insurance sky high."

"But, your captain, he knows the islands."

"Of course. What are you getting at, Denmark?"

"I've told you about my life there, as a boy, except one detail," Denmark said, pausing, allowing suspense to do its work while questioning the wisdom of telling anyone—even Adam—the rest of his story.

"Well, so, what is it? What's to be gained by revisiting your childhood?"

Just then they heard Fire Company 9, a slave brigade stationed at Inglis's Arch on Bedon's Alley, rush by on their way to fight the fire.

Though anguished, Denmark relented, revealing the part of his childhood he had left out. He told Adam of Madame's life savings— the chest and the leather bag buried beneath "his rock" on Madame's island.

While working on Adam's portico Denmark had explained to Adam and Caesar, with theatrical drama, about the tense, unharmonious relationship between Madame and her evil son-in-law, as though retelling a medieval fable. Long ago Adam had checked part of Denmark's portico story, but the absence of an island on a map where one should be caused him to question it. The new dimension Denmark now related—to the mind of a skeptic—did not inspire confidence.

"Yes, I remember the story," Adam said, thinking to himself, *a wonderful treasure tale, just like the rest of Denmark's enchanted life on a mythical island.* And yet, even before Denmark had pounded on his door that evening, Adam had already made plans to sail to the West Indies aboard the *Eleanor* at first light—to escape the wrath of his investors.

"Your boat sails again soon, right? And she'll travel within miles of Madame's whether we go or not, yes?"

"Wel I've not yet agreed. How much are we talking about anyway, in pounds sterling?"

"I can't say how much in English money. For one thing, the coins are of many nationalities and denominations, and there are gold bars too…a lot, to be sure. A heavy chest and a bulging leather bag, full of hard money."

Adam considered what problems a financial windfall could solve—if Denmark was telling the truth.

"What's my cut? What'd you have in mind?"

Denmark proposed, "Fifty percent for me, it is my money, thirty percent for use of your boat, and twenty for the crew. Fair enough?"

"I'll take fifty, it's my risk. You take thirty."

Pondering his options, though he could perhaps wait for another boat, another gamble on another partner, considering the likelihood of some better outcome he suggested a compromise.

"I tell you what; I'll give you forty, with forty for me, if you come along as owner, with authority over the captain."

Adam had been doing some thinking of his own. If there was any truth to what Denmark said, and if his captain and crew saw only Denmark standing between them and all that loot, he might never see them again. Or the *Eleanor*, and certainly not Denmark.

Recognizing that Denmark would require some time to handle his affairs Adam considered where he might hide in the interim before proposing, "Meet the *Eleanor* at the dock opposite Sally's before dawn tomorrow night, and we'll shove off."

It was only after the men shook hands on the deal and the pungent odor of smoke from the distant fire had reached the alleyway that Adam asked another question that must have by now occurred to Denmark too. "And, what if your Captain Vesey refuses you manumission? What then?"

FORTY-EIGHT

I'm Coming

Denmark left the alleyway first. He looked both ways before stepping onto a deserted East Bay Street. Once he turned inland he found a city in chaotic, manic motion. Men of all descriptions and stations in life made their way toward Denmark's destination, King Street.

A fire that had broken out in the commercial district had quickly spread to a second building before the city fire crews could contain it. Denmark managed to trail behind a man and his gaggle of slaves. Close enough for others to assume he belonged to them, but far enough behind to not draw their master's attention.

Once at the fire Denmark joined in with Fire Company 9. Two of company 9's slaves noticed him but said nothing. The number of men and the amount of water brought to bear on the flames began to win out and the remaining threat was subdued in a matter of hours. Once the conflagration seemed under control Denmark meandered over to Captain Vesey's home and slipped into the backyard unnoticed.

In the kitchen he found Nell and Ambrosia, worried. But not about the fire. They greeted him with anxious eyes and non-stop news of events that had transpired in his absence. Captain Vesey had taken up with Mary; the wealthy dark East Indian immigrant Denmark had met. He'd moved in with her at her well-equipped handsome plantation, The Grove. The women were afraid they'd soon be sold.

Nell said, "Captain Vesey say, 'Send Denmark to see me at The Grove when he returns.'"

Denmark decided to keep his good fortune to himself. Now was not the time to gloat or flaunt his luck in front of troubled women. And besides, the women's apprehension made Denmark worry too; about his own fate. About his chance for freedom.

When Denmark arrived the next morning at The Grove Captain Vesey and another man Denmark did not recognize were on the veranda surveying Captain Vesey's new domain. Denmark went around back to the servant's entrance and knocked. He heard voices inside but no one answered the door. Just as he considered knocking again a servant opened the door and then retreated. Captain Vesey appeared and told him to come inside. His new owner wanted a word with him.

Shaken by the news—perhaps Nell's and Ambrosia's fears were justified—he took off his hat and entered the large home. Captain Vesey walked ahead of Denmark and a house slave, the butler, who, now, appeared out of nowhere, walked in front of Denmark to escort him. The two stopped at the sight of Captain's Vesey's visitor in their path. Ignoring the two black men the visitor turned to ascend the stairs near the main entrance, alone. In the front parlor stood Mary, waiting, Captain Vesey at her side.

"Good morning, Denmark," the dark woman dressed in a flowing, layered white silk and cotton dress said as though addressing a friend. Her dark brown eyes were as kind and expressive as the day they had chatted at the captain's back door.

"I suppose Captain Vesey has informed you of the news; I have purchased you."

Denmark failed to conceal his surprise. Fumbling with his hat in his hand, rotating it like a wheel, Denmark could not conceal his pleasure either. He only said, "Yes, ma'am."

She began by explaining that he and Nell and Ambrosia needn't worry. Their positions within the King Street household were secure. Implying, of course, that she had no plans to sell them—and that she now owned all three of them.

After this news, spoken in a pleasant benevolent tone Mary attempted her commercial voice, taught to her by her father. "And your arrangement with the city will continue," insinuating that the income would now be passed through her hands before Denmark's meager pay reached him.

"Yes, ma'am. I'll tell them. They'll be happy to hear as much," Denmark said.

Since the subject of money and ownership had been raised, Denmark decided to waste no time.

"Miss May," Denmark began (May is the name she'd asked Denmark and her friends to use): "I have a proposal I would like to make, if I may. A business proposal."

Mary furrowed her brow and Captain Vesey stepped into the conversation, "Now see here…" But Mary raised her hand to cut him off.

"Whatever do you mean?" she said, clearly offended, feeling that her graciousness had been violated. She'd expected gratitude expressed and the conversation concluded.

"Well, ma'am," Denmark looked at Captain Vesey whose expression had turned hostile, like when Denmark had first asked about Charleston's evening drums.

Denmark measured his words, realizing that at this very moment, if he displayed the prudence and discretion Madame Chevalier had preached, the kind of life she had intended for him, free and financially secure, could again be within his grasp.

"Well, you see," Denmark decided to present material evidence to back up his words, "I've won the East Bay Lottery," Denmark said, producing the winning ticket and the signed check the old man had almost completed.

Mary reacted as though Denmark had produced a newborn baby.

"Oh, my! Let me see that!" Mary said, stepping forward to Denmark. Captain Vesey became more agitated, and moved closer as well. Mary took the ticket and check and compared them, noting the amount and the 'For' line that read: *Winning Ticket 1884.*

Mary also noted the blank, 'Pay to the order of' line. She said, "But, it's not completed. There's no name."

"Yes, ma'am. That's what I wanted to talk to you about. And…and, I'd like to buy my freedom," he said in as easy a tone as he could muster.

Mary, holding the documents, looked up into Denmark's eyes and smiled. Captain Vesey cocked his head and scoffed.

"You go down to the new Bank of South Carolina, on Broad Street. Do you know where that is? You go down there now and we'll meet you there. Joseph, ask Henry to bring the carriage around," Mary said without hesitation, expecting everyone to do as she'd asked without question.

Denmark could only manage a nod. He nodded again, thinking, and backed out of the room. The waiting butler walked him to the back door.

Denmark left The Grove on foot, walking the three miles to the bank, anxious, confused, happy and worried, seemingly all at the same time. She hadn't asked about price. She hadn't given him the ticket and check back either. He was supposed to just trust that Mary would show up and help him, rather than fill in her own name and make a deposit—denying Denmark's story. He began to walk faster. He didn't know if this was another of his best or worst days. He had to trust that yet another member of "the powers that be" would do right by him and it scared him half to death. He walked faster. Close to a run. But then slowed himself and settled into a rapid gait hoping his swift movement would not attract attention.

In his mind he questioned the conversation. Every word. Every verbal and nonverbal cue. He could just hear Captain Vesey entreating Mary to deposit the check and dismiss Denmark, sending him back to the city job. Denmark's heart beat like it would explode from his chest.

At the bank, before walking in, Denmark checked his demeanor. The struggle to compose himself almost overwhelmed him. He took a piece of paper out of his pocket. The old pass from his Dorchester trip. He folded it and held it in his hand as he walked in. The guard asked him his business and he said he had a message for Captain Vesey, pointing to him, glad to see Mary too through the windows of the bank manager's office. The guard let Denmark past him.

Through the windows Denmark could see an animated conversation taking place with Captain Vesey raising his arms as he spoke. Denmark knocked and was signaled to enter the office. Captain Vesey stopped talking.

The moment Denmark entered, Mary, seated in front of the bank manager's desk said, "Sign here, Denmark." Documents lay upon the bank manager's desk. A frown upon his face, the banker said nothing to interfere with the wishes of Mary, one of the largest depositors in his newly chartered state bank. The manumission form read:

"I, *Mary Clodner*, in consideration of faithful service, do release from the yoke of servitude, set free and discharge, a certain *Negro man named Telemaque, his Christian name being Denmark, aged about thirty-three years, my slave at this time, in confirmation of which I do now deliver this act of emancipation. The said Telemaque, Christian name Denmark, was born in Africa, and came to me after many years as the slave of Captain Joseph Vesey in Charleston, South Carolina. He is an honest, sober and industrious man, always a house servant, laborer and chandler's assistant.*

Given under my hand & seals at Charleston this *31st* day of *December* in the year *1799*. *Mary Clodner* (Seal). Also signed & sealed in the presence of three witnesses:"

Denmark's hand quivered as he read. He looked at the disgust upon the faces of the two men in the office. Mary gave a slight nod and smile to Denmark before saying, "And here. Sign this copy. And here, sign this and this…" The other documents were a bank deposit of $900 and a check paid to the order of Mary Clodner for $600. She had done it!

Mary signed the documents. The bank manager signed both copies as did another banker that had been summoned to sign Denmark's emancipation declaration. Captain Vesey then signed both as the third witness. After which Mary handed Denmark one of the two emancipation papers and a checkbook embossed with the name *Bank of South Carolina* in faux gold leaf lettering.

Denmark kept silent. He could hardly believe what was transpiring and, if it were a dream, he didn't want to spoil it.

Mary said, "Done. You're a free man, Denmark!"

Denmark remained speechless, but his expression said everything as he looked to Mary through tear welled eyes and mouthed, "Thank you."

Without thinking, still numbed by the experience, as he was leaving Denmark put out his hand to Captain Vesey. Horrified he'd done so he was afraid of its being rebuffed. But, resigned to the facts, Captain Vesey shook Denmark's hand.

Once Denmark departed the expansive office his chest felt tight as though he couldn't breathe until he made it outside of the building. Mary half expected to hear through the now open bank manager's office door Denmark yelp with joy from the sidewalk.

Instead, once on the street, Denmark folded the manumission document and put it into the only pocket of his slave pants and closed the button. Taking a deep breath of crisp winter air he looked skyward, deaf to the street noise as though river water had fill his ears, and he thought, *I'm free, again, at last* as a spontaneous broad smile appeared upon his face.

Denmark's finger twitched. "I'm coming, Koi. I'm coming," he said aloud.

FORTY-NINE

He Began to Read

The first thing Denmark did after leaving the bank was visit a tailor's shop. Outfitted in the latest fashion, on the way out of the shop's door Denmark bumped into Thaddeus. The two men's opposite shoulders collided hard enough to push the other aback. Thaddeus looked Denmark up and down but didn't say a word to him. Denmark let his expression of indifference speak for itself.

Outside, on the sidewalk, on his way to buy his children, smiles and greetings from other well-dressed free blacks were bestowed upon him. People who wouldn't have acknowledged his existence earlier in the day. A nod of the head from a woman here, the tip of a hat from a man there, and then, a slave stepped aside, into the street, rather than crowd Denmark on the sidewalk—just as Denmark had done a hundred of times before.

When Denmark knocked on 47 Broad Street, Beck's master's door, he was disappointed when another house servant answered. As he waited for the man, a grocer, to appear he considered that Beck had not answered the door because Thaddeus had been a man of his word. That Thaddeus had already purchased Beck and the children. Denmark had been away for long enough for such a change to occur.

As he was pondering the notion the grocer interrupted Denmark's train of thought. He was not quite prepared for what came next.

"Yes, what do you want?" the older man said in a gruff manner, a napkin tucked into his collar. Denmark had disturbed the family's mid-day meal.

"Excuse me, sir, Mr. Paul. I've come to offer to buy Beck, Sarah and the boys. My family," Denmark said, holding up his bank checkbook for Mr. Paul to see. He didn't know if he could afford everyone now, but with Madame's money he surely could. And without asking he couldn't know.

"Yes, I've been told of the relations," he said, by way of letting Denmark know he knew who Denmark was. He looked over Denmark's new clothes. "But I wouldn't sell a nigra to nigra for no amount," the man said, spitting disdain from his mouth along with the gristle from the greasy pork Denmark was keeping him from.

As Denmark was attempting to say, "How about I leave a check for…" the door slammed shut. Denmark mumbled to the closed door, "…an amount you can think about," before slapping the checkbook against his other hand.

Feeling dejected about his encounter with Mr. Paul and his inability to even speak to Beck or see his boys or say hello to Sarah, Denmark walked next to a source of comfort—the lending library. Thinking of his long journey to the West Indies, that night, he sought some new reading material to pass the time. The son of the wealthy and influential man who'd opened the doors to his private collection—a collection not unlike Madame's—greeted Denmark like an old friend and complimented him on his attire. Denmark, always grateful to be able to take refuge in the little shop, dropped a donation into the box at the counter after selecting a few volumes to read during the voyage.

Back at Captain Vesey's house Ambrosia and Nell cooed at his new clothes and peppered him with questions about his trip to see Captain Vesey. He would never have imagined two women more glad to continue being enslaved (at the King Street house). He explained he was going out of town for a few weeks, careful to avoid details he knew could find their way back to Captain Vesey.

That afternoon he walked over to visit with friends that gathered at the end of the workday, before the drums. He was eager to tell them of his good luck, new status and immediate plans. They often met at the livery stable on King Street where Monday Gell entertained them within the confines of the manure and horseflesh smell of the stable.

Monday was finishing his day's labor and accepted horses to board overnight.

Denmark regaled to his friends the excitement of his exploits with Adam. How Adam had helped him with his lottery ticket. About the look on the old man's face when he realized the winning ticket was Denmark's! The falling shattered glass after his pistol fired and their eluding the patrollers.

His friends laughed and offered their own imitations and renditions of the characters and events. Each more exaggerated than the last to hardy laughter and pats on the backs of each other.

Then Denmark produced the mighty document—Mary's agreement to allow Denmark to buy himself—his freedom paper. It was passed around for each man to examine in wonder. Caesar snapped the document from Peter; the shipwright who had schooled Denmark and Caesar in the finer points of carpentry. Though illiterate, Caesar appeared to study every line, including and especially the signatures that had set his friend free.

During Denmark's description of his experience at the hands of Mr. Paul, Gullah Jack broke the melancholy by making fun of the fat old balding grocer's uneven colored teeth.

"They look like the keys of an old piano I seen at the roadside, beyond the Boundary Line."

The chuckles encouraged him to continue, "And you'll see. That old man won't be long for this world. Then you can approach his wrinkly pink skinned widow. She'll sell, no doubt. She got no use for a pretty thing like Beck."

The inferred dark reference—to the sexual liberties commonly taken among masters—only quieted the men anew.

Caesar asked how much Mary had demanded to sell Denmark his freedom.

"$600," Denmark replied.

"Six hun'ered! Whew, you's dubly lucky. Triply lucky! The goin' rate for you is more like $800, and for a carpenter, more like $1000." To witch Peter nodded in agreement.

"Well, I sure wasn't going to quibble," Denmark said to raucous laughter and fresh smiles all around.

Monday had to excuse himself to accept a horse brought for new shoes and grooming. He returned momentarily and heard the tail end of Denmark telling the others of his plan to sail to the West Indies that night to seek out Koi.

Recalling Denmark's lengthy depression after her sale, Monday said, "You go and look for your woman. I would." His other friends echoed the sentiment, wishing they too were traveling somewhere, anywhere.

And so it was on New Year's Eve, 1799, two weeks after the death of George Washington. While many whites of America still mourned the Father of their country, a slaveholder, Denmark Vesey and his friends rejoiced with laughter, celebrating the freedom of their friend. A man who'd been held as a slave for more than twenty-five years. To a man Denmark's friends felt a tinge of jealousy along with the vicarious thrill of his new status. Still, his release from bondage gave them hope.

Denmark felt bad about not telling the whole story behind his journey. But he reasoned that, if successful, he could hold court again upon his return, with more to offer than just encouraging news next time. On his way "home" Denmark bought a newspaper, folded it under his arm and wondered where he might move to as a free man of color.

That night Denmark was too excited to sleep and too nervous to put the strength of his freedom paper to the test—in the hands of illiterate patrollers—before he had to. He spent his time pacing his room above the kitchen thinking of Koi and Madame's island before packing the lending library's books and his few belongings into an old bag Captain Vesey had given to him for his Dorchester trip. He then turned his attention to the newspaper he had bought and began to read.

FIFTY

The Right Time

Well before dawn, before Nell and Ambrosia even stirred, Denmark quietly stepped down from his room, through the kitchen and across the backyard. He peered down King Street, both ways. As he did a patrol rounded the corner. Denmark jerked his head out of sight. There he waited, listening to the men talk and joke with one another as they made their way down to the commercial district. Once they were gone, Denmark stepped onto the sidewalk and traveled in the opposite direction.

Mindful of other patrols walking the city streets Denmark used his knowledge of dark alleys and deep doorway recesses to avoid attention.

Once he reached the water district, Denmark realized why Adam had chosen this setting for their rendezvous. The area around the old rickety pier across the street from Sally's—a new name for one of the oldest and most notorious taverns along the waterfront—was a thieves den and runaway's refuge. Even his most ardent pursuers would think twice about hanging around to search for Adam amid the shadows and low tide stench. Adam had chosen this location and hour, just before dawn, with an idea toward discretion, not safety.

Having read the latest account of Adam's scheme to defraud his investors Denmark could understand why Adam would want to hide from the townspeople and the law. And now he had his own reasons to worry. An article in the newspaper had not only assailed Adam's integrity, calling him "a charlatan," it also detailed Adam's role in Denmark's accomplishments, as seen through the eyes of Mr. Hammer. A charge of theft "by Wolff and his nigger" was accompanied by outrage with Mary's perceived misconduct, labeling her "an accomplice." While he felt bad for Mary, she had her wealth and Captain Vesey to shield her. But an accused slave that had won the East Bay Lottery and used the proceeds to purchase his freedom would have no such capacity to thwart the designs of an unruly mob of racist malcontents bent on his destruction. Given his notoriety, Denmark arrived at the appointed hour worried for his own life—only to find a deserted ship and pier amid the waning moonlight.

The captain and crew of the *Eleanor* were still in the holiday spirit—Washington's Christmas season passing notwithstanding—and happy to while away the hours inside Sally's. Drinking with shipmates and low life strangers who may become shipmates one day they were more than a little reluctant to return to sea just yet, "What with color in the sky, such as it is."

Suddenly, Adam appeared from below deck, alone.

"Denmark. Right on time. Good," Adam said, before he noticed the newspaper held beneath Denmark's arm. Adam could tell by Denmark's expression he'd read it.

"Where's your captain, and crew?"

"You wait here," Adam said flatly as he disembarked from the *Eleanor* and walked the pier. While waiting Denmark looked over his shoulder into the darkness when he heard a noise he could not discern; a noise that troubled him. He had a feeling of déjà vu. An eerily familiar feeling. Like the one he had had that night at the bonfire celebration in Africa, just before the king's raid. He walked away from his post to approach the tavern door.

Somehow, without telling the captain of the unusual cargo they sought, Adam managed to convince the captain to rouse his crew for the voyage. However, only some of the *Eleanor*'s crew, only four of the seven, stumbled their way out of Sally's door, following the captain and Adam who were busy talking among themselves.

Outside, Adam chided Denmark, "I thought I told you…" Adam instantly quieted the tone and volume of his rebuke. He looked both ways down the wet ballast stone street covered in pre-dawn dew in front of Sally's. A fog bank began to roll ashore from the bay.

Adam then turned his wrath on the captain for failing to corral all his sailors.

"I can't force them to sail. Under the circumstances, what with the holiday merriment and all we're fortunate to have these," the timid fat cargo captain insisted.

Adam gave the captain a hard look that he then turned on Denmark to forestall any objection Denmark might echo—a look that said, *we don't have a choice; we must sail now!*

Denmark opened his mouth, but he was not only taken aback by Adam's unfamiliar demeanor—angry and scared—he was unsure as to how, or whether he should describe the noise he'd heard emanate from the *Eleanor*. He was as anxious as Adam to get underway before some opportunistic dock worker could broker the sale of information concerning Adam's whereabouts, or his. Denmark (and Adam) feared an angry mob could appear dockside any moment.

Once the skeleton crew were aboard, with Denmark's help, the *Eleanor* managed to slip into the harbor and then over the Charleston Bar by sunrise. The vessel tacked south, intent on riding the Labrador current close to shore all the way to the islands of the West Indies.

"Are you planning on a return trip, or will you stay in the Indies once we split up the loot?" Adam asked, out of earshot of the others. He was eager to change the tone of their last exchange and to avoid, or at least postpone, the topic he knew was foremost on Denmark's mind.

"I don't know yet. I haven't decided. I suppose I'll know when I, when we, get there."

The two men let the early morning views of the coast, starboard, and the vast ocean, portside, dominate their thoughts. Each man wandered the deck alone to ponder the future while the crew worked double-duty around them.

The second evening of the eleven day voyage, after dinner, Denmark broached the subject Adam couldn't escape.

"Why, Adam? Why did you deceive so many, including me, about the Yazoo shares?" Denmark no longer cared as much about the money. Even factoring in a large return of his small investment the amount paled in comparison to his lottery winnings, or his share of what he hoped he'd find on Madame's island. More important than the loss of his investment was his loss of trust in Adam.

"I didn't. I didn't, I tell you."

Denmark cut Adam off, scoffing at his answer as he looked away.

"I didn't cheat anyone. The New England company was cheated by the Georgia men. That's the truth. I'm told. I have no reason to believe otherwise. My friend doesn't hold the mendacity to do such a thing. He's assured me he will get to the bottom of the deceit. And I believe him. I've known him since our school days. He's an honest man. I believe him."

"Well, what are you going to do then? Hide out in the islands forever?"

"I need to lay low, true enough, until this matter can be resolved. His last letter, forewarning me of the scandal, said he has plans to travel south to Savannah, to file suit."

As proof of his innocence Adam said, "Look, I lost money too. I have suffered injury too. More to my reputation than anything else." He wiped a bit of saltwater spray from his face and then looked out to sea. "Besides, one wagers, or invests, only what one is able to lose, whether it be Yazoo shares, copper, gold, tin or slaves. To do anything else, to risk more, is a fools bet." Adam knew his point was lost at the mention of slaves, and he regretted his choice of words.

Denmark thought of the card table. When Adam had wagered what he knew to be most of Denmark's savings, his manumission money, on the outcome of one hand. And the mention of slaves, as a commodity, angered Denmark.

"You men...you men have the choice, to be happy or not with your wagers. Trading goods, shares and people as you please. But there can be no choice, no happiness living as a commodity, as a slave!"

Adam offered his only retort. He exposed his wrists that still bore the scars of shackles. Denmark scoffed again but let that point of the conversation go. He had another question he wanted to bring up. But he knew he would probably not get a satisfactory answer and, in truth, it was none of his business. But he had to ask. Much like he had to ask Madame about Millie's mother.

"You've been a free man. All this time, you've been a free man, with means..."

Adam watched Denmark struggle to form his thoughts and began to anticipate Denmark's next line of questioning.

"Why have you not sought out your family? Koi told me all about them. Why have you not searched for them? Why?"

Adam was right, and so was Denmark.

Adam took his time, as his reply had more to do with Denmark, and his search for Koi, than himself, and he knew it. He couldn't bring himself to dash Denmark's hopes. Not after what had transpired between them, now, and before. He couldn't tell Denmark that the odds of finding his true love were infinitesimal. He couldn't tell him the truth. So he lied, mostly.

"I've made inquiries. You know my family has had connections throughout the islands, connections that are generations old. I'm told my two sons were sold, along with Augustus, to a patron whose signature in the ledger is illegible. My wife took her own life after learning of the sale, knowing she'd never see her family whole again. As for Beulah, there was no news. And once we've concluded our business at your mysterious island, I hope to see Statia again. Look in on my ancestral home. Visit my family's gravesites and inquire as to the fate of The African and little Statia. Though, such as is the case, she is a grown woman by now."

The two looked upon the moonlit ocean swells together in silence for some time before retiring to their private cabins. Denmark opened an old favorite he had picked up from the lending library, *Gulliver's Travels* and read himself to sleep.

What no one onboard knew was that two desperate misfits had stowed away aboard the *Eleanor*—the source of the noise Denmark had heard at the dock in Charleston. The misfits bided their time, listening for the ship's story while under sail. Stealing food from the galley. Eavesdropping, lip-reading and attempting to interpret the posture of all aboard. The two tried to make sense of Denmark and Adam's arguments. Orders to the captain. And the crew's murmurs— conjectures the crew made that echoed throughout the ship at night. One sailor boasted to the others of overhearing "words between Adam and that free nigger that even the captain weren't privy to!" though he couldn't say with confidence what it all meant.

Even undermanned, in fair weather and seas, the shallow draft, sturdy but lumbering *Eleanor* made surprising time. The ship arrived at dawn one morning off the coast of Paradise Island ahead of schedule. Sensing the voyage nearing an end, the two misfits dispatched a sailor and his galley hand as they cooked breakfast. They then hid the dead men with them along with two stolen knives and waited for the right time to make their presence felt.

FIFTY-ONE

Pygmies!

Soon thereafter the *Eleanor* rounded the tip of Paradise Island and sailed over the wrecks Denmark had explored in his youth. Denmark thought of the remains of the now channel current ravaged *Eclipse*. The ship that had almost entombed him. The site of the wreck sent a shiver through him.

Previous nights' spent in Lilliputian dreams—that morphed into visions of Koi and Madame—had sustained him during the long voyage. Now, even without the aid of a spyglass, the sight of Madame's island in the distance, dead ahead, eased his mind and reinvigorated his spirit.

Just then, the misfits stormed the deck! One brandishing the bloody knife used to kill the two sailors. The misfits threw the corpses from their shoulders into the ocean. Startled and frightened as they were by the gruesome bloody scene no one was ready for what came next—it all happened so fast—the knife slashed into one of the only two sailors left, killing him and driving the man overboard. Both misfits then bared a growl of their fearsome teeth—teeth carved to a point by West African pygmies.

They were the two French sailors Captain Warret had watched swim ashore with about a hundred escaped Africans after the sinking of the *Diane*. There the two had then stolen a canoe with which they made their way south, hugging the shoreline of the mysterious continent. Through the years, with every foray inland they had eventually been chased back to the coast under threats to their lives.

On their last desperate attempt to make dry land for food, water and shelter they found themselves surrounded by a tribe of Aka pygmies.

The diminutive nomadic bushmen, armed with spears and blow dart poles—whom the sailors gathered looked upon them as an appetizing meal—had smiled through their pointy sharpened teeth at each other as they exchanged words of curiosity about their strange discovery.

Later, the Frenchmen learned the ways of the gentle short people. Moving from place to place, hunting and gathering with the men as the women built new shelters at every turn and cared for the elderly and young. Around evening meals the pygmies managed to tell their story. That they were the lucky ones. That other pygmy clans were subjugated by their larger rivals. Treated as subhuman. Worse than slaves. Sometimes eaten as medicine prescribed by a shaman.

The Frenchmen learned to use the hollow poles. They shot poisonous darts through them to kill game. They climbed high trees along with the pygmies to steal bee's honey, and danced in line with the men around bonfires, separate from the women.

The sailors also learned the method of—and perceived attractiveness of—sharpening their teeth. The tall white men had designs on the pygmy women and strove to impress them. But found themselves rebuffed even after acquiescing to the decorative enamel procedure, much to their chagrin. One night the two men forced themselves upon a woman who had refused their separate advances.

Thereafter, the pygmy men shunned them and the tribal elders soon deemed the misfits incorrigible, even dangerous. One night, the tribe slipped away from the misfits as they slept, disappearing into the forest canopy from whence they came.

The misfits finally spotted a slaver and convinced the captain to grant them passage. Working among a crew that castigated them for their appearance they found their civilization no longer felt natural or familiar to them after living so many years of in the wild jungles of Africa.

"Ahh! Arggh!" The misfits snarled to the desired effect. The others on the *Eleanor*'s deck backed still further away from the killers.

"Don't hurt me, I'm just the captain," the sniveling, overweight mariner insisted as he raised his hands, releasing his grip on the helm. "It's he you're looking for," pointing to Denmark. "He knows of the treasure."

Denmark's eyes hit Adam's.

The last word, treasure, turned heads and froze the deck. Every motion suspended; all eyes turned to Denmark. The misfit's sharpened pointy teeth grew in length as their smiles broadened, inducing nervous laughter and tepid grins all around.

Denmark used the opportunity of immediate danger to defer discussion of treasure. Pointing dead ahead, he quickly explained that if the *Eleanor*'s present course was not altered, the ship and all aboard would soon be at the mercy of the submerged reef surrounding Madame's island. The captain's fear of the misfits was replaced by the panic of sinking—weighed low by the coral reef's punctures to the hull and merciless ocean currents.

Denmark revealed a secret: that at high tide a shallow draft boat, like the *Koi*, and hopefully the *Eleanor*, can traverse Madame's semi-circle of coral reef at one location. If the *Eleanor*'s daft was shallow enough she could anchor within the protected lagoon at the base of the island. Such a tack would shield the *Eleanor* from spying eyes and put her as close as possible to "his rock." The one he pointed to.

However, as Denmark examined Madame's island while explaining the precise course for the *Eleanor*'s approach he noticed a change in the island's profile. Unfamiliar contours. Closer still, he could tell much of the foliage had disappeared. He thought of the birds. Soon, a brown fence, no, what he could see, was a wall, had been erected all around the top of the island. Built in part, no doubt, from the wood Captain Palmer once delivered and put to effect repairing Madame's home.

Madame's unclaimed, unchartered island, true to Master Thomas's grand design, had been transformed into a bacaroon, an open air slave pen in competition with the Danish West India Company's monopoly—beyond the jurisdiction of the Danish government. Or any government.

Denmark became weak at the knees and crumbled to the deck at the sight, speechless. The others helped him up, asking themselves as much as Denmark about his trepidation.

"What's wrong?" Adam asked, steadying Denmark.

"Is it the treasure? Something wrong?" the captain wanted to know.

"It's not the same island," Denmark said.

The captain misunderstood, "The wrong island?"

"No. No, it's the right island. It's just… It's just not as I remember it. It's changed."

The wall extended past, and now enclosed, the old kitchen where he'd slept for years. It continued down through the garden to Madame's grave alongside Captain Palmer's sailors.

From their vantage point, all aboard the *Eleanor* saw black heads pop up intermittently over the wall's height for brief intervals.

Little did they know of the effort required to achieve such ends.

Taking turns, slaves stood on the shoulders of another slave who stood on another's shoulders, forming a cooperative of humanity, desperate for news of the outside world. And an unfamiliar boat at anchor offshore was big news inside the crowded pen.

The door to the pen creaked open. Feeding time.

The dark faces disappeared from atop the wall as the ladder of slaves collapsed to the ground.

Two pygmies—captured like the Ewe in raids betwixt two warring expansionist kingdoms—entered the pen. One wheeled a vat of gruel behind his timid partner brandishing a spear. The starving mass of miserable people drew near, encircling the frightened little men. The pygmies especially feared a recent arrival. A hulk of a black man dressed in a white man's clothes who often menaced and laughed at them. The slaves too were wary of the recent arrival. They left him alone to brood as he pleased.

On board the *Eleanor*, once Denmark had divulged the site of the buried loot, Adam asked of no one in particular, scanning the slope, feeling captive to the misfit's intentions, "Who's to make the climb?"

"We'll go," the two misfits said in passable English, almost in unison. Everyone on deck stared up at the steep incline leading to the large boulder. It jutted out like a devil's horn, abutting the base of the wooden wall surrounding the top of Madame's atoll.

"Who's to stop the climber from continuing on…?" Adam said, regretting it after seeing the menacing looks the two men gave him in response.

"Could be any number of guards for a fortress like this," the captain said scanning the wall.

"OK, you should go," Adam said as if it were his idea all along— glad to be rid of them, off his boat. And, after all, there may be no treasure. Denmark had said as much, *the island has changed.*

Two birds, macaws, landed on the mizzenmast, at the stern, near the helm as the men discussed the perils of the climb and debated who should make it.

"Oh, we'll be back for you," one of the misfits said through a cruel laugh.

"You're a liar, koo hooo," said a voice unlike a man's, turning heads towards the birds.

The misfit who'd spoken charged and swatted at the birds who squawked and flew away, back toward Madame's island.

Denmark coached the men as they jumped overboard into the shallow water and waded ashore. Denmark knew the danger well. The rock is perched at the edge of a cliff that drops over a hundred feet to nothing but boulders and dry sand. No water reaches there, not even a high storm tide; it was barren rock.

The pygmy-toothed misfits crept up the edge of the incline like spiders, grasping tentative vegetation and other dubious choices as they scaled the height to "Denmark's rock." Close to its height but off to the side, to the right, the misfits reached a new but already well-worn path. One that encircled the entire bacaroon; to and past "Denmark's rock." The two stopped at the rock and began to dig beneath it, as instructed. What they found was a smattering of toys scattered about a degraded tin box of toy soldiers. The two looked at one another thinking the same thing—that they'd been had! Lied to, played the fool! Those on board the *Eleanor* watched, anticipating, hoping for a moment to celebrate. Instead, along with signs of commotion between the misfits they heard "Ahh! Agh!" followed by curses in French.

One of the two misfits was so tormented with anger he misstepped and slipped over the edge of the cliff, yelling out loud as he fell.

The pygmies, finished with their feeding chore, had closed and locked the pen door and sat themselves down on the trunk of a fallen tree nearby. They were admiring the view from atop Madame's island, as she once did, when they heard the same confusion as the men aboard the *Eleanor*. One pygmy turned to the other with a silent cock of his head, as if to ask, *did you hear that?*

The other misfit grabbed the fallen misfit's arm. But in the process he too fell over the side. Each now frantically clung to the side of the cliff. They finally recovered their senses and secured new footholds and alternative paths down. The men crept all the way down and swam in Madame's lagoon for a moment, happy to be alive.

Back on board, the bruised, scraped and bleeding misfits shouted at Denmark. Claimed it was all a trick. A dangerous trick at that. One pulled the knife he'd used to kill the cook and his helper and waved it, circling, challenging Denmark to make the climb, "If he weren't no liar." The other misfit said, "No. We all go."

"Who, me too?" the captain asked sheepishly. Frightened by the prospect of such an arduous and dangerous feat he said, "I'm just a bystander, with nothing to gain. Not at this point, anyhow."

One of the misfits bared his pointy teeth at the captain and said, "Wouldn't want you sailing off while your betters are all ashore, would we now?"

"But…" the captain started to explain his fear.

Denmark said, "Whatever we do, we'd better act soon. Your screams could be heard for miles, trust me. If not taken for a slave crying out, well, we could have company soon."

The misfit who'd ordered all to make the climb, thinking it safe to speak freely in French, grinning, told his mate, "We can rid ourselves of the lot of them. Leave 'em ashore. Dead or alive, no matter."

Denmark, in French, warned, "*Tu ne deviendrez pas loin sans nous tous* (You won't get far without all of us)."

The misfits snapped their heads to Denmark's French, surprised.

For the benefit of the others Denmark then said, in English, "We're in this together now, like it nor not."

Climbing the slope, all six trudged the same path taken earlier by the misfits. Denmark led the way.

Before the climbers reached the top, the two pygmies had resumed their duties. They were in the habit of each walking opposite of the other around the perimeter of the wall, meeting in the middle, at the rock, "Denmark's rock."

On the climb, once they were almost to the edge of the cliff, one of the two misfits raced around and ahead of Denmark, to the top. And by the time Denmark and the other misfit reached the summit the pygmies were each approaching the rock from either side of the men. One carried his spear.

At the sight of the sentries, one misfit exclaimed, registering his anguish, "*Pygmées! Pygmées!*" The other screamed, "*Ah Pygmées! Je déteste des Pygmées! Je les déteste!* (Ah Pygmies! I hate Pygmies! I hate them!)"

Each misfit ran furiously toward the surprised little men. Adam, the captain and the last remaining crewmember alive each aborted their trek. The captain, in an instant of haste, fell to his death. Adam studied the captain's body; straddled motionless across a large boulder way down below. Adam redoubled his grasp and carefully, slowly, began to retreat down the cliff as did the only crewman left.

With the misfits engaged in hand to hand combat against their pointy tooth nemeses, Denmark examined the scene of the dig beneath his rock. His familiar toys brought a smile to his face.

Denmark then dug deeper into the hole. Almost immediately he could see what, if the misfits had been more aggressive, more diligent, they would have seen too. The chest sat just where he had left it all those years ago. It was as though Madame's savings had been waiting for him and him alone to return to claim. Denmark opened the chest, revealing its contents, full of coins and jewelry and the leather sack of coins strewn atop gold bars. Some coins spilled out.

Denmark heard a cry concomitant with the blur of a body falling aside, past him. Then another, as each of the two misfits were pushed by their foe off the cliff; seemingly to join the captain below.

The pygmies made a quick retreat once freed from mortal combat.

In triumph, Denmark held up high the full leather bag. The two men below, about to climb aboard the *Eleanor* cheered when they saw him.

Much to his surprise Denmark heard the faint cries of the misfits. Each had managed, again, to grasp vegetation that clung to the wall of the cliff. The two scampered up the side and were soon standing next to Denmark.

Denmark spoke in French to the misfits, "Let's free the slaves. Open the bacaroon's doors and let them scatter. Their owner will be so consumed with recapture he won't have time to chase us. And some will no doubt make it to freedom, somewhere."

One of the misfits said, "What if there's more of 'em?" thinking about the pygmies.

The other said, "Good! I hope there are!"

The men's intense hatred of their former hosts was shocking. Men often hate most those they've wronged.

FIFTY-TWO

Do You Know Me?

Denmark and the misfits smashed the lock and swung open the unguarded pen's door. A whiff of foul odor stung their senses like campfire smoke as they peered inside.

The slaves' habitual response to the door opening was to move forward, in anticipation of food. The one exception was the newcomer, Moses, the *bomba* of *Paradis* Plantation. He'd claimed a corner of the bacaroon farthest from the pen's door for himself at the outset of his arrival. When he did approach the pygmies he taunted and menaced the little men even as they fed him.

When Denmark and the misfits stepped inside they saw one of the most wretched sights anyone could ever behold. A hundred or more near naked hollow-eyed souls peering back at them. Denmark scanned their faces, looking for the familiar.

Sensing no danger as murmurs of the men's defeat of the pygmies circulated, the captives dared to view the intruders as saviors. They approached Denmark and the misfits with cautious optimism. Moses shrank his stature and attempted to blend in with the other slaves as he moved close too. But his size and well clad appearance betrayed him as unique. When one of the misfits smiled his pygmy-toothed grin— pointing out Moses—all the slaves scattered and reverted to their usual frightened state of agitation.

Denmark raised his hands into the air and spoke to them in his Ewe dialect. He told the few that seemed to understand him that they were all free now. Though free to do what, he did not say. Denmark pointed to the open door and repeated his announcement before turning his back to them and instructing the misfits to leave with him. Now. They did, though the one misfit who'd brought Moses to the others' attention sent the *bomba* a stern fleeting glance during his retreat to the pen's open door.

One escaped the pen. Then another. Then a few more until the exodus became a torrent as the mass of men and women struggled out of the pen's single egress. As the crowd thinned, turned loose on the island, some splashed in the water near Madame's dock. Many gorged on the uncooked stash of slave fare gruel just outside the pen's door. Others approached the *Eleanor* on the lagoon side of the island. Some climbed aboard the *Eleanor*, despite shouts from Adam and the crewmember to stay away.

Once Denmark and the misfits were onboard the *Eleanor*, under their watchful eye, they allowed Adam and the *Eleanor*'s lone sailor to examine the loot inside the chest. An assortment of the emancipated jumped around on deck while others splashed one another in the water next to the *Eleanor*. Moses's approach frightened and scattered all those in his path.

One of the freed slaves that had understood Denmark's announcement told Denmark why—that Moses had brutally abused them in his role as *bomba* on Paradise Island. As Moses splashed through the water and attempted to board the *Eleanor* Denmark took from Adam's hand a pistol Adam had retrieved from his cabin. Denmark pointed it at Moses's face.

Adam flinched at the sudden removal of his weapon from his hand and, seeing Denmark point the pistol at the fully clothed man, said, "Denmark! What are you doing?"

"You! You will remain. You will remain to explain to your MASTER how it is that you have been set free."

"Denmark?" Moses said.

That name. The name of Madame's boy across the bay. A boy he'd seen in Road Town with Madame, came as a surprise to him. Reminding Moses of other slaves he once knew by name in the years gone by.

Equally surprised, Denmark asked, "Do you know me?"

"I know of you. You're Madame's boy. Was," Moses said in a tone meant to engender sympathy through association.

Denmark cocked the flint lock.

"Don't leave me here. That old fat Master Seymour is sure to add me to his graves."

The name Seymour struck a chord with Denmark. The name was the name of the man who'd become Madame's new business manager after Armand's sudden departure.

"Is he not the man who runs Madame's tavern and inn?"

"The same," Moses said. "And as overseer, he done taken over *Paradis* too, from Master Thomas, now resting in a shallow grave. I dug it myself. Along with a grave for Master Armand, and them three copper investor men. All in a row, next to the Frenchman what hired Seymour." Denmark couldn't know it (and Moses would never have made the connection), but Denmark's sister, Sade, rested there too. She was buried in the slave cemetery of *Paradis* in an unmarked grave of her own.

Denmark began to piece together his boyhood encounters with that man, Seymour. He already knew that the threatening bombastic recipient of Madame's dispatches was the man who'd chased him from the copper field. What he did not know was that the man who'd replaced Armand and the spy who'd accepted Madame's dispatches were one in the same. Or that Seymour was more than just a tyrant. He was a thief and a murderer too.

Though he had operated under the guise and protection of the U.S. Congress' Secret Committee as a spy, all Seymour ever really wanted was to profit from the sale of Master Thomas's slaves, the copper from the investor's mine, and eventually *Paradis*. Now in control of all of Madame's properties, including her island, turned bacaroon, and Master Thomas's entire business domain, as well as the copper mine, Seymour had succeeded beyond his wildest dreams.

Armed with this information, and a pistol, Denmark had no more use for Moses, and thinking of the many chain gangs Moses had led to and from the fields, to early graves, he hoped Moses would meet the same fate. But Denmark had no wish to put him there. No. Left to Seymour, Moses would get what he deserved.

"Back away!" Shaking the tip of the gun barrel in Moses's face Denmark repeated, "Back away! Or I'll shoot you dead this instant!"

Moses put his hands in the air and backed away onto the beach. The pygmies, who had regained their composure, appeared on the scene from their hiding place and rushed toward Moses's back, yelling and screaming at the one slave who had taunted them. They now deemed him as an associate of recent events. The pygmy with the spear charged Moses's back as though hunting an elephant in Africa.

The *Eleanor* pulled away with several freed slaves still aboard. They could not deny the emancipated for fear of arousing a mutiny among them. With Denmark at the helm the *Eleanor* managed to slip through the one depression in Madame's reef that allowed passage into the wider expanse of water leading to the Atlantic. Denmark had studied geography and navigation since he was a boy with a *someday* like this day in mind.

He could hear but did not turn to see the two pygmies' assault on Moses.

FIFTY-THREE

He's Right, You Know

With a mind and heading toward Road Town, Denmark heard the cock of the flint lock pistol—their only guard against the whims of the misfits who they now needed to help sail the *Eleanor*. It was Adam now holding the gun, pointing it at Denmark.

"I can't let you do that."

"Do what?" Denmark asked with anger in his voice.

"Let you look for her."

"What are you going to do, Adam? Are going to shoot me to stop me?"

"These are desperate times, Denmark. No, I'm not going to shoot you. Unless you make me. No, I need you to pilot the *Eleanor*. Now that that miserable little captain is dead. But I need that money, in Charleston. It will placate my investors. At least until I'm able to prove my innocence."

The moment of Adam's last word, as the *Eleanor* reached the hard winds of the Atlantic beyond the tip of Beef Island, the report of a cannon was heard. Then the splash of the ball landing within yards of the *Eleanor*. Then a second blast and another cannon ball splash near the first.

All those aboard the *Eleanor* saw a ship not far away, to the south. Her French flag flying from her halyard. She'd rounded the tip of Beef Island from the Sir Francis Drake Channel. Denmark peered through the captain's spyglass. He changed course setting sail north-northwest, to go around the tip of Paradise Island for cover and evasion.

Before rounding the tip of Paradise Island, Adam spied the extent of the French strength before handing the spyglass to Denmark for him to survey too; the close by ship was but part of an armada carrying over forty thousand soldiers. Soldiers Napoleon had dispatched. The armada, led by his brother-in-law, was sent to crush the slave rebellion led by Toussaint L'Ouverture on St. Domingo.

Denmark called for more sails to be hoisted and steered a course as close to the wind as the *Eleanor* could withstand without capsizing.

Beyond the tip of the island, with Paradise Island port side, all aboard the *Eleanor* were alarmed to see the French pursuit continue. Rather than remain on course the *Eleanor* tacked more northwest to evade her pursuer. A lone ship, a sentry among Napoleon's flotilla.

Moments later a distant roar was followed soon thereafter by another cannon ball splashing well behind the *Eleanor*, this one starboard, off the stern. Adam raised the spyglass once more to see within the shadows of Paradise Island the silhouette of a second ship in pursuit, not far behind the first. He relayed his findings to Denmark who ordered water thrown on the sails to stiffen them, to allow less wind through the porous canvas while altering the *Eleanor*'s heading again. This time, intent on outmaneuvering the French, he set course due north. Denmark hoped to put more distance between the *Eleanor* and cannon fire.

The *Eleanor* maintained her monotonous course north for days and nights on end. She rode the Gulfstream current in an attempt to stay just ahead of the French. Only the luck of favorable wind and fair seas had thus far kept her out of firing range.

One evening at the helm, in an attempt to ease the tension, Adam said to Denmark, "You know, it's in your best interest too to sooth the investors with some of your Madame's treasure."

"How so?"

"Because of your sale of shares, in the tavern. Men might come to think of you as an associate of mine. Guilty as I, I imagine."

Denmark remembered thinking the same thing while reading the newspaper article, in Charleston. Guilt by association.

But he said nothing to encourage Adam's overture. So, Adam calculated to flatter Denmark's mastery of the seas by asking him about the *Eleanor*'s course, charted by Denmark by following celestial movements of the stars. Denmark indulged Adam's seemingly innocent curiosity by pointing out his night sky guideposts.

Changing the subject, Adam then suggested that if Denmark applied his evident mastery of the seas to his new found carpentry skills—once Adam had been able to prove his innocence and regain the trust of those in the Jewish community and beyond—he might be of some service in helping Denmark, as a free man, establish his own construction enterprise.

"Once I get my troubles sorted out, I might be able to be of some assistance in that realm of business." His quiet words were meant as his bond; an example of his interpretation of *tzedakah* (an act of righteousness). "Give the matter some thought."

The two men were quiet for a few minutes.

Though afraid of the next topic, Adam addressed it.

"And, even before we departed Charleston you'd probably already thought of, but dared not admit, another fact."

"What do you mean?"

"Most of the African trade goes south of Charleston. Much further south even than the West Indies. Most slaves are destined for the fields and mines of South America."

Denmark had considered that. He'd heard and read as much.

Denmark's sharp tongue insisted, "What are you getting at?"

"So, in truth, Denmark" Adam gambled on a renewed familiarity by putting a hand on Denmark's shoulder at the wheel, "You'll never find her." Without removing Adam's gesture Denmark shot a look at him as though Adam had just sold her off himself.

"In truth, Denmark," Adam said staring into Denmark's eyes, "she's probably dead."

Denmark struck Adam so hard Adam's face hit the deck before he saw the punch. The gun bounced from Adam's hand, but Denmark did nothing to retrieve it. He and all aboard the *Eleanor* were captives of their present danger and course.

After over a week more at sea, with only brief naps at best for the only navigator captain aboard, Denmark grew so weary he had to insist on relinquishing the helm to sleep. After giving instructions to the crewmember he went below to his cabin.

In his state of fatigue as he drifted between sleep and consciousness he thought of the emancipated aboard. About their unsuspecting fate once the *Eleanor* had cleared the Charleston Bar. He considered the idea of throwing them overboard, near shore, before reaching Charleston; for their own good. Better to have a chance at freedom than to be turned over to a new life of bondage. Then, it occurred to him he could cast Adam overboard as well. And the misfits. Especially the misfits. He pondered the reaction to his scheme as he was, at last, asleep.

He dreamed a fanciful dream. One where without notice of change, everyone was alike. All manner of men and woman went about their Charleston business as shopkeepers, merchants, maids and dockworkers without regard to status or hue, as though each were calico. White men as footmen, black men as bankers. White women, some as lords of their manor, some as house maids. Black men as laborers and speculators. And no one thought the other out of place, out of the ordinary. A sideways society. Liberty and justice as a matter of course, as in "...*all men are created equal...they are endowed by their Creator with certain unalienable Rights...*" In his sleep, Denmark was as enamored with the prospects of the American declaration as Madame had been when she first read those words.

Other images flitted about his mind. In one he saw the *Mal Majeur* wagon parked outside St. Michael's. One of two children being led away by their mother ran back through the taunting, jeering crowd and unlocked the cage door before running back to the safety of a mother's outstretched hand.

In his Africa, slavery was no more. Oppression the new bane. No longer tolerated on the continent.

Then Koi came to him like a wraith bathed in porthole moonlight and illuminated cabin dust. She disrobed herself and laid her head upon his chest. Her cheek resting upon his chin, like the night they'd jumped the broom together, her image spoke. *He's right, you know. I love that you have come for me. I love you. But he's right, you know. You have to go on now. You have so much more ahead. He's right you know. And you know I'm telling you the truth. Live. For me. For you. For our people. Free!*

And he woke; the heat of the sun burned his eyelids then blinded his vision as he rose. He went topside.

Adam was observing through the spyglass the *Eleanor*'s pursuers, only to determine, at the sound and sight of another cannonade, that the source of the cannon balls was not French, but English. The second ship, the one he'd first spied in the shadows of Paradise Island was an English vessel. All along, the English ship had been firing her two nine-pounder bow-chasers in pursuit of the sentinel French ship. Only to miss and land her charges near the *Eleanor*, dead ahead of the French. The French brigantine had sailed toward the *Eleanor* only to evade the larger English brig pursuing *her*. The *Eleanor* was of no consequence to either one of the other's interests. The whole journey had been one long chase between combatants at war.

With the Charleston Harbor entrance in sight, another ship, smaller than the *Eleanor*, then two more of equal size, sailing south mistook the *Eleanor* to be in league with the nearby brigantine flying a French flag. The hated French!

Ever since word that American emissaries had been rebuffed by their French counterparts, X, Y & Z; ever since they had been asked for bribes in return for access to the post-revolutionary French government and markets, the American public had been outraged; their clamor for war with France had only increased by American and French naval clashes at sea. French effigies had been burned up and down the east coast.

Now, at the Charleston Bar, the three agitated ships, "patrollers" out to capture French merchant ships in America's undeclared, quasi-war with France, approached the *Eleanor*, hurling epitaphs at her deck.

Before Denmark, or Adam, could shout or signal a defense a barrage of gunfire, then cannon, then more cannons, opened up on them. Several of the attackers—at the sight of blacks on deck and strange pointed toothed grimaces—yelled "Haitians! Haitian rebels! Fire! Fire!" More cannons fired from all three ships at once as they passed along either side of the *Eleanor*. Those who did not jump overboard were cut down where they stood. Engulfed in flames, reduced to a wreck, the *Eleanor* drifted with her dead before sinking below swells at the Charleston Bar as her tormentors fled the scene.

Denmark awoke on shore. The surf lapping at his feet. Sand in every crevasse and pocket. The scent of low tide in his nose pressed to the beach; no one alive in sight. He traveled the shoreline, finding bodies, including one of the misfits, but no one he sought. He then came upon the pistol, half buried in the sand. He looked around him. The pistol couldn't have come ashore alone. He saw footprints at the edge of the dunes and followed the first, second, third, and then Adam rose in front of him.

An oysterman and his crew came upon the two just as Denmark discovered Adam.

"Don't shoot!" Adam yelled as loud as he could. Then as softly as he could, "Hold the gun up. Point it at me."

Adam raised his arms high in the air as though surrendering.

"Tell them who I am. That you've captured me hiding here. Without the money, at least one of us will get out of this alive. You'll be hailed a hero."

"What's that you say?" the old oysterman called out.

"Over here!" Denmark yelled, pointing the wet, sand-filled gun barrel at Adam.

FIFTY-FOUR

Man Plans and God Laughs

Days later, back in his room at Captain Vesey's, above the clatter of pots and pans below him, Denmark tried to think ahead to his next move. As Denmark paced, brooding about Koi, his still enslaved boys, and the loss of Madame's treasure, his old habit of giving in to his thoughts of Koi dominated. There was now only one story left—she's gone—and he still struggled to accept it.

As though whispered into his ear, the words came back to haunt him—*You know he's right. And you know I'm telling you the truth. You have to go on now.* Unbeknownst to him at the time, this encounter would be the last of its kind; Koi—talking in his head with a finality reminiscent of Madame's during the dark days of her illness—said, *Look out the window. What do you see? You're a free man. With money in your pocket. You're a free man! Get out of this house. Make a life we couldn't. Or don't come back, talking to me again. I'm not here every day anymore, anyhow. Man plans and God laughs. Go!*

Denmark paraphrased aloud to Koi the words he had read by a Russian writer, "You may make many people happy, but never try to take away their misery." Denmark kept his misery. His feelings of love lost. But he tucked them away where even Koi couldn't get to them. His finger twitched.

Part III.
1800-1822

FIFTY-FIVE

Pennies on the Dollar

Denmark retrieved his checkbook. He then walked down the stairs and through the kitchen past his busy companions. As he left Captain Vesey's King Street house he vowed to listen to Koi; from this day on, every day would be a Sunday.

Denmark went by grocer Paul's house on Broad Street to check on his boys. But the same house maid that had answered before said her master had sold Denmark's family to a Master Schnell. Another grocer who lived over on Church Street, number 74. And when Denmark knocked on that door he was told that not only could he not see them, he was told to not come back, ever. As it turns out, Thaddeus was no gentleman at all.

Denmark next walked over to the white's jail, on Magazine Street nearby the Work House, to visit Adam. He'd been ridden on a rail there by an angry mob that grew larger and larger every block away from the oysterman's boat at the wharfs. Still unaccustomed to his new status—a free man—after showing his freedom paper to the picket guard a block away from the prison, he was allowed to proceed. Denmark was taken aback by the fact that his request to see Adam was not derided and denied.

"He ain't here," the white jailer said before spitting tobacco juice onto the sandy ground. "They turned him loose yesterdee." Denmark tipped his hat and walked away without betraying his surprise.

Instead of going to Adam's house, Denmark walked to The Grove.

At the back door the same servant who'd answered before let him in and the same butler ushered Denmark into the parlor to wait. Ten minutes later Denmark heard heavy footsteps descend the entryway stairwell.

"Denmark. What brings you here," Captain Vesey asked. "It was good of you to capture that feller, Wolff. The whole town is still talking about it. They've all complimented me for your actions. Saying I must be teaching my niggers right."

Denmark let the insult pass with only a nod, as in agreement.

"I've come to offer you an opportunity," Denmark said.

Captain Vesey put his thumbs to his arm pits, tucking them inside his vest. He stared at Denmark a moment. "Another request for help, I see. Already," he said with an expression of superiority. But, more like a man talking to a delinquent debtor than to a slave. A subtle but significant and welcomed change—another change Denmark would have to get used to—a change of tone enough to embolden Denmark.

"Yes, well. Not exactly, sir." Remembering lessons learned in his dealings with and for Adam, that scarcity breeds attraction; that everyone wants what someone else is willing to pay for, Denmark lied.

"You see, I've come across a number of contracts for work, and I'm trying to gauge my availability to best please all of my customers." Denmark let the notion dangle for a moment like one of Adam's black curls, hoping Captain Vesey would be lured to the bait.

"Well, hold on there, now. We didn't free you just so you could profit from others at our expense. You've got to give me first dibs, as payback for that below market price my misses granted you. Don't you agree?" he said in the anxious tone Denmark had witnessed Captain Vesey take with merchants when haggling with them over the price of trade goods.

And so, Denmark's new career began. He walked away from The Grove plantation with a signed contract resting in his pocket next to his freedom paper.

Within days Denmark had set up shop in the parlor in his new home. A house on Bull Street—three blocks east from the residence of the future Governor of the state and three blocks west of the future Intendant (mayor) of the city.

Through Captain Vesey, Denmark was contracted to fill in swampy land within and beyond the city limits and to build piers along the Ashley River for new home sites there. He hired just his friends at first. But soon, as Denmark's carpentry skills and reputation for quality and timely work spread he was asked to build stables, barns and fashionable portico additions in and around the Charleston district. These projects led to more projects and in a short time he had earned a clientele large enough to require the services of still more workers to fulfill his commercial obligations. Throughout these developments Denmark hired free black artisans, indentured servants and slaves hired-out by their masters. He paid the free blacks more than they were accustomed to and slipped extra money to the indentured and enslaved; more than the wages he paid their masters. Soon he had a devoted pool of workers willing to do whatever he asked of them.

Ever since Adam's release from jail Denmark had walked past Adam's residence off King Street whenever he could. But he never saws signs of life there. Then one day, ten months after his release Adam appeared at Denmark's new home. He congratulated Denmark on his new life and success and told him of his self-imposed exile after the magistrate had set him free.

Adam then spoke in a whisper, in confidence, "Have you *searched?*" raising his eyebrows. With an almost imperceptible shake of his head, Denmark refused Adam's temptation to discuss the topic.

Adam's lips formed a small knowing smirk.

He cleared his throat and changed the subject, "I've found work for you...in the frontier district, among the lands once owned by Francis Salvador."

Denmark asked Adam, "Have you not heard the name Gabriel Prosser yet?"

The story of Gabriel Prosser—a Virginia slave who had led a failed Richmond insurrection—spread as fast as disease throughout the south, and the nation. Denmark tried to explain to Adam that no good would come of it for blacks, free or slave. That he'd already read in the newspaper of proposed new measures that would restrict the activities of free blacks like Denmark. The new restrictions would prevent him from taking advantage of Adam's connections—the work Adam spoke of for Denmark in the frontier district.

Adam shrugged and started his familiar refrain, *"Mann tracht…"* but Denmark cut him off, raising his hand and shaking his head, he said, "I know, I know…*und Gott lacht."*

Adam continued, as he was prone to do, speaking as though the matter of Gabriel Prosser had no bearing on anything remotely related to him. Which he felt was true about most everything.

"I told the judge the same thing I told you. That I didn't know about the dubious nature of the New England Mississippi Yazoo deeds. The claims against them. I told him I'd lost money in them too, what with their value having plummeted to near zero."

"What of my share, my commission?" Denmark asked, disappointed Adam had ignored the topic and weary of Adam's propensity for scheming.

"Well, same as the rest I'm afraid. But I still have confidence the investment will bounce back. Just like my friend says they will. He's not only filed suit, he's got Congress looking into the matter, even President Jefferson. I'm buying all I can. I've bought out most of my exchange partners already."

Adam put his hand into his pocket as though, perhaps, about to retrieve a few dollars for Denmark and said, "How about you then? You interested in buying Yazoo deeds for pennies on the dollar?"

FIFTY-SIX

Changing Perspective

Mary, "May" to her friends, Captain Vesey's third wife, like his previous two, died within five years of matrimony. Leaving the captain a small boy of mixed ancestry—Joseph—and a large fortune that included The Grove and all of her slaves. Like most wealthy merchants, Captain Vesey divided his time between residences in the countryside and in town. More the former than the latter. Despite repeated inquiries among the black community, Denmark never heard a satisfactory answer to account for May's death; no two explanations were ever the same.

For years after Gabriel Prosser's hanging—and that of twenty-six more co-conspirators—states that post-revolution had embraced manumissions, mostly those to the north, began to change their positions on the slave trade and abolition.

Much of the new restrictions were aimed at free blacks. New York, a state that had granted free blacks the right to vote, rescinded the franchise. Others made living in or moving into their state difficult. In Philadelphia, a crowd of angry whites chased away a group of free blacks from an annual Fourth of July celebration.

During the ensuing years Denmark looked upon the political squabbles between the Jeffersonian Republicans and the Federalists with concern and suspicion. The purchase of the Louisiana Territory was particularly troubling. More territory meant an increase in the demand for labor, slave labor; an expansion rather than a contraction of slavery.

But, in the two post-revolutionary war decades many states, including South Carolina, suspended participation in the transatlantic slave trade—ahead of the U.S. Constitution's stipulation to end it in 1808. However, in 1803, South Carolina reopened the trade. In fact, the state was soon thereafter importing more saltwater slaves from Africa than ever before.

Among the perverse and contradictory changes toward administering "the slave question," South Carolina's legislature enacted statues allowing blacks to gather for religious study and worship—part of the second "Great Awakening"; a renewed effort to assimilate and domesticate African slaves by converting them to Christianity.

In the midst of following these decisions Denmark was not surprised that—despite President Adam's material support of the Haitian rebels against the French—President Jefferson did not recognize the new Republic of Haiti when it declared independence in 1804.

He was surprised however to learn of a troubling position held by Alexander Hamilton—a man whose stance on abolition Denmark had followed and admired.

A letter Hamilton had written to a fellow Federalist the day before he died in a duel came to light; printed in newspapers. In his letter Hamilton had disagreed with a New Englander that the cure to America's ills, including slavery, was not northern succession—a notion many Federalist supported if they couldn't convince the South, including President Jefferson, to abandon slavery. The most alarming among Hamilton's words—made public two years after the fact—were that succession was "no relief to our real Disease; which is DEMOCRACY." This pronouncement made Denmark fearful of the changing perspectives in America. Fearful for her future. For the future of abolition, and therefore, the future of his people.

Amidst all the turmoil and changes in Denmark's life he made a new friend, Rolla Bennett. Rolla was a servant a few blocks away from

Denmark's new home. Soon Rolla was attending regularly held
meetings at Denmark's residence. Denmark's neighbors—well-to-do
Brown Fellowship Society mulattos and middling folk whites—grew
accustomed to these gatherings at Denmark's shop. A place of business
as well as, supposedly, worship.

Rolla frequently told Denmark and the others gathered at
Denmark's house about conversations he'd overheard while serving his
master's guests. Imitating a white guest at a recent dinner Rolla said,
"The only solution is to remove the free blacks!" A sentiment that
merely parroted President Jefferson's own words.

Rolla continued, "Another man answered, 'the very presence of
free blacks threatens our way of life. If blacks see all their color as
slaves, it will seem to them as the disposition of Providence. They will
be content with their lot. But, if they see others like themselves free,
enjoying rights and privileges they are deprived of, they will repine.'"

Next Rolla laid out competing views he'd heard as he served the
white guests drinks in the parlor after dinner.

"One man, a Yankee, described his solution as the 'diffusionist'
proposition. He said that the spreading of slavery throughout the West
would make the elimination of slavery a forgone conclusion. That with
slavery so spread out, and with a simultaneous increase in free white
immigrant labor, slavery would exist in such small amounts, it would
eventually cease to be an issue, and die out."

Denmark had read of this theory. He considered it demeaning.
Proffered by those too timid to take up the fight of abolition against
the entrenched slave plutocracy.

Another man, a man Rolla said dominated the dinner conversation
and to whom most every guest demurred, spoke at first in harsh tones
against the Yankee's prophecy. He lectured the Yankee, "Remember,
man, the black's deficiencies are innate! Slavery is, in and of itself, a
means of civilizing their beastly propensities." Then, modulating his
tone and volume somewhat he'd continued, "Because the blacks have
no capacity to administer their own freedom, it is the slave holder's

responsibility, nay his duty—and as Christians, our burden—to hold them in bondage forever…to look after them…for their own good."

To this revelation the men gathered at Denmark's house stood silent in quiet repose, pondering Rolla's words.—Not unlike the white men who'd been drinking within the Bennett parlor a few blocks away.

Despite the well-publicized fate of Gabriel Prosser four years earlier, after his attempted insurrection, Denmark's workers—chief among them Caesar—seemed to think or talk of little else. Caesar would put the odds of a successful outcome, of running or fighting, at ten to one. And when compared to the odds winning the lottery, as Denmark had done, he considered those odds to be favorable. In his Caribbean lilt, when others would talk of winning the lottery too, Caesar would opine, "light'tin don strike twice de same." As inherited property of Captain Vesey, Caesar, Nell and Ambrosia all knew their chances of manumission had died with Mary.

Having considered the prospects of escape or revolt many times as a slave, Denmark could not disparage talk of other's attempts to run away or overthrow white rule.

But now, as a free businessman, he saw the future in a different light. He had expanded his network of business to as far away as forty miles from Charleston proper. And as his contacts and projects grew so did Denmark's capital.

Denmark did not admonish rebellious talk among his work crews. Nor did he label Gabriel's failed attempt as foolish. No—to the contrary—he only wished the young man had planned better.

Looking ahead, although Denmark was very interested in the prosperity that had occurred since President Adam's peace accord with France, he continued to follow the abolitionist movement. He read everything he hoped pointed to better days, by peaceful means, for his family, friends and others enslaved. All the while counting the years, the days—observing the ticking clock—until the U.S. Constitution's ban on the Atlantic slave trade would take effect in January 1808—

thinking that, perhaps, swift progress on the issue of slavery would follow.

And amid his business and political research he came across a book in the lending library about submariner designs. Recalling the air pocket he found many years ago within the sunken *Eclipse* his thoughts turned to putting the examples illustrated in the book to good use. He began making plans to scour the Charleston Bar for Madame's treasure.

Then, one busy day while engaged in weighty thoughts, Denmark discovered treasure—on land. A chance meeting changed his perspective in an instant. Her name was Dolly.

FIFTY-SEVEN

As though Across a Flame

As Dolly gathered water on Coming Street, near Denmark's home, she looked up to find Denmark staring at her across the public well. Even as she blushed she found herself unable to turn away from Denmark's gaze.

Though ten years his junior, for some time now Dolly had been a secret admirer of the best known free black man in her neighborhood. Denmark looked whites in the eye and had the respect of his friends and neighbors. Denmark's attraction to Dolly, Koi incarnate, was overwhelming. He was devoted to her the moment their eyes met, as though he'd first caught her attention across the flame of a bonfire in Africa.

Denmark had developed a routine of meeting his boys every Sunday at the same spot where he used to deliver melons to an old woman that once she'd become blind was released from bondage to fend for herself. Denmark brought Dolly to meet them the first Sunday after, "Hello."

Beck and her daughter Sarah would sometimes accompany her boys to the market on Sundays to meet Denmark. On this Sunday, Sarah, Denmark's boys and Dolly made small talk while individually glancing at the private conversation between Denmark and Beck a few yards away.

The years had not been kind to Beck. Thaddeus had spurned her and left her to her fate; a slave in the household of grocer John Schnell. As the boy's parents spoke it was apparent to all that Beck was not pleased with Denmark's new companion. But the boys and Sarah liked Dolly's easy disposition, her humility in the face of Beck's suffering. The boys, and even Sarah, were torn between their admiration of

Denmark's freedom and success and the disparaging sentiment about Denmark that Beck was in the habit of expressing to them. Even the youngest sensed that Beck's remarks said more of about her than Denmark. Remarks made during frequent bouts of rage that camouflaged her own disappointment. Disappointment rooted in the mistakes she'd made, among the very few choices she had in life. Beck pointed out to Denmark Dolly's resemblance to Koi, whom she'd seen but once, briefly. And the disparity in their ages.

They saw Denmark shrug his shoulders as she spoke and then, smack! Denmark recoiled from Beck's slap across his face. Beck then walked away from the gathering, leaving everyone embarrassed and befuddled, without words. Denmark recovered his smile. He hugged his boys and Sarah before departing for a stroll with Dolly through the market.

Events beyond Charleston were soon to make their mark on Denmark and those around him. With Napoleon's ascension in France, ongoing hostilities with England escalated around the world. Each of the two countries delivered military and diplomatic blows wherever they could. These bouts made every other nation a casualty of the two nation's war for dominance. While the French battled mostly for control of the European continent, the English were seemingly at war with every other nation on the high seas.

And just hundreds of miles up the coast from Charleston one event occurred in the summer of 1807 that rattled all Americans of every station in life because President Jefferson compared it to the battle at Lexington.

An American frigate, the USS *Chesapeake*—setting sail to free 700 white sailors from enslavement by Barbary pirates in the Mediterranean—was fired upon by the fifty gun HMS *Leopard* after refusing the British request to board her. The captain of the *Leopard* had insisted on searching for English deserters. Several American seamen were killed. After the USS *Chesapeake* lowered her colors, the

HMS *Leopard* impressed four sailors—three of them were American citizens.

President Jefferson retaliated with a complete embargo of trade—ignoring reports that 9,000 of America's 24,000 man navy were English deserters. The President chose to disengage America from the worldwide "free ships, free goods" trade policy that had sustained the country's economy for the past twenty years.

At first the embargo merely curtailed business. But soon it all but shut down American commerce—except for smuggling—drastically diminishing the profits that paid for Denmark's projects. Once Jefferson's embargo became the law of the land— prohibiting trade with any nation—busy ports, including Charleston, became swaying forests of naked masts while gunboats patrolled the waters of the harbor's entrance. The only good that came of Mr. Jefferson's trade policy was that idled projects created more time for Denmark to spend with family and friends.

Though a slave in a separate household from "her man, Denmark," Dolly resided only two blocks away. In four years' time the couple had four children together; three boys and a girl. Their firstborn they named Denmark. The twins that followed were named for Captain Palmer and the doctor on St. Domingo who had saved Denmark's life. They named the youngest, Charlotte.

The economic straits felt by all of Charleston not only provided ample time for Denmark to enjoy his children playing in the yard of his house, they also raised the prospect that Widow Taomer, owner of Dolly and the children, might consider selling them, to Denmark, for much needed cash.

Widow Taomer received Denmark in her parlor under the watchful eye of her daughter. Between all of the makeup and perfume worn and a distinct lack of hygiene the room smelled like a whorehouse.

"Ma'am, Mrs. Taomer, thank you for seeing me. I appreciate your time. I'll get right to the point," Denmark said, looking to the pursed lipped daughter after addressing the old woman. He made it clear that he was willing to pay above market prices to purchase his family. At first Denmark suspected the old woman was hard of hearing for her expression revealed no recognition of his proposal. However, after a prolonged silence the widow said with some effort, "I'll free her and the children in my will."

Denmark smiled broadly. The daughter jumped from her seat next to her mother and left the room as though propelled by a sudden, urgent errand.

FIFTY-EIGHT

A Farce

After Denmark's visit with the Widow Taomer he felt he'd achieved the best possible outcome under the circumstances. He and Dolly and their children would have to wait. But guessing the widow's age and gauging her condition, Denmark was sure the wait would not be a long one.

The War of 1812, "Madison's War," brought a new English Navy blockade of Charleston Harbor. And a run on the banks amidst the collapse of business credit. President Madison sent Charleston into a frenzy of motion recruiting troops for the militia and the Federal army. Both in turn scurrying here and there to shore up ocean batteries and convert anything that would float into gunboats. Everyone hoarded whatever supplies could be had.

British blockades along the rest of the Eastern seaboard, from the Chesapeake to The Narrows of New York Harbor, choked off the nation from all goods including smuggled slaves skirting the 1808 Federal ban on their importation. The consequence of supply and demand fueled temptations to poach Negroes—any colored man—for sale in some other far away market.

Caesar chose this time of military and economic upheaval to make his escape. Late on a hot overcast early August Saturday night in 1814 he set out for the freedom he hoped to find far north.

Adam had a stroke of luck few would have predicted. Congress stepped in to settle the New England Mississippi Yazoo Company dispute in Adam's favor. Overnight the company's claims, and Adam's fortunes, had rebounded.

That day Denmark collided with Adam as the two men rounded opposite corners at Broad and Church streets.

"Whoa," Denmark said as the man jostled him.

"Oh, my God. Denmark. If it isn't just the man I'm looking for."

Adam took an envelope from his coat pocket and handed it to Denmark. Inside, Denmark guessed, was over a thousand dollars.

"Your commission," Adam said with a smile while Denmark finished the astonished expression upon his face. Adam explained what had transpired and told him he was headed off to the territory to stake his claim; 25,600 acres, 640 along the banks of the Yazoo River.

"You're not going to sell it?" Denmark asked without trying to hide his surprise.

"No. I'm not willing to test the ire of those I bought from at pennies on the dollar. Their jealousy might be the death of me. No, I'm heading out tomorrow…" Here he paused, head down, moving with his toe some of the crushed shell sand dust on the sidewalk. The smell of horse urine pooled at the curb wrinkled Adam's nose as he finally spoke, "I was thinking…well, maybe, you'd like to come along."

Denmark was surprised by the offer. He let his silence and lack of enthusiasm speak for itself.

"Well…It was just a thought," Adam said, trying to mask his disappointment. He didn't really want to set out on this venture alone. Then again, he knew Denmark had family ties Adam no longer enjoyed. Denmark offered his hand instead as congratulations and good-bye. Adam briefly embraced Denmark and Denmark patted Adam on the back. In another instant Adam was gone.

On a clear Monday, Captain Vesey saw Denmark on the streets of Charleston outside the grocery where Denmark's son, Sandy, worked for his master, John Schnell. They spoke of business between them and the weather.

Catching Sandy's attention, Denmark attempted to introduce the two, but was cut off and shouted down by the overbearing grocer who drilled orders into the boy's ear with the spray of his spittle. In a dash, Sandy was gone.

Beyond a cold stare delivered from a clinched jaw Denmark could do nothing to address the insult. The Captain, forever obtuse in the face of indignity said, "I'd like you to go over to the Work House. Caesar's back. Turns out he didn't get far. They found him in a chicken coop on one of the Ball's plantations about twenty-five miles north."

Denmark parked his wagon behind another near the shadeless entrance to the Work House; near an arched double doorway with guards at the ready. A wagon with two unattended slaves, both chained to the wagon's wooden frame, sat motionless; morose and exhausted in the scorching heat.

After stating his business to the guards Denmark was ordered to wait outside with his wagon.

Denmark stood closer in proximity and circumstance to the slaves in the wagon than two white men standing well out of earshot beneath the only shade in the area. That of an old oak tree between the Work House and another fortress-like prison, the nearby jail for whites.

The two slaves could be father and son in age, but their clothes and demeanor said otherwise. The man, about thirty, wore the silk and cotton clothes of a gentleman in contrast to the young boys shredded coarse slave fare. Denmark observed they'd not spoken nor glanced at one another. Rather, each held fast to their own. Reliving parts of other days in their mind.

Removing his hat and making conversation Denmark allowed a, "Mighty hot," followed by another, softer, "Sure is…Mighty hot," looking in the chained man's direction.

Taking his cue, the man sat up responding, "Yes, yes it is," in an American accent foreign to the South. Then he stopped, but kept his gaze, trying to speak with his eyes.

Denmark moved closer.

Denmark asked the high-yellow, well dressed, educated mulatto, "What's your story, sir. And the boy's?"

Henry De Bouwerij motioned his head, asking Denmark to come closer still, before he uttered, "I'm a free man. Kidnapped by men inside. You must help me."

The words resonated with Denmark more than the chained man could ever know. The words sent Denmark back to offensive memories unvisited for many years.

Denmark's grimace and sudden change in demeanor startled the mulatto at first, but let him know Denmark understood something of what the free man in chains has been through. And at least some of why.

"Do not profess your freedom to those men…not in your circumstances," Denmark admonished, speaking from experience. The bifurcation of his advice was not lost on him. His advice was nonetheless genuine, wise, and important.

Denmark's friends and associates were of the hired slave and lowly free black caste. Twice and three times removed from the poorest of whites in the city. The dichotomous stratification of status, of value and freedom in Denmark's world, hounded him at every turn. Never failing to nip at his flesh. Denmark had reason to distrust the word of a mulatto elite; like that of a slave who curries the favor of his master over his own kind. These thoughts suppressed his interaction just now like the heat suppressed exertion.

Denmark repeated, "What about the boy?"

"He was in the wagon when they put me in it an hour ago. The boy doesn't talk."

Both men looked at the mongoloid features of the child. Denmark tried French, Spanish, Gullah and a dialect of Arabic. The young boy's only response was a blank stare and a lone tear as he lowered his head.

"Sir, I am a citizen of New York. Those men inside drugged me and stole me from my life. My wife and children. We were on our way to Philadelphia. To start a new life. They went ahead of me, until I could close my business and sell off my father's farm. I had the proceeds in my pocket. I woke up in chains on board a ship. Below deck, without my coat and money. My wife, my family, won't know what's become of me. Please, I beg of you, sir, can you help me? Please!"

Denmark said, "What's your name?"

"Henry. Henry De Bouwerij. Can you get word to Philadelphia? Tell my wife, Alicia, you find me. Her brother started a newspaper there. Tell her to look for me. Please!"

"I'll do my best," was all Denmark could promise the man before the driver returned to the wagon. Now loaded with additional slaves released from the Work House the wagon began to move away down Magazine Street.

Caesar was brought out with the others, unconscious. Stinking of weeks of filth and dried blood from his daily lashes. The captain said he first heard of Caesar's capture and captivity three weeks ago. Denmark understood the rest. He took Caesar to Captain Vesey's King Street home where Nell and Ambrosia could nurse him back to health.

By the time Denmark returned from his next foray into the Lowcountry Caesar had recovered his health if not his pride.

After traveling down King Street, the main thoroughfare into town, when they reached Captain Vesey's house Caesar beckoned Denmark to join him for a moment inside as he squinted into the afternoon sun.

Caesar poured a drink from the captain's liquor cabinet, giving Denmark second thoughts about Caesar; fearing he may not be as well as he appeared. The sullen slave walked over to where Denmark was seated and handed the glass to Denmark.

Caesar began with, "Widow Taomer died yesterday." Denmark jumped to the edge of his seat, about to stand and leave. Caesar motioned for Denmark to stay seated.

"I was by Widow Dewee's place dis morning." Stalling, he offered, "Over on Queen."

Denmark knew the place, and Caesar knew he knew. Denmark froze at its mention.

Choosing his words he repeated, "De morning you lef, dat afternoon, old lady Taomer, Dolly's Ma'am, she took a turn for the worse. Dis morning I seen Dolly sold off by her relations. Your children too. De man paid a tousand, one hunerd dollars. But he couldn't buy dem all. So young Denmark, he sold to another man. For tree hunerd."

Not that the numbers meant anything. They were simply a reason why. Why they were split up.

Denmark was quiet. Eyes to the floor, his hands made fists. Caesar continued with the ugly event as it unfolded before him. As seen from his vantage point, through the arched doorway, from the street.

"Your boy, he already a man. Dolly screaming and pleading wit dat man. Saying, 'She'd be his all her days, could only he keep da boy, too.' He say, 'I don't got da money.' And da bargain was struck, jes like dat. As dey started to drag him off, your boy got loose and ran straight way to Dolly. She bent over and told him. Her face shiny wet wit tears, 'Remember your Momma. Remember your family.' De man, he yanked her arm. Telling her, 'Behave, or, I'll,' raising his arm high…Den, your Denmark, he punched the man right in his privates. De man fell to his knees, onto de flo, cursing and scratching for your boy wit one arm. As dey pulled dem apart, your Dolly and Denmark, Denmark say, he say, 'Don't cry Momma. Momma, don't cry.'"

Caesar's moist eyes met Denmark's and Caesar stopped.

Denmark left his wagon at Captain Vesey's and roamed the streets of Charleston to avoid reality. To prolong passing his family's home on the way to his.

He seemed invisible to the people on the sidewalk and in the streets around him as he passed through them unacknowledged. As though he, too, no longer existed there. The world went on about its business. Nothing had changed. To Denmark, it was a landmark day. An awakening that his dream of a good life—a home and a family, emancipation, living among society in some better way—free, all free— was never more than a daydream. A ruse. A farce.

FIFTY-NINE

Close Enough

For the next several years Denmark was not home. Not in mind at least. Whenever his boys or his friends spoke to him it was as if his head was hollowed out and his eyes were elsewhere even when they addressed him face to face.

His work suffered. He took to drink. And spent far too much time away from home, alone.

On Sullivan's Island outside Charleston in an isolated dilapidated country barn his aquatic design was taking shape.

Charleston, indeed the country, did not fare much better. In 1816, "The Year without Summer" as the time came to be known, a global cooling gripped the North American continent. It was caused by the eruption of a volcano the year before on the other side of the world. In the Pacific. The Mount Tambora volcano. Its ashen plume reached South Carolina amid the aftershocks of the New Madrid earthquake in Tennessee. The quake cracked walls as far away as Charleston and continued to do so for years as occasional tremors spread throughout and beyond its epicenter.

These natural disasters inspired sermons of hellfire, brimstone and damnation in churches across the city. And brought hardship and disillusionment to planters and farmers. Their curtailed growing season and profits were a genuine source of fear to everyone, including the slaves. Many of whom were being sold "down river" —from the mid-Atlantic states of depleted soil and resources—to the Yazoo territory.

Plantations did not have enough food to feed the slaves. So they sold to plantations opening on the frontiers in Alabama, Mississippi and Louisiana. The Yazoo lands that had three thousand five hundred slaves when Adam left Charleston now put fifteen thousand to work in the fields under the constant threat of the lash.

On Meeting Street, near The Market, Reverend Morris Brown stopped to ask, "Denmark. Denmark, are you all right? You look troubled, son."

Unacquainted with the two other black ministers accompanying Reverend Brown, Denmark leaned closer and told Reverend Brown about his family. And of free men being sold as slaves and that he feared he'd never have a life in this world. The others heard Denmark's low voice. Reverend Brown put his hand on Denmark's shoulder and for a moment they all stood silent, heads bowed.

"Will you be at the prayer meeting tonight? It's going to be in the clearing beyond Boundary Street." Asking the question was also telling Denmark the two of them would talk again later, in private.

"Denmark, I want to introduce you to these fine ministers from Philadelphia. Bishop Allen and Reverend Martin. They're with the African Methodist Episcopal Church, come to help us organize a congregation for all the meetings already going on in and around the city."

Prodded by abolitionists, and lulled by editorials depicting the enslaved as happy with their servile condition, a grandiose enlightenment period of sorts had ensued in which slaves and free blacks were to be preached to—and allowed to preach New Testament verse—while being careful to ignore the old Testament book of Genesis. This practice gained momentum as justification for, even duty to, the practice of human bondage. For slaves, the prayer meeting loophole meant a new spiritual freedom, and more opportunities to gather together during the week.

"Did you say Philadelphia?" With the memory of the sores on the man's wrists from the chains weighing on him, Denmark interrupted the visiting ministers.

Denmark grabbed the wrist of two of the men to ensure they were listening closely and told them all he knew about the man in the wagon, and the boy. In perfect Dutch, Denmark told them the man's name, "De Bouwerij. Henry De Bouwerij." The ministers mimicked an Anglicized pronunciation of the name, as "De Bowery." Close enough, Denmark believed before saying, "Yes."

SIXTY

Like a Bolt of Lightning

A fissure between the white Methodist leaders of Bethel Methodist Church and their more than 4,000 slave congregates, including Morris Brown, erupted over an issue related to the disbursement of collection plate revenue and the church's plan to erect a sanctuary over an old slave cemetery. The result was a break from the white church.

Soon thereafter, in 1818, twenty-six free blacks signed a petition to incorporate a black church on Anson Street; The African Church of Charleston.

The African Church of Charleston was so successful—drawing free blacks and slaves from every river and tributary of the Lowcountry and the Sea Islands—the gatherings so large, a second sanctuary was opened nearby on Cow Alley to accommodate the throngs of parishioners. Denmark and others accepted with resolve Reverend Brown's challenge and invitation to act as meeting leaders. To preach the word of God to smaller groups of his growing flock from all over the Charleston District.

Soon, repercussions of the financial Panic of 1819 wreaked havoc worldwide. Rice and cotton prices fell. As did South Carolina's market share of crops, exacerbated by falling prices offered by the Yazoo planters. The very planters of the Deep South responsible for the hardship sale of slaves. The vicious circle contributing evermore to the slow drain of South Carolina's slave labor, at reduced prices. A sentiment Rolla Bennett heard among the many struggling Lowcountry planters—made only half in jest across the diner table—referred to the cost of slave upkeep in the face of wholesale losses; "'Tis easier to kill them than feed them."

This period of change in all things natural, economic and spiritual did not escape Denmark. He viewed the disorientation as an opportunity. Harkening back to his first reading of a hurricane, written by a young boy on St. Croix.

This was an opportunity to recruit the black race through a plethora of firebrand religious dogma with a specific goal in mind. In French and English, Denmark drilled Old Testament verses into the hearts and minds of Christian slaves. Especially the book of Genesis, countering the New Testament propaganda preached by whites.

He repeated the Arabic words of Muslims, "The Koran teaches that the emancipation of slaves is a virtuous act." And through the spirited incantations and conjuring props of Gullah Jack, he preached to Pagan, Obeah and Animism followers of the Sea Islands in the Gullah and Ewe languages. To all who remembered life as a free African, he reminded them of it. Told them to keep it alive and well fed by hope and courage.

Denmark was soon re-engaged in building projects spread throughout the Charleston District and beyond. He developed arrangements for accommodations with small farmers for a roof or campsite wherever he could. These lengthy stays meant movement, and visits among slaves as well as masters. Learning the ways and opinions of each.

As Denmark made the rounds, working projects as a supervisor and carpenter by day, sometimes far away from Charleston, he worked the crowds of slaves around campfires as a lay preacher by night.

About this time a fire on Sullivan's Island burned to the ground the barn housing Denmark's secret submariner design.

In 1820 on a bright, fine Spring Sunday morning after Reverend Brown's sermon Rolla Bennett introduced Denmark to Susan, a free young beauty. By then Rolla and Denmark's friendship stretched back many years. Having observed Denmark's struggles since losing Dolly, Rolla thought the two might just make it as a couple.

As the congregation emptied into Anson Street, Rolla had engaged Susan Prudhomme in conversation until Denmark stepped out of the sanctuary. After the couple's eyes met for moments at a time it seemed as though Rolla no longer existed.

Denmark, enchanted with new promise, thanked Rolla with his eyes and bid him farewell in the silent dialect of men.

The couple rode out of the Hampstead neighborhood in Denmark's wagon to Wragg Square, a neutral ground park.

He'd bought a picnic lunch packed by a neighbor of the church who catered to the congregation. Admiring the day and the fine homes still growing up around the park, both felt enamored by the other's presence. Denmark pointed out the properties on which his crew of men had worked. Explaining the jobs with such precision and concentration Susan could see his hand in the woodwork of her sister's home.

"What brings you to Charleston, Susan?" Denmark asked, admiring her youthful features.

"My sister. She's pregnant, and needs my help right now," she said.

"And, then? You plan on staying on for some time? Or, do you need to get back to someone in, where was it Rolla said you were from?" Denmark said, pretending in jest as though he did not know.

"New Orleans. Our family is from New Orleans. My sister, Annie, married a sea captain. He's also a partner in a trading firm here."

Neither gentleman today had bothered to ask where she lived in Charleston. "They rent that house across the street," she said, pointing to one in a row of three identical fat white columned, two-story Georgian styled homes. A fourth one was under construction by Denmark's crew.

Impressed but coy, Denmark said with a mocking a gold-digger's smile, "And?" waiting for the "someone" answer.

"And, what?" Amused by his antics and enjoying his persistence, she said, "Oh, am I staying? Well, I haven't thought that far ahead. But, no. There's no 'someone' waiting."

As they talked Susan tried to explain the multinational influences and flavors of the New Orleans Vieux Carré. French, Spanish, Caribbean and American. She attempted to explain, without insult, that New Orleans though not unlike Charleston in many ways, had a bit more flair and freedom for all of her inhabitants.

"For example, my father, Emile Locoul Prudhomme," the French names brought a soft smile of remembrance to Denmark, "is, of course, of French descent, but my mother, Patty, is an Irish-American whose family has been living in New Orleans since before Jefferson bought it. Her marriage to my father (a member of the *les gens de couleur libre*, a Creole of color) is accepted there in a way I don't see possible here in Charleston."

Susan meant that the races mixed more freely in New Orleans. And that the size, the proportion, of the free mixed-race population in New Orleans was greater than she'd witnessed in Charleston— comparing the size of Lake Pontchartrain to Charleston Harbor as her metaphor—and, she implied over the course of their conversation, that the practice of blacks owning slaves was less prevalent, less accepted by her neighbors than in Charleston.

Denmark told her of his life in Charleston. First as a slave, then winning the lottery. And some of what had transpired since. When the conversation turned to Charleston's African Church, Denmark tried to convey just what it meant to the black community. And he told her about his previous religious experiences. He also told Susan about Madame's take on the Bible, and what he gathered Charleston whites believed. He related his communion service at the Second Presbyterian Church, along with two other blacks, a block or so from where they were sitting.

"Madame, she found it hard to preach Bible verses to me, as a slave one day and a pupil the next," Denmark's far away eyes said what he needed to regarding the old woman.

Denmark continued, this time referring to the teachings of white denominations throughout the city.

"They preach separation and subjugation is God's work. 'Servants, obey thy masters.' They have no idea what they're talking about. They put in place separate ceremony, separate seating , pews in the balcony. They even have a separate catechism book, one just for slaves—to conceal Bible verses not in keeping with their message. Half the ministers own slaves."

Denmark followed, trying to explain the dynamics of his world, "In the countryside, most of the whites just eke out a living with no help at all. When I arrive there, they see my manner of dress and know others do my labor. They hold a look in their eyes of shame and disillusionment. A black man among them better off than them. The hurt is palpable. Eased only by a gracious greeting from me, as though they were my equal, or better. It's a concession I make in return for their permission to camp, or to secure goods for my crews of workmen. But, in town, most households, black or white, own at least one if not many slaves. Why, on my own street, not only the whites, but most of the mulattos own their help. I've heard stories of how they treat them. I've been told by slaves themselves that the meanest, most severe and irrational masters, man or woman, are those new to it. Those who've never been masters before. As a British Prime Minister, William Pitt, once said, 'Unlimited power is apt to corrupt the minds of those who possess it.'"

Each, like singing to the chorus, in perfect pitch, laughed at the other's shared view of the world. Its comical characters and absurd, hypocritical customs. Denmark said a Jewish friend in town, Adam, once told him he'd stopped attending synagogue after, as a college student on leave from school up north, while visiting his great uncle's family in Charleston, he'd been asked to join the family for Seder. When he found the holy meal was to be served by the family's half a dozen slaves he declined their invitation. Taking umbrage to Jews of the Exodus being served Passover Seder dinner by slaves.

Denmark marveled at the candor and grace of the gorgeous, delicate, demure yet unabashed beauty before him. That a mulatto woman, as fair as an Irish immigrant, could speak as frankly as she'd spoken amazed and dazzled his imagination.

Their lunch complete, Denmark walked Susan to her door and asked if he might call on her. Thoughts of her and her reply mesmerized Denmark all the way home. They maneuvered him through city streets and traffic under their own power.

So encompassing were his feelings for the woman he'd just met that for the very first time since the sale of his family—at a price he could afford, but never had the opportunity to offer—Denmark rode past old lady Taomer's place in a different frame of mind.

Though he still mourned—there'd been no trace of Dolly and the children after the auction—he did not hang his head nor shed a tear as usual. Instead, a spike of anger steeled through him like a bolt of lightning.

He snapped the reins, onward.

SIXTY-ONE

Not His Mind

The baby born, a boy, making Susan an aunt, was not the reason Susan stayed on in Charleston. Rather, it was the promise of a child of her own, with her new husband, Denmark. The two were married in the African Church packed with well-wishers. She took Denmark knowing his former wives, his children, and their fate, would be now and forever intertwined with her own.

The lives of most of Charleston's slaves and free blacks soon revolved around the new church. It was their sanctuary from the oppression beyond its grounds. The Intendant (mayor) and the new Governor allowed the church latitude in its illegal activities. Ignoring both law and custom. The new administrations allowed blacks to congregate well into the night, in fine clothes, long after the curfew drum rolls were silent.

But one evening during the performance of a one act play at the church—actors parodying the roles of happy slaves, tipping their hats to buffoon massas, to a howling crowd—all that changed. The city guard stormed the building. Down the aisles and to the pulpit they rushed the sanctuary and surrounded the congregation. Shouting commands for the congregants to stay in their pews, not to move.

Among the 140 church members arrested were six bishops and ministers from the A.M.E. parent church in Philadelphia, and Denmark. Though herded by guards like cattle, the colorful parade of silk and satin through the streets to the Work House brought to mind a procession to honor the death of a fallen dignitary.

The magistrate said he would accept five dollars to escape the same whipping a slave's master would normally be charged for. Having paid their toll, the bishops and church ministers were discharged by morning. But at his interrogation Denmark stated he did not have the requisite cash in his pocket.

In the small interrogation room the gray haired old magistrate ensconced behind a rickety black table shuffled his chair. Quill pen at the ready, the magistrate snapped a request for Denmark's name and owner without looking up from his paperwork.

Denmark stood straighter as he spoke, looking ahead at the wall.

"My name is Denmark Vesey. I am my own master. I am a free man," he said. He ignored the old man's disrespect and instead thought of the last time he had declared that status—as a youth aboard the *Prospect*—and of the New York mulatto, kidnapped and chained to a wagon in front of this very building years ago.

"Vesey. Where have I heard that name? Oh, yes, Captain Vesey." Looking up, he said, "You're his slave, are you?" The magistrate asked as though encouraging a new answer.

The advice he'd given to the kidnapped mulatto in the wagon echoed in Denmark's mind.

"I'm a free man."

Denmark was whipped in lieu of $5 cash and released. Captain Vesey sent Caesar to pick up Denmark from the Work House.

Susan's tender touch soothed his wounds, but not his mind. To occupy the time while he lay prostrate, recuperating on his stomach for days amid the odor emitted from his wounds, so pungent he could hardly bare the scent, Denmark read a book by Abbe Henri-Baptiste Gregoire, *An Enquiry Concerning the Intellectual and Moral Faculties, and Literature of Negroes*. It's refutation of Hume soothed his mind a bit and served as a sort of salve for his soul.

He also pondered tattered and worn abolitionist pamphlets, articles and debates of legislation he'd hoarded in a box he kept under the bed like his childhood collection of tin soldiers hidden under "his rock" on Madame's island. Beneath a like-new copy of Thomas Paine's *Common Sense* lay a collection of faded newspaper clippings, including a copy of Patrick Henry's well known *give me liberty* speech. Denmark noted that it read, in part, *Why stand we here idle? What is it that gentlemen wish? What would they have? Is life so dear, or peace so sweet, as to be purchased at the price of chains and slavery? Forbid it, Almighty God! I know not what course others may take; but as for me, give me liberty or give me death!*

Also there, arrayed alongside the abolitionist material lay schematics of submersibles (the *Drebbel*, the *Turtle*, the *Nautilus*), and Denmark's own draft version emboldened by his experience within the bubble of air he'd encounter inside the hold of the sunken *Eclipse*. And, among the other papers, along the bottom of the pile, were articles documenting slave revolts. One read:

Of Publick Interest…SLAVES REVOLT!

On the morning of Sep't 9th, in the year of our Lord 1739, on the Sabbath, two dozen slaves stormed a store at Stono's bridge, killing the Inhabitants & Robbing guns and powder, &c. before crossing the river, south for Spain's Florida, gathering slaves to join in Killing at least 20 White Citizens in their path. Had Lt'd. Governor William Bull not happened upon the hoard & Sounded the alarm, God only knows.

Another article detailed an account of Gabriel Prosser's trial. And to Denmark's estimation, his failings.

SIXTY-TWO

His Problem

Denmark, like the reading public, could see the gamesmanship at work between the pro and anti-slavery camps as congressional interests welcomed, tit for tat, territory after territory into statehood. Mississippi for Indiana, Alabama for Illinois, and now, Missouri in exchange for the free state of Maine, carved out from an expanse of Massachusetts.

Familiar with the publications, *The History of the Expedition of Captains Lewis and Clark* and *Niles' Register* that printed Senator Rufus King's speech railing against the expansion of slavery, Denmark saw the conduct and outcome of the contest for the vast territory beyond the Mississippi River, north of parallel 36°30', as a contest of wills. As a measure, a test, of the resolve and power of the abolitionist movement in the United States.

Meanwhile, during the Christmas season, a more malevolent, local act—with personal consequences—overshadowed the holidays and the ramifications of the Missouri Compromise. The South Carolina legislature, in an attempt to quell the growth of free blacks within its borders, amended the Negro Act. The new law—effective as of December 20, 1820—forbade the emancipation of any slave, at any price, without the written consent of the legislature. For the enslaved in South Carolina—Denmark's boys, Beck, Sarah included—any hope for freedom someday, died that day.

Susan dismissed a distant stare that appeared now and then thereafter—*just part of his healing process*—she thought—*his way of dealing with his life's traumas.*

One morning, weeks later, Denmark woke up laughing with a smile on his face. As though he'd worked through to the end of some puzzle or riddle; to the end of his problems.

SIXTY-THREE

Notsie

The shutters slammed shut on the windows, all thirty-two, all at once, sending the darkened barracks into pitch black and the scurrying soldiers running into one another in a panic—the smell of smoke in the air.

Slaves had descended upon the militia Guard House at The Lines, the remnants of the old original wall stretching east to west along the northern-most part of the Charleston peninsula.

Eighty slaves sealed the shutters. Dozens more lit the cotton bales and lamp oil from nearby warehouses, setting the old wooden barracks ablaze. Almost a hundred militiamen beat on the doors, the shutters, even the walls as they scrambled and screamed for their lives from inside the burning building.

The entire structure was engulfed in flames within minutes. The fire at first illuminated the slave's presence like a torch, then as a rising sun. The glow of fire and embers on the warm, clear, moonless, sleepy summer Sunday night revealed the number of Gullah Jack's troops to be thousands; whooping and hollering as they ran away, jumping over dead sentinels and through The Lines: the time was 12:04 a.m. [SPLASH! Upon the wall of Notsie.]

A book in his lap, Governor Bennett was reading by candlelight in his quiet mansion at the corner of Ashley and Bull Streets, only blocks away from Denmark's home. Rolla Bennett ran a bayonet through the winged back chair in which the Governor was seated. The Governor gasped once—as the blade recoiled—on his way to the Persian rug covering the polished wood floor with no knowledge of the identity of his assailant. Rolla denied his first instinct—to rush to the aide of the man he'd served for many years. The man who had entrusted Rolla with the care and security of the musket attached to the bayonet.

Rolla dropped the blood stained weapon to the floor and made his way, a pistol in hand, to the front door of Intendant Hamilton, three short blocks away, passing Denmark's home en route. After a series of sharp raps on the Intendant's door, Rolla took one step back and cocked the weapon behind his back.

Soon the Intendant himself opened the door in his nightshirt. It being Sunday, his servants had the day and the night off. Rolla's appearance, given the late hour, was alarming, but not in and of itself a life threatening event. After all, Intendant Hamilton was familiar with Rolla. Not only through Intendant Hamilton's visits to the Governor's mansion, but because Rolla had some weeks earlier volunteered—in order to clear his name—to be questioned about a slave rising rumored to be contemplated among some of the Negroes of Charleston.

At the sight of his target, as Hamilton asked the matter of Rolla's appearance, Rolla leveled the pistol and fired into the face of the shocked man; the only other man, other than Governor Bennett, who had believed him. Governor Bennett had vouched for Rolla's character and repudiated his slave's involvement or knowledge of any conspiracy.

Next, retracing his steps, Rolla corralled the group of cheering slaves that had emerged from Denmark's house and backyard—down Bull Street from where the shot rang out. Denmark instructed some to set neighboring homes ablaze and to kill anyone, black or white, who attempted to interfere. Rolla commanded the rest of the men to follow him. To coalesce with Ned and Batteau Bennett's forces at the mills on the Ashley River. They were to guard the bridge over the river, on the western edge of the city; to prevent any movement designed to escape or rescue Charleston. The time was 12:11 a.m. [SPLASH!]

Denmark headed alone in the opposite direction of the now cheering armed mass of frightened, yet emboldened, torch carrying slaves. His sights were set on the inmates of the Work House and its contingent of guards there, and the white's prison, both on Magazine Street.

Despite the chaos Denmark's army of 9,000 slaves had unleashed against the city, the blocks of unlit houses between his home and the Work House were quiet. As yet untouched by violence or even alarm. A single shot heard in the dead of the night of a police state was nothing to be too concerned with. Though not an everyday occurrence, it remained, in the middle of the night, "a matter for the patrols." The church tower bells were as silent as the dead sentries in their steeples. Dispatched before the outset of hostilities.

Some homes were deserted, save the few trusted slaves left behind in the summertime migration of families to cooler climates inland. The very kind of slave Denmark had warned his subordinates not to recruit; to not trust the fate of their people to those who might betray them for white rewards. Denmark found himself strolling the empty streets and slate sidewalks, as well dressed as any Sunday, in route to the Work House as though the night were like any other Sunday evening he'd spent in the city during the past decades. But his tight chest and dry mouth dispelled that notion. Dispelled any sense of normalcy, despite appearances.

Companies of slave soldiers, thousands strong from four plantations and countless smaller farms across the Ashley River, and from the Sea Islands as far south as St. Helena, under the command of Peter Poyas, were at that moment arriving on the shores of White Point at the southern tip of the peninsula; while on the eastern watery edge of the sleeping, silent city thousands more African and French speaking slaves pulled canoes ashore along the Cooper River to meet Monday Gell and Bacchus Hammett at The Market. The time; 12:12 a.m. [SPLASH! Upon the wall of Notsie.]

Peter Poyas split his forces at White Point. Armed with stolen pistols, swords, knives, sickles, hoes and axes, he sent one column to the Work House on Magazine Street. He led the rest on a march to the arsenal and guards at the corner of Meeting and Broad Streets, across from St. Michael's Church and next to the Second Bank of the United States.

Bacchus and Monday Gell ripped boards away from The Market buildings. They revealed a hidden stash of muskets and musket balls. The bullets had been fashioned from fishnet lead weights on a mold stolen by John Vincent. They also retrieved a keg of gunpowder stolen by Bacchus from his master. And Lot Forrester, who had managed to steal a length of "slow match" from the city arsenal, grabbed the coiled fuse he'd hidden beneath a dock near The Market months ago.

Denmark made his own munitions contribution, though he hadn't known it at the time. Many years ago he couldn't pass up the chance to acquire guns and powder when the opportunity to do so presented itself. The occasion took the form of a simple accounting change—the "counting error" Captain Vesey had "discovered" years ago, and had punished Denmark for. That "punishment"—to go to work for the city—had been the key to his "freedom" to walk the streets and meet the men who now were his cohorts in mayhem. Denmark had changed the manifests of two ships carrying goods for Captain Vesey's chandler trade. The net result was the absence, without detection, of two large barrels of gunpowder and twenty-four crates of muskets. Denmark, familiar with revolutionary tales, knew of a secret hiding place within the old revered Exchange & Customs House building, located at the head of Broad Street along East Bay. Common knowledge held that the Continentals had hidden gunpowder there during the entire British occupation of Charleston. Denmark chose to hide his cache in the exact same spot, underneath the noses of his oppressors, just waiting for an appropriate occasion; like, tonight. [SPLASH! Upon the wall of Notsie.]

Gullah Jack also divided his forces. A contingent of marauders were sent to join the forces of Monday Gell and Bacchus at The Market. But the mission of the main body of Gullah Jack's two thousand recruits—armed with sharp pikes made by Pompey Haig, Jesse Blackwood and other blacksmiths—was to hold the wall at The Lines. They were to allow slave families through to the wharfs, to escape on ships, but keep all white forces at bay. If Gullah Jack could control The Lines, and therefore access to the rest of the peninsula, Denmark reasoned, victory was at hand. [SPLASH!]

Some of Gullah Jack's forces were Calvary, mounted two to a horse. Pausing at a store that sold guns on the corner of King and Tobacco streets, the Calvary broke in and armed themselves with more muskets and cartridges, while gathering more horses from nearby public stables and predetermined homes in the neighborhood. From there, twice their initial strength, they set out in search of the half a dozen patrols marching around Charleston's city streets.

As Denmark reached Magazine Street, from the other direction he could hear Peter Poyas's throng of slaves approaching the fortress-like prison complexes, as could the guards on duty. The guards were not sure of what to make of the sounds of a hoard of voices on the move, in the distance but closing-in fast.

The guards of the white's only prison soon shouted their alarm in a manner terrifying enough to arouse the attention and action of even those asleep at their posts. Then, shots were fired. The white guard's volley of one shot muskets, a hail of bullets, ripped through the column of armed, angry, determined slaves, with little effect. The slaves rushed over the bodies of their brethren and toward the company of astonished guards, who were immediately accosted and ripped apart by the remaining arriving mass of men surrounding them.

The guards at the Work House were next, and they knew it. After one dropped his weapon, they all did, on the spot, and ran like hell into the darkened streets of the moonless night, screaming like frightened children as they ran. Before leaving for his next prearranged destination, Denmark ordered his men in the street into the Work House, to free the black inmates inside.

Meanwhile, Peter Poyas approached the arsenal and city guards at Meeting and Broad in disguise. Months before, Denmark and Peter had arranged for wigs to be made, like those still worn by barristers and judges in some parts of the world. With the addition of white makeup and fine clothes as their disguise, Peter and his cohorts planned to surprise the city guard sentries. To then take the fight into the building itself; bottling up at the entrance the seventy-five guards inside with Peter's column of hundreds of slaves streaming in behind him. [SPLASH! Upon the wall of Notsie.]

Those among Peter's force not engaged in battle with the guards assumed a very important task, one only made possible by Peter's frontal assault. Led by Denmark, they stormed the Second Bank of the United States, killing its guards and robbing it of its treasure. Bank notes, pieces of eight, pounds sterling, gold and silver bullion, more than enough treasure to ensure welcoming arms for them in Haiti or Africa or South America. The sight of all that treasure made Denmark think once more of Madame's treasure just waiting at the Charleston Bar.

By now the smoke and flames of houses and businesses set ablaze lit the skyline of the city. All the slaves once assembled at The Market fanned out among the streets beyond East Bay Street and, according to their orders, began torching anything they pleased while stealing goods from stores, rolling barrels and wagons laden with food to the docks and waiting ships. Still others, guided by Monday Gell and Bacchus, searched the taverns and brothels of the waterfront district, looking for captains and crews of vessels moored in the harbor to kidnap for navigation beyond Charleston waters.

From the countryside, black women and children, old men and the infirm slaves slipped into the city. Flames transformed the white streets of crushed shell and sand into bright orange ribbons, interrupted by the shadows of those darting for safety amid the structures set ablaze.

The bodies of white men and house slaves who suffered the misfortune of encountering the rampaging, ravishing crowds of armed slaves littered the stoops, streets and sidewalks of the acrid smelling city. One master, impaled on an ornate iron fence rail, sliced from groin to throat by his slave of thirty years, his dissembled entrails wrapped around his neck, challenged all who passed to stop and come to his aide, as if anything could be done.

Gullah Jack split his reinforced Calvary in two, each squad with only one mission. To hunt down and kill the patrols. The first twenty raced off to traverse King Street from Boundary Street. Gullah Jack led his twenty horsemen galloping down Meeting Street. Encountering a steadfast target in formation at the corner of Meeting and Society, Gullah Jack and others shot and trampled the men to death, stomping on the moaning, bleeding uniforms with dozens of hooves long after they fell silent. [SPLASH! Upon the wall of Notsie.]

As the fire spread, engulfing entire blocks, the flames reached as high as a hundred feet, wrapping their tentacles around the spires of the city's landmark church steeples. Reasoning that the embers would do their best, Denmark ordered all women and children aboard the ships, first. The hundred or more skiffs and canoes ashore, at The Market, ferried slaves and supplies from ashore to ships from all ports of call—all now impressed into service by the largest slave insurrection in the history of the United States.

Denmark's instructions were clear. Set ablaze only structures beyond East Bay Street, to keep the flames from interfering with the loading activity among the ships tied to the wharfs and anchored in the harbor. Still, the glow of the flames could now be seen for miles, reflecting light from the water onto the giant hulls. With the loading of ships well in hand, Denmark ventured into the burning city in search of his family. They knew their tasks and where to go on this night. Denmark's son, Sandy, was to do his part both in the rising and to help his mother and siblings, Polydore and Sarah. Susan, pregnant with the couple's first child, knew her instructions. Denmark found his empty residence in flames.

On his return to the docks Denmark came across a band of marauders whose leader he recognized. Denmark encouraged then ordered them to the ships. But they were reluctant, even afraid, to board any boat. And so the leader of the gang of slaves bid farewell, insisting he and his brethren were going to march all the way north, to freedom. Without time to argue the point, all Denmark could do was wish them well as they all departed in anticipation of a future full of possibilities.

At the corner of Broad and East Bay, Denmark heard the low rumble of an explosion but saw no damage. It was a shell bursting at The Lines; artillery from a contingent of regrouping militia forces, buttressed by a rabble of white locals, who began fighting to break through Gullah Jack's wall of blacks in their path to retake the city.

Denmark, despite the obvious dangers, ventured to his right on East Bay rather than to the relative safety of waiting ships at the wharfs. He wanted to once more walk by, to stand in defiance of Captain Vesey's chandler shop, just up the street.

As Denmark approached, to his dismay he saw movement. A shadow moving to and fro from within. When Denmark opened the front door as though he were a customer on any other occasion, the captain fired a shot, breaking a window pane with a lead ball. From a crouched position Denmark called out to the old man, allowing time for his vision to adjust from the flash of gunpowder and the dim light of the office. A counter, the width of the room, the only physical barrier between the two men.

"Is that you, Denmark?" came the weakened and frightened voice of a once stern slave ship captain. "I thought for a moment I'd recognized you, but I couldn't be sure."

"Yea," Denmark responded. Not his usual, 'Yes, sir.'

"What the hell is going on?"

"A just rising."

The space between them fell silent for a full minute as the reality of the moment rained down on them like the dust settling at the end of a long struggle—the tenuous nature of their life together had come to an end, once and for all.

"You?" the Captain asked, breaking the silence, implicating Denmark in the insurrection.

"Yes," was all Denmark said in reply, waiting for something, he knew not what, from the old man. Twisted and dysfunctional as their relationship was, it somehow pained him to know the old man might die this way, at the hands of Denmark's soldiers.

In a sheepish tone uncharacteristic of a slaver, the captain asked, "Do you think I'll meet them in heaven?"

Though he knew the answer, Denmark wanted to hear it from him, so he responded with, "Who?"

"The ones tossed overboard, or sold at auction?" the captain inquired.

"I suspect you'll have to," Denmark replied, beginning to regret his detour.

The room fell quiet once more.

Still out of sight, in false bravado, the captain yelled, "You better get, Denmark. The Guard will be here any second to crush your devils."

Denmark offered the old man a last chance; a way out.

"We need captains to navigate. Come with us and live to see another day," Denmark said.

"Another one of your tricks, I suppose. Like feigning weakness on the docks there, that day," Captain Vesey said—referring to the *grand mal* drama Denmark acted out to ensure the Captain would have to buy him back.

"I didn't believe you then, or now," the Captain said.

Denmark, knowing what he knew then and now, still crouching near the door, experienced a spontaneous smirk in response to his trickery and the obtuse ravings of the old captain.

With that, Denmark stood erect, opened the door and walked out into the street.

As Denmark paused outside, standing still in the middle of the street amid the chaos and mayhem all around him. It occurred to Denmark that the slaver had never asked the most poignant question, *Why, Denmark? Why you?*

Unbeknownst to Denmark, the captain had secretly followed Denmark out into the street.

Boom! The old Exchange & Customs House, blocks away, burst into the sky, the flame of the explosion, for an instant, turned night into day. Amid the falling debris, Denmark fell to the street, a musket ball to his leg, well aimed by Captain Vesey in the clear illumination.

Denmark limped and stumbled to the river's edge, and went in. As he lay on his back, his face to the sky, bright stars looking back at him, Dolly and their children, Koi, his mother and father, his sister, and all of his village from Africa, followed by Madame Chevalier, Millie, Captain Palmer, the French St. Domingo doctor—they all floated by at roof-top level, waving and smiling. Then Master Thomas's bird flew by. They all passed over him as Denmark recalled that day in the river in Africa, looking skyward, his ears submerged—silence—he knew he'd made it to freedom, free at last to be with his family and loved ones.

"Wake up! Wake up!" his jailer shouted as he kicked Denmark's shin.

Denmark understood the tone more clearly than the words that awoke him from a deep slumber. By then, he and his cohorts had been imprisoned at the Work House for over a week, accused of conspiracy to incite an insurrection.

Denmark's shin pain permeated his body like the last kick he'd received from the night sentry as a young child slave, asleep beneath the reed roof overhang of his master's dwelling in Africa.

SIXTY-FOUR

It won't Stop

Thirty-four men were executed in Charleston along with Denmark Vesey. Twenty-two were hanged in one day alone. They were arrested before the rising took place; informed upon by a rat, a manservant to his master. They were tried and executed for the crime of conspiracy to incite an insurrection. Hundreds more were imprisoned or exiled.

***

"Wait. Wait. Wait till his finger stops twitching before you cut him down," the executioner demanded of his assistant.

The hangman's helper replied, "But it won't stop!"

EPILOGUE

April 14, 1865
Fort Sumter, Charleston Harbor

Robert told Aaron, "My father spoke at length during his trial, even cross-examined witnesses against him, but, oddly enough—by order of the magistrates—his words were not recorded in the otherwise meticulous 147 page court reported transcript. Nor did the courtroom scribe even mention what he looked like.

"Ironically, because he was so well respected within the white community, two weeks into their investigation the authorities had still not arrested him. They refused to believe the cries of my father's co-conspirators that Denmark Vesey was the ringleader of the planned rebellion.

"My mother, Susan—three months pregnant with me at the time the sentences were carried out—raised me alone. She never remarried.

"Names of the urban slaves; carpenters, blacksmiths, coopers, distillers, coachmen, butlers and butchers; names like Lot Forrester, Bucchus Hammett, Mingo Harth, John Vincent, Polydore Faber, Jesse Blackwood and Harry and Pompey Haig, all swore an oath, not to betray their secret discussions, under penalty of death.

"Whether my father was the author of the misconception or not, it came to be regarded as fact among the slaves that the vote in Congress in 1820 was a vote against emancipation. My father used this belief and other stories as common ground to rally the diverse cultures that existed between the Sea Islands from Beaufort to Georgetown, and in the Lowcountry from the Stono to the Santee rivers. He preached Old Testament Exodus verses he construed as parables, describing the plight of the Israelites as justification for a means to an end. Gullah Jack extolled to the mesmerized masses, 'Eat only parched corn and ground nuts de day of the rising,' and, 'any man who'd put a crab claw in 'is mout, cannot be kilt nor wounded.'

"That small band of determined souls set out to change the world as they knew it. And in so doing, change their own circumstances, and those of their loved ones. None wanted to live to see their limited liberty eroded, and none could bear to see another of their relatives sold off. To a man, each agreed, my father's strategy and goal represented the only means of change, the only path.

"Many choose to frame my father's actions within the context of race, as though he aimed his fury at white people because of the color of their skin. But my father was an African. My father's people, the Ewe, escaped from the walled city of Notsie to flee the oppression of tyrannical rulers, African tyrants. His planned rebellion was meant to escape the walled city of Charleston, to flee the oppression of American tyrannical rulers, American tyrants, *both* black and white. Like planning to end the repeated attacks of a familiar rapist, once and for all."

Still spellbound but exhausted by copious note taking, Aaron's pencil had ceased to move.

Robert explained to Aaron that while it was the view of many that although his rebellion had failed, his father, along with Gabriel Prosser, Nat Turner, David Walker and John Brown had each contributed to the disintegration of the institution of slavery—like splashes against the wall of Notsie. But in truth, there were many other blacks, the 54th Massachusetts, for example, and other whites too, Abraham Lincoln chief among them, and the might of the whole damn Union army that had finally broken through and brought the walls of slavery tumbling down.

As Robert finished his story, though anxious to have made an impression upon the young reporter, to have given a complete and just account of his father's life, his thoughts once again turned elsewhere. To the drawings, blueprints and schematics of submariner designs strewn across a table in his office; his own father's among them. And to the one tangible legacy of his father he believed lay buried, still, within the Charleston Bar.

His parting words were a final nod to his heritage. Still thinking of Madame's gift he muttered through a wry smile what had become a Vesey family mantra, *"Mann tracht und Gott lacht."* Recognizing a familiar turn of phrase from his rabbi's sermons Aaron returned the smile.

Acknowledgements

In researching the life and times of Denmark Vesey, many sources brought the work to fruition. A partial list of historical novels that entertained and enlightened me includes *The Known World* by Edward P. Jones, *The Confessions of Nat Turner* by William Styron, *Island Beneath the Sea* by Isabel Allende, *The Whiskey Rebels* by David Liss, *Sacred Hunger* by Barry Unsworth, *Pirate Latitudes* by Michael Crichton, *Someone Knows My Name* by Lawrence Hill, *Master and Commander* by Patrick O'Brian, *The Eden Hunter* by Skip Horack, *The Fort* by Bernard Cornwell.

A partial list of non-fiction that intrigued and informed me includes *The First Salute* by Barbara W. Tuchman, *Empire of Liberty* by Gordon S. Wood, *Washington* by Ron Chernow, *Benjamin Franklin: An American Life* by Walter Isaacson, *American Creation: The Triumphs and Tragedies at the Founding of the Republic* by Joseph J. Ellis, *The Classic Slave Narratives* by Henry Louis Gates, Jr., *Saltwater Slavery* by Stephanie E. Smallwood, *The Slave Ship: A Human History* by Marcus Rediker, *Denmark Vesey: The Buried Story of America's Largest Slave Rebellion and the Man Who Led It* by David Robertson, *He Shall Go Out Free: The Lives of Denmark Vesey* by Douglas R. Egerton, *Slaves in the Family* by Edward Ball, *Southern Campaigns of the American Revolution* by Dan L. Morrill, *1776* by David McCullough, *The Emergence of a National Economy 1775-1815* by Curtis P. Nettles, *Sons of Providence: The Brown Brothers, The Slave Trade, and The American Revolution* by Charles Rappleye, *The Exchange Artist* by Jane Kamensky.

This novel would not have been possible without the encouragement and support of my family and friends. You know who you are; my love and thanks to you.

Book design and cover art: Damian Huntley

Editors: Paul Dinas, Alice Osborn

Graphic Artists: Rachael Hatley and Annie Kane

Atlantic Ocean and Caribbean Islands map courtesy of David Rumsey Map Collection, www.davidrumsey.com

Charleston, South Carolina map courtesy of Historic Urban Plans, Inc., www.historicurbanplans.com